GODS OF RUST
AND RUIN

AZALEA ELLIS

Seladore Publishing

To Jared. For I am with you.

Chapter 1

No one but Night, with tears on her dark face, watches beside me.
— Edna St. Vincent Millay

I SAT UP ABRUPTLY, choking on my own blood. I jerked out of the little cot tucked into the side of the wall and spat the liquid onto the floor in a dark splatter. The heavy iron taste in my mouth added to the terror of the nightmare I'd been yanked from. My claws slipped out and I sliced through the empty darkness, lashing out at a nonexistent enemy.

A second of flailing later, I got control of myself. I was alone. The only enemy attacking me was also the thing keeping me alive, now that I lived within NIX's compound. The Seed of Chaos made me powerful enough to be valuable, while literally eating away at me from the inside.

I gagged and coughed, trying to staunch the blood flow with one hand while fumbling for the backpack shoved underneath my mattress with the other. The only light in the room came from the small diodes on a couple of sleeping electronics, but it was enough for my augmented eyes to see. I pulled out a small pouch and fumbled for one of the large, marble-like Seeds within. "I wish I was more Resilient," I mouthed almost soundlessly, pressing it to my neck. I was long past flinching at the pinprick. I sighed in relief as the Seed injected its contents into me and took hold, stopping the bleeding.

Birch, my little monster-cat companion, woke, either from the noise I'd made or the smell of my blood dripping everywhere. He let out his scratchy little meow, the sound lilting upward at the end in an obvious question. He hadn't yet displayed the ability of his late mother to share thoughts through touch, but he was far from stupid.

"I had to take a Seed," I muttered to him, my voice low in case something was listening. "I was bleeding again, but I'm okay now."

Birch bumped me with his head and licked at the blood on my forearm with his prickly tongue.

I withdrew my arm before his tongue accidentally removed the top layer of my skin, and moved to the shower in the tiny bathroom stall. I was the only one of my teammates with private quarters. The others were sleeping in a small barracks-like room across the hall from me, stacked two bunks high. I'd glanced at their room the night before, and then promptly passed out from exhaustion onto my own private little cot.

Behind me, Birch grumbled and moved to licking up my blood from the cold hard floor. He had an excessive and disturbing penchant for raw meat and blood. Especially my blood.

I turned on the water at a temperature most kindly described as "scalding" and let it wash away the sticky red residue, along with the lingering creepy feeling from my nightmare. I'd been waking up with nightmares, *from* nightmares, for a while. But they were getting worse than ever before, and I rarely went a night without them.

Sometimes, it was the monsters of a Trial coming for me, ready to rip me apart and dance with my entrails. Sometimes, it was the last time I saw my team member China, as the light went out of her eyes and she died. And sometimes, the nightmare had no form. It was the creeping mass of decay and putrefaction devouring everything in its path. A shudder, a feeling, a smell.

When I exited the shower, Birch had finished cleaning all the blood from the floor. My sheets and pillowcase still glistened with the dark liquid, but luckily, they were black. I took them back into the shower with me and cleaned the synthetic material as best I could. No one would know what had happened.

Birch called to me from the doorway of the shower, his meow still scratchy from sleep.

"It's getting worse," I murmured.

The cub padded past the open shower door and under the spray of water, then licked my knee and peered up at me with his green human eyes. Water splashed down on him and his translucent second eyelids closed sideways for protection. He spread his downy wings to better catch the warm water.

"I'm afraid," I whispered, knowing that he couldn't reveal my secret, and the rushing water would cover any other surveillance that might have slipped through my search. "The Seeds aren't working for as long as they used to."

The Seed of Chaos grew continually stronger, as Behelaino had warned me it would. I just hadn't thought it would happen this *fast*. Every time I was forced to use it, it grew stronger, but being able to display it was the only thing keeping me—and the team—safe.

The meditation technique Adam had taught me helped control Chaos, too, but I could only do so much without more Seeds. A lot more. Without them or some other way to heal myself, the outcome was obvious. I had wanted to keep my condition a secret, but I would need to reveal it to Sam, and hope that he could help me until I could find a way to fix myself.

"I'm dying, Birch," I whispered with terrible certainty, the words no more than a breath on the air.

Chapter 2

I buried my past under a sheet of old earth, and hoped it would not rise up to follow me again.

— Ilium Troia

"I'M GOING to have to find another way to fix this," I said, voice hardening as an angry determination pushed back the fear. The words came easily enough, but I had no idea how to actually do anything about the black Seed eating away at me.

I exited the shower, turned on the lights to my room and sat on the floor, ignoring the water still beaded on my skin and slicking my hair down. Fear pounded through my bloodstream, gurgling in my stomach and weakening my muscles. When Birch crawled onto my lap, I laid my hand on his side, letting his heartbeat center me.

I breathed out and started my meditation exercises. The sun wouldn't rise for a while, so I had time. I closed my eyes and breathed in deep, until I could feel the oxygen swirling in the deepest parts of my lungs, spreading into my blood. From there, it wasn't so hard to sense the tiny particles of Chaos.

I forced them into my mental room of serenity, and put their writhing darkness in my box of silence, locked inside the chest of stillness. By its very nature, Chaos hated being confined so, and wrestled with me to escape. But if there is one thing I can be sure of in myself, it is my will of iron. I do not back down.

I stayed in my meditative state even after I was finished cleansing my body, letting my heightened Perception swirl around me. I could feel Birch's little heart beating within his body, hear the electricity thrumming through the walls, and sense the cold air blowing through the vents woven into the compound.

Desperate curiosity sparked within me again. I'd agreed to join NIX for two reasons. Partially, to gain their "protection" for myself and my team. And partially because of the alien down below. Maybe, we could have threatened NIX into compliance after breaking the Shortcut and escaped to live in peace, but when I had seen the alien, that had no longer been an option for me. Not until the urge inside me that I didn't even understand had been sated, at least.

The night before, I'd searched my quarters for monitoring devices. I found many, some of them hidden more cleverly than others. I'd destroyed them, of course. Beyond that, I'd been too exhausted to even brush my teeth before falling into bed. I hadn't had the time or the energy to learn much about NIX, or the thing it was holding far below, in the bowels of the mountain. Now I did.

I sent my awareness outward through the air, leaving my room though the vent in the ceiling. It was more difficult to force my awareness to travel through substances I wasn't in physical contact with, and as I pushed farther from my body, even moving at all got exponentially harder. So I let my mind travel through the vents and hallways and spaces where air traveled unimpeded. I sensed Players as I went, an aura of sorts thrumming around them even as they slept.

Occasionally, I passed a bright spark of power that wasn't asleep. A couple roamed the halls, or the cafeteria, and farther down a group of them had gathered in a large room along the way, but my Perception of details aside from the Seed glow was hazy at that distance, and I couldn't tell what they were doing.

I slipped past, straining to hold my concentration together. Downward, level after level, until something pinged on the edges of my alertness. I ignored it. I was used to gaining levels by that point. I'd check my stats later. I strained, but I couldn't keep hold of that strange extra-sensory Perception at such distances. It snapped, fraying like mist through a shredder, and I found myself fully back in my room, my head throbbing fiercely along with my heartbeat.

I DRESSED in the bodysuit NIX provided for its Players, wearing my blood-powered armored vest underneath it. I ignored the boots, because my feet were too strangely shaped nowadays to fit into them, and the skin there was tough. I wove my damp hair into a tight braid and checked the whites of my eyes in the bathroom mirror. I'd disabled its monitoring function the night before. The blood vessels in my sclera were still red and irritated, and patches of rusty brown showed where they'd broken and bled, which made the ice-blue of my irises stand out more. At least it looked better than the disturbing bloody color the whites of my eyes had been the day before, after I'd used too much Chaos.

Before leaving the room, I pulled up my Attributes Window to see what had happened during my mental foray into the carved-out depths of the mountain.

PLAYER NAME: EVE REDDING
TITLE: SQUAD LEADER(9)
CHARACTERISTIC SKILL: SPIRIT OF THE HUNTRESS,
TUMBLING FEATHER

LEVEL: 38 UNPLANTED SEEDS: 0
SKILLS: COMMAND, CHAOS
STRENGTH: 14
LIFE: 27
AGILITY: 21
GRACE: 18
INTELLIGENCE: 17
FOCUS: 17
BEAUTY: 10
PHYSIQUE: 12
MANUAL DEXTERITY: 9
MENTAL ACUITY: 18
RESILIENCE: 22
STAMINA: 19
PERCEPTION: 20

FOR SOME REASON, my out of body awareness didn't count as
a Skill. Maybe because I hadn't gained it through a specific Skill
Bestowal. I didn't advertise its existence, and anyone who didn't
know and saw me using it just thought I was into meditation. The
couple of Seeds Commander Petralka had given me and the others
as a joining bonus weren't noted, either.

I placed my hand on the pad next to my door, and it slid open
onto the slightly curving hallway. One of the barracks doors a few
meters down the hall was also open. A Player leaned nonchalantly
against the doorway, staring straight at the entrance to my quarters. She held my gaze long enough to make it an obvious challenge, then stepped back and waved her door closed.

Birch bared his teeth at her closed door.

I rolled my shoulders to release the tension already building
there, and knocked briefly on the door to my team's room before
signaling it to open. I wasn't going to worry about hostility from
the other Players in NIX, since there wasn't much I could do about
it. Hopefully, our display the day before would keep anyone from

messing with us directly. If not, maybe we would have to put on another gruesome show with the first people to try their luck.

Within the room, most of my teammates milled about in various states of undress, some still obviously waking up.

Birch shot through the open doorway, straight at Adam. He knocked Adam back onto the low bed behind him, ruffled his wings, let out a scratchy roar, and pranced off.

Kris, Blaine's young niece, let out a delighted laugh and bent down, making enticing noises at Birch.

"Be quiet," her younger brother grumbled, scrubbing at his face. Gregor's adorable bushy eyebrows drew down into a scowl like a storm cloud.

"Why does Birch hate me?" Adam said, throwing his arms out dramatically and ruffling Sam's pristinely made bed. Which he was still lying on, apparently having given up on the idea of standing back up.

Zed laughed, leaning down from his bunk above Adam. "Birch doesn't hate you. He loves you. He *loves* to torment you."

I snickered, drawing Adam's attention, and was about to add a comment of my own when a flash of blonde caught the corner of my eye. My first thought was that Blaine was combing Sam's hair. I realized it was China, not Sam. Then I realized it was Chanelle, and her hair had been cut sometime during her stay at NIX. No doubt to make it easier for her captors to care for her. She stared blankly ahead, not seeming to notice the tug of the comb on the boy-short hair of her head, or the people around her. Everything about it was wrong. China's face, even if it wasn't really her, shouldn't be so blank. And she definitely would never have chopped off her princess-hair.

Any amusement died a cold death.

Adam's eyes followed my own, and he sat up, running nimble fingers through the brown mop of curls atop his own head.

"No luck?" I turned to Sam, who was yanking his covers back into some semblance of neatness.

He straightened and shook his head. "I can tell something's wrong with her, or was wrong at some point, but ... I can't fix it. Something's wrong with her brain, I *think*. But it almost seems as if it's natural, rather than an injury. Maybe, it's because whatever it was happened too long ago. I can't take away scars." He grimaced and looked away, but not before I caught a glimpse of the shiny wetness in his eyes.

Jacky hopped down from her own top bunk, landing way too lightly for a normal human. She was unrealistically beautiful even with her brown eyes glazed over and her hair a tangled mess from sleeping. I would have bet money that she put more than a few handfuls into Beauty, if I didn't know better. She clapped Blaine on the shoulder, causing him to drop the comb and wince from the blow. Then she patted Chanelle on the head, gently enough that she probably wouldn't have cracked an egg. "She'll get better, Sam," Jacky croaked sleepily. "We're gonna figure out a way." Then she stumbled to the bathroom, burping loudly and scratching her stomach.

"Ugh, everyone, please shut the gaping holes of loudness and stinking breath you seem to think are your mouths," Gregor said, loud and clear, just as the door opened beside me.

The room quieted for a bit, as we all turned to stare at the child in astonishment.

"Whoa," the new arrival said from the doorway. "Brush your own teeth before you start talking!" Bunny turned to me. His rumpled shirt, hair, and the slightly awkward tilt of his mouth belied the directness of his gaze. "Someone's been having bad dreams," he murmured mockingly.

I almost reacted, thinking he was talking about me, when Gregor muttered, "They're not bad dreams. I'm not an idiot!" and stalked off to the bathroom, the hems of his pajama pants covering his entire feet.

Blaine turned to Kris, a question on his face.

She shook her head and picked up the small stuffed moose

propped up against her pillows. It was old and worn. "We both have bad dreams sometimes, but Mom isn't here to make them seem less real now."

Blaine stared at her through the lenses of his glasses, his hands stilling in Chanelle's hair. "Err ... well ... I am here now. I know I cannot compare to your mother, but—"

Kris shrugged quickly, and cut him off. "We're older now. We don't need you to help us with bad dreams," she said, carefully patting her moose on the head and settling it back against her pillow without looking at Blaine.

I felt awkward on Blaine's behalf, so I turned to Bunny and gestured to Chanelle. "Do you have any idea what's been done to her? Brain damage?"

Bunny shrugged. "That's really not my area of expertise. Besides, wasn't she all 'rabies-biter,' before?" He bared his teeth and made fake claws, swiping at the air.

I stared at him expressionlessly, letting my eyes convey how utterly humorless I found him.

He lowered his hands after a few moments, "Well, I just mean, you guys did something to her, right?" He stared hard at Blaine. "You gave her something that stopped the crazy but made her stupid instead."

Blaine stood up, clenching the comb in his hand hard enough to bend the plastine teeth. "I did *not* do this to her."

"Whoa, *calm down.* You've got to admit it. You're not a doctor, you're a scientist. Maybe you didn't consider all the side effects."

Blaine's arm jerked a couple times, his hands loosened around the comb, and he went back to untangling Chanelle's hair, not seeming to notice that some of the comb's teeth were bent. "I am a genius," he said. "I did not do this." But now, his voice was calm, almost serene in fact.

I lifted an eyebrow. Blaine, calmly accepting someone disparaging his inventions or intelligence? Maybe he really was worried that he'd done something wrong. "Well, NIX has records, right? I'm assuming they were studying Chanelle and whatever it was that infected her. We need that information. Talk to whoever you need to, and make it happen," I said to Bunny.

Bunny hesitated. "That's probably classified information. Besides … they're not very happy with me at the moment."

"I'm pretty sure everything we know about NIX is classified. At this point, does it really matter? If you don't make it happen, Bunny, I'm going to." I let my expression harden a bit.

He scratched the back of his head. "Well, if you agree to get your VR and GPS chips replaced, I could probably get that information." When Jacky, Sam, Adam, and I immediately focused on him, he rolled his eyes. "*Don't be so suspicious*, guys! NIX just wants to make sure they can keep track of you without going to ridiculous lengths, and all the other Players here have working VR chips. They run the classes with them, make announcements, all that stuff."

I felt my shoulders relax just a little. That made sense. But it still didn't mean I was going to agree to give NIX even more power over the team and me.

Jacky shrugged and returned to getting ready, while Sam relaxed with an easy smile, but Adam frowned and shook his head.

Zed hopped down from his bunk. "What about me? The boss lady said you were going to remove the Seed from me. How does that work?"

Bunny shrugged. "I have no idea. The scientists are working on something. They'll let us know when they've got it figured out."

I frowned. "How long is that going to take?"

"Not long, probably. *Don't worry*," he said, meeting my gaze. "NIX will take care of Zed. Commander Petralka knows how valuable you are."

I wasn't that worried. But staring into Bunny's eyes, I realized that I couldn't tell what color they were. That was weird, wasn't it? I nodded, and he smiled, the skin around his eyes crinkling up in happiness.

BUNNY TOOK us first to the cafeteria for breakfast, where we garnered plenty of attention. Everyone knew who we were, apparently. Many had probably seen the pandemonium of our second invasion of NIX, and each had their own response. Some seemed afraid of me, and the power we had displayed. Perhaps unsurprisingly, that response was in the minority. Most watched and waited to see what we would do, like predators waiting for our guard to drop. To be taken in by NIX, you had to be valuable. And above all, NIX seemed to value those of us with monstrous tendencies. I was no exception.

I sighed. It was definitely going to get annoying if everyone didn't go back to minding their own business soon.

After we finished the gigantic and very uncomfortable meal, Kris and Gregor left to go to class, which apparently was being taught by remote schooling. I was surprised, because for some reason I hadn't anticipated that NIX would ensure the kids' continued education while holding them hostage against Blaine.

Blaine left with the kids, excited to spend time with the niece and nephew he'd been separated from for so long, and then to get his lab area set up while they were learning.

Just as Bunny was about to continue our introduction to NIX, some scientist approached and requested that Zed come with him for diagnostic testing.

"He's not going anywhere with you alone," I said automatically.

Bunny sighed loudly. "*You* are the one who asked for this, Eve. *Relax*, and let the man do his job."

Zed looked uncertainly from the scientist to me, but left with him.

I watched him leave, feeling strange. Just as he was about to turn the corner, I crouched down, touching Birch on the flank. "Go after him. Make sure he's safe," I murmured.

Birch fluffed up and raced after my brother, his claws leaving little scratch marks on the floor.

Bunny shook his head, but only sighed. "Come on, guys. Let's get you signed up for classes." As we walked, he launched into a seemingly-rehearsed spiel. "NIX is very interested in helping our Players to develop and expand the utility of their Skills. With some experimentation and practice, you may find that you're more versatile than you originally imagined, or that refinement of your control significantly increases your effectiveness."

He turned to look at Sam. "NIX is particularly interested in helping you develop your Skill, you know. It's rare that we find someone with the ability to heal others, and the juxtaposition between the restorative and destructive side of the coin is fascinating. To the scientists, you know. I heard them talking."

Sam smiled, but it didn't reach his eyes, and he met my own gaze with wordless apprehension once Bunny had turned away. I knew Sam didn't want to use the destructive half of his power any more than he absolutely had to. It was too easy to kill with. "I'd love to take some of the first aid or medic classes," he said after a pause.

"Oh, definitely!" Bunny nodded. "Adam, your Skills are pretty interesting, too. Hyper Focus, Electric Sovereign, and Animus, right?"

Adam nodded silently, his fingers sparking with tiny little flashes as he rolled a coin between them.

"It's a pretty eclectic mix. We're hoping we'll be able to help you integrate them and create some really powerful synergy."

"*We?*" Adam said. "Do you still consider yourself part of NIX?"

Bunny rolled his eyes again. "You're part of NIX now, too. God, why are you all so cynical? This is going to be an ordeal. Step one, remove stick from buttocks. Step two, sigh in relief." He smiled at Adam in that infectious way.

Adam smiled back, though it was more like a smirk on him.

Jacky snorted, and slapped Bunny on the back in approval. "Great advice. So, how's NIX gonna help *me* get stronger?"

I shared a look of amusement with Adam at Bunny's wince and stumble. Soon enough, Bunny would learn to brace himself when Jacky moved in his direction.

Bunny walked us around the circular, multi-leveled base, pointing out our classrooms, places we could go to spar mundanely or practice with our different types of powers, and places where we could go to review previous Player battles. "Players get a chance to contact relatives twice a month. Video chats are restricted to those with good behavior, so *you* guys won't be having those for a while. But as soon as NIX is able to find and contact your families, who seem to have 'relocated' mysteriously, we'll get you in contact with them. Wouldn't want them to think you died!" He laughed, while those of us with relatives still outside NIX shared looks of unease.

We stopped by one of the empty observation rooms. One wall was a big screen, and there were multiple smaller cubicle stations with smartglass tables.

Bunny used his link to activate the wall display. The guards atop the wall and down below went from mostly still to kicked-anthill scrambling, in fast-forward. Then, a small figure appeared atop the wall, as if they'd leapt up, and began to attack.

"This is us," I said. "You recorded us, from yesterday."

"Of course. There are cameras everywhere, as I'm sure you know. But these rooms are mainly used for the Players to view the official mock battles. Your little rampant destruction spree was uploaded only because you haven't participated in any of the battles yet, and I'm sure the others will be eager to analyze it."

"What exactly are these mock battles?"

"Oh, you know. Just practice in military-style fights. In the Trials, you run willy-nilly for your lives, or so I hear. In the mock battles, you have objectives you have to complete, against an enemy that looks and thinks like you, but is stronger than any of the normal human soldiers on Earth. We simulate protecting civilian groups, or taking out enemy strongholds, that sort of thing. Based on your ... 'wanton destruction,' we probably won't be having any Trials for a while, so this is going to be the main way for the Players here to gain Seeds, in addition to the occasional reward for exceptional performance in class."

"So, we fight another group of Players for Seeds, and everybody else watches how we did, trying to figure out how to beat us next time?" Sam said, staring up at the screen, where I was now fighting the Player girl and getting tossed around.

"It shouldn't be that hard," a new voice said. "You're not so special. I have no idea why Commander Petralka agreed to let idiotic traitors like you join."

We turned to the Player standing in the door.

"We're the elite," he said. "You don't belong here." He stepped forward, and a group of other Players filtered into the room behind him, spreading out among the stations.

"Watch yourselves," Bunny said sharply. Without his nonchalant irreverence, his innocuous veneer slipped away.

The Player who'd spoken looked away in an obvious display of submission, and stayed silent.

"Let's go," I said. "I've seen enough here."

As we left the room, I spread my awareness out just enough to keep track of anyone who might see our turned backs as a vulnerability. It irritated my head, and I was just about to reel it back in once we reached the hallway, when I realized a bright spot of power was following us, and it wasn't one of my team.

I turned my head, and saw Bunny exit the room.

He shook his head in exasperation. "You Players are mostly idiots, as I'm sure you're aware. Don't take it too seriously. They'll get over themselves in time, once you're all properly integrated."

I shrugged, keeping the expression from my face, and turned my head back to the front. "Where to now?"

Bunny started talking, and moved to the front of the group to lead the way again, but I wasn't paying attention.

I turned and caught Adam's gaze out of the corner of my eye. I shook my head minutely.

He nodded, the motion almost undetectable.

—Bunny's a Player.—

-Eve-

—I figured. Mind control, do you think?—

-Adam-

Chapter 3

Turn your face toward the sun and the shadows will fall behind you.

— Citron Aodh

ADAM and I discussed our suspicions through Windows, so that neither Bunny nor anyone watching though the cameras at NIX would notice. The need for secrecy resulted in a useful discovery. Instead of body movement or verbal cues, I could use a focused enough *thought* to direct my VR chip.

I discovered this by accidentally wishing to close the Window Adam had sent to me. With a little more experimentation, I found I could mentally dictate and send him a message back, without ever moving my body or speaking a word. Of course, I shared this discovery, and from there it was easy to communicate without fear.

—SHOULD WE TELL THE OTHERS?—
-ADAM-

I debated the question for a bit. They knew how to keep a

secret, but if NIX was watching our every move, lack of knowledge about Bunny's true nature would ensure they weren't able to accidentally give anything away.

—No.—
-Eve-

Adam's mouth twitched in a subtle grimace, but he nodded.

I watched the back of Bunny's unkempt head, my lips twitching as they attempted to pull back in a snarl. What good reason could Bunny have for hiding the fact that he was a Player? Or for manipulating our emotions? Any trust I'd ever had for him had evaporated quicker than rubbing alcohol. If I could just take him somewhere isolated … But no. If he just disappeared, NIX would notice. I couldn't remove him unless I either had a really good way to hide my own involvement in his disappearance, or I no longer needed NIX's goodwill.

We decided to keep a close eye on Bunny and his interactions with the others to make sure he wasn't doing anything too nefarious. We would tell them if it became truly necessary.

The whole situation left me feeling like I had ants crawling up my spine, and only made me more desperate to regain control of everything being swept up by the winds of circumstance. I had to fix whatever was wrong with me, first. Then, I could work on the reason I'd agreed to join NIX in the first place. The creature below. With more information about it, and NIX, I'd be able to figure out what to do about Bunny.

We had some free time after the group gathered again for lunch, since we weren't yet integrated into the schedule of the rest of the Players. I left Adam to keep an eye out for the rest of the team, and grabbed Sam to come with me.

Birch stayed by Zed's side, fluffing up and growling at any of the other Players or guards that came a little too close to my brother for the creature's liking.

I led Sam out into the courtyard, where people milled around, repairing damage, examining the Shortcut, and guarding the compound and surrounding wall. We climbed up onto the top of the wall, where a guard moved as if to stop us, but stopped abruptly when he saw my face.

I listened carefully for monitoring devices, and found them only on the uniforms of the guards, who kept their distance from us.

"What are we doing, Eve?" Sam asked. He looked over the side of the wall, then stepped backward away from the open air.

"I need your help," I said simply. "Follow me." I walked until we were standing over the edge of the mountain, looking down on the crashing waterfall below. The sound would help disguise our voices, I hoped.

"Are you hurt, from yesterday?" he said. "I saw that you didn't look so good, but I was so preoccupied ... with everything ..." He pressed his lips together for a moment, as if scolding himself. "I'm sorry. Where are you hurt?"

"I'm not sure, exactly," I said. "Everywhere, I think."

He laughed, then frowned in confusion when I didn't join in. "Err ... did you get really bruised up? You seem to be walking alright. Broken ribs or something? It could even be internal bleeding, with how you got tossed around." He seemed to be worrying himself more and more with every word. "Eve, you really need to stop toughing these things out and just let me know when you need to be healed. That's *what I'm here for.*" He reached forward, and placed a hand on my forehead.

I watched his face carefully. What would he find?

His eyes went blank for a moment, and then he frowned. "What ..." He grabbed my hand with his free one, and frowned harder. "What's going on, Eve? It's like ..."

"Like what? What do you ... *feel*, or sense, or whatever?" Tension leaked into my voice.

"Something is hurting you, as we speak. It's ... everywhere. It's almost like it's trying to dissolve you, or *eat* you. Your body is trying to heal itself, but it can't keep up. What *happened*, Eve?"

"I did something foolish," I admitted. "But it had to be done."

"What did you do?"

"I ate the Seed of a Goddess," I said simply, knowing he would understand. "She told me my body wouldn't be enough to contain her power, but I thought I'd have more time. But … it's getting pretty bad. It's giving me nosebleeds quite often now, and when my emotions are heightened, I can feel it become agitated. It feels … almost alive, like a wild animal, or a storm that's caged inside me. I've been putting the normal Seeds into Resilience and Life, and meditating to calm it and keep it caged, but that's not enough on its own. I need you to help me stay ahead of it."

"Why didn't you tell me earlier?"

"Because this is what's keeping us safe. I didn't want everyone to feel guilty about it, because we don't have a lot of options. And I didn't want NIX to know, because if they knew I wasn't as strong or valuable as they thought, I wouldn't be such a good bargaining chip. But people might start noticing something is wrong soon, and I can't seem to get my healing factor up high enough to overcome it, so I need some help."

Sam nodded soberly, and said, "I hope you know how stupid you are, Eve," before closing his eyes and getting to work.

Seconds passed, then minutes, as his eyebrows furrowed together, and his skin grew pale. I waited to feel a difference, some feeling of relief, but nothing happened. "What's wrong?"

He shook his head silently, continuing to strain until tiny beads of sweat broke out atop his still-pale skin and his breath grew fast. Finally, he took his hands off me, and stepped back. "I can't," he said. "I don't know what's wrong with me, but I can't fix it. My Skill just glances off. I can tell you're hurt, but I can't get ahold of the injury to pull it into myself." He shook his head desperately, as if denying the truth of his own words.

"Oh," I said, my voice almost swallowed by the wind. "Well, now I'm really worried."

THE NEXT COUPLE days were stressful, to say the least. I asked Sam to keep my condition a secret from the rest of the team, at least until I could come up with a solution of some sort, and he acquiesced, but made me promise I would let him help if he could be useful.

Sam volunteered his services to other Players who got injured in one way or another, which seemed to both reassure him that he could still heal, and to make him more anxious and motivated to keep doing it. I figured it must have been difficult not to be able to heal Chanelle or me.

The Player members of our team, even Zed, started attending classes. Zed had a lighter load of "Player" classes than the rest of us, and spent the rest of his school day with the kiddos, working on his own normal education.

I spent most of the next few days acclimating to classes and trying to perform well enough to earn some Seeds, while any free time was spent meditating and worrying about the Seed of Chaos' effects. I spread my awareness around the base when I had the chance, but I had yet to be able to reach far enough to observe the alien, though I was aware of its location below me at all times, as if it was a beacon.

The scientists came up with a way to remove Zed's Seed, and I carefully controlled my worry around Bunny, but convinced Blaine to come observe the first removal session and make sure everything was okay.

When I arrived in the observation room, Blaine was already sitting in front of the observation window, half paying attention to the scientists below. I used my link to turn on the speakers in the room, playing some loud classical music. NIX was no doubt already frustrated by my insistence on privacy for my private conversations.

Birch pressed his ears back at the noise, his tail flicking back and forth in irritation.

Blaine didn't look up from his tablet as I took a seat beside him, but I was used to that. After a few moments, he spoke casually, as if we'd been talking for hours. "I have made some progress on the diagnosis, but none on a cure. I am not sure there *is* a cure, to be candid. This may be like amnesia, or memory loss. Something we can only hope that the body fixes on its own."

I knew he was talking about Chanelle. "What have you learned about what's wrong with her?"

"The files which Bunny," he said the name with badly hidden irritation, "got for me about what happened to her were redacted. Heavily. Apparently, my clearance level is not high enough to be privy to whatever experiments they were doing. I am going to be speaking directly to the scientists in that research department in the attempt to get more information. For the time being, most of what I know, I have discovered through my own research. Meningolycanosis affects the brain. However, I am not certain that is the entirety of what was done to her. The symptoms suggest that she was infected with something slightly different to the samples I was given to work on, or that in a human host, it interacts complexly with the body. Perhaps even both. Whatever she had seems to have affected her like an advanced, mutated cousin to the rabies virus."

"What does that mean? Are you saying the serum you made to cure her didn't work?"

Birch pressed himself against the cool floor, a small whine escaping him in response to the tone of my voice.

"No, it worked. For the most part. But the damage was already done. In the samples I studied along with your blood, the Seed organisms seemed unable to recognize the meningolycanosis, and it did not attack them and thus draw attention to itself. However, samples I got from Chanelle show an almost nonexistent number of Seed organisms. Much less than I originally estimated, based on China. It seems that somehow, they were all destroyed. It was as if they were a bacteria subject to high doses of antibiotics. Without more knowledge of the timeline of what she was given, and access to research materials, I cannot be sure. Perhaps the upgraded meningolycanosis began to attack the Seed organisms, and in doing so revealed itself for counterattack, and they wiped each other out. Perhaps the anti-meningolycanosis serum I administered allowed the last of her remaining Seeds to remove the meningolycanosis, but not in time to stop their own eradication. Both the meningolycanosis and most of her Seeds are gone. How, I do not know.

"Worrying as that may be, it is secondary to the extensive brain damage. Strangely, it has left her gross motor skills intact, and she seems to be able to understand basic instructions well enough to feed herself and carry out other rudimentary functions. It is also quite a conundrum why Sam is unable to heal her. So far, this is the only ailment I have encountered that seems to elude him, except for perhaps amputated limbs and the like."

I knew that wasn't quite true. "Blaine," I said, turning to the man whose kind features sometimes hid behind his glasses and his focus on whatever fascinating thing he was working on at the moment. "Do you remember examining samples from me, after we got back from our last stay on Estreyer?"

"Of course."

"Did you notice anything unusual about them?"

"More unusual than the two different types of Seed material mixing around within you? More unusual than the subtle ways it has been augmenting your body?"

"I'm talking about the fact that the new Seed is trying to eat me alive," I said.

Blaine hesitated, frowned, and shook his head. "I did not have much time to do extended observation of those samples, as you know. And I did not bring any of them here. When you say, 'eat you alive,' what exactly do you mean?"

"That's what Sam said it seemed to be doing. And he can't heal *me*, either."

Zed finally entered the room below, and I turned my attention from Blaine to wave at my brother.

Zed waved back, but I could tell the joking smile on his face wasn't quite natural. A scientist motioned him onto an obviously high-tech examination table, which cocooned him in glass and began to display diagnostic diagrams and numbers all over the surface. The display was gibberish to me, but the scientists down below gathered around avidly, tapping away on the arched smartglass of the examination table and their own tablets.

Blaine watched them, explaining what they were doing and the readings the table was giving.

After a while, Zed got off the table and drank something green, gagging a few times and screwing up his face into an exaggerated grimace with each swallow.

When I used the mic in the observation room to grill them about it, the scientists assured Blaine and I the liquid was almost perfectly harmless, as long as they completed the rest of the procedure, and didn't stress Zed's liver and kidneys by having him drink it too often. Blaine seemed to believe them, and I was mollified.

Zed said something that made some of the scientists laugh, but I noticed that he didn't look up at me very often, and held himself too still. He was uncomfortable.

They pierced his arm and hooked him up to a machine that began to pull his blood out through a tube, presumably filtering it somewhere within before returning it to his body. After a while, he relaxed and sent me a thumbs up.

When I was assured enough he wasn't being harmed, I settled back again. "Maybe Sam can't heal certain things from Estreyer," I said to Blaine. "Or maybe there is some other sort of restriction on his ability that we just haven't come across until now."

"Perhaps." Blaine looked up from the simulations he'd begun running on his smartglass tablet, the worry on his face an obvious contrast to the unaffected tone of his voice and his academic language. "I do not know what to do, or how to help either of you," he said. "My specialty is science and engineering, not medicine. And I will assume that you do not want to bring the medics of NIX into this." He paused, and added in a low voice, strangely intense, "I would advise against it."

"Of course. I don't trust them. At all. But … maybe the solution is simple. If the meningolycanosis killed off Chanelle's Seeds … maybe she just needs more? You've stopped the meningolycanosis, so it can't keep destroying them, and the Seeds do a pretty good job of healing. Maybe even for things like the brain. NIX might have some research on that, if you could access it. I don't know if we'd be able to focus the Seeds into healing specifically, if we're planting them in her body for her, but it'd probably do *something*, don't you think? I've been using them myself, and Sam said it is working, but just not fast enough. If we could get a significant amount, maybe it could boost my regenerative growth level above the corrosive level of the Seed. Both would keep growing stronger, but as long as my Resilience and Life stayed higher than Chaos' strength, I'd be okay."

Blaine's face brightened and his eyes unfocused from my face. "Perhaps, perhaps. Like compound interest. I would rather not duplicate the circumstances of Chanelle's situation in another living creature for testing, but…" He sobered. "But I do not have access to Seed material, despite the fact that I work here now. Access to Seeds is very restricted, and I have actually already been denied my first request. I had a small sample back at my home laboratory, but that would not be enough to make a difference, and even that is out of our reach at the moment."

"Well," I said, watching Zed down below as the cleaned blood filtered back into his body, "I will just have to find a way."

A COUPLE DAYS LATER, the team was entered into our first mock battle. The battles were announced every two or three days during breakfast, and after the announcement, teams had barely enough time to prepare and move to the arena before the battle started.

I'd been shoveling food into my mouth, because if I didn't eat enough, I knew I'd be starving well before the second meal period of the day. Adam had calculated, with his signature snark, that I ate my own weight in food about once every week. I maintained that I was just going through a growth spurt, but in truth I worried that my body was trying to compensate somehow for the energy it expended fighting Chaos.

"Eve, you eat so much," Jacky said, smirking as she took a bite of the turkey leg held in her fist. "How often do you poop?"

Zed, Kris, and Gregor almost spit out their food with sudden laughter, while Sam stared at her in horror. The others were too busy talking at the other end of the table to pay attention.

Zed gave Jacky's turkey leg a high-five with his own, which somehow devolved into "sword" fighting, and meat flying everywhere.

Birch perked up and took a flying leap for one of the pieces, flapping his wings futilely as he snatched it from the air.

Kris looked at me under her lashes, as if worried that I'd seen her laugh and would be offended.

Gregor cleared his throat, smoothed his face, and pretended he'd never laughed in the first place.

I grinned, and Kris smiled tentatively back, then returned to making a snowman out of mashed potatoes and vegetables, while I resisted the urge to reach over and ruffle Gregor's hair. I knew he hated that, but sometimes he was so cute!

Then, the large screens cut into the walls lit up with the battle announcements.

Like creepy puppets all under the same master's fingers, almost every head in the room turned to look at the screens at the same time. The faces of my nine team members lined up beneath mine on one of the screens, number score and a ranking next to each of us. NIX tracked all its Players, both within its walls and out in the real world, giving them points for their actions. Like Commander Petralka had said, I had one of the highest scores ever for a Player *entering* NIX.

That was nothing compared to the scores of the highest ranked Players, who'd been a part of NIX for far longer.

"They're ranked twelve places above us," Sam murmured.

"And it's a full squad! How are we supposed to fight a full squad?"

Now that I technically had ten people on the team, we were considered a squad. Which was a nasty bit of payback on Petralka's part. When she had agreed to my demands that Blaine, his family, Chanelle, Zed, and Bunny be under my protection, she'd done so by putting them on my team. Even though none of them were fighters, and half of them weren't even Players, my command level was still bumped up to squad leader.

I turned my attention to the other side of the wall, where a screen showed the faces of our opponents, Squad Ridley, along with their ranking. *Shit.* Vaughn Ridley led a squad here? "The ranking isn't always indicative of real strength," I said weakly. It was no comfort. Vaughn had shown me how vicious he was in the Characteristic Trial, and I knew there was no way he'd lead a team any less driven or dangerous. Just alone, he had almost as many Skills as my entire team.

Adam shared a glance with Sam, and turned to me incredulously. "Eve." He drew a breath. "Over half of our squad members aren't fighters. Don't tell me you expect *them*," he gestured to the non-Players at the table, "to fight *them*." He pointed across the cafeteria, where our opponents were stamping their feet and shouting.

Zed scowled, clenching his fork so hard his knuckles turned white. "We can still help, Eve. Just because we don't have Skills and aren't superhumanly powerful doesn't mean we're *useless*. The battles use technology, too. I can use an air-burst gun just as well as you, or fly one of the airpods, or even act as a decoy for one of you to come in and surprise attack them."

I bit the inside of my lip as I watched Squad Ridley jog off through one of the side doors of the cafeteria, moving in formation. "Let's go. We don't have much time," I said.

We moved out, our ragtag bunch not moving in anything close to formation. We had *children* on the squad, and a girl in an unresponsive stupor, so any attempts to look cool and competent were doomed from the start.

Luckily, Bunny knew exactly where our side's battle prep room was, and he led us there, explaining the rules between puffs of air as we jogged. "If we win," he said, "we'll each get twelve Seeds for defeating a squad ranked twelve higher than us, plus the normal five Seeds for winning. If we lose, but impress the Moderators, we still might get a few Seeds on an individual basis." He stopped talking to breath for a few moments. "The prep room will have weapons or supplies that we can take, but I don't expect there to be anything really good, since they stock it depending on overall team rank."

"What?" I gritted out. "So, for our first battle, we take six non-combatants into a fight against a full squad, twelve levels higher than us, and they're going to nerf our supplies to match our average rank? Which includes the ranks of our *non-Players?*"

Bunny let out a little coughing laugh, his gasps for breath reminding me of my own first quests to exercise. Despite the situation, I felt a bit of vindictive satisfaction, since he'd been the one to give me those quests. "Don't be so surprised, Eve. Commander Petralka needs to save some face, and regain a bit of authority. Plus, she's probably," he coughed again, "angry at you. For all that …" He coughed again, and apparently gave up on finishing his sentence.

Adam shared a look with me, his mouth tightened into a grimace. "This does feels very … *personal.*"

Our prep room had a few grated shelves of weapons and supplies, a lot of empty space filled only with an old model airpod large enough to squeeze twenty or thirty people in a pinch, and a small screen on the wall with the battle's objective.

Bunny went straight to the screen and began to read, while the rest of us moved toward the supply racks. There were ten thin bodysuits that went over the top of our standard issue bodysuits, which were meant to evaluate when a Player had taken too much damage, and was considered "dead." One for each of us, and sized perfectly for our bodies. The bodysuit would also alert medics to come save someone, if they needed it. If someone wasn't critically injured, it worked the same way as the electrical immobilizers NIX had used on me when they injected me with my first Seed, and stopped you from moving.

The weapons were mostly nerfed, meant to interact with the monitoring suit to simulate damage and shut down mobility rather than actually harm. Killing the other Players in the mock battles was heavily frowned upon, and apparently resulted in a loss of all Seeds that would have been earned during the battle, but it did happen, since some Skills were more destructive than others. I bet it also happened when someone held enough of a grudge against someone else that they were willing to give up on the Seeds for the chance to kill them.

"The objective is to protect a group of civilians that have hidden about a third of the way into the arena, and evacuate them safely," Bunny yelled. "It's simulating some high priority targets mixed in with the civilian group. Scientists and politicians. It doesn't say what the other team's objective is, but based on ours, it's almost certainly to wipe out the civilian population, and probably to "dispatch" our team as well."

"How much time left?" I shouted.

"Nine minutes."

I grabbed one of the airburst-round guns, and hooked it onto the utility belt at my waist, along with plenty of extra ammo.

Beside me, Zed did the same with competent efficiency and a tight expression.

I didn't try to stop him, though seeing him suiting up for battle made my stomach clench.

"No!" Blaine's voice rang out, sharp enough to draw my attention.

Gregor scowled up at him, holding tightly with both hands to a gun of his own. "I'm not going in there without a weapon. I don't trust you or any of these other idiots to be able to protect me!"

Kris shifted from foot to foot, looking between her brother and her uncle. "I want one, too. We don't have to be a burden to everyone else. If we're attacked, at least we'll be able to defend ourselves." She turned to me, a pleading look on her face.

Gregor stomped toward me, still holding the gun. "I can have this, right?"

I looked up at Blaine, who was staring at me wordlessly, his expression mixed between pain, anger, and resignation. "It's best if they can help defend themselves," I said to him before turning back to them. "I'm not going to send you into battle, but if one of them comes after you, don't go down without a fight."

Blaine didn't say anything, just turned away and latched a large shield onto his arm, which clamped on and then contracted down to the size of a bulky armguard.

Sam was loading up with medical supplies and a couple shields of his own, while Jacky fitted what looked like gauntlets onto herself, and Adam filled his utility belt with ink cartridges and electrical cells, which had been provided specifically for him.

"Bunny!" I called. "Come grab a gun and a shield, at least. We're running out of time."

"Oh, I was thinking I'd just ..." He caught sight of my scowl. "Okay, okay. Battle gear it is."

I turned to Chanelle and helped her dress in the top layer bodysuit, then strapped a light pack onto her back and filled it with ammo and first aid supplies, just in case.

Birch yowled scratchily up at me, drawing attention to himself for the first time since the announcement had gone off. He reached up with his forepaws toward one of the smaller packs, and yowled again.

With a tiny smile that left almost as quickly as it had appeared, I grabbed the pack and helped him strap it on, and tossed the few remaining grenade rounds in, along with some random supplies that I'd learned through experience might come in useful, and wouldn't weigh his small body down too much.

Adam tossed the rest of the guns into the airpod and started it up. We all jumped in with only seconds to spare before the hangar door on the wall opened onto a war-torn cityscape.

Chapter 4

It is easier to break than mend. For everything I learned to heal, I
learned a thousand times to end.

— Sha Du

ADAM PLACED his hands flat on the dashboard, and closed his
eyes as little tiny sparks of electricity jumped from him into the
airpod. It took about thirty seconds, but then the craft shuddered
and took off, angling forward and shooting into the city.

"Stay low," I said. "If they're flying, too, I don't want them to
know where we are. And Bunny, you read the objectives, so you
should have best idea where the 'civilians' are. Navigate
for Adam."

I closed my eyes, letting my awareness spread out from the
ship, into the life-size, three-dimensional model of the city. One
whole level of NIX was devoted to the mock battles and the three-
dimensional printer that created the environment anew every
few days.

I didn't notice any sign of life, or the other team, which I hoped was a good thing. "Bunny," I said. "Tell me about Squad Ridley. What are their Skills, their specialties? What have people done to beat them?"

"They've never failed an objective," Bunny said. "Not completely, anyway. I know the leader has like six different Skills, or something. He pushes his team hard, and they're always training. I'm pretty sure the team is geared toward "attack" type missions. Kinda like this one, I guess. Except, you know, they're probably way better than us. As far as *specifics* go, I don't know. I wasn't the Moderator for any of them, and I haven't really paid too much attention to that stuff."

I kept my eyes closed, since my awareness was enough to notice the fast beat of his heart contrasted with the slightly mocking smile on his face as he looked out over the front window onto the city. I wasn't sure whether he was lying, or just slightly creepy.

We arrived without incident at a large building, one of the tallest in the area. The hostages were supposedly within somewhere.

I didn't like how exposed the ship was, or how vulnerable I felt doing this type of mission. I preferred when we were the ones attacking with the element of surprise, plenty of preparation, and no one to worry about protecting. We had no experience as a team on this type of mission. I directed Adam to fly the ship into the cover of a half-destroyed building nearby. "Okay," I said. "We've got to assume the other team also has this location, and will be coming soon. How many 'civilians' are there?"

"About twenty, according to the objectives."

"Okay. Jacky, Sam, Zed, and Adam. Go get them. Highest priority on the important targets, if you can tell them apart."

They nodded, and left at a run, Adam at the lead.

I hated to send so many of my competent team members away, but I had no idea if they'd encounter obstacles or difficulty of some kind, or end up needing to physically carry the 'civilians.' Their protection and rescue was the main objective of the mission, and not one we could afford to fail. I turned to the remainder of the team. "Blaine, if you needed to, could you fly this ship?"

"Not as well as Adam, but I could fly it."

"Good. I'm pretty sure there's a training program built into it. Start practicing." I paused, closed my eyes, and took a deep breath, pushing my awareness outward with a forceful swirl, like the beginnings of a tornado, quickly aborted. Still no sign of our opponents, but I could feel Jacky breaking down the door to the building, and I pushed my awareness inside on the wind, stretching to try and find the civilians. There were no signs of life, but down in the basement I found a group of robots. Little more than manikins capable of rudimentary movement, really. That was why I hadn't sensed any human presences, but those were undoubtedly the target. I sent a Window to Adam.

—THE BASEMENT.—

-EVE-

I opened my eyes, and caught Bunny staring at me curiously, his face far too near my own for comfort. "I've got a plan," I said, pushing my palm into his face and forcing him back. "Grab the extra guns."

I walked over to Birch, who was crouching near the open door of the airpod, ears pricked and teeth bared, as if daring something to *try* and attack.

"Good thing you're here," I said, ruffling the fur on his little head, and reaching inside his backpack for the spool of plastine wire and duct tape.

He growled a little under his breath, not averting his attention from the self-appointed duty of watchdog.

We knocked out the windows on the ship, and fastened the guns to them, pointing outward. We disabled the safeties, and tied the wire around the triggers, strings leading inward to the center of the little airpod.

I had Bunny strap himself down in one of the seats, and tied the ends of each plastine wire to the armrests. "When they come, Blaine is going to fly this ship off. You're going to man the artillery for him."

"What!?" Bunny squawked.

"Pull the wires for the gun you want to fire. Try to be sensible about it, and don't waste too much ammo, since I doubt you're going to want to unstrap and get up to reload any of them."

"Eve, we need this ship to escape with the hostages," Bunny said, in the tone of someone trying to reason with a crazy person.

"No. We need *a* ship. This one is going to be a decoy, and I'm going to get us another one. I don't have time for you to argue," I said. "I'm taking the kids and Chanelle with me, and we'll put them out of the way where the other squad isn't going to think to come after them. You two are going to run away and fire at them as if you've got plenty of people on board that you need to protect, and I'm going to commandeer a ship to pick up the hostages and the kids."

Bunny muttered something about not being a bait-worm, and that he should have been hiding somewhere safe, too, but I'd already turned to the kids.

"Are you ready?" I asked.

They both nodded, though Kris was pale and kept wiping her sweaty hands on her suit. Gregor's face was stony, but his eyes darted about restlessly, searching for danger.

"Blaine, do you have anything to add?" I joined him at the control panel, where he was furiously fiddling with the controls with both hands.

He grunted. "Keep them safe," he said, his attention obviously on his task. "I am going to fly this ship as if I am a desperate madman. The enemy will not have a choice but to devote some of their attention to me."

I squeezed his shoulder, and with a nod to the kids, grabbed Chanelle's hand and hopped out of the airpod. Luckily, she was pretty responsive to basic physical stimuli, so she ran along with me, though I had no idea if she actually understood anything that was going on around her.

I sent another Window to Adam.

—Take hostages to the roof. Will be doing rooftop pickup, using an enemy ship.—
-Eve-

—Risky. I'm sending Jacky up first to help. Got it handled here, no opposition to hostage pickup.—
-Adam-

I ran along at a pace the kids could barely keep up with, though Birch seemed to manage just fine with four legs instead of two. I was just turning a corner when a glint of light up above caught my eye. I dug my clawed toes into the ground, stopping so fast that Chanelle and the kids ran into me before they could stop themselves.

I scrambled back around the edge of the building, and sent my awareness out and upward. My range was much better than it had been when this faux Skill had first developed, but I still could barely reach the edge of the roof a couple blocks over and many stories up. Even so, it was enough, and I confirmed the presence of an enemy. I hadn't even noticed them move in! Did they have airpods, or had they come in on foot? If they were all on foot, my plan was going to be ruined.

I stretched my awareness to its limits, ignoring the whispered questions from Kris and Gregor as I searched for other enemies. I found none, but that didn't reassure me. "A Player from the other squad is up on the roof over there," I said. "We have to go a different way. Gregor, I'm sorry but you're going to have to ride piggyback. Your legs aren't long enough for the speed we need."

The solemn boy nodded, his lips pressed together, and climbed up onto my back without complaint, latching on with both his arms and legs. "Run fast," he murmured into my shoulder.

And I did, Chanelle and Kris barely able to keep up with my preternatural speed.

We reached one of the other tall buildings near the hostage's hiding point, and I fed the children and Chanelle through one of the seemingly long-broken windows on the ground floor. The door to the stairwell was locked. But even though I wasn't as strong as Jacky, the lock was rusted, and a few kicks and a yank with all my might broke it open. We ran, upward, step after step. A glimpse out one of the sparse windows we passed showed an airpod arriving. It was smaller than the one we'd been issued, made for attack rather than transport.

Kris was panting, her breathing ragged. When I told her to move faster, she nodded, and kept up with me, if only barely.

Chanelle was gasping for breath as well, but in an easier way, as if she wasn't really bothered by the fatigue or muscle pain I knew she had to be feeling, without any Seeds left in her body.

Atop my back, Gregor was silent, clinging tightly so as not to unbalance me.

When we got to the door to the roof, I stopped.

Kris fell to the ground, heaving. Her face was pale and beaded with sweat, and she looked almost sick. As soon as I had the thought, she leaned over the stairwell and threw up. "Sorry," she muttered, still panting. "It's just the running. I'm okay." She wiped her sleeve across her mouth, and used her arms to pull herself up by the rails of the stairwell.

"You did well," I said, letting Gregor down. "You guys are going to stay here for now, okay? I'm going to go attack the airpod out there, and once I'm finished, I'll come to pick you up in it. Shoot anyone that comes who isn't me. And don't worry, you'll be fine."

With that, I cracked open the door onto the roof, and spread my awareness once more. "Damn," I muttered aloud. Three airpods, not one. All of the attack-style variant, and closing in on the target building from three different directions.

Birch growled under his breath, hunching low at my feet.

"You should stay with the kids," I murmured to him. "Especially since you can't fly yet." On the upside, at least the enemies weren't all on foot, and there *was* a ship for me to try and commandeer, moving toward me at that very moment. I wished Blaine had a VR chip, so I could contact him and tell him it was time to go, but instead I had to wait.

Luckily, I wasn't stuck hiding against the door of the stairwell for long.

Our ship rose from the half-demolished building, scraping against the walls a little as it did so. It fired a couple shots at the nearest enemy airpod, both from the ships' guns, and from the rigged windows, and then turned at a sharp angle, racing away at top speed. Blaine handled it surprisingly well, weaving in and out among the buildings like he had a death wish.

The two airpods that had been closing in from the ten and two o'clock angle turned to follow him, already spitting shots of their own, while the one coming in from behind me, at six o'clock, seemed to actually slow for a second instead of speeding up.

Was someone inside able to sense me, maybe? I worried for a second, but the airpod sped up again, on a trajectory to pass right next to the building I was on.

I burst out of the doorway, slamming it closed behind me and running toward the edge of the roof.

The pilot must have seen me for sure, then, because the ship slowed, rotating in midair to face me.

It was too late. I jumped off the side of the roof like an animal, claws fully extended, and slammed into the side where the seam of the doorway allowed me to dig in. This close, the airpod's guns wouldn't be able to hit me.

I was digging my claws into the door, preparing to try and rip it away, when the whole door blew off and outward, with me on it. I twisted in midair, angling the door under me and looking up at the airpod, where a Player glared down at me. I had only a second to be surprised, before the door and I both hit the roof of a lower building and went tumbling.

I rolled with the momentum, tucking my arms around my head to protect it, and came to a hard stop against the lip of the roof, bruised and winded.

The Player jumped down after me, the force of her thrust making the airpod wobble for a moment before the pilot regained control. She walked toward me calmly, her eyes just a little unfocused, as if she was looking more at the area around me than directly at me.

I let my awareness wash over her, and was dismayed by how brightly she shone. I wasn't sure exactly what her Skill was, but she was strong. And obviously not afraid of me, if the slight smile on her face was any indication.

I stood up, and slid into the fighting stance Jacky had shown me. Inside, Chaos swirled eagerly, and I took a shuddering breath, trying to ignore it. I attacked first, claws out in a straight thrust toward her throat.

She slid to the side as if I was moving in slow motion, gripped my wrist, and slammed her hand toward the back of my elbow.

I panicked, I'll admit it. The thought of my arm bending backward, the tendons tearing and the joint ripping apart, was enough to make me act without thinking. Chaos bubbled up in a wave from my stomach, rushing along my outstretched arm.

She released me immediately, jumping back so hard she skidded when she hit the ground and had to stretch out a hand for balance.

My attack dispersed futilely in the air, leaving only the arm of my outer bodysuit a little ripped up, as if it had been a surge of little razors that passed. The backlash hit me. I should not have used Chaos. I hadn't meant to, but now it was only more imperative that my team won, because I'd need the Seeds to mitigate the damage.

I dashed forward, but only made it a couple steps before the airpod she'd arrived in shot at me. I tried to dodge, and in an instant, she was in front of me again, her hand smashing into my face, my solar plexus, my kneecap. She swept out a leg, knocking my own out from under me, then kicked me with a forward thrust before I even hit the ground, so hard that I flew. I once again crashed into the lip of the roof.

I rolled over, and pushed myself up, but my knee buckled and I barely caught myself. I let out a low keening moan, and unhooked my gun.

Instead of shooting at her, I aimed for the airpod. I hadn't wanted to damage its flight capabilities, but at this point, I just needed to reduce the number of concurrent threats.

My shots didn't even come close to hitting, and I was about to turn my attention to the girl, who was now sprinting toward me, when both Kris and Gregor burst out of the nearby roof's stairwell, rounds slamming out from the muzzles of their guns.

Gregor shot down at the girl, who avoided the airburst rounds just as easily as she'd avoided my claws, while Kris doubled up on my fire at the airpod, and actually got a few hits in, which caused it to tumble away out of sight.

The girl turned her attention toward the kids, and I screamed at them. "What are you *doing*? Go back inside!" I ignored the grating sensation in my knee and pushed myself toward her, hoping to distract her before she got any ideas about attacking the kids.

The airpod rose from between the two buildings, having recovered from the temporary loss of control. It shot at the ground around the kids, obviously not aiming for them directly. Whoever was inside at least had a little bit of a conscience, I guessed.

"Go back *inside*!" I screamed again, my voice breaking.

Instead, they threw a couple of the nerfed grenades from Birch's pouch at the airpod, and ducked down back behind the lip of the roof.

The force of the explosions made the airpod tumble sideways

and lurch drunkenly, but it recovered, and by then the girl was attacking me again, her hands and feet lashing out even faster than Jacky's, seeming to anticipate my every move.

—JACKY, I NEED YOUR HELP.—
-EVE-

I sent the Window with a thought, backpedaling frantically, desperately avoiding the other Player's attacks.

—I'M ALMOST THERE.—
-JACKY-

She was true to her word, leaping off the side of the civilian target building, arms and legs circling as she sailed through the air. She slammed into the side of the airpod, and then jumped off again, heading toward the girl.

The girl sidestepped just as Jacky was about to hit her, but Jacky corrected easily, touching down with absurd lightness based on how fast she'd been hurtling through the air, and spinning around to attack.

The much-abused airpod finally seemed to lose control, its side dented a little where she'd made contact.

Kris and Gregor appeared over the edge of the roof above, and threw some more grenades, which seemed to seal the deal.

I caught a glimpse of the pilot frantically manning the controls as it tumbled toward one of the nearby buildings and disappeared out of sight. I would have cheered, if not for the arrival of one of the other ships, which looked a little scuffed up, but otherwise perfectly fine. Either it had given up on chasing Blaine and Bunny, or they were downed.

The new arrival shot *directly* at the kids. It blasted them back over the edge of the roof, and they didn't stand up again. I screamed once more, and sent my awareness lashing out toward them, desperately pleading with anything out there to have mercy, and not let them be hurt over some stupid little *contest*.

Birch was crouched over them, yowling at the new airpod, real snarls managing to make their way out of his tiny voice-box.

—Sam, the kids!—
-Eve-

I sent him a Window with a map of their location along with the message, and immediately turned my gun toward the new airpod, shooting off air-burst rounds in an attempt to draw it away from them.

I felt Gregor stir, and together, he and Birch worked to pull Kris back toward the stairwell. Not fast enough. Gregor wasn't using one arm, and Kris lay limp.

I shot at the new airpod frantically, reloading clumsily when I ran out of ammo.

It wove in the air and avoided most of my shots, but didn't even bother to turn and shoot back at me. I sprinted toward the edge of the roof. I wasn't Jacky, but I thought I could make the jump to the airpod. I had to, because the kids were exposed still, and I had no idea how badly Kris was hurt. I could only pray that it was her top layer bodysuit keeping her limp, and not a serious injury or concussion.

That was when the side of the target building, where the others were traveling with the hostages, exploded.

I didn't have a chance to figure out what caused it, because afterimages of a man's body flickered in front of me, between me and the edge of the roof.

I skidded to a stop as Vaughn solidified in front of me, and then he broke into transitory multiples again, and something hit me, and tore at me, and I spun through the air, my outer bodysuit kicking on and enacting the electrical immobilizer.

I lay on the graveled rooftop and watched helplessly out of the corner of one eye as Jacky fell back, one arm already hanging limply at her side. Her head turned, and I saw the crushed cheekbone and eye socket, and her eyeball trailing out, connected only by a fleshy string. I wasn't sure if she was still conscious as her opponent smashed her literally down through the roof.

It was only a couple seconds later that the klaxon blared, declaring an end to the mock battle.

Chapter 5

Farewell Hope, and with Hope farewell Fear.
— John Milton

I GOT three Seeds for my performance in the mock battle. I wasn't sure I actually deserved them.

Adam got two, apparently for some impressive Skill work.

Despite not being a Player, Gregor got one.

This shocked Blaine at first, and then drove him to quiet rage.

Gregor agreed to give the Seed to Chanelle when Blaine explained to him that they might help heal her brain damage.

Blaine and the carrier airpod had been downed, and his suit had immobilized him while he was out in the middle of the city, with no way to check in or see what was going on.

Sam was already busy healing Kris and Gregor by the time Blaine learned what they'd done. Blaine berated the kids, white-faced as he watched Sam assume Gregor's broken arm and second-degree burns, and Kris' broken ribs and minor concussion.

We all gathered together in the barracks, after NIX's medics and Sam had done what they could for everyone. Jacky was more withdrawn than I'd seen her in a long time, and when I sat beside her, she murmured, "I'm really sorry, Eve. She just ... she was *better* than me." Sam had patched her eye socket back together, but it was still fragile enough that she had to wear a bandage around her head to keep everything in place.

I shrugged. "She was better than me, too." I was just glad she was alive. I'd wondered for a moment, when I saw her injuries.

"But I'm supposed to be the fighter, no? It's my job." She hunched her shoulders. "I'm gonna train more, I promise."

I bumped her with my shoulder, ignoring the throb it caused my bruises. "We'll all train more. Don't worry about it."

She nodded, but didn't smile.

Adam was suffering from the exhaustion of Skill overuse, to the point that he could barely move, and he fell asleep in his chair.

Zed drew on Adam's face with a marker while he slept, but his mischievous smile didn't ring true.

Sam flopped back on his cot and went straight to sleep, but even in repose his face was pale and strained. We relied on him too much, but his demands to heal what he could had held an intensity that wouldn't be denied.

Before the end of the day, what had been wary watchfulness in some of the Players turned to open hostility in almost all of them. I made sure the team knew to travel in groups of at least two or three, and turned my mind to making sure something like this never happened again.

The next day, Blaine and I went down together to one of the battle observation rooms and watched a replay of what had happened. His knuckles went white around the edge of the table when the kids left the cover of the stairwell, and when the airpod shot and hit them whatever he'd been containing snapped out of him. He smashed his fist into the table and the sides of the station's walls, glasses flying off and getting crushed mindlessly under one of his now-bloody fists.

I didn't try to stop him. I knew what it felt like to need a release, even if it hurt a bit. Sometimes, things built up to the point they were unbearable.

Still, every time his knuckles slammed down into something harder than they were, with another panting, desperate breath just on the edge of tears, I flinched. I had taken the kids, and I was supposed to keep them safe. I'd been the one to give them weapons. Maybe they would still have gotten hurt if I'd kept them unarmed, or left them with Blaine, but it seemed obvious that the way they had *actually* gotten hurt was almost entirely my fault.

When Blaine tired himself out, he dropped into one of the chairs and sat silently for a few moments.

Tentatively, I picked up his broken glasses, and handed them to him.

He put them on, though they were lopsided on his face, and one of the lenses had been shattered and was missing. "The rest of us need VR chips," he said, almost conversationally.

I was surprised enough by this that I didn't respond.

"Ones that aren't," he paused, and almost whispered, "*accessible by 'outside sources'* like the modifications I made for your team. Except we should all be able to communicate with each other freely, rather than needing to route messages through you."

I nodded slowly. "That's a good idea."

"And the kiddos need to start learning self-defense. And working out. Maybe they won't ever be able to stand up to one of you, but I want them to at least be able to fight back enough to escape." He paused again. "I am going to start doing that, too. And training with the battle technology. I cannot be useless if I am going to be an ... *active* part of this ..."

I reached out awkwardly and put a hand on his shoulder. He didn't push it off, but I struggled to find words. "Blaine ... I'm so sorry. I'll help you in any way I can. We all will, you know."

He nodded, and stood abruptly. "I am going to my lab. If you wish to join me, I will see if there is anything I can do to help *you*." He gave me a meaningful stare and strode off.

I followed him. Technically, the area was off limits, but Blaine ignored the alarms and the guards that responded to them, and eventually things settled down.

Something about the irritating sirens reminded me of the klaxon blowing to signify my team's utter defeat. I'd been out-strategized, our technology had been eclipsed, and on an individual basis, we'd been outclassed by the Players of the other team.

Blaine had a small lab, adjacent to the huge one, which contained the alien spaceship. He entered it and immediately began to putter around, muttering to himself and drawing diagrams on the smartglass screen that covered one of his walls. He'd turned on some ambient water sounds, the volume high. He took samples of my blood, claws, hair, and the inside of my mouth. While he got to work, I sat in an armchair at the corner of his lab, crossed my legs, and leaned back. I was so tired. "Blaine," I murmured, "I'm just going to close my eyes for a moment."

He didn't even acknowledge my words.

I breathed in deep and exhaled my awareness. It filled the room, and then drifted out through the vent in the ceiling. NIX had huge air shafts running through the entire base, as far as I could tell. I'd thought things like that were a cliché from the films. There was always the whirling fan blade that the character had to time and jump through at just the right moment to avoid being cut in half … or flames that shot out periodically, something like that.

But any sufficiently large industrial system that needed to cool machinery or transport air deep into the ground needed an extensive ventilation system. From what I understood, NIX also had an oxygen-scrubbing fail-safe, but it was too expensive to put in place unless we were on lockdown due to a nuclear war or some sort of airborne biohazard.

I was deeper in NIX than I'd been since Commander Petralka had taken me to see what our world was up against. Maybe … I took another deep breath, trying to calm my body, and pushed out, reaching downward through the vents, farther and farther, level after level. I passed plenty of interesting things along the way, but the thing that almost distracted me was the number of Seed-imbued people as I went farther. I was pretty sure they weren't Players. Not per se, anyway. Maybe, they were Moderators, like Bunny?

I felt my attention straining, so I ignored them and continued on till I reached a sterile holding cell with enough fail-safes to contain a herd of rabid elephants. Or an alien, I guess. Since that's what it was actually containing.

I slipped in through the small vent in the ceiling, trying not to let the strange buzzing vibration that filled the room distract me, and snap my concentration. Conversely, the clarity of my senses seemed to sharpen. I reached out tentatively to the angled metal slab in the middle of the room, and felt the huge creature shackled to it. Power radiated from him, flowing in his veins and *brightening* him in a way that had nothing to do with sight, and everything to do with whatever non-sensory Perception the Oracle had given me. I had to consciously hold myself back from thinking of him as a man, and remind myself that though he may look like a larger version of us, he wasn't human.

I focused my attention on his face, which was half-obscured by an unkempt beard, observing him in secret as he slept. Or maybe he was drugged into sedation. He looked sick enough. I pushed forward, touching the gaunt skin over his cheekbone, mentally almost tasting the clammy sweat there.

His eyes snapped open, staring out into the empty air of his room as if he knew I was there.

We had met before, in my mind.

When I had first been injected with a Seed, I'd had glimpses of this room, and thought they were a hallucination. When I was dying after my Characteristic Trial, and after my younger brother injected himself with a Seed and I'd broken down from despair, I'd met him twice more. After I'd solved the Oracle's first puzzle, I'd had a vision of Behelaino, and then a dream. And I'd worn his body in that dream. Or maybe it was also a vision. I didn't know. I felt almost as if I was slipping into his skin, the sensation dizzying, as my paradigm of the world shifted.

I still was reeling when his rage slammed into me. He shoved my existence away with a white-hot anger, and I crashed back into my body with a searing headache.

He hated me. It wasn't just anger. He *loathed* me, and me specifically.

BLAINE DIDN'T REACT to my muffled gasp as my attention returned fully to my body.

I reeled mentally for a second, almost nauseous. I stood and moved to the doorway.

The scientists were so caught up in their work that they didn't notice me, despite the dark color of my bodysuit indicating I was a Player.

I waited at the door for a while, just watching them work and looking around at the crazy inventions. The hair on the back of my neck stood up, the skin prickling. I rubbed at it. My eyes lingered on the alien spaceship. It really was damn cool, even if it was from a species determined to wipe us humans off the face of the planet.

Something prickled at the back of my mind. Maybe it was discomfort at what I'd just experienced. But instead of dissipating as time passed, it grew as I watched the scientists, and thought back to the almost ant-like crawl of people though the underground tunnels and rooms of NIX.

I realized once again that NIX had some amazing technology and resources.

But this time, that realization scared the feeling out of my fingertips.

If NIX had been better prepared, we might not have won when we attacked. They constantly drilled us, preparing us to fight against people as strong or stronger than us. How could they have been unprepared to fight against Players, their own cultivated weapons? I didn't trust Bunny even as far as I could no doubt throw his scrawny frame, but he'd mentioned that NIX was worried I might be a Player from somewhere else. If that was true, they would have been prepared for Player-level attacks. If they'd used their technology ... If they'd sent out Players to fight Players instead of weak soldiers ...

I'd been cocky, sure. But I knew now we weren't the strongest, so why hadn't they sent out a group of people like Vaughn, with armored suits and some heavier weaponry, to neutralize us? I could almost feel my brain buzzing against the muffling nature of a building headache.

Had they been afraid I really *would* be able to win against them, and then escape? Maybe ... they wanted me to *feel* like I won. Why else send expendables out to fight me?

But if so, why? What did they gain? I looked up, and around at the chaos as scientists milled around the huge lab, working at personal stations or tables, or entering and exiting the auxiliary labs that filled this whole level of the base. There I was, standing among them, having just resolved to train harder for NIX, after getting my ass handed to me in a mock battle they orchestrated.

I stumbled back, letting the wall support me, as my legs were too weak to do so. It felt as if these questions may have been hiding in the back of my mind for a while. I had been deliberately ignoring them. And that wasn't like me. Maybe Bunny had more influence than I'd thought. That was a terrifying idea, that I resolved to explore in detail. But even so, why would they do this?

If I looked at the outcome, and worked back from there to find the answer, it was easy to see that NIX got what they wanted. They now had stronger Players with special Skills under their control, and I and my whole team ended up beholden to them. When NIX was first preparing to fight off an alien invasion, they must have realized the stupid tropes in the sci-fi films weren't realistic.

No human could successfully hack an alien computer with

only their link. The aliens wouldn't have some specific weak spot so obvious a five-year-old could point it out, which one man could exploit to bring all the invaders to their knees. An alien race that had achieved interstellar travel would probably outnumber us, would definitely outgun us in every way, and lastly, outsmart us. We couldn't just increase army enlistment and train soldiers, funnel resources and fund military research. We had to get smarter before any of that would yield quick enough results.

I'd bet my life that when NIX first discovered the possibilities inherent in the Seeds they supercharged the Intelligence of every compatible candidate they could get their hands on. Those people would be working on everything from technology, to battle tactics likely to prove successful for humans, to ways to manage Earth's population up to and during an attack.

There was no way they would have botched my recruitment. I suddenly recalled Nadia saying to me that I'd escaped *almost* all of their methods of monitoring me, praising me for my trickiness. I groaned under my breath, a low, sick sound with a hint of a whimper. How could I have missed that?

Bunny. He'd come off as a bit of an ignorant rookie, working for the bad guys but just a normal person who was a bit weak-willed. But he'd been a Player all along. Or maybe, I should say that he'd been a Moderator, all along. I knew they had psychological evaluations done on all Players before even injecting them with the initial Seed, and they probably continued to develop those evaluations afterward. It would make sense for them to pair Players with a master manipulator who monitored their every move. Someone literally built to control the weak-willed. Bunny had been chosen to be my Moderator, and even now that master manipulator was on my squad, under my "protection" from NIX's retribution.

And if Bunny had been a plant, what about Blaine? Why would a genius like him, who was supposedly being *forced* to work for them, have been allowed outside of NIX? Another valuable asset, ripe for me to acquire and turn on them. He was perfectly situated to subtly guide my choices, leading us to his masters, acting as another spy, all the time. I shook my head in denial, even as I had the thought. I didn't want that to be true.

I realized what Blaine knew, NIX might know. The side effects of the Seed of Chaos might not be at all secret. My find filled with horror like a glass fills with water, to overflowing.

I wanted to deny it. I was jumping to conclusions, I must be. There had to be another explanation. And maybe there was. But I knew that no matter what truth came to light, things weren't how I'd thought them to be, and I couldn't trust anything around me. It would be illogical to do so.

How did I even know the others on my team came to me organically, that NIX had not been guiding my every action with an unseen hand? Chanelle, made important to me as the person to help me when I was alone and frightened, sending me to her sister, the girl who became my first ally and even a friend after that? Jacky, obviously stronger than the rest of us that first Trial, enough so that I would notice and remember her? Adam, who Bunny had me "save" from being caught in possession of a knife. Then Sam, who Bunny sent to save *me* when I was about to die, furthering my trust in the both of them.

I grew dizzy as my breath heaved in and out of my chest, too fast for comfort. I looked down at the link on my arm, pulling up the time. Zed was about to enter a cleansing session. A horrible certainty filtered down from my head, settling in my stomach like a living thing. I turned, almost mechanically, and sat back down in the corner of Blaine's office.

Then I pushed my awareness outward again, ignoring the headache. It took me a few minutes to travel unnoticed to the vents around the lab they used during Zed's sessions, but I still arrived before he did.

Scientists and researchers bustled around the room, most wearing white coats. I could hear them clearly, chatting as they prepared the equipment. Two in the corner worked on a glass screen set into the wall, examining the display that my Perception didn't even come close to being able to render at this range.

"This subject has been amazingly successful," one noted to the other. My heart sank, and I focused my hearing on them.

"He is Redding's brother. I wonder if that has any bearing on it, or if it's solely due to the fact that he's been forcefully kept alive through the initiation by her healer. Hawes, wasn't it?"

"Samuel Hawes. Interesting Skill if I ever saw one."

Zed's entrance cut off whatever reply the second scientist had been going to give. He smiled wide and greeted all the scientists by name.

To my slight surprise, they greeted him warmly in turn. Maybe they *weren't* doing anything nefarious, but I continued to monitor them to make sure, since the true measure of their trustworthiness was what they would do when they thought no one was watching.

They did some diagnostic scans and then ran Zed through stress tests, taking samples of everything as he ran on a treadmill, caught small balls as they shot at him from machines, lifted weights while answering their rapid-fire logic questions, and so on.

My worry morphed steadily into a fatalistic dread. He was performing more like a Player than a normal human. A weak Player, true, but they hadn't had him for long, yet. I swallowed. Maybe it was just talent. He'd always been better than me at anything physical, and he was smart.

My desperate hopes died as they laid him out on a device that looked similar to the diagnostic machine they'd used the first time. But this time, as he lay on the slab like it was an operating table, they put him to sleep. Clear walls rose up from the sides of the slab, curving over and enclosing him like a stasis chamber, or a clear tomb. They gathered all around his prone form. Then, clear tubes and needles grew from the glass all around him, piercing his flesh in hundreds of places.

I clamped my hand over my mouth, holding back a whimper. I kept the majority of my focus on the room hundreds of meters away, but took a moment to reassure myself nothing was amiss near my body. Blaine didn't seem to have noticed my involuntary physical response.

Then one of the scientists with Zed pushed some buttons, and the glass lit up with electricity, though I couldn't tell what it was displaying. "Everyone knows their task for today?"

They all nodded, and he tapped on the screens. The needles injected something into my brother in a slow, continuous stream. Each of the scientists began to tap away on their section of the screen. The machine seemed to have control over the substance, sending signals to the liquid and directing it as they wished.

Some of them worked on his bones, others on his joint and muscles, others on his very organs, augmenting his lung, his heart, his kidneys. One was even doing something to his brain.

I watched them work for over an hour, biting into the skin of my palm, which I held clamped over my mouth still. I wanted to rush out like the angel of death and kill them all. I wanted to save Zed, but I held myself back, knowing that would be the worst thing I could do.

NIX mustn't know I knew, or I wouldn't be able to save us, to fix everything.

So, I stayed silent while the needles withdrew and the machine sealed all the little holes they'd left. I watched as they woke Zed up and told him they were making slow progress removing the Seed as he gingerly moved his aching body. I did nothing as they told him it looked like the Seed had made some permanent changes for the better, and everyone smiled.

I watched Zed leave with movements slow and stiff, and rage and helplessness burst against my insides. I memorized the feeling.

Chapter 6

Do not look for my heart anymore; the beasts have eaten it.
  — Charles Baudelaire

ONCE ZED MADE it safely back to the cafeteria and sat with the
team for dinner, I released my awareness, and leaned back against
the wall with my eyes hooded, watching Blaine work. Chaos roiled
inside me, as if it could feel my distress.

Blaine seemed oblivious. He pushed his glasses up, and
absently scratched at the light dusting of stubble across his cheeks.
Too stressed out to shave for the last couple days, maybe.

I listened to the ambient sounds he'd turned on, and his earlier
assertion that we needed to keep our preparations secret from
NIX. Was that a ploy to make me more trusting, or had he been
loyal the whole time? I didn't know, and I needed to find out. The
suspicion was like a gnawing worm in my gut. I had to find some
sort of proof.

I stood up, and had to steady myself on the chair when the
room spun dizzily. I was starving, I realized, and the last meal of
the day was about to start. I considered joining the Player

members of my team in the cafeteria, but instead grabbed a few nutrient bars off Blaine's desk, and headed back to my little room while eating them, more than a little distracted from my surroundings. Thankfully, most of the other Players were also in the cafeteria, so I didn't run into anyone hostile enough to start a fight.

I hurried through the curving hallways back to my quarters. My face felt like a skin-mask, calm and deceiving, a barrier between me and the real world. I'd been so *stupid*.

Birch waited for me outside my room, posted beside my door like a little four-legged sentry. He mumbled angrily when he saw me, no doubt peeved at being left alone and waiting outside.

"Sorry, Birch," I said absently, striding through my door as it slid open and then closed behind us. I didn't turn the light on, and ripped the bedding off my little nook, spreading it onto the floor. I sat, and tried to focus despite myself. It took a while, but I searched my bedding and every inch of my room for monitoring devices. I'd done it all before, and destroyed everything I found, but I was newly suspicious, for good reason.

I turned the lights back on after finding nothing, then stopped. I looked up at the light. It was too high for me to reach normally, even with my size, but I took the spartan stool from the corner of the room and stood on it, then reached up to the light panel in the ceiling. It came open after I pried at the edges with my claws for a few moments. The tiny black camera and microphone attached to the edge of the light inside did not surprise me.

I'd never noticed it before, because its presence was disguised by the electric activity of the light when I searched for the buzzing of mechanics, and it turned itself off when the light did. I'd thought the little bump next to the veiled light was just part of the mechanism.

I detached the spying bug and debated whether to put it back and pretend I didn't know it was there or crush it. I crushed it. Whoever was on the other side would have seen me find it, and if I suddenly allowed it to stay, unlike what I'd done with all the other devices I found, my deviation would set off alarms.

Once I was as sure as I could possibly be that my room wasn't being monitored, I moved across the hall into the team barracks.

Zed was in the top bunk and sleeping already, though none of the others were there. Had he not been able to eat much? I watched him sleep for a bit, then reached up and put my hand on his forehead. The skin was hot, and when I spread my awareness toward him, I felt the strange substance all throughout his body.

He woke when I took my hand away, and stared blearily at me for a moment. "What are you doing?"

"Come with me," I said instead of replying.

He groaned. "Do I have to? I don't feel very well. I just wanna sleep."

I grimaced. "It can't be that bad," I said. "Get up and come over to my cell. I want to show you something." I tried to keep my tone light, while I conveyed the seriousness of the situation with my expression.

He frowned, then got up, stiffly making his way down to the floor and following me to my room.

"Just in case," I said, once I'd slid the door shut behind us. "I just found another hidden camera in the light fixture. I might have missed some of them in the team room as well."

He looked around the dark room in sudden distrust. "Oh. Is that what you wanted to talk about?"

"No. I want to talk about the cleansing session you just had." I could only hope that whatever NIX had done to him didn't allow them to monitor what went on around him, or to hurt him remotely. As I explained what I'd seen, and the epiphany I'd had, he sat weakly on the side of my bed, listening in horror.

When I got to my suspicions about our former Moderator, he interrupted me. "Wait," he said. "If that's true, I think Bunny is up to something *tonight*. He seemed nervous. I didn't think anything of it at the time, but Kris asked him if he'd help her to sew the button-eyes on her doll after dinner, and he said he couldn't because he had something to do. You should do your astral-projection thing and find him."

I didn't need any more convincing than that. I took a couple deep breaths, and pushed my awareness out along with the heat radiating from my body, ignoring the icepick spike of pain that shot through my head with every heartbeat. Skill overuse had its consequences.

I found Bunny in Commander Petralka's office, which was close enough to my own quarters that I had a mostly clear impression of it and its occupants. His presence didn't surprise me, but my hands still clenched in my lap, and my fingernails almost itched with my body's desire to lash out.

He was talking—*reporting*—to Commander Petralka and another man who shone with power. Another Moderator? " ... shows a continued general distrust of NIX, which is mirrored by her squad. Performance-wise, she seems to be excelling, as expected," Bunny said.

"But she still believes herself to be valuable enough for us to fear?" Commander Petralka said.

"As far as I can tell, she's overconfident to the point of being cocky. Moods have been dimmed somewhat by the loss against squad Ridley, but she's the type to focus single-mindedly on overcoming the obvious obstacle. The antagonism of the other Players will provide plenty of conflict for her to focus on in the near future. Though I'd keep an eye out for serious injury. She likes to make bold statements where everyone can see. Ridley in particular might be a target."

"And her mental state?" This time, it was the other person, who'd spoken before Petralka got a chance to.

She shot him a subtle glance of irritation, which he either didn't notice, or didn't care about. Interesting.

"I've noticed subtle signs of emotional turbulence. From the stresses of the situation, perhaps. Despite the slight instability, I see no reason for concern," Bunny said.

"Team relations?" Once again, it was the man. Something about him was a little strange. Almost as if he was simultaneously paying full attention and absolutely no attention at all to everything in the room.

"Control over the team is good, no signs of insubordination or insurrection. She has a way of making those valuable to her feel like they're … important, and from there they rush to fulfill her expectations. Even Mendell's young niece and nephew both have an obvious desire for her approval."

"Do you still believe she may attempt to take revenge on Kilburn for the death of her teammate Black?" Petralka asked. This time it was the man who glanced at her, though I couldn't tell anything from his expression.

Bunny nodded. "Any competent psychological evaluation would have told you she was lying when she agreed to let it go. She doesn't believe in forgiveness. She understands retribution, and her own value as the center of her universe. But I actually don't know if she's planning something, or just biding her time."

"You *don't know*?" This was the man.

"This has nothing to do with my infiltration capabilities," Bunny said with a mix of indignation and fear. "Eve—Player Redding, excuse me, likes to work with a certain measure of secrecy. She likes to be the only one to know all the pieces of her plan, and when she's ready, she reveals everything in such a way as to build the team's excitement."

"What about the locations of their families? Have you gotten any information about that?" the man asked.

"You mean you haven't found them yet?" Bunny said, clamping his lips shut as frowns deepened on both of the other two's faces. "Well, I haven't, because I didn't know you needed that. But I'll find out before the next report."

There was silence for a moment, and then the man waved his hand at Bunny. "You may go."

Bunny didn't wait to be dismissed by Petralka. As he walked down the hall away from her office, he muttered to himself, "Damn creepy Thinkers."

Back in the office, Petralka said, "Her arrogance is a good

thing. It shows she doesn't suspect the truth, or our strategy to subdue her if need be. I've commissioned the cell on level sub-seventeen to be readied for a high threat-level occupant."

I almost lost control of my grip on my awareness, then. But I clung desperately to the commander's office, and managed to stabilize it. I needed to hear this.

"This entire situation is precariously balanced," the man said. "It is an exceptionally delicate situation. You must do away with this volatility."

Petralka's back stiffened. "I've been doing the best I could, with the strictures on my available courses of action from *your* side. You wanted her strong? We've done what you said, applied just enough pressure to make her desperate, and now she's got a new type of Seed entirely, and it's got all the destructive capability you could hope for. You wanted her here, with room to analyze her? She's here. I can't complete two conflicting goals at once." She stood up, facing the man, though he was much taller. "Either you want the situation on lock down, or you want her to continue to develop freely."

"There are more ways to control a situation than brute force," the man said, enunciating every word. "And more ways for you to fail than just not following our instruction. Your two sources of inside information are both unreliable. This 'Bunny,' the Rabbit group Moderator. His interest lies almost entirely in self-preservation. He may nominally be doing this for the good of our world, but his Skill is dangerous, and he grows much too free with its use. He attempted to *calm* us."

Petralka's eyes widened, and the man continued. "And Blaine Mendell's loyalty was never in question. It is to his niece and nephew, and only to them. It was clever, to use his sincere hatred of us to ingratiate himself with Redding and her team, but your petty little revenge for your niece's defeat, putting those children in the mock battle? The *reason* he follows our orders is because we keep them *safe*. If we fail to do that, he has no reason to comply."

Commander Petralka pressed her lips together. "I'll say it was a warning, and a punishment for not doing a satisfactory job of keeping us informed of Redding and her team's actions, previously. For cutting off our access to their VR chips and GPS trackers. It can be used to cement his loyalty. They didn't get seriously hurt."

"And Redding's brother? If he dies …"

"He's not going to die. As long as he keeps getting the nutrient paste for the nanites, he'll thrive. My scientists are ecstatic at how well he's responding. He may be the first working solution to the lack of sufficient Seed material. And as long as we've got him, we've also got Redding. I have this under control."

My awareness snapped back to me, then, and I slumped over to the floor. The room spun around me, and I swallowed hard to keep my stomach from heaving up the previous nutrient bars.

"WHOA, ARE YOU OKAY?" Zed asked, grabbing me by the shoulder and helping me to sit up again.

Birch mewled anxiously, butting me with his head as if to keep me from falling over again.

I groaned and waited till the room stopped spinning. There would be no more extra-sensory Perception for me that day, though I wished I could go back and listen to the remainder of the conversation between Petralka and the man Bunny had labeled a Thinker. "I'm okay," I mumbled. "Just a bit of backlash from pushing too hard."

Once my stomach had settled, and Zed had forced me to take a couple headache pills that helped with the throbbing pain, I explained what I'd heard. Then I sent Zed back to the team barracks, because we needed to act normally, and both of us were feeling so wretched that sleep was necessary before we could start to formulate a plan of attack.

A nightmare woke me after a few hours. I turned on the light to push back the darkness, and lay back down, thinking of what

I'd learned, and hoping that some solution would present itself to me. I was absolutely screwed. The whole team was.

I'd been like a puppet on a string.

I sat up and reached under the mattress of my cot for my pack, withdrawing the second largest band of silver loops the Oracle had given me. With a deep breath and a roll of my neck to stretch the tense muscles, I sat cross-legged on the floor to puzzle it out.

I meditated again, forcing my brain to put all its energy into fixing what could be an answer for my problems. I strained, pushing and *pushing* for hours. And then I started to bleed, again.

My eyes caught my own desperate reflection in the surface of the first crimson drop as it fell onto the silver bands in my hands like an omen of doom. It splattered, spreading more than such a small amount of liquid had any right to. And then the next drop of blood fell, and suddenly it was a steady dribble, as the sensitive skin inside my nose succumbed to the onslaught of Chaos.

Birch mewled and tried to climb onto my lap to lick it up, but I shouldered him away, focusing my glare on the bloodied puzzle in my hands. "The Oracle got me into this mess, and the Oracle is going to get me out of it," I said. But even so, I wanted to cry.

My meditation had been helping to keep my emotions under control, but the stress of my current situation was too great. So I scrabbled with the silver bands, and tears fell from my eyes to meet the drops of blood. I couldn't help it.

I gasped, eyes widening. Pushed by the tears, my blood formed spider-web-thin lines on the bands, spreading, and converging into delicate pathways. The last puzzle, the ring, had tiny protrusions and grooves that kept it from forming up unless I matched them together exactly. This one hadn't, and I knew because I'd searched desperately for them.

What type of ridiculous prerequisite was both bleeding and crying on the puzzle before being able to solve it? I scowled at the Oracle's gift. Had she somehow known that this would happen, that I would fulfill the condition? If she really could see the future, as her name implied, maybe she had.

It took almost an hour, even after that, but I solved the puzzle, each of the bands fitting with the other perfectly, creating a woven cylinder. Nothing happened.

So, I held it with my left hand, making sure to pinch hard so none of the pieces slipped out of place, and slipped my right hand through it.

It immediately seemed to come alive, like its smaller counterpart had done, and wriggled up my forearm like a snake, clasping to the flesh. It stopped when it reached my elbow, and injected its contents into me.

My VR chip popped up with two messages a few seconds later.

YOUR NON-SENSORY PERCEPTION HAS INCREASED!
YOUR INTELLIGENCE HAS INCREASED!

Then, once again, my body was seized with pain and I spasmed uncontrollably, flailing about. I smashed my arm against the floor involuntarily, but the solved puzzle acted as a guard and stopped me from bruising it. My eyes rolled back. Flashing lights behind my lids put on a show to match the pain.

Then, I began to see, as before.

A rush of images passed, almost too fast for me to recognize them. Bright red ants swarming and stripping every ounce of flesh off a small animal, the streak of a wing passing behind a fluffy white cloud, a flash of light as a blinding sun shone fully into my eyes, and a thousand other things that passed from my memory as quick as they came.

Finally, it slowed. A moon hung over a black sea, shining silver into the depths.

A blonde man stood on the surface of the water, and he pointed downward.

My sight followed the rays of moonlight into the darkness, and I saw that here and there they connected with the beams from another orb. This one was bright and almost golden, but it was crumbling. Bits and pieces fell and floated away, mixing like blood in the water. I watched them float until they were lost in the inky darkness, and when I looked back, the orb was an eye. It noticed my presence, then, and as happens sometimes in dreams, I knew that it was my great enemy, and that it knew not who I was. I lost the sense of myself in the knowledge of how little it cared for my existence, and then it devoured me, absorbing all that I was and ever could be. And I, too, rusted away into nothingness.

I woke, gasping, to Birch on my chest.

He licked my cheek with his painfully raspy tongue and yowled full force into my face.

I groaned. "Oh, shut up, please." My head throbbed so hard I felt like I could almost hear my brain thumping against the inside of my skull. "You're getting big enough that your voice is a weapon."

Birch quieted and scrambled off my chest, hopping around on all fours like an excited baby deer.

"What time is it?" I whispered. I pulled up the answer on a Window, then groaned again. I had no idea what the vision meant, or what I was supposed to do next. And I was late for breakfast.

Interlude 1

They had taken her off the side of the road, on her way to work. It was a simple thing, to cause the pods ahead of her to crash. Her own slowed and stopped to protect her, and he ripped the door off it.

She squinted and flinched back as his body dwarfed the breach he'd created in the tiny vehicle's side.

He bent, snapping the protective straps off her shoulders.

Her eyes widened, and then she glared at him like a rattlesnake. "*You,*" she said, fairly spitting with anger.

His eyes tracked over her face, taking in the faint wrinkles—those were new—and the challenge in her expression—that was not new. He didn't respond, simply grasping her by the shoulders and yanking her out of the pod.

She screamed for help.

No one responded, or even looked their way. His companion's *blood-borne* ability redirected the gazes of the humans around, so he didn't fear their notice or reprisal.

He forced her into their own, much larger vehicle, careful not to damage her. He remembered how fragile humans could be.

Another of his companions disposed of her vehicle, and as the pods involved in the crash pulled themselves off the main road, traffic began to move again.

She didn't bother screaming at them or begging them to let her go. Her long polished nails went straight for the eyes, and she kicked at his genitals.

He turned sideways so her foot impacted ineffectually against his thigh, and grabbed both her wrists in one hand. "Calm yourself, woman. We mean you no harm."

She laughed, loudly and bitterly. "And yet, you are kidnapping me."

He settled back with a tiny twitch of his lips that someone might interpret as a smile. "It is for your own good."

She scoffed. "I've heard that one before. Bastard."

He ignored her.

Once they arrived at the compound, she was hustled away to stay with the other humans. He had not seen her since, but he found his thoughts drawn to her. It had been a long time.

Chapter 7

I have a meanness inside me, real as an organ. Slit me at my belly and it might slide out, meaty and dark.

— Gillian Flynn

I DIDN'T EVEN MAKE it out of my room before my VR chip malfunctioned. Screens flickered in front of my face, flashing with varying brightness, spreading, popping, and flying around. They were filled with random symbols, but nothing that resembled words or the stats that I'd become accustomed to. They came like a barrage, cutting off my vision with their numbers and movement.

I dropped to my knees, clenching my jaw so tightly I could hear my molars creaking. I held back a scream of fear. Was NIX somehow attacking me, or had the second puzzle damaged the chip? Seizures couldn't be good for the electronics attached to my visual cortex, to say nothing of their detrimental effects on my brain itself.

Birch yowled at me again, and then began to whimper under his breath as he pressed his body against my thigh.

To my relief, the Windows disappeared after another minute

or so. I patted Birch on the head and made some soothing sounds until he calmed down. I was about to pull up my Attribute Window, to make sure the VR chip wasn't broken, when one last screen appeared in front of my face.

ACCESS ACCEPTED. PRINCIPAL GUIDE UPDATED.
GUIDE NAME: ORACLE

I screamed, then, just a little.

FORGE AN ALLIANCE WITH ESTREYAN CAPTIVE
COMPLETION REWARD: ALLIANCE
NON-COMPLETION PENALTY: DEATH

A timer popped up, set at 24 hours. I watched, wide-eyed, as the numbers ticked down, second by second. A single day to complete the quest. I wasn't sure whether to be horrified or elated.

BIRCH FELL asleep several times just during breakfast. It was quite hilarious to watch the little creature's head begin to fall as he succumbed to sleep, only to jerk awake again repeatedly.

His antics amused the whole squad, but did little to distract me from the timer in my peripheral vision. I'd tried to dismiss it, but neither actions nor words had any effect on it, and it remained like an omen of doom.

A thorough examination of my VR chip's Windows and information also showed a couple significant changes. The Skill Window was one.

CHARACTERISTIC SKILLS

TUMBLING FEATHER (KINETIC CLASS): INCREASES
GRACE AND AGILITY. IMPROVES SENSE OF BALANCE

AND MOTION. SKILL EFFECTS WILL EXPAND AND
STRENGTHEN WITH PLAYER GROWTH.

SPIRIT OF THE HUNTRESS (SPIRIT CLASS): INCREASES
GRACE, AGILITY, PERCEPTION, FOCUS, PHYSIQUE,
AND STAMINA. NAILS EXTEND AND SHARPEN ON
COMMAND. INCREASES CHANCE TO LAND ON FEET
AFTER A FALL. AGGRESSIVE TENDENCIES INCREASE.
SKILL EFFECTS WILL EXPAND AND STRENGTHEN
WITH PLAYER GROWTH.

SKILLS

COMMAND (MUNDANE CLASS): ALLOWS LEADER
ACCESS TO THE TEAM MANAGEMENT WINDOW.
LEADER CAN COMMUNICATE WITH TEAM MEMBERS
THROUGH GAME WINDOWS, SEE LOCATION OF TEAM
MEMBERS ON TEAM MANAGEMENT MAP, AND IS ABLE
TO ACCESS BASIC GAME INFORMATION OF TEAM
MEMBERS.

WRAITH: INCREASES PERCEPTION. SENSES EXTEND
BEYOND THE BODY, GIVING A COMPREHENSIVE
UNDERSTANDING OF SURROUNDINGS, AND
MARKING AREAS OR BEING OF POWER ACCORDING
TO DEGREE. SKILL EFFECTS WILL EXPAND AND
STRENGTHEN WITH PLAYER IMPROVEMENT.

CHAOS (GODLING CLASS): LATENT ASCENSION
POTENTIAL. GIVES ACCESS TO THE PRIMORDIAL
POWER OF THE GODDESS OF CHAOS.

THE ORACLE RECOGNIZED that Perception Skill I'd found so useful, and there was some actual information about Chaos.

The second change was the Attribute Window.

STRENGTH (14): ABILITY TO EXERT PHYSICAL FORCE.
AGILITY (21): PHYSICAL ABILITY TO INITIATE QUICK-TWITCH MUSCLE MOVEMENTS.
MANUAL DEXTERITY (9): ABILITY TO UTILIZE FINE MOTOR CONTROL.
INTELLIGENCE (20): ABILITY TO REMEMBER DATA AND EMPLOY REASONING.
MENTAL ACUITY (18): ABILITY TO THINK AND DRAW CONCLUSIONS QUICKLY.
FOCUS (17): ABILITY TO CONCENTRATE ATTENTION ON A SPECIFIC ISSUE.
BEAUTY (10): PHYSICAL APPEARANCE, CONFORMING TO THE WISHES OF THE PLAYER.
CHARISMA (12): MEASURE OF INFLUENCE OVER OTHERS, BASED ON ATTRACTIVENESS AND FORCE OF PRESENCE.
GRACE (18): ABILITY TO CONTROL THE FLOW AND CONSEQUENCE OF BODY MOVEMENTS.
RESILIENCE (23): ABILITY TO RECOVER FROM DAMAGE AND MENTAL AND PHYSICAL EXHAUSTION.
STAMINA (19): MEASURE OF HOW MUCH PHYSICAL OR MENTAL FORCE CAN BE EXERTED BEFORE BECOMING EXHAUSTED.
PERCEPTION (24): ABILITY TO SENSE BOTH THE PHYSICAL AND THE IMPLIED.
LIFE (28): MEASURE OF HOW MUCH DAMAGE CAN BE ABSORBED BEFORE DYING.

Physique seemed to have been rolled into Beauty, and there was a completely new Attribute. Charisma. I'd never put any Seeds into it, but if I calculated based off the total number of levels it already had, it had something to do with Beauty and Physique. Not so surprising, but Charisma seemed *much* more valuable than either.

There was also no indication of any "unplanted" Seeds, or even a space for it.

Zed's eyes caught mine several times during the meal, and I knew he wanted to talk with me, but we both knew it wasn't safe till we could be sure we weren't being monitored.

I watched both Bunny and Blaine surreptitiously. Our former Moderator seemed lively and carefree, joking around with Kris and Jacky easily, while Blaine had bags under his eyes, and had brought a smartglass tablet to the breakfast table with him, so that he could continue working on his latest project.

My claws scored lines in the back of my plastine food tray as Bunny yawned, then poked Chanelle in the side when no one else was watching. His continued presence was like a bloodsucking tick burrowing into my skin, which I couldn't even attempt to remove yet. Blaine, I could at least sympathize with. Bunny had no excuse.

When breakfast was over, Zed tried to move toward me as we left the cafeteria, but Blaine got to me first, using the noise of all the Players around us as cover for his words. "I have looked through your samples," Blaine murmured to me. "I destroyed them, and erased the data. I am sure NIX has access to my devices, and I didn't want to leave evidence of your condition for them to find."

I stared at him for just a moment too long, but he didn't seem to notice. Was his secrecy and paranoia toward NIX a ploy to get me to lower my guard, or was he truly eschewing his duties as spy? "What did you find?" I asked.

"Not much more than Sam. The Chaos Seed material seems to be attempting to drag your body toward entropy on a cellular level. There may be a way to combat it through 'mundane' means, but I have not been able to think of any. I considered the modified meningolycanosis as a way to combat them, but there's no discernible way to target it to one specific type of Seed. And seeing what it did to Chanelle ... I believe I am understandably reluctant to suggest such a thing. There may be others besides Sam who would be able to heal this with a Skill, but NIX would be made aware. The only viable solution is likely to be what you already suggested. Overwhelm its destructive capability with Seeds in the healing Attributes."

I'd suspected as much. And at this point, I'm not sure I would've trusted Blaine if he had suggested anything else. "Thanks for trying," I said simply.

"I have also started preparing the modified VR chips to implant in the kiddos, myself, and the others. Whenever the rest of the team is ready, I should be able to enable communication in their chips so that you don't need to relay messages for any of us."

"Okay," I said. "We'll set something up, maybe in a couple days. We can't be too obvious about it."

He nodded and left, ignoring the rule about traveling alone.

I spent a tense day slogging through classes and meals while worrying about completing the Oracle's quest.

Birch ended up taking several naps during my classes, which some of the Players around seemed to think was cute. One tried to pet him when I was distracted, and he woke up immediately and bit them. His human-like eyes glared at them in a manner that I imagined was somewhat disturbing, especially with his little pointy teeth glistening red.

No one tried to touch him after that.

During our shared Battle Tactics class, I sent a Window to Adam.

—NIX WIPED ALL YOUR DATA ON THEM, RIGHT? ALL THE STUFF WE TOOK OR CHANGED BOTH TIMES WE WERE ABLE TO ACCESS THE SYSTEM?—
-EVE-

—YES.—
-ADAM-

He looked at the smartglass screen in front of us with an almost comical load of sadness and frustration.

—You know the...*stuff* down in the basement?—
-Eve-

He looked up at me, and then back to the screen, matching my deliberately casual expression.

—Yeah?—
-Adam-

—Do you remember if there was anything about it in the data you downloaded?—
-Eve-

—The first time, I only modified some of the data, never downloaded it. And the second time, I didn't have it long enough to look through it. When we agreed to join, you know NIX force-wiped everything I had. I'd tried to keep some hidden, but they did a wonderful job. I'm considered a high-priority risk for the information systems now. I'm not allowed to access them outside of classwork or the allotted hours I work with Blaine, and they monitor my logs.
—

-Adam-

He paused a second, and then sent me a second Window.

—Why? Is something happening?—
-Adam-

—Yes. I've got to find a way to get down to it

WITHOUT BEING CAUGHT. I'VE GOT AN IDEA HOW TO DO IT
ALREADY.—

-EVE-

—THEY'VE GOT THE SURVEILLANCE SYSTEM WORKING
OVERTIME. WE'VE PROVED IT FALLIBLE TWICE, BUT YOU
BETTER BE CAREFUL. DO YOU NEED HELP?—

-ADAM-

—NO. MY METHOD REQUIRES MY SKILLS, SO I HAVE TO DO IT
ALONE. I'M NOT PLANNING TO GET CAUGHT, SO DON'T WORRY.

——

-EVE-

He looked at me doubtfully, but I was already lost in speeding thoughts.

At the end of the day, back in my room, I moved my little stool over to the vent in the corner. It was smaller than a lot of the other vents around NIX, but it was significantly bigger than it probably would have been, if NIX wasn't cut into the depths of a mountain. I measured it carefully, then compared it to the width of my own shoulders.

I wouldn't be able to move my arms and legs, but if I could find a way to avoid needing to climb until I reached the larger ventilation tube that my own fed right into, I could make it. I crouched low, then sprang upward, grabbing onto the metal grate with my clawed fingers. I held myself suspended with one hand as I reached out with the claws of my other hand and unscrewed the nine rods holding the grate to the ceiling. I hid the grate and the rods in my bedding, turned off the light, then returned to the stool.

I jumped again, with my arms held close to my head and pointed straight up toward the vent. My shoulders hit the sides with enough force to bruise, but the tips of my claws caught on the edge of the main vent system. I had to let go, because I didn't have enough space to wiggle my way up.

I pulled over the small table and balanced the stool atop it, as Birch watched curiously.

My feet had changed significantly after getting the Spirit of the Huntress Skill, so much so that wearing shoes was difficult. The toes were too long, and with a little extra push, they grew claws, making it a simple thing to grip the edge of the stool for balance. The little extra boost activating the Huntress Skill also gave me the necessary power to fully reach the bend in the vent. I scrabbled with my claws, and managed to drag myself up and into the larger duct.

Birch mewled pitifully and scrabbled up atop the table and then the stool, and with a motion familiar to cats everywhere, wound up for a seemingly impossible jump. His tiny body launched up toward me, and I caught him by the forepaws, helping him over the edge.

"Be quiet," I whispered to him. "We can't get caught."

We crawled through the metal-walled vent slowly, pausing at the grate over the team barracks. A quick foray with my extra-sensory Perception told me my brother was sleeping within. It took me longer than I'd expected to navigate through the three-dimensional maze. Partially because of the monitoring devices I discovered hiding around some of the corners in the ducts. I cursed spectacularly in my head, glad that I'd been sensing my way ahead and had noticed them before they noticed me. I ended up having to take several detours to avoid them.

I would have been dripping with sweat if not for the cool air pumping through the shafts in a less-than-gentle breeze, and even so I was panting from all the spread-eagled climbing and descending I had to do, taking roundabout paths to avoid the sensors on the more maneuverable shafts. If not for the days of climbing mount Behelaino, I might not have been able to do it.

As I grew nearer to the alien's cell, a buzzing sound, like a variation of white noise, filled the air and brushed insistently against my skin. It ran just beneath what I might have noticed if my Perception wasn't so heightened. As it was, I could feel the hair on my arms vibrating along with it. By the time I entered the vent that connected to his cell, it was strong enough to feel in the metal under my fingertips. I'd noticed the buzzing when I'd sent my awareness down before, but not when Commander Petralka had brought me to look at the alien the normal way. Was he causing it, or was it something NIX did?

I drew my knees up to my chest so Birch would be able to fit beside me if he wanted to, and poked my head forward to peek through a slit in the grate.

The man met my eyes, glaring up at me in complete awareness.

I jerked back without thinking, as if he'd slapped me. When my heart stopped squeezing with a combination of shock and fear, I leaned forward again, and met his glare. "Don't make a scene," I whispered, almost inaudibly. "They'll come." Could he hear me? I'd heard him speaking English in the vids Commander Petralka had shown me, so I knew he could understand.

"Why should I not?" he said. His voice was hoarse, whether from disuse or from screaming I didn't know, and his mouth formed the words strangely, lilting with an accent I didn't recognize.

It must be an Estreyan accent, I realized. The realization that aliens existed hit me anew, as I realized how absolutely bizarre my current situation was.

"I doubt you are supposed to be here," he said, voice low. I hoped whatever microphones they had in the room were also affected by the white noise, and wouldn't pick up on his murmur.

"I am definitely not *supposed* to be here. But you must hate them, too. Why would you alert them?"

"You are *one* of them!" He growled up at me, lips curling back from his teeth in a feral snarl.

I shrank back. I couldn't help it. My body knew that he was a predator, and compared to him, I was prey. Great. Make an alliance with someone who hates me. No problem. "I'm not one of them. They have power over me, and they're using it to try and control me."

He scoffed, a sharp huff of air through flaring nostrils. "You wear their clothing, sleep among them, and train among them. You are just another of the ..." he paused here, as if searching for a word he couldn't find, "two-legged maggots." The machines to one side began to beep more rapidly, an obvious warning. "Your kind is a horrid race, matched only in your natural weakness by your capacity for cruelty."

I opened my mouth to argue with him, and then closed it. What was I going to say? Just one look at the red, raised flesh around his cuffs, the tubes running in and out all over his body, and the sunken, bruised skin under his eyes would have made me a liar. I looked down at my own claws, which I hadn't retracted. They were evidence, too. "You're right," I said instead. "My kind is cruel. And compared to you, we are also weak, no doubt. I can feel it in the air and the way the hair on the back of my neck rises when I just look at you. But my kind also have a saying. 'The enemy of my enemy is my friend.'"

He relaxed, one deliberate muscle at a time, and the machines calmed. "Why are you here?"

"I am here *right now* on a quest given by the Oracle. I am here *within NIX* ... because they manipulated me and predicted my decisions. They somehow knew that I would agree to stay, if I knew that you were being held here. But I learned that they're betraying me already, and have plans to stab me in the back in other ways. I think they might have been lying about quite a few more things, and I'm hoping you can help me."

"The Oracle?" he said, ignoring the other parts of my explanation.

"Well, that's what she said her name was. She was made of stone, and every time she moved she made music, and she used these birdbaths that played music and sent shadows of herself to fight me ... ugh." I groaned. "I'm not making any sense. The Oracle is a stone ... creature, from your world, who gave me three puzzles. I've just solved the second one, and it involves you."

His eyes widened, and for the first time since I'd arrived above his holding cell, I felt like I had the upper hand. That might have been nice, if I hadn't been so desperate for him to provide something other than shocked silence.

"You ..." He stared at me, his eyes narrowing, but not quite with hatred. He didn't continue with whatever he'd been going to say.

"Is it true? That your kind is going to attack our world?" Why had the Oracle told me to make an alliance with him?

The alien snarled at me once again. "Yes! My warriors will come for me. We will come in force and raze your cities to the ground like the ripe grain of a field. Your putrid maggot species will be wiped from the face of this planet, no more to defile it." The machines were beeping at him again, this time more urgently, and I waited a while for him to control himself, and them to calm down.

I could take a hint. Hatred for humanity was a trigger subject. Since I was a human, I was a little worried about the likelihood of completing the quest.

Birch decided that was the moment to come forward and peek through the vent beside me. He let out a chattering sound, and curled his claws around the metal of the grate.

"A ... tailos?" the alien said, almost breathless.

"Yes! One of the Trials NIX sent us to was in their habitat. The retchin—you're familiar with those?" At his nod I continued, "They were attacking, pretty much wiping out all the tailos. We fought back but we lost. The leader gave me her egg to protect, and after we got back to Earth, Birch hatched." Mentions of his world seemed to be the key to negotiating with him.

He was staring up at Birch and me with no hint of a scowl. "When you met the ... Oracle. Did she reveal anything to you? Did she speak with you, when she bestowed upon you the three gifts? A message, or a task?"

"Err, not really. She said I'd proven myself worthy, gave me the puzzles, and said some platitude about walking in the midst of tribulation and not wavering," I said, but he stared up at me as if waiting for more. "The first puzzle led me to a ... mountain-woman named Behelaino. From her, I got a black Seed, that I'm pretty sure she called Khaos." I enunciated the "K" and "H" separately, as she had done. "She warned me that it would destroy me, but I thought maybe I was *supposed* to take it, and that it would help me do what I needed to, so that I could save ... save us from NIX." I hesitated for a moment. "But it's destroying my body. So, I solved the second puzzle, and had another vision, which you were in. Then, the Oracle connected to the Virtual Reality chip that NIX implanted in my brain, and gave me a quest to come see you. I was hoping that with your background, you might have an idea about what I should do to save myself. I can't heal fast enough to keep up with Chaos' growth, even though I'm putting all the normal Seeds from the Trials into the healing Attributes."

"The 'normal' Seeds?" His voice turned into a growl. "Your kind have made a horror of the Bestowals, as you know, and yet you continue to reward yourself with the theft of my blood. You force the blood-covenant on me in pretense of a bond ..." his voice grew hoarse with the strength of emotion, and guttered out.

I blinked at him. "Your blood?"

He strained against the cuffs again in sudden rage. "You pretend innocence, when I know you take my blood willingly, though I have not consented! You are despicable. I wish destruction on you and all your progeny, till the sun falls from the sky." The full force of his presence, his rage, was back again, making it hard to think beyond the instinctual need to protect myself from imminent death.

Birch growled at him, wings flaring out to make himself seem bigger.

"Your blood is what makes the Seeds," I muttered, managing to ignore his outburst. My mind was exploding like a firework. "They're not making Seeds, they're ..." I looked at all the tubes puncturing his skin, running outward like a splayed mass of tentacles to the machines. "Harvesting them," I whispered, finally. I focused harder, letting my Huntress Skill sharpen my eyesight, until the faint shimmer of the substance within the tubes was clear. "Oh my god," I said aloud, inanely.

"But ... how do they keep you here?" I wondered aloud. "If the Shortcut takes anyone with the Seeds in their system, wouldn't you escape back to your homeland every Trial?"

"Is that what they tell you? That my 'Shortcut' takes all who have a blood-covenant with me?"

I knew the answer without him saying it, from the look on his face. "It doesn't. That's a lie. They have complete control over who stays and who goes." I pressed my forehead against my knees, staring down at the dark fabric of my bodysuit. It meant that they didn't even *need* to cleanse Zed to keep him from the Trials. I wanted to throw up. How stupid could I have been?

He stared at me, his expression unreadable, but at least no longer radiating fury. His head jerked a few inches to the side, his eyes going distant. "They are coming. You must leave now, human. Come talk to me again soon."

I didn't need any more prompting than that to start moving away, but paused, turning my head back to the grate I could no longer see through. "What's your name?" I asked.

"I am Torliam, son of Mardinest, of the line of Aethezriel."

"I'm Eve Redding," I said, moving away again but sure he would hear me. "No fancy titles."

He said something else, but I did not hear him past my own pounding heart and the incessant buzzing.

In the corner of my vision, the countdown timer disintegrated.

Chapter 8

Someone I loved once gave me a box of darkness. It took me years to understand that this, too, was a gift.

— Mary Oliver

THE NEXT DAY, I talked to Adam, bringing him into the loop about my recent discoveries. NIX's puppeteering, the experimentation on Zed, the second vision from the Oracle and the subsequent strange behavior of my VR chip, and the alien far beneath our feet.

Adam seemed to be unsure how to respond to the influx of ulcer-inducing information. His hair stood on end from a building static charge, and he took the time to give me an all-purpose, "I told you so," for all the times I'd ignored his pessimism and paranoia. "It's not paranoia if they really are out to get you," he said, lips turning up at the corners just a bit.

I raised an eyebrow. "Is that the important thing to be dwelling on right now? Yes. You were right, *some* of the times you were suspicious."

"I notice that you can no longer say, 'acted crazy,'" he said pointedly, letting the electrical build up jump between the fingers of his hand in miniature arcs of lightning.

"We need to deal with Blaine," I said, sobering Adam handily. "He's useful, and I'm pretty sure that he really does hate NIX with a passion. It's just that our previous offer wasn't good enough to make him actually put the kiddos in danger. We need to present him with a more ... *persuasive* argument."

During our free period, the entire squad moved to the courtyard to get a workout and training session in, under Jacky's leadership. The courtyard was really more like a huge, artificial caldera. It was the best place to talk unobserved by NIX, because the wide-open space was free from the mics around the walls, and at such a high altitude, the wind always seemed to be blowing, even better for not being overheard.

Instead of joining in, Adam and I drew Blaine away from the main group. "A storm is coming," Blaine said. "I can smell the ozone in the air. Quite interesting, you know. A similar smell is created when ..." His eyes flicked between Adam's and my own face. "What is this about?"

"Do you remember the first time we met?" I asked.

"Yes." He chuckled a bit. "You all burst in, asking who I was working for, and willing to do anything to get me to talk." He held up his hand, the crushed finger of which Sam had healed.

I turned to him more fully, looked him in the eyes, and said, as significantly as I could, "*I know.*"

He stared at me for a second, and then his eyes dilated visibly as he sucked in a ragged breath. Blaine was anything but dense. He understood exactly what I meant. He straightened. "I knew you would find me out."

That surprised me. I shared a quick look with Adam. "Then why did you do it?"

"You know why." Blaine looked to the kiddos, who were laughing with Birch as they followed Jacky's instructions. "I had no choice. I could not risk it, not when I was wagering with their lives." He paused, and then added with difficulty, "Are you going to kill me?"

I tilted my head to the side, studying him. "I would have a hard time hiding the fact that I'd killed you." I smiled kindly, for the benefit of any watching us. "But I don't think I'm going to have to worry about that. I *did* already know why you lied to me, and to all of us. I just wanted you to say what's really important to you out loud."

"You would hurt *them*?" Blaine's voice grew gravelly.

"Would that make you loyal to me?" I was doing my best to exude a sense of calm that I didn't actually feel. I noted every twitch of his facial muscles, the tone of voice, his body language and breathing, watching for any reaction that could help me navigate the conversation. "I don't think it would. It certainly hasn't made you more loyal to NIX, has it? When Petralka put Kris and Gregor into our mock battle, so that they could be hurt? Did you know she did that as a chastisement, because you actually *did* turn off our VR chips and GPS trackers, instead of just saying you did while allowing them to have access?"

Blaine seemed to be trying to find something to do, or say, his body fidgeting while his eyes stayed locked to mine, the glasses making them look just a bit larger. If he were a film actor he'd play a kind kindergarten teacher. He was handsome, but unassuming. A face you could trust.

"I've learned quite a few things that might interest you, Blaine. I, too, bargained with Commander Petralka, for the safety of someone I care about. Someone defenseless. A few days ago, I watched secretly as they *experimented* on my brother with *nanites*. Trying to overcome the limitations imposed by the fact that NIX can't create their own Seeds, and most of the population can't assimilate them without dying. As I understand, they've tried before. Subjects have died. In fact, the scientists are excited that he might be the *first* functional alternative to the Seeds."

Adam interjected then, with perfect timing. "Gregor swears those nightmares he has are real. What if something is happening to them, under NIX's protection? Even if it isn't, how long do you think that will last? How much will they try to get away with, while you continue to 'protect' the kiddos with your loyalty?"

Blaine paled even further.

"I want to keep us all safe," I said. "I'm coming up with a plan, but I know I'm going to need your help. For real, this time." And that was all it took.

ZED THREW an angled punch toward my kidney, which I avoided by twisting my body in a way that most gymnasts couldn't, and landed a glancing blow with the side of one of my clawed feet.

"Point for me." I grinned wolfishly, and bounced up and down on my toes a couple times.

"This is obviously unfair," he said, though he didn't let that deter him from attacking again. "How am I supposed to compare to an alien mutant woman?"

I slipped past him and kicked the back of his knee, which made him stumble but not fall. "I don't know ..." I twisted and caught his neck in the crook of my elbow, bringing his head down to thoroughly tousle his hair. "Maybe you could use some of your cyborg powers?" I said, just loud enough for him to hear.

He struggled free and took a moment to straighten his now-tangled hair. "You've taken this too far. I hope you're prepared for my retribution," he said with mock seriousness.

I slid my feet apart, settling into horse stance like a kung fu master. I beckoned him with one arm outstretched. "Bring it."

The whole team was sparring toward one side of the courtyard.

Jacky directly instructed the less experienced, while the rest of us practiced on our own, except for the occasional comment from her.

Kris and Gregor were learning to attack viciously in ways that might give them the opportunity to run away from a stronger opponent.

Blaine and Bunny were being forced to hit a punching bag in endless repetition, which Blaine took to much better than the petulant Bunny.

Blaine had kept to his word about making sure both he and the kiddos were better able to defend themselves if need be, and during the times I'd followed him with my awareness for the last day, he hadn't done anything obvious to betray us to NIX. He was exhausted from working so hard, and I believed in the fact that he was on our side fully now, though it would be a while before I could let my guard down around him, even if I did understand why he'd made the decisions he had.

Adam and Sam were sparring in a way that gave both of them practice with what they needed. Adam created Animated ink constructs, mostly animals, and set them on Sam, who could feel free to attack without fear of harming something that could actually feel pain.

Birch had volunteered himself to help Sam defeat the animals, and was also happy to rush in and attack Adam with tooth, claw, and a not-quite-fearsome roar if he saw the opportunity.

After Zed got tired enough to need a water break, I wandered over to watch the spar between Adam, Sam, and Birch. Adam had a variety of materials spread out around him, both different inks and different surfaces to draw upon. He was already panting from exertion, though except for the rare times Birch had gotten past one of his ink constructs, he hadn't had to fight physically, and in fact had barely moved. "Have you come to distract me?" he asked, bright red paint dripping from the artist's paintbrush in his hand.

"Just curious. You can ignore me," I said, as the saber-toothed monkey he'd just created attacked Blaine, while swatting Birch away with its two tails.

"I don't mind. I'm almost out of juice anyway, so this'll be over soon. I know you have questions, it's written all over your face."

"Well then. Why are you using so many different supplies?

And I know you don't even need to use a paintbrush or canvas. Or ... a cafeteria food tray," I said, noting what he was painting on.

"Turns out, my Animus Skill cares about stuff like this. This is mostly a fun experiment, but I've been experimenting more seriously in the Skill Handling class, and it turns out that various factors affect the quality of the constructs I can produce."

"Really? Like what?" My own Skill Handling class had been an exercise in *avoiding* using my Chaos Skill as much as possible, while working on Spirit of the Huntress and Tumbling Feather freely. I'd definitely frustrated the instructor and the scientists who'd come to "help," but they were under the impression that I just had a bad attitude, not that I was afraid of killing myself.

"It doesn't like plastic, most of the time. Either to paint with or on. Dry mediums don't work, it has to be paint or ink. It has a thing for metals, the harder or more precious the better, it seems. The constructs increase in quality when I spend a little more time on them, but that seems obvious. And a couple other things, but it's pretty inconclusive so far. There must be some sort of rule behind it, but I haven't figured out what it is yet."

"That's fascinating," I murmured. Did my own Skills have similar functions that I'd never noticed? I didn't have a chance to ask him any more questions, as a heavy *thwump-thwump-thwump* filled the air, signaling the approach of a heli-pod.

The heli-pod hovered above one side of the courtyard, waiting as a section of the concrete ground opened up to the hangar down below. People began jumping out, which would have been dangerous for a civilian. Two of them carried a cot between them, which held a body covered by a white sheet.

My eyes widened as a tall, thin man launched himself out, floating just a little too far in a way that reminded me of Jacky.

The commotion drew attention, and other Players filtered out of the various doors to the courtyard, or watched curiously from the rows of glass wall and windows.

"Is that ..." Adam asked, standing up slowly.

"Yes." It was the man who'd killed China. The man I'd dubbed the "snake," and a mortal enemy.

He smiled and stretched, and did not notice me among the others milling around the outside of the walls.

Jacky and Sam came over to us, dragging Chanelle, Blaine, and the kiddos with them, while Bunny watched nervously, and then sidled over to put our group between himself and the new arrivals. "Maybe we should leave, guys," he murmured, just loud enough for my augmented ears to hear him.

"He's back," Jacky whispered.

Zed moved closer to my side, Birch balanced precariously on his shoulder. "Is that the guy you told me about?"

Adam nodded. "Stay away from him. He won't hesitate to kill you if you give him an opportunity."

"Are you going to do something?" Sam asked, looking at me.

I looked around, and noticed the soldiers stationed in the courtyard. There were other Players all around who already didn't like us so much, along with what I assumed were the man's teammates. They would attack with pleasure, if I tried to start something in such a public space. No, we couldn't attack him now. We would never succeed, and with the amount of power in attendance, I might not even get close. The knowledge maddened me.

I carried rage under my skin like a second being. It whispered of gleeful destruction in the intervals between my heartbeats. "Yes. I am going to. But not now."

Chapter 9

Terrible things happen to good people every day.
Consequentially, I am not one of the good people.
I am one of the terrible things.
— Marianna Paige

"I'M LOOKING FOR A NEW RECRUIT!" China's killer called out.
"One of my soldiers was too weak to cut it, as you saw." He
gestured toward the door his other teammates had taken the body
through.

The clamor grew, as people chattered excitedly to themselves.
A few overheard snippets of conversation revealed that the man
was called Kilburn. In fact, at least some of the other Players
present had connected our history, and were looking between him
and my team with greedy little eyes.

"I'll sign up for that spot," another familiar voice called out.

I turned to see Vaughn pushing through the crowd. The heli-
pod sank into the hangar below, and as the cement closed back up
after it, it seemed as if the whole courtyard had grown quiet with
anticipation.

"My unit is elite. Are you sure you won't just end up as the next body bag?" Kilburn asked, his smile stretching too wide across his face. Did normal mouths have that many teeth?

"I have no intention of dying any time soon, if ever," Vaughn said.

"Your intentions don't mean much to me. I need someone who can prove they won't weigh me down." They were both speaking loudly, no doubt for the benefit of the crowd.

"You'd like to fight, then?" Vaughn smiled with enough charm to make me shudder.

"No. That would be silly. And you'd die. I want to see you fight *her*." He swung an arm around and pointed straight at me. Apparently, he hadn't been oblivious to me at all. "A friendly little spar should do it? You can stop if you get her to vomit blood."

Vaughn followed the line of Kilburn's finger to me. "Oh. Little Miss Spirit-type, the famous Redding. We met recently, didn't we?"

To my surprise, Blaine was the first to move forward, drawing something shiny from his pocket and pointing it at Vaughn. "Stop there. If you want to spar, you will do so under NIX's established rules."

Adam fingered the ink and electricity cartridges at his waist.

Jacky popped the knuckles in each of her fingers individually, glaring at Vaughn in obvious threat.

Vaughn looked around at the guards in the courtyard and atop the wall, who were far outnumbered by the Players. "I don't see any of the guards trying to stop us. I'm pretty sure that means they're okay with it." I was pretty sure some of them were actually Moderators, or maybe even Thinkers, but he was right. "And that gun isn't going to stop me," he said. It's meant to be nonlethal for *normal* Players. I don't mind fighting all of you at once, but Eve, you could save your teammates if you'd just come out and fight me one-on-one. Wouldn't you like a chance to redeem yourself after the last time?" He stared at me intently, and then his expression morphed into surprise for a half second, and maybe even a little concern.

Then I felt the warm wetness on my upper lip. I slapped a hand to my face, covering my nose. "Oh, shit," I muttered. "It's no big—" my words cut off as a wave of pain cut through me. I felt dizzy and nauseous and like my blood had just begun to spontaneously boil, all at the same time. That side effect was new. I took an involuntary step back from him, half-stumbling.

Unfortunately, Adam turned around at that moment. His eyes took in the blood flowing around my cupped fingers, the expression of fear and pain on my face, and then cut back to Vaughn. "He just attacked Eve," he said urgently. A logical conclusion, I guess, if you didn't know the truth.

Jacky roared like an animal, lunging at Vaughn with a rage that I'd rarely seen in her before. She grabbed him by the arm before either of us could say anything, pushing and pivoting at the same time.

Vaughn went flying, sliding back through the doors to the cafeteria, and Jacky stomped after him, her footfalls causing noticeable tremors in the ground beneath our feet.

Players scattered to get out of the way, moving towards the outer walls of the courtyard.

I stumbled forward to stop Jacky, but the pain was still sliding through my veins, radiating through my muscles.

"Jacky, please—" Blaine called, pointing his gun down and away from Vaughn, now that she was standing in between them.

"He attacked Eve!" Jacky snarled, her face flushed and eyes wide. She kicked out at Vaughn, and he jumped back further into the cafeteria to avoid her.

It seemed fortune was not on my side at the moment, because Sam laid a hand on me, and then shook his head in desperation. "Eve, I can't do anything—"

That was all the rest of them needed to hear, I guess.

Adam's eyes flickered between my face, and the blood, and my hand, braced on my knee to help support me. Within a second he'd snapped open an ink canister and surrounded me in a shield bubble.

"Wha—" I mumbled, sputtering blood away from my lips. "You guys, stop it." But they either didn't hear me within the bubble, or they were ignoring me. I tilted my head back. My nose didn't stop bleeding, but at least the blood ran down my throat instead of spilling all over the place.

I tried to relax past the pain, but couldn't, as it was different than the usual injury. I didn't feel hurt, I felt sick, and I couldn't ignore it. It faded away after a few more seconds, and I focused on the microscopic organisms of the Seed of Chaos in my blood. I calmed them perfunctorily, as quickly as I could, but it was a slow process at the best of times.

I took a portion of my awareness and pushed it outward, ignoring the fear bubbling up hotter than ever in the back of my mind. I gasped.

It hadn't been more than a minute, but the team was being decimated by Vaughn. I'd known he was strong, but they were no match for him.

Adam had stepped in to help Jacky, leaving the shield which was imprisoning me to fade away when it expired.

Sam was a few yards away, popping Blaine's shoulder back into place. The kiddos were on the edge of the crowd with Zed and Chanelle, being guarded by Birch, who was snarling at anyone who even got close to them.

As soon as Sam was finished with Blaine, he ran back toward Vaughn, who dropped forward as if about to smash his own face into the ground, then flickered out of existence in the gap of a half second, his body alternating between flashing brightly with light and disappearing in the blotchy spot of darkness that marred the vision in the light's absence.

Sam barely noticed the flicker of distortion above him in time to throw himself out of the way.

Vaughn popped back into sight, and seemingly, also back into plain old existence, just as he touched the spot where Sam had been.

Jacky jumped back toward Vaughn, bringing her hand forward like it was a hammer, while a small flock of ink birds pierced through the air, emerging from behind her and darting around in a pincer movement toward him.

Vaughn hummed under his breath, low enough I might not have noticed if I hadn't felt the vibration with my outstretched senses.

The vibration of his hum split from his throat, and a vibrating after-image pushed forward from his body.

When Jacky touched it, barely sinking into it, her skin bloomed bright red. The feeling of it in the air was like when your teeth grind together, or the way you feel when you hear nails screech across one of those antique blackboards teachers used to use. I was pretty sure her skin had just been ripped apart beneath the surface.

Jacky snatched her hand back like it'd been burned, and the ink birds disintegrated as they hit the after-image.

The after-image split in two, and then those split in two again, each of them humming a slightly different note. Vaughn had surrounded himself with a shield of sorts. One of his copies lashed out at Sam, brushing its vibrating fist against the boy as Sam yanked Jacky backward.

Adam flashed forward, two ink rods held in his hands, almost like swords. He managed to slip through the copies and clip Vaughn across the side, but Vaughn blinked out in a flash of brightness again, and Adam had to throw up a quick shield in order to escape. Adam was tired already, coming close to exhaustion, and it showed in the pale skin of his cheeks and lips, and the way he panted.

On a positive note, Vaughn's vibrating copies disappeared along with him, and didn't reappear when he flickered back into existence behind Sam. "You're good," Vaughn said. "But you're not good enough." He slammed a fist into the side of Sam's neck, dropping the boy like a sack of potatoes.

Vaughn looked down at the red crystals growing out of the side of his fist, where he'd touched Sam. "Ouch," he said, and flickered into existence behind and to the side of Jacky. He kicked her in the ribs hard enough to send her flying in my direction.

She softened her own landing, but didn't get up fast enough, and he began to hum again, bringing the copies out as he moved toward her.

Adam was running towards us, but he would arrive too late.

I let out my claws and raked them across the blackness in front of my face. I knew Adam imbued his Animations with the characteristics he desired when bringing them into the world. His shield was meant to keep things out, not trap something inside. It was already close to evaporating, and so when I attacked it from within, it ripped and disintegrated.

I ran forward, the claws on my toes scratching on the hard concrete beneath my feet with every step. I threw myself toward Jacky, who was doing her best to regain her feet before Vaughn kicked her in the ribs. Again.

I slipped around one of his after-images with a quick feint, and smashed my foot down on the front of his leg, trapping hit foot on the ground without doing any real damage. "Stop!" I snarled, my voice ripping through the noise of the crowd and echoing off the walls. The sound died down as people quieted to catch every second of this new development. "This is over."

Vaughn laughed and stepped back, dragging his trapped leg away from me.

I shook my head at Adam, telling him silently to stay away. Anger had become my frequent companion, since that first time NIX had taken control of my life. It had deepened and grown along with me, and now it strengthened me with its familiar hot-and-cold chill.

"*Can* you end it?" He cocked his head to the side like a bird. "I saw what you did to little Petralka and the Shortcut. I've wondered about you since then, but I've never seen you go all-out again."

"Eve, he's strong," Jacky groaned, and I heard her spit onto the floor.

I jumped to the side, feinting, and when the copies nearest me lunged forward to block and attack, I spun back and slipped through the opening I'd created, slamming my claws toward his chest and closing my eyes. At least he wasn't clairvoyant, too.

His eyes widened, and he flickered just as I made contact, so brightly it would have been blinding if I'd seen it without the protection of my closed eyelids, and disappeared. The vibrating copies disappeared along with him, but once again didn't reappear when he flickered back into existence a few feet farther away.

I lifted the hand that had touched him, showing the blood on the very tips of my claws. There was surprised mumbling all around from our audience.

He laughed, then, and started to hum this time before flickering. His copies took a split second to reappear every time he changed location, but this time they stopped me from properly getting out of his reach or counterattacking, and where they touched me my skin fell off.

Just the first couple layers, but it seemed with every attack the damage grew. My bodysuit couldn't withstand the vibrations, but it did act as a temporary shield. My armored vest beneath it stopped his vibrations easily, simply spreading the energy along its whole surface. Unfortunately, it only covered so much of my body, and the rest of me was vulnerable to his Skill.

I let the pain sharpen my instincts. I twisted and turned around his copies like an eel swimming through the air, slashing at him when I could get close enough and using my ability to keep track of him and his copies at the same time, even if I couldn't see them all with my physical eyes. I knew I couldn't keep it up for more than a couple minutes at most. I was fighting against my instinct to unleash Chaos into the area around me. Despite the side effects I'd been dealing with only a minute before, I'd half

AZALEA ELLIS

convinced myself that I could release it just for a split second and end the fight.

It was to my enormous and hopefully secret relief when Commander Petralka stepped into the courtyard. "Freeze!" She roared, rage suffusing her voice. "What the hell do you homicidal imbeciles think you're doing?"

Zed lifted both hands and pointed to Kilburn and Vaughn. "They started it!"

COMMANDER PETRALKA SCREAMED A BIT MORE, and sent all the onlookers scrambling away, then berated Kilburn, Vaughn, and my team. She seemed quite suspicious that I was going to try and attack Kilburn, or vice-versa, and sent us back to the team barracks, while she kept Vaughn and Kilburn behind to chew out.

Once Sam woke up, he healed Jacky, Adam, Blaine, and I, and the tension in the muscles around his eyes only grew.

Kris and Gregor wanted to know why the whole incident had happened, and I left it to Adam and Jacky to explain it to them, while Zed slipped in sporadic comments meant to distract them from their fear and uncertainty. The way Kris held her little moose to her chest made something inside me squeeze with regret, and I turned away.

Bunny sat with Chanelle in the corner of the room, trying to get her to play a card game with him, with a total lack of success. Eventually, he got up and clapped his hands together. "You guys are way too mopey. Lighten up!" he said, looking at the kiddos.

They smiled, a little, and then he turned his power on the rest of us. "'Now is the time to get stronger, so this doesn't happen again!' Eve, isn't that your line?"

I felt a new little bud of determination well up within me. I wondered if I was getting better at detecting his intrusion, or if perhaps the Oracle's second gift had made me a little more aware, with the Perception boost it granted. The foreign emotion was one-dimensional. It held none of the desperation or fear that my real determination was tinged with. "I've got a plan for that, actually," I said. My claws itched, and I relaxed my fingers so that they didn't slip out and display my feelings toward him outwardly.

He smiled, oblivious to the thoughts running through my mind, or the nature of my plan. "Great. Care to share?"

"It's going to involve a lot of training. Bunny, I noticed that you didn't participate in the fight. Blaine's an unpowered adult just like you, but even he did his part." I ignored the narrow-eyed look Zed shot my way. "I want to make sure we're utilizing all of our members to the best of their ability. Maybe we could get you a gun or two, like Blaine? Or knives, if you prefer?"

"Err, that sounds ..." Bunny coughed. "Eve, don't you think I'd just be a liability? You don't want to put the other members in danger if I screw up during a fight, do you?" He stared hard into my eyes.

I frowned, deliberately letting my eyes glaze over, just a bit. "Hmm ... maybe not. But ... what if you put someone in danger because you can't protect yourself?"

"I'll stay out of the way, don't worry about that," he said.

When I nodded, but then frowned again as if I'd come up with a new argument, he quickly found a reason to leave the team barracks.

It took the rest of the night for me to get everything into place. Aside from the kids and Chanelle, who went to sleep early, the rest of us had a conversation about what I'd learned recently. I'd hesitated whether to reveal Blaine's duplicity to the others, but Adam took the decision out of my hands.

"They need to know, we all need to know, so that we can make sure it doesn't happen again," Adam said, not flinching from Blaine's obvious discomfort.

"He is right," Blaine said. "It is better if everyone is aware of the dangers. One or two people cannot keep watch for the entire group." He explained his real assignment from NIX.

Jacky almost punched Blaine, but Sam stopped her. When she

learned of Bunny's much more serious transgressions, her anger was directed in full force toward him.

The next day, after dinner, Sam and Zed stayed in the team barracks with Kris, Gregor, and the still-unresponsive Chanelle, while the rest of us crowded into my tiny room, where Sam had left Bunny in an artificially induced sleep.

Blaine did some relatively minor surgery on Bunny while he slept. For good measure, we brought in a chair and tied Bunny to it.

I assisted Blaine instead of Adam, who was still upset with Blaine. I'd come up with this plan as the best option under impossible circumstances. I didn't trust Bunny, but if he died, it would undermine the team's safety. I also couldn't just leave him alone, because then he might directly sabotage our future efforts by reporting on us. Because we would definitely be doing things NIX wouldn't like. Hopefully, the Thinker was right, and Bunny was selfish enough for my plan to work.

A quick shock of electricity from Adam woke our Moderator up. He looked around frantically, but caught on to the situation quickly. "What's going on? You guys don't want to hurt me, you know. I'm on your side! And I know NIX would think it was weird if I suddenly disappeared. Eve." He turned the force of his gaze on me. "I've helped you so much. Why are you doing this? I thought you looked out for your teammates?"

I felt compassion burble up inside me, strong enough to almost choke. I ignored it. I'd done plenty of things that made me feel bad, when the stakes were high enough. Compassion wasn't going to change anything. "Do you feel that soreness on the back of your neck, Bunny? Right under the hair line?"

His eyes grew wider with desperation. "You *have* to let me *go*, Eve!"

I frowned sadly and shook my head. "I want to. I really do. I think you *know* that, Bunny."

He swallowed.

"But I can't let you go. Because you've betrayed me, and that means there are only two options."

"What are you talking about, Eve? Guys, help me out, here! She's crazy!"

Jacky pinched herself on the thigh, and didn't release the skin as she spoke. "Eve is crazy. And if she's crazy enough that she thinks you have to die, I'm going to help her." She took a deep breath, and released the crushing grip on her skin. "Whoa."

Adam frowned for a bit, but otherwise didn't react, keeping to his role as the administrator of the intimidating, silent stare.

Blaine turned to me, looking down at the smartglass tablet in his hand in horror. "Eve, this *is* crazy. We just planted a bomb in his head—"

"What!?" Bunny almost screeched.

"I don't think I can go through with this," Blaine said.

I gestured to Jacky, who slapped Blaine lightly across the face, rocking his head to the side.

He looked shocked, then lifted a hand to the bright red imprint she'd left. His expression hardened, then, and he glared at Bunny. "On second thought, I think I can." Pain helped to break Bunny's influence.

"You're very dangerous, Bunny," I said. "Turning people's emotions against them? That must be so useful for you. I mean, you even used it on Commander Petralka and the Thinker, when you met with them the other night." I waited for that to sink in.

Bunny didn't say anything this time, but began to struggle against his bindings.

"The problem is, your power isn't invincible. It's best used subtly, and on people who have no idea that you're capable of such a thing. Once someone finds out ... well, you're a threat. Insidious and self-serving." I leaned in. "I think those are the exact words the Thinker called you after you left your little meeting with him and Petralka." Kind of true, if not exactly. "If people can't trust you, the only option left is 'removal.'" I lifted my fingers up for the air-quotes.

By that time, he'd stopped struggling, and was pale and sweaty.

"They ... how do you know that? You could be lying. You're just making all this up to try and get me to admit to something that isn't even true!"

I raised an eyebrow. "I know that you told Petralka I, 'don't believe in forgiveness.' That I, 'understand retribution, and my own value as the center of the universe.' A bit extreme, don't you think? I can be forgiving. If there's a reason."

"What—what do you want?"

"To smash your head in till I can see the white meat," Jacky muttered, which caused Adam's mouth to curl into a small smirk.

"NIX has been telling us Players some lies, Bunny. Some of them you probably know about, but I'm not sure. Like the fact that they're experimenting on my brother?" I said.

His eyes flickered away, "What? No, I didn't—"

"Lying," I said. "You're lying, so just stop there." I took a deep breath. "But that's okay. I can forgive you, because you're going to help me make sure my brother's safe. I really hope you agree to this. And I hope you can keep your word. Because I'm going to have to make sure you don't reveal this conversation before NIX kills you. That's going to be a big drain on my resources. Someone will have to monitor the devices we put in your skull all the time. Then, if you decided to talk about this conversation as a bargaining chip to convince them to keep you alive, I'd have to blow your skull apart from the inside." I grimaced.

"I'm probably going to have to do most of that work," Adam muttered. "It's a waste, if you ask me. We should just take him up to the wall and toss him off into the river below, and blow up his head on the way down, just in case."

"I can help," Bunny said quickly. "And I know how to keep my mouth shut. But whatever you're doing, you have to keep me safe. Take me with you—keep me on the list of people you're shielding —whatever. You have to promise me."

"If you're useful enough, why would I want to get rid of you? There's no chance of you influencing my decisions anymore, so you don't pose a danger in that way."

DESPITE MY EXHAUSTION after everything that had happened, I crawled down to see Torliam again that night. He was once again awake and waiting for me when I arrived. His eyes met mine, and he dipped his head in a subtle nod.

"Hello again," I said.

"You have given me much time to ponder, since our last meeting."

Perhaps being shackled there with only his mind to keep him proper company, time probably seemed to pass slower. "It hasn't been that long, and I've been busy."

"Tell me about the vision you received from the Oracle. The one that I was in."

"I've actually seen you in both my visions," I said hesitantly. "And when NIX first forced the Seed on me and I had the initiation sickness." And maybe a few other times, but there was a strange look on his face, and I wasn't sure it was wise to continue.

"What did you see?" His head strained forward, as if he could will himself out of his shackles and off the slab. He paused, as if hesitating, and then continued with a sneer, "I do not wish to speak of your mind touching mine, or your incredible disrespect."

Sheesh. "The first time, it felt like I was living one of your memories, or something. It happened directly after the vision that led me to Behelaino. You were in Estreyer." I paused, feeling uncomfortable. "This time, you were in the actual vision. There was a moon shining over water. An ocean, maybe. You were standing on the surface of the water. You pointed me down, and I followed the light of the moon into the water to this gold colored orb. But it was actually a giant eye, and I was like a bug in comparison to it ..." I shuddered at the remembered feeling of turning to rust.

"A giant golden eye, you say? Perhaps the God of Knowledge? He has been removed from mortal contact for a long time, now. Are you sure that it was *me* you saw?"

"Yes, it was you. I leaned forward eagerly myself. "Do you think this God of Knowledge might help me? With my Chaos problem?"

"The God of Knowledge is a counterpart to your Goddess of Chaos, who seems to have allowed you to ascend, if your story is to be believed. Behelaino, as you called her. The God of Knowledge has removed himself from the presence of mortals, but if there is a being in existence that knows how to save you from your own stupidity, it is he."

I ignored his continued insults, too elated by the idea that I may have found the solution to at least one of my problems. "I'll just need to find a way to get to him, then. The Shortcut is broken for now, but maybe that's where we'll be going when it's fixed …"

"No, the 'Shortcut' does not connect to his domain. It will not allow you to petition him. It is a weak tool meant to take our young to be tested when traveling far from home. The Trials connected to by my device are simple, and relatively easy, the gods lenient in accordance to their weakness. A commander works with them to shape the Trials. Usually a parent, but in this case, it is likely one of NIX's people. I am surprised, in fact, that it allowed you to connect to a manifestation of Chaos. That particular manifestation must have been much, much weaker when the destination point was originally established. You would have to travel halfway around the world to reach the God of Knowledge, or travel to Estreyer another way, and even then, it would be a long journey."

My brain wanted to be caught by the fact that someone from NIX had not only been the Examiner who explained the rules of the Trials to us, but had actively worked to shape them. Which meant that they might have been able to affect the horrific death tolls. And yet, more than half of us died within them. I blinked hard, and moved on to the currently relevant information. "Another way? Is there a way for me to get there besides the Shortcut?"

"There are other ways, but I will not be revealing them to one of your kind."

My eyes narrowed as I thought of a way around his reticence. Is this what the Oracle had intended? It was *insane*. I opened my mouth anyway. "But *you* could use them, if you were free?"

Some of the energy seemed to go out of him, and he lay more heavily against the slab. "Once, I hoped so. No more. I have found hope is only another form of torture. Until my kind return for me, there will be no escape."

"But you *could*, if you were?" I said, pressing the point.

"Yes." His eyes had caught on my expression, and seemed to be searching it for meaning.

"You have something I need ... and I have something you need," I said, my mind tumbling down all the paths that could lead to an answer.

"What do you have that I need? I cannot even move."

"I need to fulfill the vision the Oracle gave me. And *you* need ... to escape from this place."

I said the last part slowly, each word tripping over my lips separately. I needed a way out from under NIX's crushing thumb, too. I ignored the little voice in the back of my head that was screaming how utterly demented I was to even think of releasing a creature like Torliam.

"You make promises you cannot keep." He looked away from me, the muscles around his mouth and eyes tightening. Maybe even the inkling of hope he drew from my face and words was painful.

"You'd be surprised at the things I can accomplish, when I set my mind to it." I was still thinking, rapid-fire. I would have to take the whole team with me, as they wouldn't be safe on earth with NIX. But maybe, if we weren't constantly being subjected to a Trial, and had someone as strong as Torliam with us, Estreyer wouldn't be so bad. It might be safe there, for Zed, the kiddos, and the rest of us. At least until we could find a way to be safe back on Earth. I reminded myself of the team members' families, including my own mother. I still had to do something about that. But if I could make sure they were safe ... "This might actually work," I said aloud.

"The surprise in your voice does not inspire confidence," he said wryly.

"You just made a joke!" I couldn't help my small smile of excitement. Now that I could see a possible path out of this horrible mess I'd gotten everyone into, a little bit of the metaphorical crushing weight removed itself from my shoulders.

"But ... This new method of getting to Estreyer, does it scramble electronics like the Shortcut?"

His halfway-pleased expression curdled. "Why?"

"My brother is filled with nanites, which I'm worried may be affected. NIX has been experimenting on him. Without consent." That was partially a lie. If I could bring some of NIX's air-burst guns, maybe a hoverboard or two ...

"The incompetence of your race causes the 'scrambling,' as you say, of electronics. Your brother will be fine."

"And a hoverboard, maybe? There will be children coming. I don't think they'll be able to keep up on their own."

"*Children*? You wish to try and escape this place while protecting children?"

"I'm not going to *leave* them, so there isn't much choice, is there?"

He grunted. "As I said, your race's simple devices will be fine."

"And you can make sure we're not dropped in the middle of a Trial? We'll go to somewhere relatively safe?"

"Relatively."

"Once we're there, how long will it take us to get to this God of Knowledge? I've got ..." I realized what I was thinking. I *knew* the God of Knowledge would be strong, and if my time on Estreyer had taught me anything, it was that everything within that beautiful world wanted to kill you. The vision the Oracle had shown me didn't suggest he would be a pacifist, either. Even *she* had beaten me like a ragdoll, to prove my worth! And yet, there I was, planning to essentially repeat my first attack on NIX. I was unprepared. The *team* was unprepared, and it would get someone killed.

I swallowed down the shame. "I've had to fight pretty much everything I've ever met on Estreyer. Do you think it will be the same here? Is he the communicative type, or the 'crush you like the puny mortal you are' type?"

"Mortals who hunger for growth and power do petition the gods and attempt to prove their worth, but it is rare to succeed. Occasionally, they do succeed, and are given a Bestowal. These are your 'Skills.' The God of Knowledge is one of the few greater gods, and if he is where I suspect, a large portion of his strength will be gathered in one place. You will not find yourself winning a fight against him. I doubt you'll be able to persuade him to help at all. You can only hope that he doesn't kill you if you fail."

"That's not useful. You'll have to help me prepare." I said decisively. "This has to work, because I'm not going to die." That was the alternative, if I couldn't find a way to fix my power or myself.

A violent shudder rolled through him, as if he'd gotten cold, and when he murmured again his voice was quieter. "If you help me break the blood-covenants that have been forced upon me, I will help you fulfill the Oracle's vision, even if I must battle the gods to do it. This I swear."

"The blood-covenant, that's what you were talking about before. What exactly is that?"

"When you take my blood and mix it with your own, it forces a bond on me. I wish to be rid of your kind's defilement."

I ignored the barb, "If you do that, will the Seeds still work for us?" As a normal human, I'd probably die instantly within Estreyer.

"Breaking the bond is not pleasant, but any blood your kind have stolen from me will remain in your weak bodies."

"Okay, it's a deal. What measures have they put in place to keep you here? I need to know everything so I can make a plan to get you out."

He took a deep breath and began to speak. "I have a constant stream of paralytic pumping into me, and they are constantly draining me of my life-blood. They have found the perfect balance, where they harvest as much as possible, up to the limit of where it would begin to affect my power's ability to replenish itself. They hold me shackled, as you can see, and if I become too active, they will stun me with electricity and spray a different mist-sedative. This room is completely reinforced, and even if I were to get out of my shackles, I could not escape if the door were not open. I am watched for signs of rage or the possibility of my escape. There are listening devices throughout the room, but I have caused the air to buzz so that they are impotent. The floor tiles are set to detect my substantial weight pressing down on them, and this table knows if my weight leaves it. And lastly, the table has clamps running along the length of my spine. It breaks my spine from the bottom up, letting me heal over the course of a few days, and then breaking directly above the previous break, till it reaches my neck and starts back at the base again. It is a never-ending cycle of pain and paralysis. They have just started back at the base of my spine. I can move my arms and upper torso, but never my legs."

He wiggled his torso to show me, grimacing. "Many of these precautions are due to my previous escape attempts. I have tried everything I can think of. And even if you do manage to get me out of this room, we would need to retrieve my ship to make it half way around your world before I can take us back to my homeland."

My eyes were wide, as I imagined my spine being systematically broken, over and over, just to keep me securely imprisoned. I suppressed a shudder, and vowed that I would do my best not to be placed in the cell on sub-level seventeen that was being prepared for me. "That is daunting. But you didn't have me before. And I come as a package deal with my team. Now, please explain in *detail*, as best you can, how all of the security technology works. And hurry up, I've got to get to bed soon."

Chapter 10

The devil asked me how I knew my way around the halls of hell. I told him I did not need a map for the darkness I know so well.
— T.M.T.

THE NEXT MANY days were a stressful, sleepless blur of plotting and secretive preparation. All of us had our own tasks to carry out, and after the initial burst of arguing and apprehension when I'd revealed the plan, we'd gotten to work with a vengeance.

Bunny hadn't argued quite so much as he might have, because he didn't know the real plan. He thought we were going to steal the ship and escape, but had no idea that we were also bringing NIX's alien, human-hating captive with us. I kept an eye on Bunny, or had one of the others do so, as much as possible, and attempted to make sure he believed the observation was constant. But I didn't trust him, especially because, out of the whole team, he was the only one who'd joined NIX willingly, and condoned its actions.

He'd been searching for more information on the location of my mother, and the other relatives Blaine had relocated, without any luck. "NIX doesn't know where they are. Or if they do, they're doing a really good job of lying about it. *We* don't know where they are, or at least if you guys do I'm not aware of it. It literally seems as if they've dropped off the face of the Earth," Bunny said.

I wasn't sure if that was a good thing or not. On the upside, NIX didn't know where they were, and couldn't find them to hurt them. On the downside, we didn't know where our relatives were, and they'd disappeared. Though, if ever there was a woman who could fend for herself, it was my mother. I wasn't self-deceiving enough to pretend I cared about *other* people's families, but I hoped worrying over their own wouldn't affect my team members' work.

Blaine had finished augmenting the new VR chips and set the rest of the team up with them, then modified the settings so that every team member could communicate freely with the others.

When Bunny was out, we gathered in the now unquestionably debugged team barracks and discussed the more controversial part of my plan. I sat at the table, with the others lounging around in the few loose chairs, or on the bunk beds.

"What does it mean, that the Oracle is connecting to your VR chip now?" Adam asked. "I mean, the alien wants to kill us. What if she's on his side?"

"Then we're pretty much screwed, because as far as I can see, getting off Earth is our only option," I said. "And we can't do that without him. Not unless we want to wait till the Shortcut is finished, initiate the kids as Players, and then have it drop us all in the midst of a Trial." It didn't need to be said that that plan wouldn't fly.

"That may be, but what about surviving while we're there?" Sam said.

Blaine leaned forward. "The kids and I do not have the ability to just tear any opponents apart with our bare hands. With the release of the electronic restrictions, I have been gearing the ship up for conflict situations. The missing things will be noticed eventually—we know NIX keeps track of inventory—but if we do this right, we will be gone before they notice. By the time we leave, I hope to have enough to supply the whole team. We will be able to augment any strength deficiencies with technology."

Kris' stuffed moose was on her lap. "We've been practicing. Running and with the guns. I know we're not like you guys, but we'll be able to take care of ourselves better."

Gregor grunted. "If they really have been experimenting on us all this time, maybe we'll be just fine protecting ourselves." He shot a dark look toward Blaine.

"I have found no evidence that they have done anything to either of you," Blaine said. His mouth tightened when Gregor rolled his eyes.

Sam looked toward Chanelle. "Well, maybe … if there are other aliens we can get in contact with …" He hesitated for a moment. "Maybe they have a Skill or some technology that can help Chanelle."

Jacky brightened. "Whoa, great! It's weird seeing China looking like that, even if it really isn't her."

Adam ran a hand over Chanelle's short hair, making it rise with static electricity. "China would have wanted us to try, at least."

"And we will. But right now, we need to finalize the preparation. We don't have time to waste." My voice wasn't loud, but it brought everyone's attention back. "This is a complicated plan, and we need to make sure that we've got redundancies in place, in case something goes wrong. The point is that our preparation will stymie NIX at every turn. I want backup plans to counter their backup-backup plans. Zed is going to need 'nanite nutrient paste,' enough to last him for a long time, just in case. How are we going to get that?"

Blaine had a few ideas about sneaking some away and stashing it in the ship ahead of time, which Zed volunteered to help with.

"You should hide weapons on your body or in your clothing," Gregor said. "In case they try to capture you or have some way to keep you from using the powers and weapons they know about."

"That's actually a really good idea," I said. "No such thing as overkill, when we're dealing with NIX. Seriously, they've been so far ahead of us this whole time. If this is going to work, we all have to step up our game. I want everyone to come up with ideas. Blaine, you may be helping to implement some of them."

"I will prepare more stimulant pills." He sighed, taking off his glasses to rub his bloodshot eyes.

"It won't be much longer now. Adam, how is the research on that cell in sub-level seventeen going?"

"You'll need our help once you're in there, but it's still the most direct route to the alien."

"Okay, good. There are a few more kinks to work out with the plan to jailbreak Torliam, but right now I want to focus on the Seeds."

I flattened my hands on the table. "How are we going to steal them?"

DAYS LATER, while I was in the vents talking to Torliam, he turned his eyes to me and said, "They are starting it."

"Starting what?"

"The Shortcut. I can feel it beginning to call out to my blood. It is being set in motion."

"Oh, shit." I turned my body to the side, and moved along the ducts away from Torliam's cell. "It's too early."

We'd been preparing our breakout and spying on NIX through both Blaine and Bunny, so I knew NIX planned to use the Shortcut as soon as they had it working again. But electricity wasn't enough to get the floating rings spinning again, so they had to use some other way. I hadn't thought they'd be able to do it so quickly. We weren't ready.

As I scrambled, carelessly puncturing the walls of the duct with my claws to gain speed and maneuverability, I sent out Windows to the team.

—They're starting the Shortcut! I think we're all about to be taken to a Trial. If you're not where you're supposed to be, get there now! —
-Eve-

—I'm out of bounds, Eve. Halfway to the generator. There's no way I can make it back in time.—
-Adam-

Why was he doing that *now*? We hadn't planned for him to augment the backup generator yet. If the Boneshaker pulled him away halfway through using suction cups to crawl through the vents, he'd be caught. NIX would want to know exactly what he was doing in such a suspicious location. The plan would be blown apart. "Damn it, Adam!" I ground out. I sent a Window to the whole team.

—I'm going to stop the Boneshaker. Or at least delay it. It's probably going to cause a scene, and we may be forced to escalate our timeline.—
-Eve-

I crawled faster, my arms and legs moving like a spider as I skittered back to where I'd come down from. I ignored the team's alarmed responses. I was lucky, in multiple ways. If it had been only a little later, after curfew, I would've been in my quarters, and had no idea what was going on until the Boneshaker started.

I dropped into my room, and raced out the door without even reattaching the ceiling grate, only sending a quick Window to the others, asking one of them to replace it and hide the evidence, just in case. A couple guards tried to stop me along the way, but I barreled past them as if they weren't even talking.

I slammed the cafeteria doors open onto the lit-up courtyard. Kilburn stood on the grating around the sphere, his arms raised high as he forced the pieces of the Shortcut to move. They were gaining momentum.

I almost laughed. At least I wouldn't have to worry about holding back. "Kilburn!" I screamed. "Stop!" I knew putting the plan into motion early was dangerous, but allowing him to continue was unacceptable. Even if Adam weren't in danger, I would have been worried. The Trials were an unknown danger, one the team and I weren't prepared to deal with at the moment. It would be all too easy for NIX to have a "treat" planned for us over there, and if NIX decided to continue with the charade that anyone with Seeds was subject to the Trials, we'd also have to protect Zed and Chanelle. As it was, I didn't have a choice. At least by stopping the Shortcut's revival, I was choosing the danger I had most of a plan in place for.

Kilburn turned his head to look down at me, pausing his manipulation of the alien device. "Oh, if it isn't the little trouble-maker. Am I going to have to keep you in line again?" He turned his attention back to the Shortcut.

I rolled my shoulders and cracked my neck in an imitation of Jacky. Then, I fully extended my claws and sprinted forward. I jumped, and hit the side of the concrete tower that supported the sphere. By that point in my life, I had plenty of experience climbing things. A few seconds later, I tossed myself off the top of the railing, straight toward the snake.

His eyes widened in surprise, and he turned his hands from the Shortcut toward me. But before he had time to react, I unleashed Chaos in a concussive wave. Anger fueled my power, and his skin bubbled and broke as he was flung backward. The edges of my Skill clipped the Shortcut and threw off its orbiting rings. I knew I probably wasn't a match for him. I didn't have the luxury of holding back, even if there would be consequences.

The screech of bending metal was familiar, and I allowed myself a small twinge of satisfaction. It would be a few more days, at least, before it would be repaired again.

He didn't even hit the ground, instead stopping in midair like some sort of superhero, and rising back toward me as if he'd bounced off an invisible trampoline.

It was my turn to stare with wide eyes.

But I didn't wait for him to reach me, instead hurling myself at him again. I jumped feet first, my toe claws reaching for his neck.

I was on track, but before I could slice his neck open like the belly of a fish, he twitched his fingers and suddenly my legs wrenched to one side and I was hurtling toward the ground in an out of control spin. I righted myself, thanking that little boy whose name I never learned for the Tumbling Feather Skill. I landed on all fours, my joints screaming in protest.

Kilburn cursed as he landed back on the railing above, snarling. "I'm going to play with you until they force me to stop," he said, not even breathing hard. "That is, if you're still alive by the time they get here." Sirens screeched in the air, and though the guards posted on the walls weren't intervening, I knew it wouldn't be long before reinforcements came to back him up.

I turned and ran in the opposite direction. As I scrambled atop a nearby roof, I felt a sense of deja-vu. I wasn't trying to escape, I just needed a more advantageous position. One that didn't have my enemy looking so far down on me.

I'd done some research on Kilburn since joining NIX, and watched as much footage of him in action as I had time for. From what I understood, he had some control over kinetic energy. Basically, he could control movement. An extremely versatile Skill, and one he used ruthlessly, along with what was no doubt a half-dozen other, slightly less powerful Skills. But he had to have a range limit.

I ran farther away from him still, hoping to get out of the range of his Skill. I looked over my shoulder when I reached the far edge of the roof, and almost smiled to see him floating quickly down toward the other end. Now that he wanted to kill me, he'd follow me. It was doubly advantageous, because he gave up his position on higher ground, and if I could drag the fight out long enough, Adam would be safe back in the team barracks.

I felt Kilburn move with my awareness, and a flicker out of the corner of my eye was all the warning I had. I lashed out instinctively, and that might have saved me.

He bowed forward bonelessly, moving his abdomen out of my reach.

Another swipe, with my left hand, slashing across the skin of his forehead. Blood spilled down, into his eyes, and he blinked, trying to clear it away.

I lunged sideways, claws digging into the roof beneath and leaning so far forward I felt like I might fall. Away, away, had to get away. I could feel the power gathering.

A second later the arm I'd cut him with was breaking, as he twisted and flung it away with a twitch of his fingers and a flex of power.

My arm twisted and pulled in a dozen different spots, and I tried to spin with it to alleviate some of the damage, but instead ended up sprawled on the ground. My left arm from the shoulder down was mangled, twisted several times around like an ice cream swirl, the skin split, the bones and joints shattered, and my fingers pointing outward in different unnatural directions from the lump of flesh that had been my hand.

I gasped, feeling like I couldn't breathe. Then I screamed in horror, shrieking with all the strength in my lungs, the sounding grating against my throat like sandpaper. That wasn't my arm. It couldn't be. It was just so incredibly *wrong*. Not what an arm should be. Not what the arm I needed had to be.

Then the pain hit, and my screams stopped abruptly. Pain had always allowed me to focus, but I'd never felt pain like this. And to be honest, I'd never felt fear quite like this. China's blue, dead eyes flashed in my mind.

The snake turned to me, angrily trying to keep the blood running from his forehead out of his eyes. He seemed to be glowing with power, which my panicking brain thought for a second might mean I was seeing things. Then I realized it meant I was about to die, as he lifted a hand, fingers curled and trembling with anger.

I raised my own hand, the good one, and unleashed a counter-attack as his power lashed through the air. There was a split second where time seemed to slow, as it so often did when I was about to die. Everything I had moved outward through the air, and things stilled for a second. Then every cell in my body contracted and burst into pain with what must have been an almost audible *thump*, and we both began to scream.

His bodysuit and skin rippled under the force of my attack, as if he stood in front of an overwhelming gust of wind. Then the fabric and flesh began to crumble away, blowing off him like he was made of dust, as my power disintegrated his existence.

He *moved* then, flinging himself backward like he was being sucked through an enormous straw.

Was he dead? Probably not, but I felt like I was on my way there. I tasted blood, my ears were ringing and half-plugged with it, and my lungs shuddered as I breathed out. This had not gone quite according to plan.

IT HAD SEEMED A LOT LONGER, but the fight had only taken a couple minutes, and before I could even think of rallying my strength, I heard Commander Petralka's faint voice snapping orders through the ringing both inside my ears and outside from the sirens. Their response time was quicker than the last time I'd made such a big scene.

A couple people wearing a different uniform than the standard Player bodysuit, but who must have been heavily Seed-augmented, jumped to the roof of the building I lay incapacitated atop. On her orders, they dragged me down, jostling the mass of pain that had once been my arm.

I almost passed out, but instead of slipping away into darkness, my mind spun dizzily, the relief of unconsciousness not to be. "I took off his face," I slurred up at Nadia Petralka, who I thought might be glaring at me. I wasn't sure, because the red tint I kept blinking away made it a bit hard to see.

"What have you *done*?" she snarled at me, and I was sure she was glaring. "One of our most *valuable* assets ... if he dies—" she seemed literally too angry to speak.

The Thinker man from her meeting with Bunny appeared then, taking her by the elbow with his fishy fingers and drawing her away. They gestured to me, voices agitated, but I couldn't focus enough to hear them clearly, even though I knew it was possible with my enhanced senses. The man's voice raised, "... cell isn't even fully prepared yet! ... Spinning out of control, and you ..."

She responded, " ... half-dead, no way she'll be putting up a fight. We have time."

While they talked, the two who had brought me down from the roof examined my injuries and shot a vial of something into my neck.

"Go 'way," I said, still slurring. But when I tried to lift my good hand to bat at them, I found that my body wouldn't move. It could have been from injuries, but I was betting they'd just paralyzed me. My face chilled in the breeze, and I realized suddenly that my face was wet for some reason. I wasn't crying, was I? I was tougher than that, surely. I let out a tiny wet cough, and promised myself I wouldn't do *that* again as pain swept through me with the movement of my chest.

They stepped back, and one lifted his hand and encapsulated me in a bubble that pulsed faintly red, which only added to the crimson tint of my world.

Oh, that didn't bode well.

Nadia returned, scowling at me through the red bubble. "I ought to have you executed," she said, little dots of spittle spraying from her mouth. "You would be, if this were a standard military operation."

I tried to raise a defiant eyebrow, but I couldn't feel my face to tell if it worked.

"You may be valuable to us, but don't think you're untouchable. It was a mistake to give you such a long leash. You've deliberately disobeyed my orders, and proven yourself a danger to our operation." She dug her nails into her own palms, fingers clenched so tightly they'd turned pale. "Damn Thinkers," she muttered, turning her head away from me. "I *would* have you killed right now if your body wasn't useful to us," she said, quieter this time. She crouched down outside the bubble and met my gaze. "But I, too, have my orders, and your body is useful. You'll wish it wasn't, soon. You'll think back to today and wish I'd had you killed immediately. Because you *will* be useful to us. But you've proven you can't be managed with anything but a stranglehold." She stepped back, and nodded to the pair of differently dressed Players.

One lifted their arm, and the bubble rose, taking me with it. It buzzed unpleasantly along the skin touching it. As they walked behind Nadia, my head rested awkwardly against the side of the bubble.

Once again, I had an audience of Players, watching from the windows and a few open doorways. I wish I could say it was surprising, the number of faces which bore a look of satisfaction.

I caught a glimpse of my own reflection. Ouch. I would have winced if I could. The wetness I felt on my face was blood, as the red liquid dripped from every orifice in my skull. It dripped from my ears and nose, and my eyes were completely crimson around the blue irises, leaking blood instead of tears. I tasted it in my mouth, and every breath rattled with it. My left arm was swiftly turning purple and swollen under its own layer of leaking blood.

Apparently, I'd gone a bit too far with Chaos. I needed to get it under control. But I didn't have any more Seeds on me, and I didn't currently have the luxury of time to meditate. I wished I could pass out to escape the pain, but I wasn't sure I'd wake up again if I did.

My bubble followed Commander Petralka down into the

bright white bowels of NIX, and I did my best to stay alert and memorize our path and the placement and type of security measures. I would match it up against my mental map later.

Nadia passed me off to a guard when we got down to what I was pretty sure was the seventeenth basement level. "Here," she said. The word was ominous, and final, like the dust rising from a demolished skyscraper after it crumbled in on itself.

One of my captors met my eyes for a moment, and I thought I saw a spark of sympathy. Then they moved me into a small, cold white room, and the door slid shut behind me. The bubble popped, and I flopped onto the floor, eyes rolling back momentarily from the pain of being jolted. I struggled to stay conscious, noting vaguely that the air buzzed around me. What looked like thick white steam shot out of tiny holes in the wall near the ceiling. I'd seen that before, I knew, but I couldn't remember where, for some reason. I felt dizzy.

I started to separate from the pain, and with the distance came profound relief.

Then oblivion claimed me, and I knew nothing.

Chapter 11

In the midst of winter, I finally learned that there was in me an invincible summer.

—Albert Camus

THERE WAS *PAIN*, and cold, forcing me to wakefulness. I really wanted to escape from it. I couldn't, and that made me want to huddle up in the corner and sob. Instead, I opened my bleary eyes. Blood crusted together my eyelashes, and I had to blink a few times to free them. I ended up staring at a nondescript metal door. My ears buzzed, and despite lying on the floor, I felt dizzy. Abruptly, my stomach rebelled, heaving bile up onto the ground so hard I felt like the convulsion were trying to turn me inside out. It hurt, but the involuntary movement that aggravated my wounds hurt even more.

The distinctive smell of stomach acid only partially masked the scent of raw, bloody meat, which I knew was coming from my own body.

My eyes traveled to the side as I instinctively avoided following that train of thought any further, and I saw a plain grey pouch lying on the concrete floor, underneath a metal flap cut into the wall. A nutrition packet.

Despite my earlier nausea, my body cried out for sustenance with a strength that overwhelmed even my pain. I forced myself to inch across the floor using my good arm and weak nudges from my legs. I tore the cap off the nutrition pouch with my teeth, and squeezed some of the normally disgusting mush into my mouth with the cold-stiffened fingers of my good hand.

Yes. Yes, this was what I needed. I breathed a sigh of relief and continued to suck. After a few swallows, my agitation calmed, and I slowed to sips so as not to upset my stomach. I didn't want to be forced to expel the meager rations. And they were already making me feel better.

I closed my eyes and breathed shallowly, as the deeper breaths made me move more, and caused proportionate pain. As the nutrition mush settled, it seemed to push the pain away. It must have had some sort of pain relieving substance mixed in. I understood vaguely that might not be a good thing, but I couldn't bring myself to care past the wonderful feeling.

As my mind stopped cringing away from the sensations haranguing my physical body, I was able to clear up some of the Chaos I'd released in my earlier attack. I could only suppose that the sedative mist they'd knocked me out with had somehow also resulted in calming Chaos, either directly or through the enforced absolute calmness of my body and mind. Because I probably shouldn't have woken up again, *ever*, with that amount of power used and the damage to my body.

I didn't get very far with wrangling Chaos, because before I knew it I'd eaten the whole nutrition pouch, and then the world slipped away again.

WHEN I WOKE up the next time, another food pouch lay on the floor next to me, and the pain had separated into distinct sections.

I wasn't sure if this was a good thing or not. My head throbbed like my brain was trying to hammer its way out of my skull. My eyeballs, nose, and pretty much all the soft tissue inside of my head burned like I was grinding salt into an open wound, and my stomach simultaneously ached with hunger and threatened to force bile up my throat. My arm, however, hurt less, which I wished was a good thing. It ached deeply, throbbing with every beat of my heart, like my head, but the pain had decreased. I tried to wiggle my fingers, and found I couldn't.

Damn it. That was bad, I knew. Not that nerve damage was surprising, at this point. I might be in danger of being poisoned by my own putrefying flesh. The classes I'd taken recently in combat medicine and first aid flashed through my mind. But I had no tools, no supplies. I was trapped in a room by myself. There was nothing I could do for any of my wounds, except meditate and hope my Seeds were strong enough to heal me.

Somehow, I doubted the Seeds could do a thing for my arm.

I picked up the food pouch, bit off the cap, and slowly started to suck up the nutrient slush. It started to numb me, the sedative doing its job, so I backed off even though I was absolutely starving. I couldn't afford to keep sleeping.

"Display time," I muttered aloud, and my VR chip obligingly popped out a small Window. I mentally waved the warning away. It was ten in the morning, which meant I'd been in the cell approximately ten hours.

I wondered what was happening to the rest of the team. Had Adam made it back in time? Had they been captured, like me? It had been part of the plan for me to cause trouble, be captured, and locked up down here, but not like this.

If what I knew of NIX was true, they would want to use my team in the field, not lock them up. It was a pattern with them … and wasn't it crazy that I was *hoping* to be blackmail material? If Petralka thought she could control my team without locking them up or torturing them, she would. I hoped.

With that thought, I mentally interacted with my VR chip and tried to send a message to the whole team, asking for a status update. The Window pulsed faintly, but failed to send. I grew dizzy as my brain seemed to vibrate. What the hell? Maybe my concentration was too shot to interact with the VR chip properly.

I opened my mouth and croaked, "Send Window to all team members." There. It couldn't fail to understand voice commands.

Except it did.

UNABLE TO CONTACT SUBORDINATE VIRTUAL
REALITY CHIPS.

The Window popped up over the message I'd been trying to send, and the hair on the back of my neck rose as the dizziness increased. I'd slurped up the last of the nutrition mush without realizing, and my stomach decided it really would like to throw up, but I fought the urge.

I panicked for a bit, I'll admit it. Then I turned my mind to analyzing my suddenly disastrous current circumstances. I ran through the functions my VR chip was supposed to have, and determined that it was functioning properly, except for anything that required outside input. Which meant that it wasn't broken, and despite my worried thoughts, whatever was in the nutrient pack probably hadn't interfered with the chip. That was both good and bad. Good because I could still eat them, and bad, because whatever was blocking my chip was beyond my immediate control.

The buzzing dizziness was coming from outside my head, as opposed to a side effect of a concussion or the like, I was pretty sure. I wouldn't take a stacked bet against NIX implementing some sort of signal scrambler, perhaps based on the vibrations around Torliam's room. Damn. I almost wondered if it could get any worse, but stopped that thought in its tracks. It didn't do to tempt the gods of irony.

I was getting tired, and that was making it hard to think. I shook my head and set aside that problem for a few minutes while

I meditated to suppress Chaos again. I needed any edge I could get, and letting my body deteriorate from the inside any faster than absolutely necessary was unacceptable.

By the time I finished, my eyelids felt like they were trying to bench-press a hundred pounds every time I blinked. Damn it, I was tired.

I examined the room. My cell was similar to the one Torliam lived in. White, made of a stone or concrete-like substance, with small holes around the ceiling that had sprayed gas down on me. The solid metal door fit snugly into the wall on either side. The major difference between my room and his was that I wasn't stuck on a metal slab or attached to any machines. The room was completely bare, and my cell had a metal flap in the wall, through which someone had no doubt dropped the nutrition pack.

I scooted closer to it, and tried to pry up the metal flap. It opened easily, but I couldn't get my arm into it any farther than the wrist, because opening the flap's hinge caused another flap to tilt up behind it. Instead, I tried sensing past the flap using my Perception. The square metal opening slanted slightly upward just behind the flap, and then turned sharply up, then turned again to point straight parallel to the ground, opening up into the outside hallway. It created a skewed S-shape. There was no way a human arm would bend properly to fit through that, even if the flap opening didn't guard itself.

I wasn't disappointed by this realization for too long, because I passed out again, leaning against the wall with my good shoulder.

THIS TIME, I woke up when the silvery food pouch landed in my lap. I pressed my ear up against the metal opening and heard footsteps. "Hello?"

The owners of the footsteps, two people, I thought, didn't respond. But they stopped for a moment before continuing on. I immediately dove into my senses, pushing outward through the small duct and following the duo out into the hallway.

They exchanged meaningful glances with each other, and when they were a bit farther away, one murmured to the other, "Increase the dosage of food sedative for Redding, and the strength of the inhalable for the operation. She's displayed an unusually fast adaptation to the narcotics. Waking now is …" He looked as if he was doing calculations, but continued after a few moments, "almost *twenty percent* faster than expectation."

His partner glanced back at my door. "Well, at least she'll be dependent on them soon. Anything to decrease the likelihood of escape from that one is a good thing, in my book."

"Yes, but the sedatives are damaging in high doses. Her condition will deteriorate more quickly than normal."

His partner shrugged as they continued to walk away. "She's going to be 'gelded' soon anyway. Should I increase the dose in the next nutrition pouch, in prep for the surgeon? We won't have to worry so much once the VR chip is replaced with the penal conditioner model and she's locked down to a table."

"No … we want her on an empty stomach for the surgery. Just make sure the calculations for the inhalable sedative are properly adjusted."

"What about …"

The buzzing grew too strong, and my concentration too weak, for me to hear any more. I wasn't in top shape, to say the least. But I had enough to know I needed to make a move, and fast. I had no desire to meet this 'surgeon' and have him update my brain hardware.

I glanced down at the silver pouch in my lap and reluctantly away. I couldn't sleep. Judging by their conversation, by the time I would normally get the next nutrition pouch, it'd be time for surgery. Which meant I had a few hours, at most. They would knock me out with the aerosol sedative before trying to enter the room or mess with me in any way. I couldn't take advantage of them opening the door and allowing me to attack and free myself.

I needed to be gone before they arrived. How?

I had planned to be down here, and planned to have to escape. But I'd also planned more time to prepare, and hadn't expected NIX to do quite such a good job of detaining me. As counterintuitive as it might seem to be locked up in order to pull off a jail-break, and the fact that I had vowed I'd avoid being put in this cell at all costs, it had made sense.

Torliam's room was physically and electronically reinforced to the max, as was the whole level he resided on. The security wasn't unbreachable, but any way we would have broken in by force would have alerted NIX to our plans too early. To break in and *then* break out again would have taken too much time. It was faster to get NIX to take me down to Torliam themselves, so I could work from within the prison level.

We'd had a plan. It depended on use of our VR chips. Once I was down here, with everything else already prepared, I'd contact one of the team and give them directions through the vents to my cell. They'd bring me one of several stashes of supplies hidden among the vents system to enable me to more easily break out, before I was incapacitated any further, like Torliam.

Then, Adam would use the connection in our VR chips to lead me through forcing the door to Torliam's room open from the outside, which was the only way it opened at all.

So, without the VR chip, I didn't have a way to escape from my cell, or to open Torliam's. I'd tried to make sure redundancies were woven into the planning, but we were still working on it, and I hadn't anticipated *this*.

I let the tension flow out of my shoulders and brought the food pouch to my mouth with my good arm. I bit off the cap and took a single swallow. I didn't want the sedative to knock me out, but I needed the energy, and a bit of pain relief. Plus, I was just starving. Literally. I examine my arm critically as I lowered the pouch to my lap. My body was wasting away, almost in front of my eyes.

No doubt my Seeds were desperate for fuel, and had turned

the only place they could. The almost non-existent fat deposits had been burned away first, and then they'd turned to my muscle. The bones of my wrist stood out sharply against thin, pale skin, and even small movements exhausted me.

I needed to get out of my cell, and into Torliam's. Working with what I had, how could I make that happen? I put my aching brain to the test, leaning my head against the coolness of the metal flap. It was so cold in my cell, but my head was hot, and the metal soothed some of that.

There was an extremely high chance the team hadn't been able to continue preparing after I was locked up, so I could only count on the things we'd already done. Adam had been in the middle of the critical mission. If he'd finished it, we might be able to pull this off. If he'd gone straight back to the team barracks, I was screwed.

It took me over an hour of thinking, with occasional slurps of my nutrition pouch for pain relief, to come up with a plan. It was reckless, and it was dangerous. And as far as I could tell, it was my only option.

A focused examination of my cell from where I sat revealed a few cameras, and no blind spots, per se. But if I tucked myself into the wall, they would only be able to see my back. I took another swallow of my nutrient pouch and turned toward the metal flap, blocking the view of it from the cameras.

It was a struggle to get the claws of my right hand to come out, like it hadn't been since I first gained the Skill. But after almost a minute, I had claws again. My body suit was in the way, so I disconnected it at my waist.

I brought my hand to my stomach, under my belly button, and sliced into the skin. It bled sluggishly, but I ignored that and slipped a clawed finger under the skin. I could feel it tugging and separating from the layer of connective tissue and muscle below with teensy little snaps. I shuddered, and felt light headed for a second, but continued wiggling my finger below the skin of my stomach till I felt the pouch there and pulled it out.

The malleable plastic was slippery with blood, but the surface was intact, and the fluid inside undisturbed. Thank goodness. Though, I would have known if something went wrong with the tiny package, at about the same time my organs started to dissolve.

Thinking back on it, hiding a hyper-concentrated acid under my skin before getting into a fight might not have been the best idea. But Blaine had designed the pouch to be sturdy, and if Kilburn had ruptured the pouch with his power, I would have been dead anyway, from being turned into human hamburger. And Gregor and I, along with Jacky and Zed, had all agreed that hiding an undetectable secret weapon under my skin was a really cool idea. Just like a spy film. Which, I also realize, may not have been the best indicator of the soundness of the idea.

But it was going to save my ass, now. It didn't show up on scans as anything other than a fat deposit at the base of my belly.

I very carefully brought the cap of the small pouch to my mouth, and twisted the lid off. I kept the cap in my mouth, in case I finished with leftover acid and needed to reseal it.

I palmed the bloody pouch gently, and slid my hand under the flap. My hand hit against the rotating metal barrier, and I carefully squeezed out a thin line of liquid across the base of it. In a few seconds, the acid had eaten through, and the blocking flap toppled backward. I slid my hand farther through, being careful not to brush my arm against the acid eating a useless hole through the bottom of the small metal tunnel.

My arm started to shake, and I breathed deep, focusing on keeping it steady and strong. I only had one chance, and not a lot of time.

When I came to the first bend in the tunnel, I squeezed a line of acid out along the edge, using my awareness to guide me. I almost despaired at my own weakness. Just using my claws and the Wraith Skill at the same time was a struggle.

It took me almost an hour to turn the ninety-degree angle leading out into the hallway into a gentle slope, but the acid ate through the metal and stone of the wall valiantly. My good arm had gone past the point of burning pain into numbness at being forced to stay steady in the awkward position. Finally, I drew another thin line of acid along the metal of the outside flap opening from the hallway. It ate away the metal, but I didn't touch the flap, and it stayed precariously in place. I hoped the dissolved line wasn't noticeable from the outside.

Then, I waited.

Chapter 12

They are all gone into the world of light, and I alone sit lingering here.

— Henry Vaughan

THEY SPRAYED the aerosol sedative without warning, white mist shooting from the holes in the wall around the ceiling.

No doubt, they expected me to have completely passed out by the time they arrived, my struggle to reach out of the small vent futile. If I had not had the acid, they would have been right. I was much too weak to utilize Chaos, and they probably knew it.

I pressed my face to the vent and used careful application of my claws to slightly displace the covering on the outside wall. This was dangerous, and I could only hope they didn't notice from the outside and ruin my whole plan.

I held my breath for a while as the sedative shot down, and then slumped bonelessly against the wall, my face pressed against the opening of the vent, resting on my arm. I breathed slowly, sucking in the fresh air from outside the room. I was sure I'd still get a bit of the aerosol sedative in my system, since I didn't have an airtight seal to make sure I only took in air from the vent, but hopefully it wouldn't be much.

After a few minutes, during which I pretended to be knocked out, I heard footsteps coming down the hall toward me. Four people. They stopped outside my door and talked among themselves for a few moments while two of them entered in a code to the keypad and let it scan their eyeballs to confirm their identity.

The door slid open, and I withdrew my arm from the tunnel and flung myself at them, the claws on my good hand out and ready. Two of them carried stun batons. I knocked one of them out with a kick to the face, and flung away the baton of the other before she could turn it on.

Three enemies remaining. But I was already tiring, dizzy from the sudden movement. "Freeze!" I snarled. Stupid, I know, but I hoped they'd be shocked and unsettled enough to listen to the authority in my voice without thinking about it.

They froze, and I used the opportunity to its fullest. I stood straight and tried to look imposing, despite my bedraggled state and mutilated arm. "You can't outrun me," I said calmly. "Your bodies are not fast or strong enough. Back up against the wall and raise your hands. If you run, I will kill you, immediately." I flexed my clawed hand for emphasis. "But I can be reasonable."

Two of them exchanged glances, perhaps of disbelief. The alarms began to sound, alerting the compound to my actions. I hoped my team realized what it meant, since a quick attempt to send a Window proved I still couldn't contact them. I had less than two minutes before the guards converged and forced me back into my cell.

"I need an escort," I said. "And the key to the alien's door."

The surgeon choked, took a step back and shook his head. "We will never give you access to the threat against Earth."

"Yeah, I was expecting that," I said. "I guess you'll have to help against your will." I crouched down toward one I'd knocked out and stepped on his hand, pressing his palm flat against the ground. Then I used the last of the acid to remove his hand from his arm.

He jerked and screamed, waking from the pain.

I continued resolutely, watching as the liquid ate away at his wrist joint and corroded through the tendons. Blood pooled on the ground, but I soon had his hand detached from his body. Then I turned to face him. "Okay, that's the fingerprints. Now for the eyes."

He tried to scramble away from me, cradling his mangled stump against his chest, sobbing incoherently.

"Stop, please." One of the surgeon's other assistants whimpered, looking as if she wanted to step forward from the wall and stop me.

"I don't like doing this either." I sighed. "It's pretty disgusting. But I need a way to get through the doors down here, and you guys refused to help me." I knew I didn't have much time left before the deployed guards reached me. I wished I was strong enough to just force a couple of my captives to help, but I wasn't.

When I began to dig into the man's eye socket, I guess his screams got to the rest of them.

"That won't work!" the surgeon yelled. "You need our eyes intact, so that the pupils dilate when the scanning light shines in them. You can't just kill us."

Oh. Well, crap. I looked down at the severed hand and eyeball in my hand and let them fall to the floor. The poor medic beneath me was quivering incoherently, and the stench of his piss burned in my nostrils. I sighed. Time to bluff some more.

I stood up and grabbed the surgeon, yanking him away from the wall. "Thanks for the info. I'm pretty sure I'll be able to use my Skills to keep your head alive for a few minutes, with or without your body," I lied. I pressed my claws into the skin under his ears, hoping that panic would be enough to make him forgo his common sense.

It was. "We'll take you! I'll open the door!" He gasped, eyes squeezed closed.

"Let's go, then." I waved at the other two, who were still cowering against the wall. "Now!"

That snapped them out of it, and they ran ahead of me, moving faster at my urging.

I could hear the footsteps of guards behind us. Thank goodness the medics had snapped in time. No doubt NIX had given them training about what to do in the event of a break out, attack, or other emergency situation. But when a situation changes from a hypothetical to the immediacy of seeing your coworker de-eyeballed while he screams ... priorities change. People do things they never thought they would, given the right motivation. I should know.

Guards turned the corner in front of my little group, guns at the ready. The medics screamed and skidded to a halt, which gave me enough of a shield and distraction to get close to the guards before they attacked.

I raked my claws across one's eyes, and then grabbed his forearm with that same hand and turned. A bone in his forearm snapped and punctured through both his skin and the fabric of his uniform, but his hand stayed wrapped around the trigger, and the gun was facing his fellow guards. I used the familiar trick, squeezing my finger around his own and spraying them down with tranquilizer darts.

They dropped like puppets with their strings cut.

Well, at least I knew they were aiming to sedate, not kill me. So far.

I released the gun, and punched the screaming owner of the gun in the back of the neck. I wasn't good enough to use Jacky's signature neck chop, but he stopped screaming and joined his unconscious friends. Hopefully I hadn't killed him. I turned back to the medics and waved impatiently at them. "Don't just stand there! We've got places to be."

One of them let out a gasping sob, but they continued running, leading the way to Torliam as I directed them.

We arrived at his section of sub-level seventeen, and they used their verification to get us through the security block.

The sound of the alarm changed then, becoming more screechingly urgent. I wasn't sure if it was because of my current location, or because my team was implementing their part of the escape plan up above.

I could feel Torliam's presence through the wall, a kind of thrumming energy that pushed against my skin like phantom waves. I almost itched with urgency, as I thrust one of the surgeon's assistances toward the security pad. "I know the code just as well as you do," I growled. "If you use the fake one …" I let her imagination fill in the rest. "And don't think I'm not aware that different keys have to be pushed with different fingers."

Her knees were shaking, but she gave a stiff nod and entered her code, then let the pad scan her eyeball under my intense scrutiny. The surgeon went next, and though he was more hesitant to open the door, my clawed hand resting gently on the back of his neck was all the encouragement he needed.

The huge, incredibly reinforced slab of a door slid open, revealing the back of Torliam's restraints.

The medics probably knew about the cameras that watched Torliam's room, connected to monitors far away from NIX's main base. That fail-safe may have been the only reason they agreed to open the door, even considering my threats. The fail-safes assumed that NIX's security system had been compromised, and negated the ability of those within NIX to affect the compound through any electronic method. In other words, when the second set of people watching through the cameras saw where I was and what I was doing, and how NIX had failed to stop me, they took over.

I'd barely gotten Torliam's door open when they shut down the main generator, cutting off the power source to the whole compound. The lights, sirens, and ventilation cut off, and in the sudden, absolute silence, I could hear faint yells and screams from other prisoners.

I held my breath and counted to ten. A deep, rumbling explosion sounded off below, the vibration traveling through the floor and walls around me, from deep beneath my feet. I almost lost my balance and a couple of my captives let out ear-splitting shrieks, but I ignored them, letting out a breathless, loud laugh.

I stopped laughing when I realized that I sounded a bit like an evil villain. "I'm going to have to give you a raise, Adam," I murmured aloud.

SABOTAGING the backup generator had been Adam's assignment the night before when I'd been captured, but I hadn't been sure if he'd managed to complete it or not.

"Do not enter the room," Torliam said. "I do not know what you have done, but my cell has protections of its own. It is not de-fanged." Despite the warning, his tone was tight with suppressed excitement.

"Just sit tight and wait. I'll have you out soon." I instructed my VR chip to send a Window to the team, and this time there was no backlash.

—STATUS REPORT, TEAM. —
-EVE-
It only took a few seconds for the replies to bombard me.
—KICKING ASS OVER HERE. HURRY UP AND JOIN US! —
-JACKY-

—ARE YOU OKAY? WE COULDN'T CONTACT YOU EARLIER. WE'RE IN THE LAB DEFENDING THE SHIP. —
-ZED-

—CURRENTLY HOLDING THE LAB, DEFENDING FROM ATTACK. THE PLAN IS IN PLACE. SHOULD BE ABLE TO HOLD POSITION FOR THE NEXT TEN MINS. WHERE ARE YOU? —
-ADAM-

—ARE YOU OKAY?—

-Sam-

—Powering up the ship with a backup generator. We'll be ready. The kiddos are already inside, safe.—
-Blaine-

—I'm okay. Down here with our friend from outer space.—
-Eve-

I thought for a quick moment, then sent a message to Zed.

—Come down and pass me the breakout supplies. Be quick, be safe.—
-Eve-

Zed would be least useful to the team in defending the lab from the rest of NIX, and in helping with any last-minute escape preparation, but he was more than competent enough to help me at the moment.

A few minutes later, Zed broke the relatively weak grate in the ceiling, making sure it didn't fall to the floor, and pushed the supplies through. They floated toward me, balancing gently on what Jacky had dubbed the "hoverboard," without touching any of the equipment, or the pressure-sensitive floor. "What's that stuff all over your face?" Zed asked, bringing out a flashlight.

"What?" I grabbed the board out of the air and stepped back further into the hall, then dug into the supply pack for the numbing spray. We'd thought Torliam might need it, along with a few other medical supplies. I shook the can and applied it liberally, coating my entire left arm. It helped a bit. I popped a stimulant tablet into my mouth for good measure. I could crash after we were gone. Then I straddled the hoverboard around the middle with the supply pack held in front of me, and floated into the room, my good side angled toward Zed. "Don't shine that right at me. You'll kill my night vision."

"It looks kinda like … dried blood." His voice trailed off.

"Oh, yeah. I overused my Skill a bit. It's got a bit of backlash if I don't control it properly. Some of the small blood vessels in my face probably broke. It's no big deal, kinda like a dry air nosebleed. Doesn't even hurt," I lied.

"Oh." He didn't sound satisfied, but thankfully didn't pursue that line of conversation. "Who are those crying people?" Zed asked, shining a flashlight on the forms huddled outside the door.

I glanced over my shoulder. "They're the people who were going to do some surgery on me for NIX."

The two assistants were crouched by the wall next to the door, but the surgeon was pressed against the door separating Torliam's section from the rest of the level. He was banging futilely on it, calling for help.

"Do you think I should kill them? I'm not sure they're really a threat to us anymore," I said.

Zed's eyes widened, but he hesitated, and then shook his head. "Not if we don't have to." He laughed. "My life is so surreal. Here I am, breaking my sister and an alien giant-person out of a top secret base cut into a mountain. And I'm wondering whether we should kill the hostages or not."

The hoverboard brought me around to the side of Torliam's restraining slab. I maneuvered around the tubes and wires coming out from him and met his eyes. "You'll get used to it," I said absently, my concentration shot by the look on the giant's face.

Torliam's eyes were wide and feverishly bright, and his muscles tense as if he wanted to thrash against his bonds but was holding himself rigid instead. "You … are here. This is beyond my expectations," he said.

I grinned, trying to relieve some of the tension caused by the sheer force of his presence. "Don't tell me you're impressed *already*. I'm just getting started. Sing my praises when we get to Estreyer." I gripped the hoverboard tighter with my thighs, and then dug in the supply pack.

His eyes tracked my every move, unblinking.

"Shine the light over here, will you?" I waved to the side of the slab. "I've got to disable this first."

Zed swung the light, but stopped on me instead where I'd pointed.

I frowned up at him. "Don't shine the light in my eyes. Over there!" I pointed again.

Zed ignored me. "Eve, what's wrong with your arm?"

I glanced down at the appendage that hung uselessly off my shoulder. The pain flared, just thinking about it, especially when I breathed in that raw meat smell again in full force. I squeezed the hoverboard tighter between my thighs and warded off a wave of dizziness. "Oh, yeah. I got a bit hurt while fighting Kilburn. He was reactivating the Shortcut."

"A *bit* hurt?" Zed's voice rang out, and Torliam turned to scrutinize him instead. "I ..." Zed fell silent for a moment, and when he spoke again his voice was quieter, calmer. A bit of the ice I imbued my own tone with when I was angry sounded in his words. "You should have called Sam, instead of me. You are severely injured. This could endanger our escape."

I smiled up at him, squinting against the beam of light. "Logic. I like it. It's good to see you're adapting your arguments against me."

"I'm not joking, Eve! You're hurt bad." His voice rose.

"I can make it. We don't have time to heal me right now, and Sam's undoubtedly got plenty to deal with up there with the rest of them. We'll have time for healing once we're away. Otherwise we're all as good as dead anyway. Now hurry up and shine the light where I need it. We're wasting time."

Zed complied. "Well, then you better hurry up so we can get out of here and Sam can do his job," he said through clenched teeth.

Torliam watched as I pulled a pouch of acid out of the pack. "How will you bypass the safeguards of this cell?"

I spoke as I took the cap off the pouch of acid, partially to ease the tension, and partially to distract myself from the pain and weakness sabotaging me. "I know the security measures in here aren't dependent on the rest of the base. They've got it rigged to kill, under pretty much any circumstances. Guess they thought it'd be better to eliminate you than chance your escape. But I've got a team of really smart people, too. This room may have its own backup generator for security, but in the case of forced takeover, the base loses direct control and access to the main generator. Almost the entire rest of the base is dependent on the backup generator that just exploded below us. Which means that the doors are all stuck closed. If the guards want to get to us, they're going to have to blow their way through every single checkpoint, or find a way to get control returned to this base. That gives us the time we need to get you out."

I squeezed a thin line of acid on the seamless metal surface supporting his slab. "This will give me access to the inner components of this table that's got you stuck here. Please don't move around too much. I'll be working with some sensitive stuff, and I don't want it thinking you're trying to escape and setting off any safety mechanisms."

The acid did its job, and I took off the sheet of metal it had eaten through, and placed it gently on top of a machine that was attached to Torliam by tubes inserted into his skin in multiple places. Then I had a thought. "This is the one that filters your blood, right?"

"Correct."

"Hmm." I maneuvered the hoverboard gingerly around, examining the controls. "It's like a fancy version of those old dialysis machines, right, Zed?"

He looked at it for a second, peering down from his cramped space in the vent. "Maybe? I may have wanted to be a doctor, but I really don't know too much about them. And I can't tell much by looking at it from afar. Why?"

I traced the tubes coming out from Torliam to the ones going back in, and then leaned down to see a large tube full of golden shimmer. Drop by drop, more of the Seed material joined it, being filtered from his blood. "I really don't know what I'm doing," I said. "But if I do this …" I flipped a switch, then pushed a few buttons when the screen on the machine lit up. "I think it might run backward."

I leaned down again, and sure enough, the golden liquid was being slowly sucked out of the tube instead of entering it. I turned to Torliam. "Can you feel anything?"

He clenched his fist, the wrist of which had one of the many tubes entering it. "My strength is being restored. I … I thank you, Eve of the line of Redding." He looked over at another machine. "That one pumps the sedative."

I took the hint, and pinched off the tubes leading from that machine, since I didn't see an obvious "off" button. "By the time I've got you off that slab, hopefully you'll be a bit stronger." We might need his strength, because from the dizzying waves of cold that washed over my body, it seemed like my own was failing.

I took out what looked like a gun, but had a cartridge on top filled with a clear liquid instead of bullets. "This is a binding agent," I said, peering into the complicated guts inside the base of the slab supporting Torliam. "It's going to lock the pressure sensors on the slab in place, right where they are now." I reached in and began to squeeze the trigger slowly, fighting against the dangerous tremors in my hand. "So, when you get up, this thing will think all your weight is still on it, dispersed just like it is right now."

I finished that relatively quickly, warning Torliam again not to move, so that the binding agent could activate and harden.

"I would not do anything to jeopardize our mission. Place your faith in that. I desire nothing more at this moment but to be free of this *thing*, and to be rid of this place," he said.

137

When the binding agent had dried, I twisted to look up at the clamps rooted in the slab, which dug into the flesh of his back along his spine. I could see where dried blood had run down into the tiny seams around the metal. I grabbed one and manually wiggled it with my fingers, and he grunted in pain. "Hold still. There's a catch down here, I think I can draw the clamp right out, but it's probably still going to hurt." I used a claw to pry open the catch that held that half of the clamp in place, and then grabbed the whole base and pulled.

Torliam stiffened and let out a prolonged groan as I drew on the clamp, his voice mixing with the squelching sound as the metal withdrew from his flesh.

I pulled it all the way out through the slab, and brought it out of the bottom into the light. "Umm … no wonder that hurt. Are you alright?"

"I can endure whatever pain necessary. Please continue."

"That's not exactly what I meant." I pointed to the tip of the clamp, which had an angled notch cut into it. Like a fishhook, the tip of an arrowhead, or a serrated knife. It was designed to hold in place, or to mutilate the flesh if drawn out the way it had entered. "I just ripped open a chunky hole in your back."

"That's disgusting, Eve," Zed said.

Torliam glanced at the bloody half of a clamp I held in my hand, and then quickly looked away, focusing on my eyes. "Your people are indeed well versed in the art of torture, I have learned. Do not back down from what must be done."

"Well, maybe I can detach them from the slab instead of detaching them from your back. We'd still have to extract them later, but it would probably be better to have Sam do it, instead of me. He's my healer."

He nodded. "If you can."

So I used the rest of the acid to eat through the metal keeping the clamps from sliding upward through the holes in the slab. Torliam continued to watch my every move, which was slightly unnerving. "Zed, tell me about what's happened while I was down here," I said.

"Well, when you got taken, these really strong Players grabbed all of us and brought us to individual rooms. They almost caught Adam out of bounds, but he made it back in time. We were all talking among ourselves using those awesome VR chips, even though we couldn't see each other, and we kept trying to contact you. We made sure to do it all mentally, no hand or voice signals, and Adam basically walked me through the whole interrogation."

"What did NIX want?"

"Oh, basically they threatened us that your life depended on our good behavior. We were right about that, at least …"

I nodded. When I had to start the plan so early, I wasn't sure that NIX wouldn't retaliate against the rest of the team. We hadn't put any protection in place for the others yet. I realized Zed had trailed off, and glanced up at him. He was looking off to the side, jaw clenched as he remembered.

"I would prefer to never get captured and put in an interrogation room again," he said simply.

Torliam snorted at that, with some amusement that I didn't share.

"Were you guys still being held when I set off the alarms?"

"Yeah. Kris and Gregor actually broke Adam out with one of those non-lethal guns Blaine's been having them practice with. Then Adam killed some people and busted Jacky out, and with the two of them … well, you know how she is. It was like watching a superhero film. NIX didn't even have time to react. Everything locked down, but we got to the lab before you set off the second alarms, and then the backup power blew itself up. When I left, they were killing the guards who'd already been guarding inside the lab after the scientists evacuated."

"I see." I'd have to thank the kiddos, and Adam. If not for his guidance of the team and their actions, we might all be in a very different position right now. "I *really* have to give that guy a raise."

"Do you pay us?" Zed asked archly. "Isn't zero multiplied by two still … zero?" He pretended to count on his fingers.

I shot him a mock glare. "Well, I see *someone* doesn't want their holiday bonus."

"Sis, you should know by now that you can't influence me with your grubby scheming. Bribery?" He lifted his nose in mock disdain, then grinned at me. "What type of bonus are we talking, here? 'Cause, you know, I might be convinced of the error of my ways. I could even tell the others that we're being paid with non-material coin. The coin of friendship and rainbows and all that." He rubbed his hands together in a caricature of greediness.

I had to stifle a laugh, but my amusement was quickly snuffed out when I ran out of acid. "Damn it!" I hadn't finished removing the binding on all the clamps. I looked up to Torliam, who looked faintly bemused by our antics. "Sorry to say this, but I'm out of acid. Looks like you're gonna have a few more holes in your back till we can get you to Sam."

"Do it." He took a deep breath and seemed to brace himself. "And hurry. We must not waste time. Only the gods know what scheme our enemies are executing as we tarry."

I began to rip the remaining clamps from his back, wincing in sympathy. I'm far from squeamish, but even so, inflicting that amount of pain on someone not my enemy was a bit beyond my comfort level. Luckily, there were only a few left, and I finished quickly. Then I released the shackles around his limbs. "Okay. Do you have the second hoverboard, Zed?"

He quickly floated it down to me, and I caught it and held it beside the slab. "You should be able to move your arms, and anything above the level where your back was most recently broken. We need to take those tubes and monitoring patches off you, then get you onto this. You'll float out of the room with me, so we don't set off the pressure sensors in the floor. Ready?"

Torliam nodded. "I have been ready for years." He used his arms to push his torso up, suppressing any reaction to the pain it must have caused, and ripped away the myriad tubes, patches, and wires still attached to him.

"Swing your legs over first. I'm going to need to adjust the resistance. These things aren't exactly made to support people of your ... considerable size."

Zed coughed. "Sis!" He gave me a cheeky grin. "I'm shocked. I thought you were a lady!"

I sighed. "Get your mind out of the slums." I couldn't resist, though, and added, "And whatever gave you the impression I was a lady? Surely it wasn't something I said or did?"

Torliam's lifted his legs one after the other with one arm, supporting himself with the other, and I adjusted the degree of strength variation from the hoverboard's output. "Do not reprimand your sibling. She is only stating the obvious," Torliam said. "My enviable size is no secret. In fact, it is legend among the females of my homeland."

My mouth fell open, and I stared at him.

Zed's voice was choked with disbelief. "Hey, Eve, I'm pretty sure our giant extraterrestrial friend here just made a dirty joke. Did you hear it, too?"

"Erm." I coughed, busying myself with the hoverboard. "It's either a shared hallucination, or you just got one-upped."

Torliam didn't respond to our commentary, too busy hoisting himself onto the hoverboard, which dipped frighteningly under his weight, and then righted itself.

I took a quick moment to grab the blood clotting powder from the pack and messily shake it over his back.

Then Torliam and I floated out the door to his cell, unmolested. Unfortunately, it was at that point that my body gave up on me, the stimulant pill ran its course, and I lost consciousness.

I PASSED in and out of darkness, as if my life was a strobe light, catching only brief snippets of what was going on around me.

Torliam, jamming the modified stun baton Blaine had created for this very purpose into one of the doors that blocked the hallway, forcing it open.

Blackness.

Zed, towing me behind him as he raced through the halls.

A brief lance of pain as my hoverboard idled into the wall and jostled me. Zed was shooting air-burst rounds at a group of Players, dodging their return attacks of bright light. Two of them were down on the ground. A bright blue mist drifted past me from behind, but I slipped back into darkness before I could see what it did.

Blackness.

Zooming through the larger vents, Zed riding ahead of me on my hoverboard, steering us. His forehead had been cut, and blood covered one side of his face.

The hoverboard falling out from under me, my stomach rising into my throat as Zed slammed both feet into the grate, ripping it right out of the ceiling.

Something light blue wrapping around me and steadying me on the back of the hoverboard so that I didn't fall off.

From above, the view of the huge lab, one door blown open, smoke bombs spewing into the air, burning my lungs even so far up. From the hallway, one man stepped forward and knelt on one knee, with what looked like a small rocket launcher on his shoulder. His fellows closed in around him, some kneeling and some standing, holding up their shields shoulder to shoulder to guard him.

We dropped down next to the ship, near the doorway. Adam threw up a shield of black ink, and then another one a couple feet behind that one, so that there was a double layer of protection.

The rocket smashed against the first barrier with a *boom* so forceful it half-deafened me, and pushed me back with its force. Shrapnel exploded forward, peppering the wall and ceiling behind and around the team and ship. Adam's first shield was gone when I looked down again, and the second disintegrated as I watched.

He sagged, curly hair plastered to his forehead with sweat.

Jacky shouted in rage, grabbed some clunky metal thing off a table near her, and threw it like a discus, making a whole spin before she released it with frightening speed. It flew straight at the guy with a rocket launcher, and smashed him backward out of their little human shell formation and into the hallway behind.

By the way his chest had caved in, I'm pretty sure he was dead.

Sam was busy trying to heal Blaine, who was standing beside Adam in a huge, skeleton-only mecha suit. Blaine's leg had a hole in it, which was leaking some blood, probably from a bullet wound. Blaine waved Sam off, and moved his arms back till the elbows connected with a metal pack the rudimentary mecha carried on its back, which loaded ammo into the arms. He extended his arms forward, let out a battle cry, and the mecha shot its own little rockets at the formation of guards, blowing them backward to land amongst tons of their other downed comrades. Damn. That thing was pretty cool.

I floated down past the catwalk to land behind Jacky. "Guys, if you're finished playing around, we really should be leaving already," I groaned.

Another blank of darkness.

Zed grabbed my hoverboard to steady it against the wall as the ship lurched about, and then we were through the ceiling of the wrecked lab, rising up out of what used to be the ground of the courtyard. "Guys, I'm debating having secret aircraft hangars open up out of the ground when I get my own evil lair. What do you think?" he said, voice strained.

"Cliché," Jacky said with a snort of derision.

"Turret guns incoming," Blaine said. "Both air burst and armor piercing rounds. They had better not work, or ..." He cut off, as a huge explosion rocked the ship's balance.

I watched as the pieces of gun, wall, and bloody chunks of the gunman flew through the air.

"They will think twice about shooting now," Blaine said.

Jacky whooped and pumped her fist in the air, jumping and floating for a little too long to be natural. "Hell yes! Keep blowing yourselves up, suckers."

Zed gave Blaine a respectful look. "You did that?"

Blaine coughed and lifted the faceplate of his mecha suit to adjust his glasses. "Merely some simple sabotage to their weapons. They test and clean them once a month, and since it was highly unlikely they would have any reason to use or inspect them outside of that timeframe, I set it up so that pulling the trigger would result in the gun backfiring. With the power and amount of ammo those guns carry, it causes quite an explosion."

Another gun turret exploded as the ship gathered speed, shooting away through the air, over the mountains and river below.

Jacky nodded wisely. "Boom." She demonstrated the explosion with a hand motion.

Birch stood on the edge of the control station next to Torliam, growling out through the front-facing window.

Bunny moved up from wherever he'd been in the back of the ship, likely making sure he was protected with the kiddos and Chanelle, surrounded by the more cushiony, protective supplies.

He saw Torliam's back, seated at the control station at the front of the ship, and paused, just staring.

"What … have you *done*?!" Bunny said, his voice rising.

There was a moment of silence, and I felt a sense of foreboding rise up, helpless to do anything about it.

"It's an alien! It wants to destroy the Earth!" Bunny screamed at me, then reached behind himself and pulled out the gun from his utility belt.

I lifted my good arm, but I was too far away to stop him.

Chapter 13

Go forth into the hollow lands, where the fears of men live.
— Ateus of the Fall

SAM, who'd been standing disregarded next to Bunny, stepped forward while everyone else was still hesitating from shock. His left hand grabbed the wrist of Bunny's gun hand, forcing it down while twisting painfully, and his right hand shot out in a straight punch that rocked Bunny's head back.

Bunny wobbled and jerked away, leaving Sam holding the gun and looking almost bewildered by what had just happened.

"Back down," Bunny snarled at him.

Sam went hazy eyed and dropped the gun, stepping away with his hands raised.

Bunny lunged toward the energy cell hooked into the wall, and began to pull on it. "Stay away!" he screamed.

Torliam roared and half-turned toward him, reaching an arm out.

I felt a wash of fear, partially artificial, and partially because

Bunny was sabotaging our escape. If he removed the energy cell, the ship would crash, with all of us inside it.

I navigated my VR chip with a flicker of thought.

Bunny's head exploded. Brain matter splattered outward.

His body tottered for a second, then fell backward.

Blue mist sputtered and died away from Torliam's hand.

Adam wiped goop off his face, and turned to me. "I told you we should have just killed him in the first place."

I grunted. "We couldn't have gotten away with that. Now it doesn't matter."

"Toss him through the waste dump," Adam said. "Good job with the gun, Sam, but your Skill is needed." He waved a hand to me, Torliam, and Blaine, who was silently using a med kit to deal with the bullet wound in his own leg.

Zed spoke up. "Eve's hurt bad. She needs to be healed ASAP. Her arm's ... I don't even know what to call that. And she looks like she's been starving for weeks." He scowled at me.

Sam stared wide-eyed at the body, blinked a couple times, and then turned to my arm. He took a deep breath. "Okay." He dug out a small medical kit from one of the supply packs.

Blaine went to the back to check on the kids and keep them from coming out while Jacky disposed of the body.

Adam looked out to the rear of the ship from one of the small windows cut into the rippling walls. "No immediate pursuit, but I can only imagine they've got trackers on this thing. They'll be after us soon."

"No human ship will catch my Lady Ladriel," Torliam said with pride. He was still riding the hoverboard, but was using his legs to maneuver it, so Sam must have fixed his spine while I was blacked out, though it looked like all the rest of his wounds remained. Then Torliam did something, and the force of our acceleration rocked me. "Lady Ladriel" began to shudder at the speed. The vibration was almost soothing, like being inside the belly of a big purring cat, except that I knew I was actually inside the belly of a small ship that had been hit by a bomb, and then inexpertly patched up by people who didn't even understand how it worked.

"I'm hungry," I said weakly. "Could I get a nutrition bar?"

Sam waved Zed aside and out of his way, taking charge as he only did in situations like this. "Did they feed you? Your body's been eating itself, obviously."

"They fed me some. But the food was drugged."

Kris peeked around Adam's side, obviously curious about my fearsome battle wounds, and Gregor joined her. "Here," she said, handing me a nutrition bar. She took one look at my arm, and drew the bar back. "Oh." She tore open the wrapping, and then held the bar up to my mouth hesitantly.

I let her feed me, while Sam used some tiny scissors and an equally small set of clamps to cut away the sleeve of my uniform, and then peel it painfully out of the crusted blood and open wound that was now the surface of my arm. It hurt. A lot.

The kiddos gasped, and Gregor looked from my arm to his own much smaller one.

"Goddamit, Eve," Zed said. "What did you *do?*"

I kept eating, because somehow the pain only made me even more ravenous. "Got in a fight with Kilburn," I said, a few crumbs spewing out of my mouth.

As Sam revealed more and more of the injury, there were sporadic gasps and groans of horror from the onlookers. I resisted the urge to roll my eyes at them, but decided not to look down at my arm just yet, because I knew they weren't overreacting, and I didn't want to think about it.

"Oh, Eve ..." Adam said, his face falling. "I'm ... *god.* I shouldn't have ..." He seemed, for once, at a loss for words. "This happened because of me."

"Damn," Jacky said succinctly.

Torliam even turned his head to see what the commotion was about, but I couldn't read his expression before he turned back to the controls.

"Not your fault. It was always the plan for me to cause a little havoc. I just went for the overkill." I grinned, but I was afraid it came out looking more like a grimace.

Gregor's little eyebrows were scowling as always, but this time with concern. "Can you even fix something like that?" he asked Sam, in a tone that was more demand than question, crossing his arms over his chest.

Sam laid his arm on the top of my shoulder and closed his eyes for a second to analyze the wound before answering. "It will be difficult," he said, instead of a true answer.

For the first time since I'd first gotten the injury, I couldn't stop the fear from slipping into my conscious mind. What if this was permanent? I hadn't known until just then how much I was counting on him to make everything better, to just ... fix me.

"Hurry up, then!" Zed said.

Sam scowled at the group. "Stop pressuring me." He took a deep breath, and some of my pain just ... went away, like it had evaporated through the connection of his skin on mine.

I sighed and released some tension I hadn't even known I'd been holding.

"Urgh!" Sam grunted and pushed through the others, throwing himself towards the small waste removal station at the back of the ship. He fell to his knees and threw up noisily into the basin. The smell of vomit had hardly started to spread before the ship sucked it up.

I wondered inanely where the vomit went. And where Bunny's body went. Did the ship eat it? "Are you okay, Sam?" Maybe something was wrong with the wound. Maybe something about the snake's Skill meant Sam wouldn't be able to heal me. And just like that, the tension was all back.

"I'm fine." He stood up, wiping his face, and spitting into the basin with a small amount of ration water. When he came back to my side, he was still pale and breathing hard, but he returned to normal as I watched. "It's just ... the pain. I didn't even take a lot from you. How are you still conscious right now?"

A low whimper forced itself from Kris, and tears fell out of her eyes before she angrily scrubbed them away with her sleeve and turned her head away.

"I'm okay," I said, forcing my voice to sound like I meant it. "I was out of it for a few hours, under sedation. But then I needed to be awake. Don't worry about numbing me or whatever. Just work on the actual injury—that's the important part. Besides, when you fix that, the pain will follow suite."

Sam clenched his jaw and nodded. "Someone get the numbing spray from the med kit. Something is better than nothing, at least," he said. He healed my arm, bit by bit, as Adam covered my entire arm and every new piece of exposed flesh with the substance. Because of the way my arm had been twisted, Sam had to untwist it to heal it. And because he couldn't heal all of it at once, it was excruciatingly painful for parts to twist back into place while the pieces adjacent to them were still mangled. Fragments of bone slid through muscle to reattach themselves to each other. Old, clotted blood seeped out of my flesh as the skin and muscle moved, separating themselves from the marbled-swirl-cottage-cheese mess they had been part of.

I tried not to scream, I really did. But I couldn't help it.

Sam apologized over and over, white-faced and straining as his own flesh mimicked my injuries in little patches, but I gritted my teeth and told him to shut up and stop worrying about me.

Adam's hair was floating around his head in a big curly halo from all the times he'd run his fingers through it while nervous static jumped from his skin.

Kris was crying silently in the corner, while Blaine tried awkwardly to simultaneously comfort her and shield her from the sight and sound of me.

Zed knelt beside me and held my good hand, and let me squeeze his fingers so hard they would probably be in danger of breaking, if his bones weren't reinforced by those bastard nanites. But from the way he gritted his teeth, maybe the nanites weren't standing up to my Seed-enhanced strength. I figured if I did break his fingers, at least Sam could fix them later.

Torliam pushed away from the controls.

He moved the hoverboard with skillful pressure from his legs, obviously having acclimated quickly. He was scowling, and despite the fact that he still had holes along his spine in some places and the backs of metal claws poking out in others, he was imposing enough that those standing around stepped back.

Adam quickly realized what he'd done, and moved forward again, as if to insert himself between Torliam and me.

Torliam glared at him. "She will break her own teeth, grinding them like that. Move."

Adam scowled and didn't move, but Torliam shoved past him. He snapped of the strap of a nearby pack, folded the padded fabric over, and forced it past my lips, between my teeth. He settled it back between my molars. "Bite down. It will help."

I bit down, and nodded my thanks to him, panting through my nose.

Zed pushed some sweat-dampened hair back from my forehead, and then Sam started again.

I learned a new appreciation for Sam. What must it take, to willingly mutilate yourself, over and over, for someone else? Then, Sam jerked backward, and stared down at where his hands had been in horror.

I didn't want to look, but I did. I don't know what I'd been expecting, but five little spots of red crystal sprouting out from my skin like a fungus, where the fingertips of one of his hands had been? I was speechless.

My eyes tracked up to meet his, and he shook his head back and forth, taking another step back. "It was an accident," he said. "My Skill … it just … *slipped.*" He was stuttering, almost, holding his hands away from himself as if afraid of them. "It's been difficult, lately. Like it's pushing back against me when I try to heal. It's been getting harder to push through, but nothing like that has ever happened before. I *didn't mean to do that.*"

"Maybe you need a break," Jacky said.

"But what about Eve?" Zed said. "You're only halfway through!

And the Estreyan dude has holes in his back! Also, Blaine got shot."

"We have Seeds," Blaine said. "In the back. I could only carry two cases, but they may ensure infection does not set in, at least. I cannot use them, but my wound is relatively small. I can treat it myself. And perhaps the Seeds will give Sam the energy he needs to continue."

I looked to Torliam, and though his knuckles were white and the skin on his back had a slight sheen of sweat, he didn't say anything, or turn around.

Blaine directed Adam to retrieve a metal briefcase, which clanged much more heavily on the floor than its size would indicate. Inside were row upon row of Seeds, nestled individually like eggs in a carton, and stacked atop each other. A quick calculation told me it held at least a few hundred Seeds.

I took the slobber-soaked, well bitten strap out of my mouth and grabbed a handful of the sparkly treasures. "I wish I had more Life," I muttered, ignoring the sharp pricks as the six or so Seeds injected their contents into me. I dropped the empty spheres to the ground and grabbed another handful. "I wish I was more Resilient." I repeated the process again, then waited as the side effects swept through me, signaling that the Seeds were "planting" themselves in me.

Torliam let out a sharp puff of air that no one but me seemed to notice.

Sam did the same, and went to sit hunched over in the corner.

After a few more minutes, and quite a few more devoured nutrient bars, I felt a little better.

Kris looked around, and frowned. "Where's Bunny?"

No one said anything for a few moments.

"He decided he was on NIX's side after all," I said.

"So he decided to stay behind?" she asked, clenching her moose.

"Yes," Blaine said, staring hard at me. "He decided to stay behind."

Gregor's eyes narrowed, and his gaze tracked from face to face, analyzing our expressions.

Sam shifted and avoided his gaze.

Gregor's eyes stopped on my own face, and he raised an eyebrow.

I raised my own in response, just a little. He was smart enough to figure it out for himself.

His expression flattened out, and he gave me a small nod. "He was weird, anyway," he said to Kris.

I grabbed a handful of the bars and moved to stand beside Torliam, still eating. It seemed like my stomach would never be sated, even with the bland chewiness I was swallowing en-masse. I ripped the wrapping off yet another bar, using my teeth and the fingers of my good hand. I waved the bar teasingly under Torliam's nose. "Aren't you hungry? I bet they starved you to keep you weak down there."

Something tightened in the skin around his eyes, his tangled beard moving as he ground his jaw under it. "They will be following. Tracking us. We have little time, and I refuse to go back."

I, too, would be afraid to return to a tiny little prison deep beneath the surface of the earth. I could understand that, and I knew what he needed to hear. "Eat," I spoke more softly, leaning down so I was closer to him. "You need to build up your strength. If you end up needing to fight …" I was confident he understood.

He reached forward and grabbed the bars from my hand, ripping one open and biting into it. The ship continued hurtling over the ocean, unconcerned. Overhead, the clouds parted sporadically, beams of sunlight shining down and making the water glow. We stood in silence, and then he spoke in a soft voice, his lilting accent making his words seem almost like poetry, in a way I'd never heard from a human. "It has been *irimael* since I have seen the sun. It is not my own, yet somehow, it is comforting to know that the light of a distant star shines brightly on its own world." He sniffed in a way suspiciously reminiscent of tears, and I carefully didn't look at him, in case that would embarrass him.

Sam's voice came from the back, unsure and exhausted, "I'm feeling better. Let's try again."

I looked down at Torliam's back, a few meaty holes in row with the huge hooks still pressing into him, threatening his spine. "Come away from the controls and let my healer help you," I said. "If it comes down to it, your condition will be a lot more important than mine. Sam can heal me once we're safely away."

Torliam nodded sharply and conceded his spot, moving over to the sleeping nook in silence.

Adam moved up to take the spot at the control panel, but Blaine protested. He had emerged from the mecha suit, which was sitting crouched in the back corner beside our supplies. "I can pilot the ship," Blaine said with a smile and contrasting narrowed eyes.

Adam shook his head. "Haha! I'm the master of electronics, alien or human. This is my thing."

"I am a genius, a mechanical engineer among other things, and I know more about the alien technology than everyone else but … perhaps *one* person on this ship. And that person is not you," Blaine said firmly.

Jacky snorted. "The boys both wanna drive the cool alien plane," she said to Kris, who had thankfully stopped crying.

"Ahh …" Kris grinned, nodding wisely and crossing her arms over her chest.

"Childish," Gregor said, adding his own nod.

"Come on, Blaine." Adam pointed an accusing finger toward the powered-off suit in the back. "You've got a freaking warrior mecha suit! I think I should at least get to fly the ship."

Under the weight of that argument and all our stares, Blaine gave in.

I ate and drank till I was stuffed, sharing the pack of food bars I'd opened with Torliam, who ate stoically even while being healed. I drifted off at some point with Birch purring next to me, barely aware as Adam draped a blanket over me.

Interlude 2

Someone had hit the woman. A purpling bruise spread across her cheekbone, darkening where it surrounded her eye.

His heart thumped, and he turned to the man who held her arm in a vice grip, undoubtedly bruising her tender flesh. "What happened?" It came out an accusation.

"She attempted to escape, Eliahan. I found her climbing over the inner wall, to the east." The man rubbed a hand across his jaw, where already fading red lines marred the skin.

"And she fought back, so you hit her. A human woman who could never be your match in battle," Eliahan said, letting the words roll out as slow as mountain honey.

His compatriot flushed. "She fell, when I was forcing her back down off the wall. I did not hurt her intentionally."

The woman yanked away from him, and he let her go, shooting Eliahan a guilty glance when she rubbed gingerly at her arm.

"I will take her back," Eliahan said. "And you would do well to remember that these people are our guests, not our prisoners." He pretended not to notice when the man muttered that the "guests" weren't worth their efforts. Eliahan offered the woman his arm as they walked away.

She refused. "I know what you've done," she said abruptly. "How could you? They're only children."

Her accusatory look made him feel oddly guilty. "I have done many things wrong in my life. What exactly is it you accuse me of?"

"Kidnapping our children! The other families were talking about it. How their children started acting strange, and kept getting injured, and then just disappeared. You've been running some sort of...cult, or militant recruitment group. I didn't even..."

He frowned. "I believe you may be mistaken. It is not us who is taking your children. That is an organization called NIX. We have you here to protect both you and your children."

She seemed to deflate. "So someone *did* kidnap them? I'd hoped..."

She had hoped that he would refute her accusations? He shook his head. "They are being trained for war, in ways you cannot even imagine."

She was silent for a moment, and then surprised him. "Well, what are you going to do about it?"

When he was silent, she stopped and turned to scowl up at him, hands on her hips. "Eliahan, you damn well better be doing something to fix this."

Chapter 14

Awake, arise or be for ever fall'n.
—John Milton

TURBULENCE WOKE ME, as the ship rattled and pitched a couple times.

"Oh, what have the humans done to you, Lady Ladriel?" Torliam muttered, frowning down at the ship's controls. His wounds no longer oozed blood, though they were quite raw, and at least all the clamps had been removed from his back.

"How long have I been sleeping?" I asked.

"Not long," Adam said. "Twenty minutes."

"Any signs of pursuit?"

"Not yet, but there's no way they're not tracking the ship. And it won't just be our base coming after us. They could be sending pursuers from anywhere in the world. We've been gone for slightly over an hour. If this ship wasn't so fast, they probably would have caught us already," he said, fingers running along the cartridges at his waist, as if reassuring himself they were still there.

"Has he revealed how we're escaping, yet?"

"The alien? No. I don't know why he won't just tell us, at this point. There's no way we're going to reveal it to NIX."

"Stonehenge," Blaine said.

"What?" I asked.

"Based on a few basic pieces of information, like our flight trajectory, size of the alien ship, and my basic knowledge of geography, I believe we are headed for Stonehenge. Our historians have never been able to unquestionably deduce its purpose. Perhaps it is some sort of portal, to those who know how to use it."

Torliam grunted, from the front. "Your historians are imbeciles. Though your race dies off so quickly, it is no surprise that you cannot properly bequeath information to your offspring."

"I will take that to mean I am correct," Blaine said, slightly smug.

"If that's true, at this speed we'll be there in about … five minutes!" Adam said.

"Do we need to prepare anything, Torliam? Pack up, etcetera? Or will you be able to send the whole ship through?" I moved up to stand beside him.

He was tapping at something on the control panel, and didn't seem to hear me. He muttered something in his own language, face growing increasingly more expressionless, if that's even a thing. Then he just … sagged. "It is damaged, according to the ship's sensors. The array is completely broken. It will not work."

There was a beat of silence, and then the interior of the small ship burst into noise, everyone questioning him all at once.

I was stunned into blankness for the space of a couple breaths. Then I calmed, and my mind started to race. If we couldn't escape using Torliam's method, NIX was about to catch us.

I raised my hand and said, "Quiet."

The others complied, but turned to stare at me expectantly. As if I had an answer.

"How long do we have until NIX gets here?" I asked.

"I estimate we have about thirty minutes," Blaine said, "if they are employing their absolute fastest aircraft. And I see no reason why they would not, judging by the current situation. If they have sent word to others to cut us off, perhaps half that."

That wasn't enough time to escape, even if we had a way to do so, which we didn't. And even if we could we had nowhere safe to escape *to*. "We have no alternatives," I muttered to myself, eyes darting around in thought. "Tell me about this array. Stonehenge? What does it do? How is it broken?" I turned to face Torliam. He hesitated a moment, so I snapped, "We don't have time for this! Tell me."

"That place ... the stones. They are an array that was laid down by my people when we were last on this godforsaken planet, thousands of years ago. There is a matching array in Estreyer, and this one can be used to access that one. Each can be used to transport the contents inside the circle instantly to a counterpart. But some of the stones are broken, or out of place, and some are even *missing*."

"How does it work? In a general sense, I mean. We don't have time for an alien science lesson."

"Vibration," he said simply. "I would cause the stones to vibrate, and their waves would travel across even endless space, faster than light, to pinpoint the location of the counterpart we want to access. Then ... I do not know how to explain to one with such a rudimentary language and ..." He stopped when my eyebrow rose in impatience. "It would *pull*, and we would be there, and NIX would not reach us."

"Okay. Stonehenge is made of what we humans call bluestone. Does it have to be bluestone? Could we fly somewhere and pick up some other rocks real quick?"

"They must be 'bluestone,' and they must have been prepared with the ... 'marks' by my people."

"Is there somewhere else we could go? Any other arrays like this that aren't broken?"

"There were few arrays, even before. Your world has little of worth, and we abandoned travel here long ago. The record of the array placement was not kept. When my exploratory group arrived, we did search out some arrays, but most were either also broken, or seemed to be an attempt by humans to copy something they did not understand. I did not know this one was broken."

"Most? Was there a working one, then?"

"Far from here. But it is small and rudimentary, and would not transport us all. And … I do not know if Lady Ladriel could make the trip. She is failing."

Well, screw that. I wasn't leaving anyone behind. I considered going to pirate the stones of that smaller array, but I realized that by the time we got there, loaded up the stones, and got back, NIX would have caught up long before.

I paced around, trying to will myself to come up with an answer. We couldn't run for much longer, and we really weren't strong enough to fight.

"Did you come here using the array?" I stopped and looked at Torliam again.

"No. They are disabled from our side. We cannot access Earth from Estreyer. My team flew here, the long way."

"And Lady Ladriel won't make it."

"Even if she could, we would all starve to death before even getting halfway. We do not have the preparations." He looked like a taut wire, ready to snap. No doubt I did, too.

I did *not* want to be caught by NIX. I could barely imagine the trepidation he must feel, considering the type of torment he'd endured for *years*.

"What do I need, what do I have, and how can I use what I have to get what I need?" I muttered under my breath, the words tripping on each other on the way out. My eyes passed over teammates.

I stopped, staring at Adam for a long moment. "Could you make a passable replica of bluestone with your Animate Skill?"

His eyes widened as everyone else turned to stare at him, too.

"Your Bestowal, the 'Skill,' allows a short-lived mimicry of something, borne out of ink?" Torliam asked. "I have only seen it in action against NIX as we reclaimed Lady Ladriel."

"Well, yes, basically. It can bring something I've imagined and painted with ink to life, for a short while."

"I do not think that will work," Torliam said. "We might attempt it, but without the intimate knowledge of how our arrays work, I do not think it would be possible for you to replicate their effects. Or, perhaps, to hold the mimicry for long enough to complete the activation."

My faint hope evaporated. "Is there any fix for it? Or a work-around of some sort?" I asked.

Torliam didn't answer my question right away, but his face lost its expressionlessness. "I …" He tapped at the screen faster, symbols unlike anything I recognized from Earth flashing across its surface. "It would be dangerous. It will require us to calibrate the array to ourselves *specifically*."

"We will have to try," I said. "While Torliam is working on that, the rest of you, start gathering supplies. Anything you can carry, in order of importance to our survival on Estreyer."

"Food first, or supplies?" Zed asked. "Will we be able to gather food on Estreyer, wherever we're going?"

"There will be animals, and vegetation where we are going. And another ship," Torliam said, meeting my eyes with understanding. "Smaller than this one, but it will carry anything we can bring to it."

"Can this ship fly on its own? If we send it out back over the ocean?"

"I hunted Lady Ladriel myself. She is the highest quality, and retains a small portion of her own instincts. If we tell her to go, she will go. And she can fly under the water, though a bit slower. Can your ships do the same?"

"Blaine?" I asked. He was the expert.

"Perhaps some of them. There are prototypes, but they do not compare to the speed of standard airships. If we are lucky, they will have to deploy other airships, or aquatic ones, to follow," Blaine said quickly. "But if you are planning to abandon the ship with most of the supplies inside, I must caution against it. I was already unable to fit as much as I wished into this … creature's …" he paused for a moment, seeming distracted as he looked around at the rippling walls, "… amazing cargo space. But I have already optimized based on what will be most useful for our survival. If we leave any more, I will not even have tools!"

"You'll have to make do without them, then. We're dropping off at Stonehenge, and the ship's going on without us. There isn't time for any more. And even if there was, we'd still have to be able to transport it to the other ship. We have about two minutes, Blaine. You'd better hurry."

Everyone scrambled to grab the important supplies—each team member's pack, the two cases of Seeds, some medical supplies and extra cartridges of ink and electricity, and Zed's nanite paste, which I ensured they didn't forget.

Lady Ladriel slowed as we approached Stonehenge, sliding so low to the ground it seemed like she was brushing the grass. On Torliam's order, the back of the ship opened up like a tube, and we were all sucked out by the force.

My Grace allowed me to land on my feet, thankfully, because a tumble would have been torturous to my half-healed arm. Blaine's mecha suit allowed him to do the same, with Kris and Gregor. Jacky carried Chanelle on her back, along with a huge backpack and enough side satchels that she was almost buried under them, though she didn't seem to have any problem with the weight. Blaine's doing, most likely.

Lady Ladriel shot off at an angle, the hull closing back up. Hopefully, she would draw NIX off for long enough for us to get off Earth. If we *could* get off Earth.

We ran toward the towering boulders of Stonehenge, and Torliam immediately got to work. He commandeered Jacky, and Blaine with his mecha suit, to right some of the fallen stones and move others back into position, while rearranging others.

I could almost smell the stress hormones in the air, wafting off everyone's skin.

Kris, normally quiet, snapped at Gregor. "Stop grinding

your teeth!"

When Sam kept fidgeting, Adam growled at him to, "Stop looking so guilty!" despite that he himself couldn't keep his hands still, and his hair was floating about with a life of its own.

Sam pointed this out, which didn't help Adam calm down, but did incentivize him to stalk away from the other boy toward me.

"How's the pain?" Adam asked.

"Manageable," I said. "As long as I don't move, nothing hits the arm, and I stop breathing."

My attempt at humor didn't coax a smile out of him. "Once we get there, Sam can take some more Seeds and try again. This array thing better not cause any more injuries. Whatever's going on with Sam, I don't think we can rely on him to heal them."

"We'll make it work," I said, watching as the stones glowed with strange Estreyan symbols flashing across their surface.

Torliam was almost feverishly focused, hurrying around as he used the surface of the stone like a smartglass tablet. "We must calibrate the array, now. Everyone, gather with me!"

We did as he asked.

"Hold your hand over the stone," he said. "We must give our blood."

Blaine frowned at him. "Our blood ... is it taking a DNA sample?"

"We have no time for questions, human!"

I stepped forward first, and held out my good hand.

Torliam waved his own hand, and a misty blue light shot out, scoring a thin line across the back. He grabbed my hand and rubbed the wound on the stone, spreading my blood in the pattern of an Estreyan symbol. The stone lit up along those lines, and when it dimmed, my blood was gone.

"Hurry," he said, eyes on the horizon. "NIX may not be fooled for long. We must not tarry."

The others followed suit, and then we gathered ourselves and the supplies in the center of the circle.

"Is this safe?" Adam muttered.

Torliam ignored him, still scanning the skies, and then he began to sound off the stones.

I shivered as the vibration traveled through me. Torliam explained that the sounds were a type of coordinate, each of them establishing a different parameter of location, far beyond simple latitude and longitude.

They felt kind of like the Boneshaker, but more powerful and less … teeth-grinding. My eyes caught rapidly growing dots on the horizon. Our pursuers.

But the waves were already thrumming through my body till I couldn't think of anything else but them, overlapping and merging and crashing … then we were gone.

I KNEW we were in Estreyer first because there were no clouds to obscure the blistering sunlight. My eyes teared up at the burning sensation, and I slammed them shut till they could adjust. I wasn't nauseous, like I had expected.

"Whoa," Kris said, looking around in wonder.

Even Gregor lacked his customary scowl.

"Is everything so *big* here?" Zed asked. "It's like some primordial paradise world."

We'd arrived within a circle similar to Stonehenge, but much better maintained. It was surrounded by tall yellowed grass. Only Torliam, myself, and Blaine were tall enough to see over the top of it, and Blaine only because the suit boosted his height by a few inches.

Torliam said something in Estreyan, and fell to his knees, his fingers digging into the dirt convulsively.

The smell of greenery and peaches hit me anew as my eyes adjusted to the alienly vibrant colors, and I realized that I, too, would be enamored of this stunning world, if my experience of it had not been tainted by terror and death. But I wasn't the only one who was more watchful than awed.

Adam, Jacky, and Sam stood facing outward warily, each of us with our back toward the others, facing into the unknown. This world killed the inattentive.

I spread my awareness out, sensing our immediate surroundings for danger.

Birch sidled tentatively closer to the edge of the stone circle, nose twitching.

"Stay close," I said to him, though I hadn't noticed any monsters or obvious hazards, except for the slightly disconcerting realization that literally everything around me glowed almost imperceptibly with power. "It's dangerous."

His ears lowered, but he moved back toward the group, taking his disappointment out on Adam with a swipe to the leg as he passed.

"Why?" Adam sighed. "I just want to be friends."

Birch let out something that sounded surprisingly like a human snort, and flicked his tail at Adam. He crouched down and jumped, landing on my good shoulder with enough force to rock me, then rising up with his hind legs on my shoulder and forepaws pushing at the side of my head, so that he could see over the top of the grass.

I rolled my eyes in commiseration with Adam.

Torliam rose from the ground, tilted his head back, and wiped his face while he breathed in deeply. "I am home," he said. He turned to me. "I thank you, Eve of the line of Redding. This will not be forgotten."

"You're welcome," I said awkwardly. "So, where's this other ship?"

"Not far. The other ship is no match for my Lady, but it will do. If we walk slowly, we will make it before the sun sets."

"Let's go, guys. Load up," I said.

Blaine strapped an impressive amount of supply-laden packs to his suit, challenging Jacky for the spot of most supplies carried. He seemed to be walking fine, so I figured either Sam had been able to heal the wound in his leg, or Blaine's suit was doing all of the work for him.

The rest of the team grabbed one or two packs each. I tried to grab my own, but Adam and Zed reached out to stop me almost simultaneously, and I gave up without much of a fight. My arm hurt, and I felt weak already. My skin still stretched tight over my bones, and probably would for a while. I pilfered one of the supply packs Jacky was carrying, which contained what limited food supply we hadn't abandoned, and took another handful of nutrient bars. My body needed fuel.

Birch had his own little pack, which he seemed quite proud of. We filed out into the sea of grasses, Torliam leading the way. We heard the sounds of a far-off monster scuffle, and then some pained yowling as one of them lost the fight, but we couldn't see it, and it was beyond the range of my Wraith Skill. After walking at a quick pace to keep up with Torliam for a couple hours, we crossed the path of a gigantic snake.

It turned to look at us when the grasses parted on it, but after a quick staring match with Torliam, it slithered off, its huge muscles rippling.

"A largely harmless creature," he said. "Though I do not doubt it would consider you humans a pleasant meal." I'm pretty sure he was smiling at that thought, though I couldn't see his face.

Shortly after that, we arrived at the edge of the field and entered a wooded area. I was relieved to see that the trees, while gigantic, weren't the same type as those twisted creations of the first Trial I'd been in. I'd had my share of dreams about those spores feeding on the still-living bodies of humans, growing into vaguely human-shaped colossals.

After another hour of walking the sun began to slant sideways through the trees, which opened up onto a clearing, within which was another ship, smaller and clunkier looking than Lady Ladriel, and an Estreyan-sized log cottage.

I looked between Torliam and the cottage, and for some reason, was startled. Despite what I'd seen of Estreyer, all the technology and the abandoned cities, somehow I'd never imagined the aliens, Torliam's people, living in houses that weren't so different from a human's.

Torliam inspected the clearing for danger while we waited at the tree line, and then let us into the cottage. He was obviously familiar with the area, and I wondered if this had been his house before he came to Earth. The inside was sparsely furnished, and covered in dust and Estreyan-sized cobwebs. There were also a few Estreyan-sized spider corpses lying at the edge of the wall.

"Gross," Gregor said with a shudder, but he still leaned in close to examine their hulking appendages. He held his hand up to the body, then grinned over at Blaine. "It's bigger than my hand! Even bigger than my old pet tarantula."

Torliam waved a hand, and that blue mist burst from him again, dispersed thinly, and caused a violent gust of wind to blow through the cottage, gathering the dust and cobwebs along the way and forcing them out through an open window.

Adam and I shared a look of curiosity. Was that a Skill? Or was it just what came from being so full of Seeds that people could harvest you for them?

It didn't take long for us all to spread out in the cabin, which fit the group at least semi-comfortably because of the large scale it was built on.

"Rest," Torliam said. "We are safe for now, but you may find you need your strength later."

I didn't have any objection to that. I was exhausted. I sprayed some more numbing solution over my arm, reassuring Sam who apologized profusely when he saw me doing it. "It's okay. You need some sleep, too."

"I'll finish healing you in the morning," he said. "I promise. Whatever it takes, I'm going to fix your arm."

I fell asleep almost immediately, just leaning up against the wall with a couple packs for cushioning.

A bad dream jerked me to wakefulness after a few hours.

Torliam was also awake, sitting at the wooden table with his back to me. Had he slept? Or had he awakened like me? The thought that maybe he had nightmares too made me uncomfortable.

"Your people will have been searching for you," I murmured, "right?"

His head spun around toward me, but he didn't seem surprised that I was awake. "Of course." It was almost a whisper. While I'd slept, he had cut off the messy beard that NIX had allowed to grow untended, and trimmed his blonde hair so that it stopped just above his shoulders. Together, it went a long way to making him seem more human, and less like a crazed, killer giant. "But it would have taken them a long time. The members of my crew who escaped would only have arrived back here an *irimael* or so ago to alert my people of my circumstances. As I said, they could not then simply enter an array to travel back to Earth. We forced our way through to here, but the other way cannot be used by our people."

"Why not?"

"It is forbidden." His tone was final, and I took the warning not to continue that line of questioning.

"Why would it take years for them to alert people back here as to what was happening? Didn't any of the others have one of those Shortcut things in their ships? Or some other form of faster-than-light communication?"

He frowned down at the table, and then sighed and turned back to me again. "It is coincidence that my ship carried what you call 'the Shortcut.' I rue the day I decided not to discard it before the trip. Neither my crew nor myself were still at the level of needing access to such low-leveled Trials. None of the others carried something similar. And ... there is a ... *disconnect* in space, between your world and mine. The ship's communications do not travel past it. I do not know what your people would call it. Surely you have noticed that time seems to flow differently?"

When I nodded, he turned back to the table. "I had hoped that after returning here, I would be able to contact my people, but it seems the communications system on the old ship in the clearing is broken," he said, shoulders slumping.

I sat up more fully. "Is that a problem? Can't we just fly the ship to wherever we need to go?"

"It means that no aid will be coming. We will have to make our way to the capitol by ourselves, or find some other way to contact civilization. This ship does not have the fuel to make it all the way to the capitol, and it will be very dangerous if we have to stop somewhere in the middle. The lands away from civilization are wild."

I groaned and knocked my head against the wall behind me. If Torliam thought an area was dangerous, the rest of the team would probably be vaporized on contact.

IN THE MORNING, Adam and Blaine joined Torliam in trying to fix the communication device in the old ship.

While they were doing that, Sam got back to work healing me. Kris came over to hold my hand, but I wouldn't wrap my fingers around her tiny ones, because I was afraid I'd squeeze too hard and break them. Instead, she handed me her moose. "I know it's just a stuffed animal. But he always makes me feel better when things hurt and there's nothing I can do about it. He'll make you feel better, too."

Gregor nodded. "Kris lets me borrow him sometimes. It's stupid, but it does kind of help."

I smiled and thanked her, then bit down on one of the pack straps, and tried not to scream. She had to go outside the cabin with the others, when it got to be too much for her. Gregor stayed behind, kneeling on the ground next to Sam and me, watching the healing process in grave silence.

I'm not really sure how long it took before the pieces of my wound crying out in pain were less than the ones that had been healed, but by the time he'd finished Sam's skin was disturbingly pale, and his hands were trembling.

When he took his hands away, my arm was straight, and I could flex my fist with only minor discomfort. I grabbed a nutrition bar from my little stash and offered it to him, looking at the marbled scars across my arm.

He accepted it silently.

"Are you all healed?" Gregor asked, reaching out tentatively to touch the skin.

When Sam was finished with the bar, he said, "I've done everything I can. It's not perfect. The amount of damage was … ridiculous. And something is wrong with my Skill." He added in a whisper. "But you should be okay, and you'll be able to use the arm. I recommend you take some more Seeds for Resilience and Life. I think I need some time to recover. Maybe whatever's wrong with me is just backlash from Skill overuse. This *is* the most healing I've ever done in a short period of time." He didn't sound completely convinced.

"You should rest," I agreed. "Eat something and get some more sleep."

He acquiesced, going to the corner to curl up with the supply packs and a blanket.

I found the two cases of Seeds, and handed Gregor the moose so I could carry one case in each hand. My left arm ached at the effort, but it *worked*. I experimented with slipping my claws out, and though they were now a slightly darker shade than the ones on my right hand, they were as long and sharp as ever. I was going to be okay. I spared a look and a silent offering of thanks for Sam, over my shoulder. Without him, half the team would be dead several times over.

Outside, I gave Kris back her moose with a word of thanks, and the two kids accompanied me, along with Jacky, and Zed, as I moved out beside the house, in sight of the Estreyan ship where the others were working. I counted the Seeds, making sure none were missing except the ones I knew about.

Jacky leaned forward eagerly. "Are you going to divvy them up between us?"

"That's the plan," I said. I counted two hundred and sixteen spaces for Seeds, in both of the cases. I'd taken twenty-four while on the ship, but that left four hundred and eight remaining. It was an amazing reserve of power. Enough to make a real difference. "Blaine came through for us," I said.

Jacky knelt beside me, staring at the rows with a similar mix of awe and greed. "I guess I can forgive him for ratting on us all this time."

"If we divide these evenly, there will be eighty-six for each of us, including Chanelle," I said. "I've already had twenty-four of my share."

Jacky looked over to Chanelle, who was sitting in the grass not far away, patting the ground like a toddler. "You think ... those could make her better?"

"Maybe. We'll definitely try," I said. I left silent that they could also be the difference between life and death for me. That wasn't even taking into account the power differential they represented, and how much safer the entire team would be if its Player members were stronger.

Torliam, Adam, and Blaine exited the small ship shortly after, looking crestfallen.

"We weren't able to fix it," Adam said, as they made their way to us.

"There is another communication array north of here," Torliam said. "It, too, has been abandoned for a long while, but it may still be operational. Or, we may be able to use pieces from both to create a single working device."

"Will the ship be able to make it that far?"

"We will get close, at least." He stopped near my little huddled group, eyes dropping to the Seeds. His upper lip rose on one side, in the beginnings of a snarl. "What are you doing?"

"We're divvying up the Seeds," I said, standing slowly. The hairs on the back of my neck were rising. "I know they're technically yours, but our bodies don't just create them at the rate yours does, and we're weak enough that they'll make a significant difference."

He scowled at me, a look I was becoming all too familiar with. "A blood-covenant is not something for you to throw around so lightly," he said, snarling fully now.

I felt the muscles in my shoulders tense up in response, but I didn't blink. "The deal we made was for you to help me. My team is also under my protection. Since we humans are weak, as you so love to remind us, you are just going to have to deal with us using the Seeds. What other way could we have the strength to fulfill the Oracle's vision?"

"Your *weakness* is not an excuse to *violate* the life blood of another. That is something that only the worst of my kind would do. When they are discovered, they are killed."

I hesitated, but pressed forward. "You are going to break the blood covenant anyway. This won't even affect you as soon as we're back in your hometown."

He stepped forward, towering over me. "I will not allow you to do this. My power is not something that can be shared among the masses like a cheap … sex-worker."

The pressure was a physical thing, brushing against my skin, pressing on my mind. My fingers trembled. I closed them into a fist to stop the movement. "These might be the difference between Chanelle regaining her mental faculties or not. You had no problem with me using them on the ship earlier. I assure you, we're not taking this lightly. We need these."

"On the ship, it was a matter of life and death."

I was gasping for breath, the sunlight burning my eyes as they dilated involuntarily. My claws slipped out. "It's a matter of life and death, still!" I snapped, pushing back against whatever force he was creating. "You know that! I need the Seeds to stay alive until we can get to the God of Knowledge." I bared my own teeth.

The pressure released with a snap, and Torliam stared at me for a moment, fists clenched and breath heaving. He stomped away without another word, slamming the door to the cabin behind him.

I let out a shuddering breath of relief, rubbing my sweaty palms on my thighs.

"You're dying?" Adam asked, glaring at me along with everyone else except Zed and Blaine.

Chapter 15

There is beauty in the ending day.
— Ember Wiles

"I'M NOT QUITE sure how to say this," I said honestly. "There have been some ... issues going on with me, with the Seed of Chaos that I got from Behelaino."

"'Issues?' As in, it's killing you?" Adam demanded. He looked around. "Where is Sam? Did he know about this?" he said, hair floating up.

I motioned for him to calm down. "It's not Sam's fault. Whatever's wrong with me, it's not something he can handle. I'm not sure if it's because of the problems he's been having with his Skill, or if it's something specific about whatever is wrong with me. Or maybe he's just healed me too many times already, and there's a limit. Obviously, he also can't fix Chanelle's brain damage."

"But he knew about this, and he didn't say anything?" Jacky said.

"I asked him not to, at least until I had some sort of plan to fix it. There's nothing any of you could have done. But you don't need to worry, because we have Seeds now, and with enough of them I'll be able to just heal myself. It might even turn out that loading up enough Seeds in the healing Attributes is a permanent solution."

"Do you actually *believe* that will be a permanent solution?" Zed demanded. He knew me a little too well.

"I don't know. I think the God of Knowledge might be the answer. That's the question I was asking when I solved the Oracle's puzzle, and that's the vision she gave me."

Adam shook his head. "How do you know the vision is in response to anything you asked? They could be completely unrelated."

"I don't know that. But I have to try."

Gregor spoke up, in a small voice. "But ... you seem so strong all the time. And you're the one that saved us from NIX and got uncle Blaine to us. How are you dying?"

Blaine, who had kept out of the argument, patted Gregor on the head.

The boy bit his lip and looked down at the ground, scowling.

Jacky had been shaking her head slowly, but then stopped and spat on the ground. "I've been at my total worst around you. Sniveling and shaking and I didn't know what to do, and I asked you to help me. I *trusted you* to help me. But when it came time that you were down and sick and needed help, you didn't come to us. You didn't come to me."

"Ahh ..." I opened my mouth, and closed it again, then reached a hand out to her.

She jerked away.

"I do trust you," I said. "I just didn't want to worry you when there was nothing you could do that wouldn't make our situation worse. What good is it, just to tell you that I might be dying and there's nothing you can do about it?"

Jacky stepped back toward me, then, jaw clenched, lips pursed, and hands fisted. "No," she said in a low, forceful voice, physically threatening despite the fact that she was significantly shorter than me.

"I'm not totally useless. I coulda done something. I got Seeds, Eve! In the classes. If you woulda told me you needed them …" She jerked away from me. "What kind of friendship is that?" She left, stomping off with footsteps that crushed the grass and sunk into the ground, her power activating, perhaps unconsciously, in response to her feelings.

My arm lifted again, the hand reaching out as if to stop her, but I said nothing. I didn't have any words that could come out in response to her own.

"You're incredibly stupid sometimes, Eve," Adam said. "There's no way in hell we're going to let you die because of it, though. Take your damn Seeds."

BY THE CONSENSUS of the rest of the group, I was allotted half of Chanelle's Seeds, because if thirty-six Seeds in Resilience wasn't enough for her to show obvious improvement, any more than that would be a waste. Blaine and Sam had decided that they would give her one Seed every couple days, attempting to plant it into Resilience for her, so that a sudden influx didn't shock her system, and they would have resources remaining to change strategies halfway through if necessary.

Though Torliam scowled, he didn't say anything more about our use of the Seeds. However, he would also barely meet my eyes, and the more relaxed version of him that I'd been growing accustomed to was gone.

I stashed Chanelle's thirty-six Seeds at the bottom of my personal pack, along with the third gift from the Oracle. They would be there in case of an emergency, in case I ended up needing more Seeds in a non-healing Attribute, or if Chanelle regained her mental faculties and needed them back.

With the other Seeds, I did a mass injection into Resilience, and Life, with a moderate amount also going into Endurance, and a few others sprinkled around in the areas I thought I might find useful, and that would be harder for me to increase the old-fashioned way.

The rush of so many Seeds planting themselves at once had me shivering hot and cold, in alternating waves. I stumbled my way into the corner and huddled up under the blanket, curling up among the packs in the fetal position. Perhaps using sixty-two Seeds at once hadn't been wise. But the whole point of this was the hope that overpowering my healing aspects over a short period of time would allow them to outpace Chaos, both in healing, and in growth factor.

Jacky forced Sam to examine me, but he assured her I was okay.

When the effects were past, I pulled up my Attributes Window.

PLAYER NAME: EVE REDDING
TITLE: SQUAD LEADER(9)
CHARACTERISTIC SKILL: SPIRIT OF THE HUNTRESS,
TUMBLING FEATHER
LEVEL: 38
SKILLS: COMMAND, WRAITH, CHAOS
STRENGTH: 14
LIFE: 52
AGILITY: 21
GRACE: 18
INTELLIGENCE: 28
FOCUS: 23
BEAUTY: 10
CHARISMA: 15
MANUAL DEXTERITY: 9
MENTAL ACUITY: 23
RESILIENCE: 50
STAMINA: 19
PERCEPTION: 24

I felt better than I had in a while, though I was so ravenous that Adam teamed up with me to hunt some of the smaller creatures of the nearby forest, and we brought them back to the cabin and cooked them, so that we didn't blow through our food supplies. I put weight back on fast enough that it was noticeable over the course of a single day or two.

A couple nights in, while we were all gathered around a large roast, Zed turned to me. "After all this is over, and you're cured, we're going back to Earth, right? Because Mom's still there, and we don't even know where she is."

I swallowed, a bit reluctantly. "Yeah. Maybe by then we really will be strong enough to keep NIX from messing with us. I'm sure Mom is okay, so don't worry about her. She's never met a situation she can't 'manage.'" I twitched my mouth into a halfhearted smirk.

"Do you think your mom might be with my parents?" Sam said. "I'm worried that we were trying to make them disappear, and then they really did disappear."

"Probably." I nodded. "Best guess is that someone out there has a grudge against NIX. But whoever it is hasn't said anything, and there haven't been any threats. I'm hoping that's a good thing."

Adam shook his head. "It could just as likely be that your parents are being harvested for their Player-producing genes by one of NIX's enemies or counterparts."

Sam paled. "Do you think that's what's happening?"

I interjected before Adam could make us all feel even worse. "There's nothing we can do about it, if so. Whether we have to protect them against NIX or someone else, we're useless at the moment. Once we can do something about it, we will."

Sam and Zed didn't bring it up again, but they didn't look happy.

After we were all well rested and recovered, we packed up. As we filed onto the smaller, clunkier ship that sat in the clearing, Torliam's eyes followed Chanelle, who was unresponsive, but followed the group's gentle commands. "What is wrong with her?"

I stood back with him, watching her. "She's … a bit like you,"

I said. "NIX experimented on her, and caused some damage to her brain."

Torliam's lips curled and he spat on the ground. "*Humans.*" It was a curse word, coming out of his mouth.

"I think the Seeds might be able to heal her," I said, as nonconfrontationally as I could.

He looked at Chanelle for a long while, and the anger faded away, replaced by a distant look. He entered the ship without another word. After a few minutes, Torliam lifted us off. If the ship's clunky design and worn-out body hadn't clued me into its quality compared to Lady Ladriel, the flight did. It was noticeably slower and shakier.

Zed stood behind Torliam, curiously watching as the giant man piloted. "How long till we arrive?"

Gregor groaned and rolled his eyes from the back. "You're *already* asking the stereotypical, 'Are we there yet?'"

Zed scrunched up his face and stuck out his tongue at Gregor, then grinned when the small boy huffed and looked away with his nose in the air.

Torliam released a small smile at their antics. "It will be many days before we arrive at the fort. This ship is little better than an old children's toy. We will not be stopping, because we are about to enter the Dark Lands. It is much too dangerous."

"Dark Lands?"

"They have been abandoned by my people, left to the monsters and … other creatures. They are hazardous even to my people, so for you …"

Zed laughed. "Yeah, yeah. I can guess what you're going to say. Us puny humans would all be slaughtered within mere moments of encountering the fresh air outside the ship."

Torliam gave a single nod. "Indeed." But I noticed that once again he failed to hide his smile.

Zed leaned over his shoulder again. "Can you teach me how to fly this thing?"

"Perhaps."

We flew for hours, and I took the spot up at the front beside Torliam, meditating under the light of the brilliant sun and rolling clouds. I turned my awareness inward, wondering if this was also a function of my Wraith Skill, and leisurely imprisoned every drop of Chaos I could find within myself. When I finally opened my eyes to the sunset, I was relaxed, almost languid.

That relaxation didn't last for long, as the first thing I saw was Torliam's tense face, looking outward toward the horizon. Dark clouds were gathering on the very edge, above a slight glint that I thought might be water. Torliam was pushing the ship fast enough that it shook uncomfortably.

"A storm?" I asked.

"Yes. But I do not think it is the type of storm you mean. Things have worsened in the time I have been gone." He pushed the ship a little harder. "I will try to outrun it."

"Can this thing fly in a storm?"

"No. But we cannot land here."

I leaned forward and looked down. I'd had my awareness focused inward instead of on my surroundings while meditating, so I gasped when I saw the forest of feathered metal spikes below us. They followed the path of the ship, swaying, and turning towards us like sunflowers toward the light. Or, more likely, like some sort of carnivorous plant following the movement of its prey.

The storm on the horizon moved faster than I thought possible, drawing near to us. I could hear the wind screaming. And I mean that literally. At first, I thought I was imagining it, but the sound was unmistakable. "What is it?" I stared at the mass of dark writhing clouds that seemed at times to have the shape of grasping hands, borne on an unnaturally fast wind.

"There is no word for it in your language. It is a storm that thirsts for blood to add to its waters."

Jacky had moved to look out the front viewport beside me, and her knuckles went white as she clenched her fists. "Gimme a monster to fight any day. *This* isn't …"

I nodded my understanding. "Same here." The ship lurched,

and my insides went with it, my throat tightening in fear. I was no stranger to fear, and if I was honest with myself, it was my constant companion, but it had been a while since I'd faced the special brand of it Estreyer induced.

The ship lurched again, and I bit my lip to keep from making a sound and giving myself away. My teeth fit perfectly against the thin scar I had on the tender skin on the inside of my lip. The pain of the bite was familiar, and helped me to unclench the death grip my hands had on the sides of my seat.

"We will land there," Torliam said, pointing with his chin to a spot past the forest of spikes where boulders sat scattered about on the barren ground. The ship lurched again as a portion of the storm cloud lashed out at our tail end. "Prepare to abandon the ship. We must hide amongst the stones."

I nodded quickly, and took the opportunity to occupy myself with something I could actually affect, instructing the team to put on the packs and make sure everything was tied down to them securely. We had some plastine rope, and we all worked together to tie a piece of it to ourselves. I hoped if we were heavy enough, we'd be able to withstand the force of the winds outside better, or at least someone who was could keep another from being blow away.

"Seriously?" Gregor said, his voice rising. "We're going to abandon the only thing keeping us safe from *that*?"

"The ship is meant to fly, to be carried by the wind. You may stay inside it while it does so, if you wish," Torliam snapped. He half-crashed the ship down amongst the boulders, and threw open the door. The wind flooded in, assaulting our ears with its shrieking. He let out a roar in response, but though it was defiant, I recognized the fear in it.

And that terrified me, more than the storm itself.

Chapter 16

How can I be substantial if I do not cast a shadow? I must have a dark side also if I am to be whole.

— C.G. Jung

I USHERED the team out into the gale, following right behind Torliam in a defensive formation. Strong and heavy people were positioned on the outside, with the ones who needed protection moving within the makeshift shell. I moved at the side, with Zed on my left, because I knew I wasn't strong enough to protect our back. Even with the packs weighing me down, the wind almost lifted me off my feet, so I hunched down and dug the claws of my toes into the ground for a tiny bit of extra purchase.

I knew I put on a facade of bravado for others. I needed people to believe in me, so my team would listen and follow my lead, and my enemies would fear me and hesitate to attack. I'd even hoped that if I told the lie of my own fearless power enough, it would become the truth. I had started to believe it, a little bit. But now we were back on Estreyer.

We ran, hunched over to make smaller targets, and I kept a firm grip on Zed's sleeve, just in case.

Adam threw out shields to the left and right to impede the wind, while Chanelle stumbled along next to him.

Blaine used the size and weight of the mecha suit to curl protectively around the kids.

Jacky brought up our rear, weighing herself to the ground.

I risked a glance back to make sure she was okay, and saw the cloud form a funnel and reach down to the ship, sucking it up into the roiling mass. Like it was a toy.

Jacky screamed something at me, but I couldn't hear her.

I shook my head and turned back to the front, then screamed myself when I saw the wing of dark mist swinging toward us from the side. Luckily, no one could hear me, either.

I ducked down farther as it swept over us. I opened my eyes wider instinctually as my vision was obscured. The sky had been darkening, before. Now everything was true black. My ears ached from the noise of the screams all around us. I tightened my grip on Zed to make sure we weren't separated, and pushed my awareness outward.

Faces swam in the darkness, attached to formless bodies with cutting wind for hands. One swam past my vision, large and open-mouthed, as if it was moving to devour me, and along with it, a scythe-like whip of wind cut towards us from the side, formed from the dark mist.

Torliam turned toward it, with Adam mirroring him when it smashed against one of his shields and obliterated it, but the others didn't even know it was coming. At its height, it was literally positioned to cut them in half, separating torso from legs.

I attacked, slashing out with a combination of claws and a rush of Chaos that followed my movement. I wasn't holding back. I had too much to lose, and with the Seeds I'd taken and the others stashed in my pack, I'd be more than able to mitigate the side effects.

The scythe disintegrated with my attack, and the face focused on me for a moment, but looked more surprised than angry or pained. I tried again, on a nearby figure moving toward us, with the same effect. Or lack of effect, as the case may be. Maybe this storm was too similar to Chaos to be hurt by it. All I could do was return it to its amorphous state, not destroy it.

I noticed a couple of the team were starting to veer off from the course Torliam led, unable to see him or the rest of us, so I broadcast a Window to everyone, containing a constantly updating mini-map. It showed the location of the rest of the team, and the highest-priority dangers as the cloud formed attacks around us.

Zed reached into the holster at his thigh and pulled out a gun. He shot into the amorphous mass, bullets that cut through it for a while before being commandeered by the strength of the wind, and turned back on us. I sent out an alert of danger in their path, and Adam tossed up a shield to stop their progress.

—Bullets not working. It spits them right back.—
-Eve-

—How about an explosion, then?—
-Zed-

He pulled out a small cartridge from his utility belt, and loaded it into the gun. The recoil knocked his hand back, but whatever he had shot detonated in the midst of the cloud in a ball of fire. The flames were quickly sucked up and disappeared, but the screams turned angrier.

—Duck! I'm zapping the area.—
-Adam-

I didn't even think, but threw myself to the ground immediately.

Torliam stayed standing, but I figured he could handle himself either way.

I closed my eyes almost too late. Despite the eclipsing mist, when Adam let loose I saw the back of my eyelids in a bright red flash.

—DAMMIT, ADAM! MY EYES!—
-JACKY-

When would she learn to close her eyes? This happened every time.

The lightning cut through the wet cloud with light and heat. Despite the fact that electricity hurting a storm-cloud seemed counterintuitive, it screeched so hard I wondered if my ears would bleed, and thinned out around us for a good distance.

Torliam used the opportunity to point to a big rock outcropping in the distance, and I read his lips scream the word, "Go!"

I scrambled to my feet, still clutching Zed's sleeve, and grabbed the blinded Jacky around the arm, hauling her up and dragging the both of them forward. The cloud was already thickening again, so I put a big beacon on the mini map where a rock outcrop jutted from the ground, and rushed toward it.

Another scythe rushed toward the more spread out group, from the other side. Too far for me to reach with Chaos, moving too quick. It was going to hit Blaine, and Kris and Gregor along with him.

But I had forgotten Blaine had a VR chip of his own now, and could see the threats signaled on the Windows I'd sent, just like the rest of us. He spun, using the artificial strength of his mecha skeleton to send the two small bodies flying toward my side of the circle.

His momentum carried him around, and as the scythe of wind slashed at him, his suit let out a burst of fire from the hands. It didn't catch the entirety of the attack, and he flew backward. The split plastine rope that had been connected to him waved about in the wind like a fire hose at full pressure. He was beyond our ability to rescue by dragging him along behind us, now.

Zed and I each grabbed one of the kiddos before they could hit the ground or smash into one of the many surrounding boulders.

I wrapped my arms around Gregor, and screamed, "Hold on tight!" into his ear.

Adam was pale and his long limbs seemed to be dragging, but he closed in behind us, throwing up shields to cover our retreat.

Debris whipped through the air, striking the shields, and stabbing at us when they got by.

Some hit Gregor in the cheek, and I tugged him closer and barreled forward with him tucked to my chest, head down and arms wrapped tight around his small body to provide protection.

A piece of severed rope, only a few inches long, tore through the air almost faster than my Skill could perceive. It entered Sam's stomach from the side, slicing through it like soft cheese. He ran a couple more steps before falling.

Adam paused for a moment to grab the extra rope around his own waist, looped it under Sam's arms, and dragged Sam behind him.

They were moving too slow, Adam without the strength to drag Sam while keeping himself and Chanelle safe, and Sam too preoccupied with trying to keep his guts from spilling out of his torso to help.

Blood spread out on the ground behind them. The stones were … absorbing it. No time to worry about that, either.

Jacky lunged away from me, grabbed Sam around his knees and shoulders, and carried him forward, faster than Adam had been able to drag him.

Behind us, Torliam turned and began to walk backward toward us, as if he would single-handedly hold off the storm. Then he began to glow. Not like radioactive glow-in-the-dark, but a shining pale blue light that wafted off him in visible ripples.

Then he swung his glowing arm, palm flat, and sliced with it toward the darkness, as if his arm extended far beyond the tips of his fingers, and was really a blade. Whatever power he was using sliced into the cloud with a faintly luminescent edge, and the storm shrieked again and drew back, giving us a few more moments of respite.

The storm gathered itself, tightening as if preparing to shoot forward in retaliation, but Torliam used the edge of his glowing palm to cut a line across the back of his opposite forearm. His blood splattered against the rocks around him, thrown about by the wind. What the hell was he doing?

The clouds sprang forward, formed like curving hawk talons that dwarfed even his Estreyan size. But before they reached him, the rocks around him tumbled together, smashing against each other with such force I could feel the shockwave, even if I couldn't hear it.

The boulders formed a humanoid shape that reminded me slightly of Behelaino's rock golems, only much bigger. The stone creature took the brunt of the storm's attack, and staggered backward. But it had given Torliam time to escape, and he dashed toward us, not even looking back. As he ran, all around us the boulders began to tumble together, and the stones rose on two legs, moving to face the storm.

Torliam quickly overtook my escaping team, grabbing Blaine with one arm and dragging him along as he passed. He escorted us closely the rest of the way to the center of the stone outcrop. Once we were within, it protected us from the wind.

We all huddled together within the surrounding rocks, crouching down and covering our ears with our palms. I made sure with a tight burst of the Wraith Skill that everyone was alright, then did the same.

—EVE, ARE WE GOING TO BE OKAY?—
-GREGOR-

It was the first time he'd used his VR chip to talk to me.

—Yes. You're going to be alright.—
-Eve-

I didn't tell him to trust me. Instead I smoothed my face into a mask of certainty, as if this whole situation was nothing more than an irritation to me. He was a child. I'd never let him know how completely my expression was a lie. Because even if I was afraid, I wouldn't let him be hurt. That, at least, was the truth.

Sam huddled in a corner, shaking and gasping as he pushed his insides back through the open slice, and applied pressure.

Zed and Jacky worked together to bandage him up the mundane way, and Sam kept muttering, "I'll heal, I'll heal," over and over again.

The rocks fought with the storm, releasing some sort of power that turned the mist to pebbles and forced it to the ground. Eventually, the storm retreated, and when it did, the boulders settled back to the ground, rolling apart.

Torliam let out a shuddering sigh, and gave the rest of us a despairing look. "Your combat abilities are all woefully lacking. You are so weak, I cannot imagine how you managed to survive thus far."

"MY POWER HAS BOUGHT us protection, and your friend's blood has paid for time. We may stay here through the night, but no longer," Torliam said, crouching over and trailing his six fingers over a stone, almost as if petting an animal. The cut on his forearm was already healed. "The stones will require more blood if we do, and none of us wants to pay their price, believe me."

"Is there any safe place near here?" I asked.

"No," he said simply. "If we can pass the chasm of the North, we might stay in the guardhouse for the night, tomorrow. But it is a long journey for people with such short legs. And as we have just seen, I am too weakened to protect you all, when we encounter danger." He gestured in Sam's direction.

"I'm okay," Sam muttered weakly. "I can heal it. I just need some rest."

Jacky stared at him for a moment, then turned on Torliam. "You should train us, then, no? If we're too weak to make it, you should train us till we're stronger. You're a warrior or whatever, right?"

Torliam snorted. "I have no desire to waste my time trying to strengthen a group of humans."

Jacky protested, but he didn't relent.

Later that night, the ring from the Oracle, sealed around my left forefinger, glinted in the brightening moonlight as the second moon entered the sky. I noticed Torliam glancing at it.

"It was the first gift from the Oracle," I volunteered. "She gave them to me as little interconnected loops, like a chain. I had to figure out how they all fit together, and once I did, they shrunk onto my finger, injected their contents into me and gave me the vision of Behelaino," I hesitated, "and of you. Now they won't let go."

"It is a symbol to those who might meet you," he said. "You have solved the second one, you said. Where is it?"

"It's …" I narrowed my eyes. "You're pretty interested in this."

"I have been studying the Oracle and her sister since I was barely a man. And now, I see a gift from one of them with my own eyes, on the body of a human." For once, he didn't say the word "human" with a sneer.

"You know … I'd be happy to talk about all this stuff with you. Like the visions the Oracle gave me, the quests, the third gift that I haven't solved yet …" I waited for a beat as he turned to look at me. "But it won't come free. We'll exchange answer for answer, and only *while* you're training at least one person from my team."

Jacky's head snapped around to look at me.

Torliam's eyes widened, and for the first time I had ever seen, he laughed without malice. "You bargain like a *skirling*. I will accept your offer, though I wonder if you will regret your words once you experience my training."

Jacky didn't seem daunted by that at all, so I let him teach her first.

I sat by the sidelines, talking with Torliam while they sparred out on the boulder-strewn plain.

He was brutal, and seemed to prefer showing Jacky her mistakes by exploiting them, rather than verbal explanations. He asked me to detail the first vision I'd had, and listened intently, though it didn't seem to affect his fighting performance at all.

"Why did you come to Earth?" I asked.

"There is a Sickness, on my world." The way he said it capitalized the word in my mind. "A plague. Many of my people have given up hope for our salvation, as our world dies. But I refuse to believe we cannot be saved. There is one who can stand against the abhorrent—that which causes the Sickness. Its enemy is the Champion, a god who had disappeared some time beyond living memory." He threw an almost lazy punch at Jacky's stomach that sent her flying back despite the guard she put up. He waited to see if she'd get up again for more. "I have studied long and hard, and I believe he may be on your world. Most did not agree, and I was scoffed at for my theories. But, I am the younger son of a powerful family, and my mother granted my request for a small unit to quest for him, though she thought I was a fool. We flew through space for years to reach your planet, but I was not able to complete my mission before your people attacked. I did not expect your race to have advanced far enough to do more than cower in fear, but even so I sent down my ambassador with gifts to treat for nonviolent passage."

His words were heavy. "She was killed. And then your people attacked."

I frowned. The media had told us that terrorists had caused the massive destruction of targets all over the world about seven years ago. According to NIX and Nadia Petralka, it was really caused by the skirmish between the Estreyan group and our militaries, when they sent an experimental invasion group. But in her version, we hadn't been the instigators of the hostility. "That's not what we were told …" I murmured.

His eyebrows rose, then fell again, into a deep glare. "I do not lie, *human*. Not about this, especially. Your people generated the enmity between us, altogether unprovoked."

Jacky ended their sparring session not long after.

I did my best to commit what I'd learned from watching them to memory, then stood up for my own beating.

He asked about the second and third gifts, and I rolled up my sleeve to show him the armband around my right forearm, with a promise to take the third gift out of my pack later so he could examine it.

When it was time for my question, he grimaced, so I went for something neutral that wouldn't make him angry again. "Tell me about your world. The gods, the Seeds, you know. How does it all work?"

He stared at me blankly for a moment. "That is hardly a simple matter, material for a single question or answer."

I grinned brightly in response, imitating Zed, who Torliam seemed to have taken more of a liking to than the rest of us.

Torliam caved. "Very well. But you cannot ask me to continually clarify my statements until you end up getting answers for which you have not paid."

I nodded.

"You have learned some of these things already, I do not doubt. This world, as a whole, is formed of the gods. The Champion, the one who molds, guided them to meld together and create the earth and water and the forces of nature. The gods embody principles of existence, and many of them take a physical form or two to interact with each other and us. Beyond them, there are greater forces of existence, but they are more like …" He sighed. "Laws? Absolutes. They do not interact with us. Perhaps they do not have a consciousness like our own, and do not even notice our puny existence among the vastness of … the 'every-thing.'" He lifted his arms and flung them wide to explain the word he was missing, gesturing out beyond ourselves, to the sky and wider.

"The universe?" I supplied, jumping toward him and attempting to slash at his neck.

He grabbed me by the arm, and showed me how he could have broken it, if he wanted. "Yes, that word suffices. In any case, I cannot tell you much about them. My knowledge is focused more on this world and its problems, its history. When you learn to read, you can read about what our scholars have theorized yourself."

I resisted the urge to point out that I already knew how to read, just not his language, and 'would he please not make every-thing into an insult?'

He smirked at my expression. "The mortals of this world, such as myself, traveled here along with our gods many thousands of years ago. This world sits at a junction, a place where travel is made easy. You will have to learn more about science before you can understand that.

"This planet has layers of a type, unlike your planet, on which life only dwells on the single mundane surface."

I didn't understand what he meant, but I resisted the urge to do the very thing he'd asked me not to by prying for an extended explanation. I dodged an elbow to the temple, and earned a small nod of approval from him when I kicked at his knee in the same motion.

"Most of my people have retreated to the cities, where there is safety in numbers, as the world itself grows more dangerous, and our numbers decrease. To gain strength, we train and study, and if we feel we are ready and willing to risk our lives, we will petition the gods. This is what you call a Trial. We prove our worth before the gods, and if they think us worthy, they will give a Bestowal. From what I understand of NIX, the Bestowals are what you call Skills. And very rarely, a god will find among us mortals one that shines bright with promise, and deign to give them a portion of their … *life-force*. They grant patronage, and give the mortal a chance to ascend. This … I wonder that the manifestation of Chaos did not do this for you," he said, searching my face for understanding, or maybe confirmation.

My eyes widened. "Um … yeah? She did. I'm pretty sure. She said something about welcoming me as a godling. Honestly, I didn't think she really *meant* it like that." My mind raced at the implications. "What does that mean for me? Obviously, it's not going so well. My body can't handle the power—it tries to kill me on a daily basis."

"My people would spend hundreds of years strengthening themselves before ever seeking to ascend. Of course your puny human body would not withstand it. Your lifespans are as short as a *light-bug*. You are like a walking corpse to my people." He stepped forward, both hands attacking in a blur of punches and jabs that sent me scrambling backward, without even attempting to block or slip past them.

"You're not being helpful," I said through clenched teeth.

He stopped, and raised an eyebrow, and I realized he'd pushed me back against the side of the jutting outcrop, leaving me nowhere to run.

I jumped up, as far as I could, and pushed off the rock behind me with my legs, claws out to ward off the attack he threw to meet me in mid-air.

"If in fact you did gain her patronage, it does not mean you are a god," he said, spinning around to face me.

I raised an eyebrow of my own now that his back was to the rock wall.

He snorted, and simply stepped forward, a few quick blows forcing me to retreat again. "You have a *chance* to move beyond the mortal, if you can cultivate the power and, of course, stay alive. Unfortunately, I have no way to help you, as I do not know of anyone with your history, and I am no healer. Perhaps there will be records we can dig up in the capitol that will give some hint. If not, there is no being in existence that would be more likely to know than the God of Knowledge. *If* he will concede to help us, you will have your answer. If it is possible."

"Do you think he won't help?"

"He left the mortal world long ago, his only physical manifestation settling in wilderness. Many think he is searching for the answer to the Sickness. I have heard of the occasional person going to quest for a Bestowal from him, but I have not heard stories of any who have succeeded in recent history."

That was worrying, but the Oracle had shown me that vision, so I could only hope that my answer would come out of it. We spent a couple more minutes sparring, which mostly consisted of me either running away frantically or getting the stuffing pounded out of me.

Jacky didn't smile at me or clap me on the back when we returned to the center of the stone monolith, but she nodded, and we both nursed our bruises in semi-comfortable silence.

WE LEFT before the sun fully rose over the horizon, the kids stumbling and rubbing at their eyes. There had been nightmares during the night, and no one had gotten enough sleep. Sam was still pale, but when Zed took off the bandage, the wound had sealed over on its own.

Blaine worried about sepsis, but Sam gritted his teeth and assured him that his healing ability could handle it.

We traveled in defensive formation again, Kris, Gregor, and Sam alternately walking or riding the one remaining hoverboard until it ran out of solar charge. We were all on edge, alert for attack and aggressive toward the slightest sound.

We walked all day, ate while we walked, and took few breaks. I even ordered that anyone moving away from the group to relieve themselves take someone with them. It'd be just *wonderful* if someone walked away to pee and never came back.

Finally, we arrived at a huge chasm. Wind whipped along it, singing as it sliced along the corners of the jagged rock. It put me on edge, but this wind didn't sound like it had a mouth. The sounds it made were simple whistles and roars, made by its speed.

We walked north, then, until we arrived at a spot where the chasm narrowed. It bore the remnants of a broken bridge.

"This was once the bridge of middle North," Torliam said, "and we must cross it."

It was obvious that the bridge had once been a beautiful, arching structure that was an accolade to Estreyan architecture, made of marble or something like it. But it was broken now. Only the ends remained, and between them stretched almost a mile of yawning chasm. On the other side leaned a half-crumbled tower, made of the same stone.

Blaine frowned. "Why has the bridge not been repaired? I am no expert, but it seems this damage happened some time ago."

"The bridge was destroyed intentionally, to stop the creatures of the lands beyond from following us, when we abandoned the middle North."

"Why would you abandon an entire section of your planet? With the kind of technology you are able to field, I imagine that you could handle some aggressive wildlife."

"My people are not as numerous as they once were. Resources needed to be consolidated. The lands near population are much safer and more bountiful than where we are going. We will rest there tonight," Torliam said, pointing at the decrepit tower. "The last time I was here there was still an inner room that had not been breached. It will be safe."

"How?" Jacky asked. "Even I can't jump across something that wide. And none of us can fly, last I checked." She narrowed her eyes at Torliam. "Can you?"

"Not as such. Even at my strongest, I could not cross this with anyone else in tow. Birch might ferry us across, if he were bigger. At one point, the line of Aethezriel was known for their tailos mounts."

The creature let out a peep, making me wonder once again exactly how much English he understood.

"The hoverboard might be able to make the trip across," Blaine said. "Though it would need some modification to deal with the high winds, and without the sunlight, it would not have enough power for more than a single trip."

"I might be able to Animate a connection between the two remaining ends of the bridge," Adam said. "But I don't think I could hold something that big long enough for us all to get across.

"I can carry someone," Jacky said. "And we've got Seeds left, right? Except for Eve. A couple more into Strength and Agility, and we can just sprint across."

"We can do the rope trick again," Zed said. "Like you were telling me about when you had that Trial with the ratmen, remember, Jacky? I'm not as fast as you guys, but I'm pretty sure I'm faster than a totally normal human, and if I can't make it, you can just pull me up."

"My suit is damaged," Blaine said. "If only I had had the time to complete the protective covering before we left ... I do not know that I will be able to keep up with a Player's level of supernatural speed, but I would be heavy enough to cause issues if you were to have to pull me up along with the suit."

"Just take the thrusters out of the hoverboard and use those," Gregor said. "Eve can carry me, and Adam or Jacky can carry Kris and Chanelle."

I suppressed a chuckle at the boy volunteering me to serve as his mount.

Blaine stared at him for a second. "Yes ... that might work." He smiled, and pushed up his glasses. "You have potential as an engineer," he said with poorly concealed pride.

Gregor rolled his eyes.

Adam got to work brainstorming bridge structures with Torliam. "You will add blood to the ink, of course," Torliam said. "How long do you estimate that you can hold the mimicry?"

"Why would I add blood to the ink?" Adam said, taken aback.

"Is yours not a significance-based Skill? I assumed …"

Adam's eyes widened.

"Do not tell me that you are unaware how your own Skill functions," Torliam said flatly.

"I've been experimenting, trying to figure out what makes a difference and what doesn't, but I hadn't been able to come up with such a broadly applicable rule yet. Tell me more. Are you familiar with other 'significance-based' Skills?"

"We do not have time for an extended lesson at the moment. However, some Skills are affected by the … importance, or the … implications of *how* they are used. When you spend your time carefully designing your creations, using the highest quality materials that have the most significance to you, if I am correct, it will make a difference in the nature of the creation."

"Like when you Animated your tattoo," I said. "It was strong enough to hold back the attack of a volcanic Goddess."

"Blood is a fitting sacrifice when you do not have anything more convenient, or when the situation is dire," Torliam said.

While he and Adam continued to work on that, the rest of us set up a few meters away from the edge of the chasm and timed our running speeds.

Birch joined in, frantically flapping his wings. He failed to take off from the ground even a little bit, which made sense, because his wings hadn't even turned completely to feather yet. They were still in the awkward half-fluff stage. After quite a few attempts, he mewled pitifully and lay down, legs stretched out fully to the front and back, neck resting on the ground.

"It's okay, Birch," Kris said. "You're growing fast. Soon you'll be big enough that people can ride you while flying through the sky, just like Mr. Torliam said."

His ears perked up, and he turned to her, his human-shaped eyes projecting curiosity.

She began to weave tales of his future awesomeness and bravery to him, and it wasn't long till he was sitting straight up to listen, interjecting with little sounds every once in a while.

"I'm pretty sure he actually understands what she's saying," Zed murmured to me as I watched in bemusement. "Does that count as discovery of the *second* sentient alien race?"

"I'm not sure he'd be the second one we've met," I said. "But I think he is sentient, to some degree. His mother communicated telepathically, through touch. Maybe he'll be able to do that when he's older, too." A small explosion drew my attention.

"Nothing to worry about," Blaine said, waving away the smoke. "I know what I'm doing."

After another quarter hour of frantic preparation by some people and worried waiting by the rest of us, we tied everyone together with the same plastine rope as before. Adam had been able to re-fuse the severed pieces, and assured me it would be just as strong as the original. Those who made it across, which would likely be Torliam, Adam, Jacky, and hopefully me, would pull the rest of the team up when the bridge gave out beneath our feet.

When Adam was ready, we all got a running start, sprinting toward the edge of the bridge which ended on the open air. I carried Gregor strapped between me and the pack on my back so that my arm and legs were free to pump mostly unimpeded. Torliam had Chanelle, and Jacky had Kris.

Adam ran a little ahead of us, and when he reached the edge, he threw out a spray of ink, which formed out in front of him into a narrow platform, connected to the real bridge's broken supports.

The team followed him unhesitatingly, in order of fastest to slowest. Torliam kept pace behind Adam with seemingly little effort, Chanelle's weight barely impeding him. The rest of us were straining.

Adam probably could have gone faster, but an unforeseen problem popped up. He couldn't form the ink quickly enough to keep up with his speed, and so he didn't draw too far ahead of us.

It was a problem, because it meant no one might make it across in time, and thus the slower people wouldn't have anyone to pull them up when the ink construct disintegrated.

We were about three quarters of the way across when Adam

shot a look backward over his shoulder.

—The beginning's gone.—
-Adam-

He began to form the platform tilting upward, so that as the unconnected piece of ink bridge beneath our feet began to fall, we would run up it and stay at the correct level. It was a good idea, if a desperate one.

Torliam let out a familiar blue glow, then, and the mist reached around, to buoy up the ink. We still sank, but not as fast.

Adam reached the edge first, shooting forward and leaving room for Torliam to cross behind him, then Jacky. I leapt the last bit, the edge of my foot barely reaching the jagged lip of the broken bridge. My momentum carried me forward, though, and I tumbled over the edge, doing my best not to crush Gregor between the pack and my back as I rolled.

I stood immediately and lunged forward to combat the sudden tug I knew would be coming on the rope tied to Blaine, Sam, and Zed. Torliam let me slip by him, grabbing the rope behind my back and pulling on it.

The abrupt yank on the rope knocked my breath out, and almost made me throw up. But my claws dug into the ground, and I kept straining forward.

It took less than a minute to pull up the rest of the team, and though they were a little banged and scraped up from smashing into the slightly jagged edge of the chasm, we were all alive. Blaine probably would have made it across with the help of his salvaged thrusters, except that he had started out behind the most of us, and there hadn't been enough room on the ink bridge for him to pass anyone. Even so, lifting him while the thrusters pushed him upward wasn't any more difficult than lifting a fat man would have been. Totally doable.

I was just about to let out a sigh of relief when Adam's eyes rolled back in his head, and he collapsed.

Chapter 17

I want to touch the fire in the sound.
— Pablo Neruda

SAM, who looked ready to sleep for about a year straight, pronounced that Adam was just extremely exhausted, suffering backlash from Skill-overuse, and low on blood. None of which Sam could do anything about even if he wasn't using all his healing on his own wounds, since Adam wasn't actually injured. Adam would have to recover the old-fashioned way, and would be able to move with the rest of us in the morning, though he would probably be even more grumpy than usual.

When I slid the pack off my back and untied Gregor, he wrapped his little arms around my waist and let out a sobbing breath into the material covering my stomach. He hadn't made a single sound as he rode on my back all the way across, not even when I'd made that final desperate leap for the edge.

But I realized now that he was shaking, his knees trembling so that he could barely support his own weight. I hesitantly patted his head, petting him a little as if he were an animal. "You're safe," I said in a soft voice. "I said you would be, didn't I?"

He nodded mutely into my stomach, then began to cry. He struggled to stop, no doubt embarrassed to lose his usual adult behavior, but didn't quite succeed.

I felt a bit inept, but I just petted him some more and stood still so he could hide his face in my bodysuit. He was just a kid, after all. A kid that looked like he might be seven shouldn't have to experience situations like that.

Kris noticed before Blaine did, and came over to join in our impromptu group hug, while their uncle watched them with a pained expression on his face, and took a single step towards us before shaking his head and stilling. He stood there awkwardly, but when Gregor finally let go, Blaine made a comment about how interesting Birch was, and was able to draw both kids into playful speculation about riding the creature when he got bigger, whether or not they would need a saddle, and if it would be uncomfortable. Obviously, he'd been paying attention to their interests.

I smiled at Blaine over their heads, and he smiled back, though it was strained.

We spent the night in the still-intact room of the tower, and ate through a large portion of the supplies we'd brought with us. I didn't suggest rationing it, because we would surely need all the strength we could get, traveling through the Dark Lands.

Shortly after we left the bridge, sparse, prickly trees began to grow, becoming taller as we walked farther into them. They didn't affect our line of sight, and were so scraggly they barely impeded the passage of the sunlight. Torliam didn't say anything, but I was watching carefully as he grew tenser and began to twitch at every sound.

Birch sensed it too, and kept growling low in his throat.

Finally, Torliam stopped us, hand raised silently in the air as he looked around. Something was up ahead, though I couldn't sense far enough to tell what it was.

He pointed to the side, and we began to circle around in a wide arc, as silently as possible. When had we stopped speaking aloud, resorting to nonverbal cues in fear of being overheard? Probably about the same time Birch stopped growling. After a certain point, you knew when it was time to run and hide rather than stand out.

Eventually the ground sloped upward, and the trees gained some more leaves, beginning to resemble evergreens.

I reached the top of the ridge first, and caught sight of what we were avoiding.

An … amalgamation. It was settled in the center of a huge web, which stretched across the valley of scraggly trees, covering the easy path through that we had avoided. Its top half looked like a particularly lumpy-skulled monkey. The bottom was that of a spider, oval-shaped and eight-legged.

I froze unconsciously, sinking down so that I could barely see over the fallen tree trunk in front of me. The others followed suit, crawling up to look out over the edge.

The creature quivered in place, hunched down, and wrapped around on itself. The web shivered outward from the center, shaking a group of much smaller spider-monkey creatures that were huddled near the edge of the web, watching the big one.

It lifted its head slowly, as if its muscles were creaky from disuse, and turned toward the huddling group of little ones.

They flinched back, monkey faces grimacing in obvious fear.

It stood, shrieked, and waved its arms, and chased them off the web. Its stick-like, hairy legs worked in tandem to propel its body at an absurd speed. It picked up a gigantic club off the ground, obviously made out of a tree trunk big enough to match its size, and waved it at them for good measure, still screeching. Was it shooing possible competitors away from its territory?

Its shriek hurt my ears, like nails on chalkboard mixed with a rusty grinding sound. Its body was emaciated and pale compared to the proportions of the little ones, except for the stomach of its monkey part, sitting above the junction of primate and arachnid. The stomach was grossly distended, the fur peeling off and skin stretched taught like a balloon that was one more breath away from popping.

Its legs seemed to lose control then, some of them pushing forward, and some moving back and tangling with the others. The creature crashed to the ground, and flailed around with its club till the trees trembled and even more of their leaves fell off. Then, it was on its feet again and skittering back to the web, which it shot to the top of. A few seconds of calm silence passed, and then it tore into the web with the club in its monkey arms, its spider legs, and even its teeth. Foamy spit slobbered out around those fanged teeth and a lolling, blue-purple, swollen tongue.

Once the web was hanging in tatters, it stopped again, head swiveled towards the still-running little ones. Then it shot off after them.

It fell on a straggler first, the club smashing into the thing's head and pulping it, instantly killing it.

The big one didn't hesitate, literally falling onto the smaller corpse, and tearing at it with hands and teeth. It didn't chew, it just shoved pieces of the little one down its throat and swallowed.

The other small spider-monkeys screamed with all too human voices and expressions of terror when they noticed the fate of the straggler, and ran away even faster. But it was no use, because it left that one behind half-eaten, and did the same to another, and another.

The big one screamed out, a continuous keening wail. The sound was muffled every time it stuffed a chunk of flesh down its throat, but never cut off completely.

Torliam laid a hand on my shoulder, making me jump in surprise. "Let us go. Before it is through with them, and turns its attention toward us," he whispered.

I nodded, and we hurried away, circumventing the whole area without another peep.

Birch jumped atop my shoulders, digging his claws uncomfortably into my arm.

I gently moved Birch's paws and placed my hand on his head reassuringly.

When he judged us far enough away, Torliam stopped. His shoulders slumped a little in apparent exhaustion, and his eyes didn't quite focus on me, staring bleakly into the mid-distance. "Those were its children."

"What?"

"That was your first glimpse of the Sickness that infects my world. The creature was driven mad, till it could not recognize the difference between that which it loved and hated. Hunger overruled everything, until it devoured its children for the false hope of extending its own life. The Sickness is a traitor within you, turning you against all that you hold dear." He walked forward again, and only shook his head when questioned.

That night, while Jacky and Blaine were on lookout, I sparred with Torliam, and we exchanged answers again. "Tell me more about the Sickness," I said, perhaps slightly more imperiously than he preferred.

His eyes fell to the ground, and then rose again, locking on mine as he savagely pressed the attack. He knew defense was my weakest area. "The origin of the Sickness is unknown, even to me. If ever my people had the knowledge, it has been lost. But all know that it is the most … abhorrent thing in existence. It hits the weak and the strong with indifference, and even now, we do not know exactly how it spreads, because we cannot see it, only its effects. It seems to spread more quickly if one is in contact with an infected. Sometimes. And yet, it may also strike a lone hermit, who has not met another mortal for decades. We have found no way to guard against it, even after thousands upon thousands of years. It defies us, and takes all that we love from us, as if mocking our futile struggles to defeat it."

I made the connection. "It took someone from you," I said, my voice soft.

"My younger sister." His eyes grew distant, and the rage that had bubbled up when talking about the Sickness receded. "By the time she was born, my mother had ascended the throne."

I wanted to interrupt, because I was pretty sure he basically just told me his mom was royalty, which would make *him* royalty, but I restrained myself.

"My sister was groomed to lead from infancy, and the knowledge that the world loved her burned from her skin almost visibly. Everyone who met her doted on her."

I remembered the dream I'd had, after solving the Oracle's first gift. I had been someone else. I felt with a certainty that person had been Torliam, and I had witnessed his dream, or his memory, of a beautiful young girl, who he was describing with every reminiscent word.

Then, his expression deadened, and began to speak in a clinically detached tone. "The Sickness affects all of life in different ways. It manifests in us as wasting disease, accompanied by a mental … dissociation. I believe that is the word. Hunger increases, a desire for living flesh, particularly that from a strong, intelligent creature. The diseased person's love and emotional connections putrefy, and everything they once loved or cared for becomes something they wish to consume. To destroy. I once saw a woman bite off the cheek of her partner, in her madness. The spark that makes a person what they are is deadened, and eventually leaves behind a creature that wishes only to destroy, desperate to prolong the life of the flesh husk wasting away around them."

He took a deep breath, and continued is a more clinical tone. "The body begins to die from the inside. Blood in the stool. Darkening veins. The limbs thin, while often the stomach bloats out grotesquely. The rate of degeneration increases more rapidly as time goes on, while in the beginning the infected may not show signs for some time. The Sickness is both the horror and the shame of our people, and our world."

He was silent for a while, and I considered what it would be like to watch Zed go through what his sister must have.

His arms dropped, and he released his fighting stance, turning away from me and walking toward the edge of camp.

I watched him as he walked away, wishing I could reach out my hand and stop him, tell him I had seen his beautiful young sister and I was sorry. But I didn't. I couldn't. I stayed silent, and he left.

WE TRAVELED for a few more days before anything else eventful happened. Sam regained his strength, the wound on his stomach leaving nothing but a scar. We had a few small skirmishes with the local flora and fauna, but nothing too exciting. We'd almost run out of food by that time, and it had been growing colder the farther north we went, so we jogged for the added benefits of faster travel, training, and the warmth it generated internally.

We were constantly on guard, though, and the tension was almost as draining as the physical exertion. Our packs were light with the lack of food, and we'd been hunting the local wildlife when we could, and foraging what few plants Torliam knew to be edible.

One afternoon, I was just about to suggest we stop and see if we could find something for a midday meal, when a whistle tore through the air, followed almost instantly by an arrow.

We scattered, some dropping to the ground and rolling, some slipping behind nearby trees. I jerked Zed and Chanelle behind a tree, and Jacky went *up* a tree, hiding herself in the foliage and literally dragging Kris and Gregor with her. I cursed myself for not keeping my awareness constantly extended. I'd been doing a quick scan to the limit of my reach every hour or so, so whoever was attacking must have come upon us quickly.

Chanelle let out a small sound of unhappiness, but I ignored her. Sam and Blaine had been slowly re-introducing Seeds into her system, and there seemed to be a response. She wasn't close to being normal, but she wasn't quite so catatonic, either. However, in situations like this, that wasn't helpful.

I sensed outward, and saw that our opponents already surrounded us on three sides, and were circling around behind us. They shone with power, kind of like Torliam did, in that extra sense Wraith provided me with.

—WE'RE SURROUNDED. EIGHT OF THEM. STRONGER THAN US.

—

-EVE-

Adam grimaced and threw up shields twice his height around us in a wide circle, roughly defending the group's location, though it also stopped us from being able to cleanly attack.

Torliam, the only one who hadn't scattered immediately at the warning shot, shouted something in his language, loud and imperious. Our attackers slowed, as if startled.

After a few seconds, someone shouted back, and Torliam lifted his arms and started to glow, that light blue luminescence wafting off him like thick smoke.

There was another shout, and Torliam turned to Adam. "Lower one of your shields. They are from a small village near here. I will talk with them, there is no need to engage in combat."

Adam looked to me for approval before complying, but Torliam waited patiently.

An Estreyan moved forward from between the trees, riding atop an ostrich-like creature. He stopped just outside the gap Adam had created in the shield line.

Torliam said something, puffing out his chest and somehow managing to look down on the man, despite his lower position on the ground.

The man scowled, but seemed unsure.

Torliam waved to us and spoke some more, seeming even more irritated.

One of the bird-rider's companions joined him, and they

spoke in murmurs that I could hear clearly but couldn't understand a word of. Then the first guy nodded, and said something.

"They will escort us to the village," Torliam said. "Lower the shields."

Adam shook his head. "How do I know they won't attack us when I do?"

"*My* people believe in honor," Torliam said, the inflection carrying an obvious insult.

I considered for a bit, then released Zed and Chanelle, and stepped out behind the tree to stand next to Adam. "Go ahead," I said. "They might be helpful, if they're friendly. And if they decide to attack right now, I wouldn't bet on our odds."

Adam grimaced, his hair lifting due to the tension-driven static electricity escaping his body, but he complied.

The Estreyans, probably a patrol group, closed in around us, eyeing us with some distaste. We all looked a little ragged.

One of them motioned to the tree, and with a bit of rustling, Jacky and the kids fell out of it with a startled yelp.

The Estreyan who had waved his hand smirked at them, but I noticed that they all kept their mounts a safe distance away, as if worried they might get dirty from touching us.

As we began to move, I kept my awareness spread out, and noticed the looks the Estreyans shot each other when they thought we weren't looking. They were afraid.

IT TOOK about an hour to reach the village at our jogging pace, though the riders could no doubt have gone much faster on their own. I'd tried to ask Torliam what was going on, but he refused to be drawn into conversation, just shaking his head silently. The trees thinned, allowing the huge, flat-topped village wall to be visible from far away. It towered above everything, and seemed to be made of whole, huge tree trunks stacked flush against each other. Cleared land circled the village, probably for farming or livestock grazing. And for visibility from the sentinel towers spaced into the wall at intervals.

The sentinels stationed there noticed us, and by the time we passed through the guarded gate into the village, others had gathered along the edge of the street, or were peeking through their windows. Visually, the place reminded me of a mix between old-timey log cabins and Asian architecture. Wood seemed to be the primary building material, but the buildings had peaked roofs that swooped down, and the aesthetics were beautiful in their simplicity.

Estreyans stopped and stared as we passed, going silent in waves that radiated outward. They dressed in thick, baggy clothing that seemed to wrap and tie around them, rather than being fitted or held up by belts. Both the people and the buildings were a bit shabby, as if they'd stopped having the resources for repairs or new materials a few years ago. Or maybe they'd just stopped caring.

One woman stared out at us, and I could feel a palpable aura of despair wafting off her. It had to be Skill-related, and judging from the way others avoided her, they could feel it too. But it wasn't just her. Despair was elsewhere among them, though less obvious.

A young woman, barely out of childhood, stared out from an alley between houses, the bags under her eyes so prominent they looked like bruises. No one would look at her, and if they accidentally did, they looked away quickly. One mother even crossed the street with her child to avoid the young woman.

My senses were still extended a few yards beyond the group, and I could tell that the villagers were powerful, compared to us. I felt vulnerable under their stares, and had to resist the almost subconscious urge to slip out my claws and bare my teeth at them. My hair stood at attention, my skin prickled, and I felt like I was walking willingly into a pit of writhing snakes. There was danger here, all around us. It felt like the intro to a horror film, or maybe the aftermath of a war film.

Torliam damn well better know what he was doing, I swore

silently. He was the only one who really knew what was going on, and if he screwed up or betrayed us, I was going to flay him alive with my claws.

The patrol brought us to a large, almost mansion-like house, and stopped outside while the leader sent someone inside. Whoever lived there was obviously important. No doubt they would decide our fate.

Many of the Estreyans we had passed on the way had followed, eyeing us curiously and murmuring amongst themselves. Perhaps they had never seen people as small as us before. Or maybe they just weren't used to outsiders.

The person who had gone inside returned with a very old woman, and a female who stood unobtrusively off to the side, perhaps a servant. The old woman was so wrinkled she almost looked like a half-dehydrated, human-colored raisin, but she stood straight, and I could sense the power in her. This creature, woman, whatever she was, could destroy my group, literally, within the space of a few breaths if she tried.

Obviously, the villagers respected this elder, too, because they fell silent when she appeared.

Torliam half-bowed to the elder, and when the elder nodded back, he began to speak.

At this point, I really wished I could understand the language, because the tension was high, and I was standing there like an idiot, trying to understand what was going on by voice inflection and body language. I glanced over at Zed, whose eyes were darting about, taking everything in.

The leader of the patrol group spoke then, obviously arguing against whatever Torliam had said. He waved his hand toward our group and spoke angrily, and some of the other patrol members and people in the crowd nodded at his words, murmuring softly.

Torliam's shoulders tensed, and I felt my own follow suit.

Zed grimaced, and then looked back to the elder expectantly.

—ARE YOU ACTUALLY FOLLOWING WHAT THEY'RE SAYING?—

-Eve-

Zed's eyes jumped to mine, startled.

—I'm definitely understanding more of this than I should. I can't catch the words, but I feel like I have a vague concept of what some of them mean.—
-Zed-

Torliam spoke again, waving his hand in the air to punctuate his words, and resting it on my shoulder, guiding me to take a step forward and stand beside him.

I met his eyes in surprise. What did he want? I couldn't speak the language, so how was I supposed to plead our case?

I copied Torliam's bow toward the elder as best I could, which for some reason caused a bit of murmuring in the crowd. When I raised my head, I saw the elder look at the sparkling multi-banded ring on my left forefinger.

Then she looked at Birch, huffing in amusement when the little creature growled at her, ruffling his little ragged, fluffy wings in a hint of threat.

The elder looked back to me, looking me up and down in a way I would have said was ogling, if she wasn't so *deadly* focused on me.

She spoke, finally, and nodded back at me, the same slight tilt she'd given to Torliam. That made the crowd murmur again, but she silenced them with her words, turning back to her doorway. She said something to her female attendant, who bowed respectfully.

Whatever it was the elder had said, the leader of the patrol didn't like it, and raised his voice in outrage.

The elder gave him a single look and a few soft words, and the younger man backed down.

He shot a glare at us when she turned away again.

"We have been granted asylum," Torliam said simply. "We will lodge in this ... how do you say it? Residence?"

I raised an eyebrow. I was pretty sure there'd been a little bit more to it than that. "I need subtitles," I muttered.

The attendant waved at us to follow her inside, and the patrol leader glared at each of us as we passed by him.

I made sure to hold my head high and stare unflinchingly back at him. It wouldn't do to seem cowed or weak. Predators could sense that, like sharks smelled blood in the water. And if the creatures of Estreyer had something in common, it's that they were all predators.

"What was the argument back there?" I murmured to Torliam.

He hesitated for a bit, but finally said, "They have secluded themselves to try and avoid contact with the Sickness. The villagers were worried that we would bring it in from outside and pass it to them."

I knew I still wasn't getting the full picture, but he clamped his lips together and moved further away from me. I'd have to ambush him later and get the truth out of him. Perhaps if no one was listening in he'd be less tight-lipped.

The attendant led us to a short hallway, and motioned toward the doors lining the hall, indicating the rooms were to be ours. I directed the weaker members of our group toward the middle doors, flanked by stronger members.

I wish I could say that being within civilization again eased my mind. But that would have been a lie.

THE ELDER'S female attendant let us rest for an hour, and then gathered us for a meal in one of the larger rooms near our hallway. When we had finished stuffing ourselves, she said something in Estreyan and motioned for Torliam and I to follow her.

He seemed unconcerned, maybe even a bit eager, so I went along with her request.

I sent him a questioning look behind her back.

"She is taking us to the bathing room," he said. "We are the ones highest in honor among the group, so we go first."

A bath sounded wonderful. "The others aren't going to have to use our dirty water or anything, right?"

"Do you bathe in each other's water on Earth?" he asked, mouth drawing down in disgust.

"No, but I hear we used to, before technology advanced."

"Rest assured, we passed that point of technological advancement *long* ago." He shook his head, as if exasperated. At the attendant's word, he split off to enter the male section. "We also separate the genders for bathing," he said with a curl of his lip that was more joke than sneer.

Birch followed me into the bath, and after we were finished scrubbing and soaking, the attendant gave me new, warmer clothes to wear over my armored vest.

A quick stretch of my Wraith Skill told me Torliam had already finished his own bath. His signature was faint, a few streets away.

Birch meowed plaintively at me, so I took him outside to relieve himself and go for a little walk, heading towards Torliam. Birch had fun sniffing about, until we passed a pair of boots airing on someone's porch. He sniffed them, growled at the scent, then crouched over them and pooped right down the mouth of one.

My jaw dropped, and I looked around to make sure no one was watching. "What are you doing?" I whispered harshly at him.

He flicked his ears back and ignored me, peeing into the other boot. When he was finished, he ruffled his feathers and pranced off with a distinctly self-satisfied hop in his step.

"Were those the patrol leader's shoes?" I asked, following him.

Birch flicked his tail.

I suppressed a snicker.

We caught up to Torliam pretty quickly, though my relaxation leeched away the longer I was outside.

Torliam turned to me with some surprise, and the younger

Estreyan man he'd been talking to slipped away. "You look better when you are clean," he said. He did, too. In fact, I realized this was the first time I'd ever actually seen him bathed and groomed.

"You're all … dignified," I said.

"I *am* the son of a queen," he said, but there was no malice in his voice. When Birch grunted up at him, he leaned over so that the creature could hop atop his back and scramble up to sit on one shoulder.

"What was all that about earlier? With the meeting in front of the elder's house?" I said.

"Some of them did not want us to stay, but I was able to convince the elder to grant us asylum. We are under her protection, as long as we are under her roof. Did you not comprehend this earlier?"

I bared my teeth at him. "Exactly how did you convince the elder? And exactly what do my gifts from the Oracle have to do with it?"

His stride hitched, almost imperceptibly. "It is law that should one of my line require asylum, the people must grant it. This would have been enough, ordinarily. But the fear is strong, here. It is one of the most insidious side effects of the Sickness. The uncertainty, never knowing when it might strike, or if it is already lying dormant in yourself or one you love, is difficult. There is no single way the Sickness spreads, and there are some cases where our best healers and scientists do not know how it could have done so. In some people, this uncertainty leads to them fearing anything and everything, whether there is true danger or not."

"This is fascinating. Don't think you can avoid my second question, though. You knew the elder would find the puzzle bands significant."

"Gifts from the Oracle are rumored to have been given to those with a great task or destiny to fulfill, in the stories so old almost no one remembers them anymore," he said, reaching a hand up to push the dirty blonde hair off his neck and rub the tense muscle there. "In this situation, I thought the elder would be knowledgeable enough about Estreyan history to notice them. Long ago, when my people first came to your world, it is said that some of them found the small beings on your planet pleasing, and had relations with them."

I narrowed my eyes. "Had *relations*? You mean they had sex with the humans."

"Yes. It is unfathomable, I know. Nevertheless, you may be the descendent of one of my people's lines, and I was reasonably confident she would deduce that."

As in … I'm part Estreyan?"

"Of course. How else would you survive the Seeds? They are of my world."

My eyes widened. When he put it like that … "Wait. But my brother doesn't have the gene. He wouldn't have survived the initiation if not for Sam."

"You are sure he is your brother?"

"Yes!" I said, but realized I'd never considered that question before. We had the same dark hair and tall build. I raised my hands, fingers splayed wide, and looked at the scars on the edge of both pinky fingers. "I was born with an extra finger on both hands," I said. "And an extra toe. I didn't even think about it being somehow connected to your people. On Earth, it's just considered a mutation. My mother had them removed, so I wouldn't be considered strange."

"She … cut off your fingers?" He said in a low voice, staring at me in shock. "Just so you could be more like the other *two-legged-maggots*?"

"It wasn't malicious. She didn't want me to be strange, to have to deal with the social stigma of being different. But my point was, Zed didn't have any extra digits. And she … was so happy about that." I muttered the last bit, a tendril of doubt wriggling into my thoughts. Why didn't Zed have the gene?

Torliam seemed to guess my thoughts, or maybe their path was just obvious. "You are most likely extremely distant descendants. It is possible, and even likely, that the human gene just dominated over the Estreyan in your brother's case."

I nodded. "So, every one of the Players is part Estreyan?" I didn't know our father, and for the first time in a long while, I wondered about his whereabouts. Was he like me? Or was it my mother who had passed on the gene?

I waited for Torliam to answer my question, but instead of talking he turned to look down the street.

I followed his gaze to the group of Estreyans gathered to one side. I'd been so focused on our conversation that I hadn't been paying attention to the mounting tension up ahead. Voices were raised within the group, and outside, people turned their faces away and scurried on.

I was reminded uncomfortably of the first Seed I'd ever taken. I'd been so sick, just left on the side of the road, and everyone around me looked away and pretended they couldn't see, if they were kind. If they weren't, they'd sneered at me and swerved away in disgust.

Bodies shifted, and I caught a glimpse of the young woman I'd noticed earlier, shoulders hunched up, head tucked down. She flinched as someone threw an egg at her dark hair.

Torliam sped up, calling out sharply in Estreyan.

I lengthened my stride to match him, preemptive adrenaline surging through my veins.

Chapter 18

The night has a thousand eyes,
  And the day but one;
  Yet the light of the bright world dies
  With the dying sun.
  —Francis William Bourdillon

WHEN WE REACHED THE GROUP, Torliam spoke again, his voice low and angry.

One of the villagers spit toward the girl and laughed, and Torliam thrummed with power, light wafting off his skin as he activated his signature Skill.

The girl said something, her voice small but defiant.

Whatever she'd said, it enraged one of the women on the inside of the circle. She raised her hand and stepped forward, swinging her arm for a powerful slap.

The girl just closed her eyes and cringed, so I stepped forward, bringing both hands above my head to catch the blow.

The older woman gaped down at me, and didn't seem to know whether to be shocked or angry.

I guided her hand down slowly, keeping my eyes locked on her face, while my awareness swirled around searching for any danger I couldn't see.

Torliam said something, and her eyes moved to my glittering armband, then to him, then to my eyes.

She drew back, the angry flush draining away from her face, leaving it unnaturally pale. She bowed to me, picked up a basket, and hurried away with no more than a glance over her shoulder to the young woman. "Damn, I *really* need to learn Estreyan," I muttered.

Torliam waved his hands at the others, and the blue mist pushed them back, giving them the impetus to disperse. He turned to the girl, using more of that endlessly versatile mist to help clean the egg out of her hair.

Birch grabbed one of the girl's shoes, which I hadn't noticed was missing, and brought it back to her.

She smiled, then sniffed back tears as she slipped the shoe back onto her dirty foot.

Her murmured conversation with Torliam was interrupted by the patrol leader from yesterday, who called out angrily and stomped up.

He shoved himself between the girl and Torliam, forcing her behind him. His fists were balled up, and he glared at Torliam in challenge.

The girl laid her hand on his shoulder and said something that made him relax, pointing to Torliam, and then to me.

There was a moment of awkwardness, before he gave a small bow to Torliam, and then to me. He didn't smile, and he didn't exactly look *grateful*, but there was respect in his eyes, at least.

As he walked away with the girl, I turned to Torliam. "So, what was that about?"

"She is his sister. Her husband died of the Sickness. Some of the villagers are afraid she will spread it to them. They have been trying to drive her out, though the elder has openly stated that there is no evidence you will contract the Sickness just from proximity to one who has it, or has been exposed to it."

"I really need to learn Estreyan," I said.

He stared at me till I grew irritated. When he finally opened his mouth to speak, I prepared to snap back at him, but he surprised me. "You should learn to defend yourself," he said thoughtfully. "Both in word and in action. I am already teaching you how to fight better than a half-drowned pup. Any companion of mine should at least be *literate*."

"You're so kind," I said sarcastically.

"My benevolence is renowned." He grinned at me, the expression making him look much younger, and taking the sting off his insults.

I turned to Birch. "Why do you let him insult me like this? You'd think a good tailos would at least bite him a little."

Birch looked to me, and then to Torliam, and let out a little grunt.

AFTER THE INCIDENT, the villagers were a lot more accepting. Or respectful, at least. Zed took to spending all his time among them, and quickly charmed them with his "tiny" size, quick smile, and willingness to make a fool out of himself miming things as he learned their language.

It turned out one of the nanite chips NIX had implanted in his brain gave him an unfair advantage in that field.

Blaine speculated that they had been attempting to develop an artificial version of Skills to go with their attempt at Seeds.

Zed couldn't actively tell when the chips were working, but he was picking up the language supernaturally quickly, especially with the constant practice.

In contrast, I was quite frustrated with my own progress. My Intelligence was way higher than it had been back when I was a normal civilian, but after a couple days of intense study, I was still barely learning rudimentary vocabulary and child-level sentence structure.

Even Blaine and Gregor were better at it than me, and neither of them had Seeds at all, which was pretty depressing.

Torliam said there would be time to learn, since the village didn't have a communication device—they had purposefully isolated themselves from the rest of Estreyan society—but they did have a supply convoy that would be heading to another village that did have a comms system. It would be a while before the convoy left, but we had been invited to travel with them. In the meantime, Torliam planned to teach me and the team how to fight, and how to speak and read the language, for those who were interested. Once we had a basic understanding, he said we had been authorized to search through the village's store of knowledge for information about the God of Knowledge and the Oracle, so there was added incentive.

I was sitting at the edge of the training fields outside the main wall. It was mainly open fields for sparring or practicing with the more destructive Skills, but some of them had trees or stumps to attack, or different types of terrain.

Adam had created a bigger version of Birch out of ink, and Kris was riding atop it, shrieking with laughter as she raced the original Birch across the field. Adam called out a warning, and she dismounted before the construct disintegrated, immediately begging him to, "make another one!"

Zed plopped down beside me. "Guess what I just learned?" He kept talking before I had a chance to speak. "They have a healer!" He nodded at my look of surprise. "Yeah. They were being sloppy with the new arrowheads, and Egon dropped some molten metal on his foot. They shooed him right off to the *healer*. I don't know how this person's Skill works, or if they'd be strong enough to fix what's wrong with you and Chanelle, but what if they can?"

I scrambled to my feet. "That's wonderful, Zed! Do you know where they are?"

He shrugged. "I can ask one of the villagers."

We went back to our hall of the elder's house, and found Blaine and Sam both sitting with Chanelle.

Blaine was tinkering with a small ball of metal, using tiny little tools that looked more like metal toothpicks than anything, and he didn't even look up when we entered.

"She's making mental associations!" Sam said without preamble. "She can tell the difference between red and blue, and point out the correct one when I show her an example to match up with. Not every time ... she gets distracted, but this is progress!"

Zed told him about the healer, and Sam grew quiet, then stood up. "I'm coming with you. Maybe ... maybe this healer can help figure out what's wrong with my ability, too."

The healer turned out to be an old man with one of the nicer houses. He was a bit suspicious, but after Zed introduced us, and the man got a close look at my gifts from the Oracle, including a valiant attempt to make the ring come off my finger, he let us into his house.

He tried to work on Chanelle first, making her sit in a bare spot on his stone floor that had diagrams drawn all over it. Then he stared at her really hard. He questioned Zed, eyes widening at the response. He shook his head sadly in the universal symbol for "kids these days," and returned to staring at her. Eventually, he shook his head again and waved her away with an irritated "harrumph!"

"What does that mean?" Sam asked.

Zed talked back and forth with the man, and said, "I don't know all the vocabulary he's using, but I think he's saying that any wounds caused by the direct touch of a ... higher power?" He shrugged, "They aren't something he can heal." He talked with the man a bit more, waving his hands about and miming things to convey concepts he didn't have the words for. Then he said, "So, if a god punches you in the side and breaks your ribs with its fist, you can probably be healed. If the god uses a 'power' attack—maybe like a Skill?—then a wound that breaks the skin is way harder to heal. I don't know if I'm really understanding the concept, but in any case, he can't fix Chanelle's brain."

"Maybe that's why I can't help her," Sam said, relief tinting his voice for a moment. "But it doesn't explain the backlash, and the way I can't control if I heal or hurt someone anymore."

I sat in the middle of the circle next, while Zed explained what was wrong with me.

The old man's eyes grew bright, and he peered at me even harder than he had Chanelle. He asked questions about how I'd gotten the Seed of Chaos in the first place, how I'd been using it, and what effects had come from the Oracle's gifts. By the way he suppressed an eager little smile, I had a sneaking suspicion that he wanted to know these things so he could gossip about them later, rather than because they would help him diagnose or heal me.

Finally, he sat back and shook his head, stating something final, from which I caught the word, "die."

Zed looked pained, and asked him a question before he translated the answer fully into English. "He says you're going to die, if Chaos does not stop attacking you. And as it is the direct power of a god causing your condition, there is nothing he can do about it. He said he knows of no healer in the world that could heal you, though there may be a couple who could keep you alive a little while longer. There is a healer in the capitol who may be able to help. Ifkana of the Panacean. He recommends we go to Ifkana when we get to the capitol."

Sam heaved out a sigh. "It's not my fault, thank goodness," he whispered. When we both turned to stare at him, he straightened. "Not that it makes what's happening any better! It's just—I felt like a failure. I mean, I'm supposed to be able to fix things like this, and I couldn't, and I've been so *useless* lately—"

I interrupted. "It's fine, Sam. This was never your fault." I had decided to take the Seed of Chaos on my own. Even with the warning from Behelaino. I stood up, and walked out of the center of the painted diagrams. "Your turn, now."

Zed once again explained what was wrong to the healer, who sprinkled white powder on Sam's head.

When the healer's back was turned, Sam sent me a disbelieving look.

—HE JUST DUMPED CHALK ON ME. IS THIS OLD GUY
PRANKING US?—
-SAM-

I smothered a laugh, and shrugged.

Finally, the old man threw up his hands, said, "Agh!" and shook his head before turning to yammer at Zed, who translated as he talked.

"He says, we come to him with unsolvable problems, do we try and mock him? The fair haired—blonde—one is not a healer. He's not going to be fooled by us. Or maybe we're stupid—"

"Wait," Sam said. "What does he mean, I'm not a healer?" He pressed his hands to his thighs, and met my eyes for a second. I knew we were both thinking of the same thing. His Harbinger Skill was of the Ruination Class.

"He says it is a balanced power. You must take what you give and give what you take." Zed shook his head. "What does that even mean?"

Sam didn't wait for him to ask the old man. "I can't heal … unless I offload that damage somewhere else?"

"Yes, basically," Zed said, after translating the question and receiving an answer back. "He says you are unbalanced, and your power will turn against you if you try to change its nature, or to leash it."

Sam didn't speak again until Zed had thanked the healer profusely, we had left his house, and were walking down the street. Then Sam stopped, and turned to me. "I don't want to kill people, Eve." His voice broke on my name.

"We'll find some other way," I said. I wasn't sure I believed it.

But we'd definitely try. Even if I hadn't cared about Sam at all, the team couldn't afford to lose its healer.

———

IT GREW colder over the next couple weeks, and the green things started to wither away. I trained with Torliam and the others every day. He thought I was sloppy and relied on my Grace too much, rather than actual skill. He also thought I was weak, slow, tactically incompetent, and remarked repeatedly how generally amazed he was that I was even alive to learn from him. And I *was* learning.

It had made me respect him in a new way, because even if your blood was *pure* Seeds and your bones were made out of steel, it would still take thousands of hours of practice to be at his level as a fighter. He knew what he was doing, and he knew what I was doing wrong. The only downside was that he liked to show me what I was doing wrong by showing me once, maybe twice, then beating it into me.

He didn't say it, but I thought I had a talent for battle, because I learned quickly, almost instinctually. Even Torliam couldn't fault me in that.

Sam had tried attacking Adam's Animations with the destructive side of his Skill, but the relief of "pressure" from doing that was apparently close to negligible. He didn't want to hurt animals unless he had to, so he attacked plants, taking two other people from the team with him as he ventured into the forest, making things wither, explode, crystallize, and quite a few of the other destructive effects he'd absorbed over his time as a Player. That worked better, though still *very* slowly. Still, it was a solution that didn't involve hurting anyone.

I learned enough Estreyan to inch my way through their texts. The library held everything from old books to these cool little chips that could project information right into the eye of the "reader." They were one of the surprisingly few examples of advanced Estreyan technology I'd seen in the village.

Blaine loved the library, and seemed to be trying to gorge himself on the information equivalent of eating an entire blue whale. He may have been succeeding. Unlike me, he picked up the language with astonishing ease. I mean, I had already known he was a genius, but the way he worked with science seemed more like magic to me. This was something new, and I felt a healthy dose of respect and morose jealousy for his brain.

All of us who could read spent hour upon hour in the library, searching for relevant information about the God of Knowledge, and my problem. I had never been more grateful for my boost to Intelligence, because I don't think my progress would have been possible otherwise. In fact, I'd had quite a few spontaneous level-ups to my mental Attributes while learning, and even to my Endurance.

All of the electronically archived things were searchable by keyword, so finding reference to the God of Knowledge or the Oracle wasn't the problem. Finding relevant, *new* information about either of them *was*. They didn't make public appearances very often any more, it seemed.

I found a picture of a mural with the God of Knowledge's name on it, and showed it to Torliam.

Rather than being mildly interested or explaining the background behind it like I'd expected, he stared at it, frowned, and stared at it some more. "There are old paintings," he said. "From before the God of Knowledge removed himself from the presence of mortals. I have seen them, in my research into our past. He had a temple once. There is a painting of him in it, quite like this, the roof open to the sky, people supplicating before him, and golden rods shooting into the sky. Golden light stretching into the sky ... everything within it ..."

"What?"

"Within the range of his divination. I think those were the words. All that lies under the light is within range of his power."

"Why didn't you mention this before?"

"I—" He closed his mouth, and opened it again, with a small

frown. "I had *forgotten*. It seemed insignificant." The words were fairly innocuous, but he shot me a look of silent alarm, wide eyed and tight lipped. His skin had paled, and his jaw was clenched so the skin stretched over it a bit too tightly.

It made me realize how weak he still must be, after what NIX had done to him. He was easily stronger than me, but I could only imagine what he must have once been. What he would be again. A creature with enough Intelligence that forgetting something was an anomaly.

"I have studied this before ..." He pressed his lips together. "I have spent my life studying these things, trying to find a cure for the Sickness. They say that he secluded himself to do the same. *I have studied this before, and I have forgotten.*" His expression spoke as much as his words.

I kept my expression as neutral as possible, trying not to show my alarm. He had forgotten something important enough that it was dangerous, which meant something had *made* him forget. "How far does the light stretch?" I asked. Were we even now within the god's range?

"I do not know. But we should be wary."

That was worrying, but it didn't change the vision I'd received from the Oracle.

Torliam's head jerked to the side, staring at the blank wall with such a horrified expression that I sank into a crouch with my claws out, hair raising in alarm.

I snapped my awareness out to search for the danger, but found nothing unusual. "What's wrong?"

He didn't have to answer me, because the black cube that formed in front of my face, asking if I wished to enter the Trial, explained everything.

Chapter 19

Be like snow. Silent and cold.

— Citron Aodh

I GOT a barrage of Windows from my teammates who had seen the cube. I told them not to worry. Enough time had passed on Earth for NIX to fix the Shortcut, and they had sent their Players out on a Trial. No big deal.

Even so, the others gathered in the library with Torliam and I. Perhaps it was a subconscious thing—safety in numbers.

"How could you tell?" I asked Torliam. "You knew a Trial had started, even before the cube."

"I feel all those that I have been forced to form a bastardized blood-covenant with," he said simply. "The disconnect between your world and mine had given me some blessed relief for a while, but now they are here, spread all over the weaker lands in groups." He turned back to me, relaxing somewhat. "I hope they are all annihilated before the gods of those Trials."

Over the course of the next few hours, Torliam announced when individual Trials across the world ended, removing their still-living Players from his consciousness. It grew late, and most of the group's tension leached away in favor of fatigue, but Torliam didn't relax.

"Is something wrong?" I asked.

"One group remains. Too much time has passed. It is not likely they are still in a Trial."

"Maybe they're trying something like what my group did, escaping NIX's clutches by camping out over here. Or maybe this is a special expedition, not Players sent to petition the Trial gods. I heard they've been trying to do research about your world, pick up old technology, etcetera," I said.

Torliam was slightly pacified, but as morning came, and then evening again, and they had not left, he grew distracted and ever more on edge. That tension spread back to the rest of the team. When he revealed that the Players had begun traveling in our direction, we lost any sense of ease we'd gained since coming to the hidden village.

The other Players moved closer over the next few days, till we were all on the brittle edge of fear and anticipation, and constantly asking Torliam for updates. We speculated that they were tracing us somehow, and NIX had sent a retrieval team for the valuable assets we represented. Or an assassination team.

Then, I had an idea. I sent Windows to the team and sent Birch to retrieve Torliam, and all of us except Kris and Gregor met in the library. I spread out a large map on the floor. "Point out where we are," I said to Torliam.

He did something to a little metal tab on its corner, and the drawings on the map wavered, the contents changing, flashing through different settings like it was diving downwards through them. "It shows the main layer now, which we are on. Somewhere around here is the village." He pointed to a blank spot, with no dot or label to indicate that people actually lived there.

I eyed the map, picking out landmarks and labels. "We started … here?" There was no marking for the Estreyan Stonehenge, so I was pointing to a blank spot.

"Yes."

I drew my finger haltingly along the map. "And the God of Knowledge is somewhere around here?" I waved a big, vague circle to the northwest of the village.

"Yes."

"So … what if they're not coming for us? I think they have no idea we're even here."

Everyone was focused on me, and Adam crouched down beside me to look at the map himself, already catching onto my meaning. "They want the God of Knowledge? How would they even know where to look?"

"NIX has been piecing together information about Estreyer since the beginning," Blaine said.

"Or …" a horrible thought filled my head. "Somehow, they got the information from me, or one of us."

"I did not say anything," Blaine said.

"I didn't mean by betrayal. What if they … have mind readers, or something? I mean, would that be such a crazy Skill?"

Torliam shook his head. "Skills such as that would not be gained from the lesser gods. At *most*, their Thinkers have extrapolated information based on data."

"However, this might have indeed been incited by you, Eve," Blaine said. "You were able to gain power by going directly after a god, and then used that against them. They would obviously wish to level the playing field, or at least make up in some small way for the great loss they have incurred from our escape."

Never mind that, I couldn't allow them to ruin my chances of getting aid from the God of Knowledge. "We need to follow them," I said aloud, my eyes focused on the vague area of the map where the god resided.

"Are you crazy?" Adam said.

I FROWNED AT ADAM. "There's no way I can just let this

happen without having any idea what's going."

"It could be dangerous, Eve! Why can't you just stay safely away? I know you have this burning need to be in the middle of things, but—"

"I'm dying. As far as I know, the God of Knowledge is probably the only one who can help me. I can't just let another team of Players go after something so vital, completely unsupervised! And don't worry, I'm not going to drag the whole team into it. Just me, and …" I looked around at them, judging their suitability for this mission. I'd promised myself I wouldn't put them in needless danger by rushing into an unknown, potentially dangerous situation like I had when China was killed. "And Torliam."

"What!?" Adam, Sam, Jacky, and Zed said in unison.

Chanelle whimpered, frowning at the heightened tension.

"This is a stealth mission. Recon. There's no need to bring everyone along, and it will be safer if people who don't need to be there stay behind."

"Wasn't the plan to get stronger, and maybe get Torliam to rustle up some reinforcements from his royal family, *before* you went rushing off to confront another god? The last time this happened, we had to fight. Sam almost died!"

"*Exactly.* You guys don't need to do this again. You'll be safe, whether or not I complete my vision."

"I've been training, every day," Jacky said, clenching her fists. "And I still have a lot of Seeds left, if I need them. It won't be like that mock battle, or when Vaughn beat us. I can be useful, Eve." Her voice was hard, but her eyes were almost begging.

Adam nodded. "She's right. What if you meet the other group, and they're hostile? If they're from NIX, they're almost certainly going to be hostile. If you *do* get into trouble, you might need help. We all have different skill-sets, and that's what makes us so effective as a team."

"There's no way you'd let one of *us* do something stupid like this by ourselves," Sam said, crossing his arms over his chest like that was the end of it.

"It's dangerous," I said weakly. "This is one of the strongest gods, and I'm almost certain he isn't going to be friendly, if the vision was correct. I plan to observe from as far away as possible, but if some of the things Torliam and I found are correct, even that might not be safe."

Adam ran a hand through his hair. "You do realize why that's not a good argument?"

Zed spoke, finally. "You're the leader of this team, Eve. But you're not the boss of me. I'm coming. And you don't need to worry about me. I know you hate what NIX did to me, but at least I can protect myself now." He turned to Jacky. "You need a hand packing up?"

She relaxed a bit, and nodded sharply. "Yeah." She didn't look at me as they left.

Blaine pushed his glasses up, and met my gaze. "I think you are foolish to even consider going alone, but I will be staying in the village with the kiddos. And Chanelle, of course. If something were to happen, they will need someone to protect them. And my first loyalty is to my family." There was a question in his voice, almost like he expected me to protest.

"That's fine! I would *prefer* you stayed here."

He nodded, though the sad little look he sent me wasn't at all subtle, and left.

Sam went to follow after Zed and Jacky, but looked at me uncertainly, and then shot a questioning glance at Adam.

Adam waved a hand at him. "I'll keep an eye on her and make sure she doesn't try to escape. Go pack."

Sam nodded, and left.

"Seriously?" I groaned.

"Don't pretend you weren't thinking about escaping," he said, grabbing me by the arm. "Come on, we both need to pack, too."

Torliam grabbed Chanelle by the hand, and pulled her along with Adam and me. "Your underlings are not very obedient." I could hear the grin in his voice.

"I'm not a servant," Adam snapped.

"Not a very *good* one," Torliam said, shaking his head.

THE WHOLE TEAM was ready to go in less than an hour. We already had packs ready with the supplies we needed. Add some water and food rations and we were finished.

"Do you have to go?" Kris said, picking up on the tension of our group, as we stood around outside the back of the elder's house.

"Knowledge is power," I said. "It's too dangerous *not* to go."

"That's ironic," Zed said.

Sam frowned. "Wait. If he's the God of Knowledge, does that mean he knows everything? Won't he know we're coming?"

I shrugged "If so, he *already* knows, so what difference does it make?"

Blaine frowned at me till we left, and the kids made me promise to communicate back to them with the VR chips.

Birch had grown big enough that we had to adjust the straps on his little pack. His wings were less fluffy than they had been, though I suspected it would be a long time before he could attain any significant speed or distance when traveling through the air.

The villagers gathered to watch us go, chattering amongst themselves. The news about what we were doing had gotten out, and they seemed to be excited about my "quest."

We set off at a light jog, Jacky and Zed both grinning crazily at each other as the villagers called out well wishes to us. "I can't say I'm averse to a little bit of fame," Zed said.

Adam and I rolled our eyes at him.

For the first few hours of running, we didn't communicate, except to relay what little information we had on the God of Knowledge, and to warn the others about the columns of light that seemed to be his power. I wore warmer Estreyan clothing over my vest, but the chill still slipped inside, and my breath fogged in the air.

Birch ran beside us for a while, but quickly tired from keeping up the pace and moved to a lazy spot perched on top of my backpack, claws dug in and wings furled so as not to affect my balance.

Torliam navigated for us, traveling diagonally toward the other Players on an angle that would have us catching up with them in a little over a day, if nothing changed.

The terrain morphed from the evergreen forests that had surrounded the secluded Estreyan town to rolling mountain ranges, interspersed with wide, lush valleys. Crystal clear streams and lakes speckled the valleys, and the greenery was sprinkled with tiny early-winter flowers.

I'm not sure if it was because of Torliam's presence, but the only large wildlife we saw was at a distance, and none seemed inclined to attack us. The solitude only heightened the ethereal beauty of the place.

Further out, these strange ... *growths* started to appear on the plants, in between the crevasses of the rocks. They looked like golden rods, or columns, reaching out toward the sky from every high place. They shone with a strange, harsh light, throwing shadows that were unnaturally dark. It should have been beautiful. Instead, it was creepy, like watching maggots crawl out underneath the lid of someone's wide open eye, eating live flesh instead of waste. It felt like they were watching. I could almost feel the light, sinking through my clothes, my skin, maybe even my *thoughts*.

Something was wrong.

Torliam felt the same. I could tell by the way his eyes never stayed still, drawn to the formations though they struggled to look elsewhere—anywhere else.

Birch growled, the sound low in his throat and constant.

"Sentinels? Like from the mural?" I whispered to Torliam as we ran, letting my words ghost out along with my breath.

He nodded, grim-faced.

My heart rate picked up a bit, and I had to force my claws not to come out in response. We traveled in silence again then, except for Torliam occasionally re-orienting us toward the other group of

Players. The farther we went, the larger the rods grew. Some of them looked like they had been boiled, bubbles forming from the surface. Those ones were always shorter, as if they had been stunted, and everything around them was long dead. Once, a column crumbled away near the bubbles as we passed, seemingly unable to bear the vibration of our footsteps.

Menace prickled in the air. To my Wraith Skill, the columns glowed with power, similar to the way strong Players did, or the rocks and water of Behelaino's mountain.

We stopped for the night on the side of a mountain where the rocks on either side provided a modicum of shelter, not long after darkness descended. We ate a cold meal of rations. There could be no fire, of course, and though the technology for portable hand-heaters no doubt existed on this world, we hadn't brought any. With how low-tech the village seemed in general, I wondered if they even had any.

Birch crawled inside the front of my borrowed clothes, burying everything but the tip of his nose away from the biting cold. He pressed his face against the side of my neck. His cold, wet nose touched my skin periodically, and the water in his breath condensed into a clammy sheen, sucking the warmth extra quickly out of that area.

I tucked my knees up against Birch's back, and wrapped my arm around them, trying to present as little body area to the outside as possible.

Torliam took the first watch, but with the occasional sounds of monsters in the distance, and the biting cold that I was completely sure had frozen the inside of my nostrils, I couldn't sleep.

"Lean against me." Torliam's low voice came out of the moonlit darkness. "Back to back. Soldiers do it, in my world. We can share each other's warmth, and if I arise because of a threat, there will be no need to shake you awake."

I shuffled over to him, ignoring Birch's annoyed grumble, and pressed my back against his much larger one, then tucked myself back into a ball. Heat radiated off his alien frame, and I relaxed a bit in the warmth. "Thanks," I muttered, before dozing off.

He woke me after a few hours and we switched places, me facing outward into the unknown of the night. I'm not sure if Torliam slept or not, but Birch crawled out of the front of my clothes and into Torliam's for the extra warmth, so I was a bit colder until my watch was over.

We rose with the sun, stretching and preparing for another long day of traveling.

Jacky wiped a runny nose on her sleeve, then punched Zed in the arm when he said, "Eewww!"

"If you catch a cold, I can heal you," Sam said to her. "But if it's not serious, I'd better conserve my energy."

"No," Jacky grunted. "M'fine."

Birch crawled out of Torliam's clothes, but when his paws touched the ground, he hopped around in shock at the cold and then jumped to me, begging for me to carry him with little pitiful mewls.

I scowled at him. "What kind of pet abandons their owner to the cold half the night and then wants to be carried in the morning?" I muttered.

He blinked at me, wide, human eyes looking completely innocent. He mewled again, this time even more pitifully, and lifted his front forepaw for a few limping steps, as if it was injured. Then he stopped and looked back to me, obviously wondering if I'd bought his 'poor-little-kitty' act.

I sighed gustily and held out my arms to him, once again tucking him into the front of my clothes with only his head peeking out under my chin. "I guess I forgive you."

Torliam snorted loudly, and when I shot a narrow-eyed look at him, he shook his head. "You are a slave to his every whim," he said. But he reached out and briefly scratched the top of Birch's head, somehow-warm fingers brushing against my chin in the process.

Adam stayed silent, and glared at everything for pretty much the whole day as we traveled.

I'd been sending sporadic Windows to Blaine and the kiddos, but the farther we traveled, the higher on a mountain I had to be before they would go through. I knew there was nothing they would be able to do to help if something went wrong, but being cut off from outside communication made me antsy.

It was late afternoon when Torliam stopped us. "We are drawing close to them, and most likely also converging on *him*." He drew two lines on the ground to represent our path and the path of the other Players, and circled our future intercept point.

We proceeded slightly slower after that, wary of being noticed by either the Players or the god. My awareness was strained to its limit, and felt a bit sore, like a muscle I'd stretched too far and too long. But it was useful, because I could feel the ambient energy shining through the air as we approached something gargantuan and powerful, though still too far away for me to sense directly.

"We shouldn't get any closer," I said.

Torliam nodded, then pointed to the top of a nearby mountain that was taller than the rest. It would be a good vantage point.

We all climbed up the back of the mountain in tense silence, hurrying now to get high enough before the other team either reached the God of Knowledge, or the sun went down and reduced visibility.

We reached a good vantage point and moved around to the side of the mountain so that we could peek out behind a rock.

"We'll watch the rear," Adam said. "I don't trust this place." Adam and Sam stopped a few feet down, and turned to face outward.

It was about thirty minutes before sundown, and the shadows of the mountains stretched long, and grew longer almost fast enough to track their progress.

I poked my head over the rock in front of me, and looked down onto the God of Knowledge for the first time.

Chapter 20

Rage, rage against the dying of the light.
— Dylan Thomas

THE GOD'S valley was covered in gold. The shrubbery seemed to be made of it, as did the rocks and dirt, from the floor to halfway up the surrounding mountains. Golden columns shot up high, weaving and connecting together almost like a ... shrine. Or like an open-air, majestic chapel, with one column shooting from the joining point of the others, reaching *high* into the sky.

The god himself looked like a huge, Greek statue made out gold, more *human* than the other two gods I'd seen. Or maybe, more Estreyan would be a better word. No human was quite that perfectly sculpted. Or that gargantuan.

His back was turned to us, and I had an absurd curiosity to see whether his ... *bits*, were realistically proportioned, or baby-small like the statue of David.

I pushed that thought out of my mind as I saw that he faced the other team, who had come from the far side of the valley.

Torliam's arm pressed against mine. His eyes were wide and intensely focused down below. Tension fairly radiated off of him.

As I turned my attention back to the uneasy meeting down below, I noticed the valley wasn't quite as flawless as I had first thought it.

Some of the columns had crumbled away, or were affected by those strange stunting bubbles. The God of Knowledge's left arm was peeling like he'd been a victim of the worst sunburn in living history, one of his knees chipped away at the bend in the back of his leg, and his molded illusion of hair left dust trails every time he moved the slightest bit.

I frowned. It almost looked like he was rusting. But gold didn't rust, did it? The thought tickled a half-formed idea in the back of my mind, but I was so focused on the scene below that I didn't pay attention, and it slipped away.

The Players, moving toward the god from the far side of the valley, had brought less than a full squad. Or maybe, some had died along the way. The ones I could see looked a bit bedraggled, and some had minor injuries.

I squinted, doing my best to see more clearly against the light of the setting sun on my face.

One of the Players stepped forward, away from the rest of the group. He was probably speaking, but I was too far away to hear. He dropped to one knee in an obvious show of respect.

Was that ... Vaughn? A shiver of cold wracked me as I noticed another familiar face. "It's Kilburn's team," I murmured.

"If I didn't wanna do it myself, I'd wish goldilocks here would just kill him," Jacky murmured back. It was the first unnecessary thing she'd said to me since we left the village.

"I know why you have come—cuddle." The God of Knowledge's voice resounded out and upwards from down below, loud, smooth, and almost nondescript in its perfection. It was like an amalgamation of so many pleasing voices blended together that the end result was unremarkable. But ... "cuddle?" Was that an Estreyan word?

I looked to Torliam for confirmation, but he just shook his head with a frown, and gave a one shouldered shrug.

"You think—apple—gain power from—" That time, he just cut off, like a recording where the sound glitched out. "What arrogance! Instead, you will—hairless—my sustenance. Give thanks for this opportunity to—beefcake—a role in maintaining my strength."

I'm pretty sure the group down below wasn't expecting that any more than I was. They lost a couple precious seconds exchanging looks of wary confusion. It was more than enough time for the god to act.

They all suddenly went stiff, and wide-eyed. Vaughn was kneeling, and just low enough that his face was in the shadow of the mountains, unlike the others. He was only illuminated by the strange glow from the golden beams.

I saw his eyes flash with two pinpricks of reflected light, like a nocturnal animal.

The god strode forward smoothly, only the tiniest limp apparent from his decaying knee, and picked up two of them by the neck. They didn't react, and he tossed them bodily over his shoulders, into the area surrounded by columns that I had earlier thought of as the chapel. Two more followed them, but the fifth, he didn't throw.

He clamped down hard with one hand on her arm, right below the shoulder, then twisted right below that point, like taking the cap off a water bottle. Then he *tore* the broken arm away, and raised the bloody end to his mouth, letting the blood drip down into it.

The pain seemed to have released his victim from whatever trance she was in, because she started jerking and screaming. But she didn't reach for her shoulder, or even try to escape his grip. Instead, her remaining hand tore at her own eyeballs, digging at the soft flesh till they were just bloody, pulped holes in her face, blood streaming down her cheeks like tears.

The arm stopped streaming blood, and he bit into it, bone and all. I could see the edge of his jaw from behind, chewing slowly and swallowing like he was at a formal dinner rather than holding a hysteric human in his hand and eating her raw flesh. His too-perfect voice vibrated the hairs on my skin as he moaned in pleasure.

I was frozen, my own mouth seeming to alternate between dryness and the overabundance of saliva that prefaced violent vomiting.

Jacky must have felt the same, because she ducked back down behind the rock, vomiting in the quietest way she could manage.

The girl's teammates weren't reacting, still caught in their trances, until suddenly one of the taller columns broke for no apparent reason, crumbling at the base and falling to the ground.

The Player closest to it jerked, a single sharp spasm, and then *screamed*. Voice cracking, and then breaking, then gurgling on his own bloody vocal cords.

Birch grabbed the back of my pants and kept tugging, as if trying to drag me away.

I'd heard screams like that before, in the Trials. Humans reach a certain point where the thing that separates us from animals just … breaks. We lose ourselves. And then, sometimes we scream like that.

Chapter 21

Darkness, once gazed upon, can never be lost.
— John Milton

THE GOD DROPPED HIS SNACK, and moved to throw the screamer and the others who were still frozen into the chapel.

Torliam laid a hand on my arm, and the warmth of it startled me out of the trance I'd been held in, as I watched the creature down below so easily conquer the humans.

My eyes met Torliam's, and as one, we turned to go. But I looked back.

Vaughn was running frantically, apparently freed from whatever had been holding him and the other Player, who was still screaming. He saw me. A moment of confusion, then comprehension, then hope. He mouthed "help" at me, the word silent from this distance, though it must have been a scream.

No. No way was I going down there to try and save them. "Run, guys," I barked. "Run away!" I pushed off the rock in front of me, moving just a little too high above the edge.

The god stiffened, even as I turned, as if we were a spider that

240

he had just felt running over his neck. He turned toward us with a speed that would have disabused me of any notions about his humanity, if I'd had any.

I saw his face for the first time, and it forced that last little bit of fear into me. Except for the nose and mouth, it was a smooth face. He had no eyes. No place where eyes would be. Just smooth, featureless gold. As if whoever sculpted him had forgotten the most important part.

The light hit me before I could continue my spin. Everything around me grew bright, the colors standing out even more vividly, tinged with a glowing golden hue, and the world slowed.

The brightness grew, until it overwhelmed my vision, burning into my pupils, and scorching the back of my retinas with cold instead of heat. When I was a child, I touched a piece of dry ice that was making the fog at a Halloween party. It was so cold, the skin of my fingertip fused to it instantly, and it *burned* me, just as well as touching a glowing hot coal would have. This was like that.

It burrowed past my retinas, in a scorching path straight for my brain. I had a single moment of panicked rejection, a "No," sounding in my mind, but then it was inside.

The brain doesn't have pain receptors, or so they say. Yet, I could feel the little maggots burrowing through my thoughts, like a physical sensation. They searched, and they found.

Memory exploded through my consciousness, along with a strange dreamlike *understanding*.

I was young, small, and thoughtless. I called another girl stupid when she made a silly comment in class. She clammed up and turned away from me, pointedly ignoring and avoiding me for the rest of the day. I never saw her after that year, because she moved to a lower-income district when her mother died.

I was afraid, weak, and useless. Chanelle helped me, standing beside me in my first Trial. If she'd never met me, she would not have slipped in the blood. She would not have died with her throat being ripped out by a rabid fellow Player, and would not have left her sister alone to rely on me.

I was stressed, untrusting, and protective. I told Zed to leave me alone, pushed him away, and did my best to extract him from all the new areas of my life. As the new areas, the ones where I was a Player, took over my *entire* life, I tried to push him out of that, too. He felt abandoned by the person who had been a best friend and unloved by someone he had thought cared unconditionally. He kept coming back for more abuse, desperately trying to fix whatever problem had caused it. He wondered if maybe he'd been wrong about how close he and I were. He sat in the corner of his room, slumped over, shoving fists into burning eyes in a failed attempt to hold back shameful tears. And then he got up again, and kept trying till he no longer expected a different response.

I was desperate, and selfish. I purposely took advantage of China, because I wanted her strength to protect me, just as her sister had done. I convinced her to trust me, to work with me, and even rely on me. Then, like her sister, she died. Protecting me. Her hand held out in a vain attempt stop the oncoming threat of Kilburn's power. Her body twisting, her eyes meeting mine for the last time.

I was terrified, panicking, and selfish. I twisted the last piece of the puzzle in my hands into place, releasing myself from my cage. Across from me, the girl, who had been just as frightened as me, screamed as the black stone turned to devouring mist, sinking through her skin, and corroding her from the inside. She could feel her bones giving way first, dissolving till they could no longer support her weight, then her muscles, tendons, organs. She screamed until she could no longer scream, watched me until her eyes were gone, too, and was in the end thankful that even with all that, she had lost, and not allowed herself to become a monster just because of fear.

The snippets of memory and understanding hit me, one after the other, an onslaught of the times I'd made the wrong decision, hurt another person, caused pain and sorrow and death. And I was forced to not only to remember, but to understand. I saw the connections, cause and effect, and I *knew* the pain I'd created as if

I'd had to endure it myself. I knew it like a lover, like the feel of my fingers, like my own reflection in the mirror, my ice blue eyes blazing back at me.

I hurt.

So bad.

And it went on and on, until suddenly, I was torn away. I could feel the cold maggots trying to keep their grip on me, but slipping away, back out through my eyes with a ripping sensation.

MY VISION DIDN'T RETURN at first. Wind whipped past my ears, a warm body pressed against me, arms wrapped around me, Birch yowled, and I tasted blood in my mouth. I'd bitten my tongue.

A loud sound passed through the air, cutting through the sound of the wind, and it took me far too long to process it. It was a roar, sounded in the melodious screams of thousands of smooth voices, too loud to be human. My body vibrated painfully at the sound, and my eardrums pretty much just gave up.

As my vision returned through dark spots like I'd been staring into the sun, I realized that Torliam had tackled me off the side of the mountain, and we were falling. It was eerily similar to the end of my first foray into NIX, and Adam's tackle that saved me from the same fate as China. That had happened because I made the wrong choices.

I had the horrible feeling that something similarly terrible had just happened, but I was too mentally overwhelmed to figure out what had gone wrong.

Each moment passed at a bovinely slow pace, but I realized finally that there was no river to break our fall, and we would no doubt soon crash into the unforgiving rocks below.

I caught a blurry glimpse of Birch, his claws digging into Torliam's back, wings flapping frantically, trying to slow us down. It was futile. He wasn't even big enough to fly.

Where were the others? Had they fallen? Were they trapped in the light, too?

Torliam began to glow. It wasn't like the glow of the golden helixes, rather it was ripples of visible sky blue that looked almost liquid, a physical thing instead of ephemeral light.

Then, suddenly I was jerked sideways, and then immediately sideways again. He must have been jumping from rock to rock as we fell to slow our fall. Then, a sudden drag had my insides protesting at the change in inertia. I was flipped so I could see the ground past Torliam instead of the sky for half an instant. One of Torliam's arms released me and ripped Birch around to my side, on top of him, and then the three of us met the earth.

The impact almost knocked me out. It did knock the breath out of me, even though Torliam had cushioned the fall with his own body.

My teeth had smashed together when we hit, and my left arm had been jerked around a little bit. It ached, from shoulder to fingertip. A horrible sense of foreboding rose in me as the rippling light disappeared. I ignored my lungs' screaming for air, and peeled my body upward.

My vision had gone wonky again when we hit, but it normalized quickly when my brain settled in my skull. I looked around at the small but relatively deep crater surrounding us.

Torliam must have created the hole with his power, somehow, along with slowing our fall. And cushioning both Birch and I with his own body.

Adam, it had to be, was sliding down the mountainside inside a black ink box with a sled-like curve on the bottom. I hoped Jacky and Sam were with him, because I didn't see them anywhere else. I would have called out, but I couldn't talk, as my lungs had yet to regain the ability to breathe.

Torliam's eyes were closed, his face screwed into a grimace.

I stabilized myself on his chest with my good arm and used the left to check his pulse at the neck. It was still beating strongly, and another quick check confirmed he was still breathing. I rolled painfully off him toward Birch, who had bounced and rolled off to the side from the rebound of our impact.

Birch lay on his side, belly rising and falling shallowly as he breathed in and out with quick little pants.

I laid my hand gently on his side and stretched my Perception out, into his body, looking for what was wrong.

He had fractured bones in the wing he was laying on, and a good amount of bruising already forming. His eardrums were ... ruptured? I could feel a bit of blood beginning to seep out of his large, tufted ears. I guess it wouldn't have mattered if I could speak, because he couldn't hear me anyway.

I lifted my hand and placed it gently on top of his furry head in reassurance, fighting to regain my own breath, and take stock of my own injuries. My left arm hurt, deep and *aching*. There were consequences when humans got turned into hamburger—consequences even miraculous healer Sam couldn't get rid of.

My chest and stomach ached, a sour, burning sensation. I realized inanely that it was *emotional* pain. Guilt. Regret. Uncertainty. I would have scoffed at that, but it truly, seriously hurt to the point it distracted me from my physical injuries. What had the god done to me?

More blood filled my mouth, and I spat it out, along with a large, jagged chunk of tooth. My eyes caught for a fraction of a second on the white bone amongst the bloody spatter, and moved on. No time for that now.

Bruised ribs on myself as well, and one of my knees had slipped past Torliam's side and hit the ground in our fall. Kneecap broken, but not completely shattered. I still couldn't hear anything, except for a faint, metallic ringing sound.

I felt a bit dizzy, and wondered if that was because of my ears, or if perhaps I had a concussion. I shook my head to try and clear it, which instead sent a throbbing wave of pain through it. No *time* for this! How long had it been since we hit the ground?

I scooted over to Torliam and slapped his cheek lightly. No doubt, he'd taken more impact than either Birch or I, but he was also an Estreyan. I needed him awake, and in commission, if I was going to make it out of this. And I didn't have time to wait for him. The unjustifiably beautiful monster in the valley behind us could be preparing an attack, either by physically coming after us, or using his golden growths.

Adam scrambled down into the hole, Jacky and Sam half a second slower than him. Adam threw up an ink shield over the top, drowning out what light remained. Sealing us away from the light of the sentinels.

That was why Torliam had created a hole, I knew. But in battle, if you couldn't move, you died. And we were trapped within.

I felt Torliam's groan under my hands. I sent a Window to Sam, in lieu of verbal instruction.

—TORLIAM IS HURT. PRIORITIZE HIS HEALING.—
-EVE-

While Sam placed his hands on Torliam's exposed skin, I reached out as far out as possible with my Wraith Skill. It hurt my brain, and I had a sudden surge of nausea, but I could feel the blindingly bright power of the god on the other side of the intervening mountain, along with many other smaller points of power where the helixes burst from the ground.

The god's power was surging, probably with anger, but he didn't seem to be physically coming after us, at least not yet. And the golden light didn't reach us where we were.

Torliam's eyes opened, and I drew back my focus, blinking to clear the blurriness.

Jacky had broken a glow stick, and its eery light made our huddled group visible.

The distinct taste of tears washed away the blood on the tip of my tongue, and that's when I realized I was crying. I didn't even try to stop, because I knew I couldn't.

Torliam frowned when his eyes met my own, and I said, "Are

you okay? Can you move?" He didn't have a VR chip, so I hoped he could understand me. It was strange to feel my voice box vibrating, and know that I was speaking, but not actually be able to hear myself.

He nodded, and then immediately winced at the movement of his head. But he rolled over anyway, then rose to his hands and knees.

I saw his lips moving, and interrupted whatever he was saying. "I can't hear you," I said. "My eardrums are probably ruptured. You weren't out long, less than a minute, I *think*. I'm not entirely sure. I may have a concussion. The God—*it's* not coming after us, yet." I realized suddenly I was almost shouting, and tried to lower my sound output, which is harder than you think. "We need to stay out of the light." I shook my head. "You know that already, sorry, I'm rambling. But we do need to move, it's not safe to stay here. And Birch is hurt," my voice broke, more tears spilling out of my eyes.

I used the gauze wrap I'd brought since Sam's healing ability was limited, and bound Birch's wings to his body. Only the one was injured, but I couldn't find a quick way to secure it while leaving the other free, and figured just the one wing wouldn't be useful for anything anyway.

Birch woke up while I was doing that, likely from the pain, and I whispered to him, "You're okay. I'm just making sure your wing doesn't get hurt anymore. We've got to move, soon. Can you walk on your own?"

He struggled to his feet, and his mouth opened, though I couldn't tell what type of sound he was making. He touched his nose to my hand, and something foreign flashed in my mind. Two human legs, blurry facial features—blue eyes, dark hair—a strong smell, and the feel of warmth.

I jerked my hand back in horror, until I realized that it had been Birch behind the images, not the god. The little creature's "first words." I regretted that I didn't have time to celebrate the momentous occasion.

Then the very ground and air around us vibrated, and my ears screamed again. All of us except Torliam winced bodily and hunched over, me with my palms to the side of my head, leaning over Birch.

When the incomprehensible sound ended, I uncurled and opened my eyes to find Torliam crouching over me, just as I was crouching over Birch. He laid his hand on my back, and said something.

I shook my head silently. "My ears aren't working," I reminded him. I considered putting a couple of the Seeds I'd been saving into Resilience, but almost discarded the idea. I had so many Seeds in that Attribute, I doubted a couple more would make much difference to my eardrums in the short term. Then I remembered that those Seeds were there to offset the effects of Chaos, and were most likely busy doing that, with nothing to spare for injuries caused by outside stimuli. Maybe a couple more *would* help. Besides, I'd probably be putting them into Resilience or Life soon anyway, as Chaos grew stronger. This wasn't an injury I wanted to waste Sam's reserves on, especially not when I could use the VR chip to communicate with most of them.

So I went ahead and dug three Seeds out of their secure place in the center of my pack, and put them into Resilience. I barely noticed the side effects, except for a vague sense of physical relief.

Torliam shuddered when I injected them, and I slipped the empty Seed shells back into my pack awkwardly. He didn't react further, other than a tightening of his lips, so I tried to put it from my mind.

I was so mentally scrambled, it wasn't hard. I couldn't stop seeing the things the light had pulled from my memory and explained to me in unflinching bluntness.

Torliam laid his hand on my arm, causing me to jump and bring my focus back onto my immediate situation. Damn, what was wrong with me?

He leaned forward and placed his lips behind my ear, and I stiffened despite the pain it caused me to do so, freaked out in a completely different way. Then, his lips started to move, and I felt the vibration of it in my skull. He was talking, and with a little push of Perception, I could understand him even without my eardrums.

"The god said that we might hide from his light until we grew too weak to resist him, or come out when desperation settled heavy on us, and be captured then. I believe he expects us to remain trapped here. I have remembered some of the research I did before, and from what I know of him, he is not one to move from his seat of power in a physical way. He will try and trap us in his light, but if we can escape that, perhaps we will live."

I nodded. "But how do we escape *light?*"

"In truth, I do not know. His power is made to pierce defenses. It reaches brightest into the darkness, transfixing through any shields of deceit. It speaks well to your underling's concentration that his constructs were able to shield against it."

"But we're safe here, with the earth surrounding us, right?"

"In essence. His light travels straighter than most. The ... bouncing off of things? It does not happen as much. It is not like sunlight, or manmade light. It is meant to travel far and straight. Does that make sense?"

I nodded again, though I wasn't quite sure. Maybe the light from the golden columns was like a laser. I sent Windows to the other three explaining this.

Sam put his hand over my knee, touching my skin through the torn fabric there. My kneecap shifted, and whatever had been broken fused back into place.

I let out a sigh of relief.

—IT'S ONLY A BASIC JOIN. IT WILL BREAK AGAIN IN THE SAME SPOT IF YOU'RE TOO ROUGH WITH IT, TOO SOON.—
-SAM-

Jacky inched over to me, when he was finished, and found my hand in the dark.

—Are you okay? Sorry I didn't drag you away soon
enough. I didn't even know what was happening.—
-Jacky-

I squeezed her hand.

—I'm okay. Can't stop crying, though. That thing did
something to my head.—
-Eve-

The ink covering over our little nook evaporated, and Adam
tossed out another shield, but in the brief moment of twilight, I
saw his wide-eyed look of exhaustion.

I questioned, and he answered.

—Whatever that light is, it's attacking my shield. If
we weren't dug into the ground, I don't think I could
keep this up.—
-Adam-

"If we had something to *reflect* the light, instead of trying to
block it?" I murmured aloud. "But I didn't bring anything like
that. And my Skills aren't any good for something like that."

Torliam's head lifted, then, and his eyes met my own, obviously thinking quickly. "I am of the line of Aethezriel," he said,
touching me so I could interpret his vibrations.

—Why doesn't he have a VR chip, again?—
-Adam-

Wraith could feel the scowl on Adam's face, which I ignored
along with his question, in favor of the more pressing matter.

"Okay…? You told me your last name before. What does that
have to do with anything?" I frowned. "I really hope this name

sharing isn't some type of before-death ritual for you guys, because I'm damn sure not giving up."

"Aethezriel is not my *name*. It is my *line*. My ... ancestry. It is the line of power that has been passed down since ancient times."

" ... Your Skill? Is that what you're saying? Aethezriel is the power you have?"

"Aethezriel is my ancestor, who mated with a god. But, your meaning is correct."

I tried to think of the implications of what he was saying, but I couldn't concentrate. I lifted my good arm and wiped away the line of my tears, sniffing to clear my nose. "So why is that important? Can you get us out of this?"

"My power comes from the god of the upper air. It is a greater power, like your own Chaos. It is the bloodline of a god with a wide domain. There are many aspects—interpretations—of the power, if you know how to draw them out. One of them is *light*."

I smiled then, a sudden relief coming over me. "Oh. Well that sounds promising."

"As your incompetent scientists may have discovered, light is quite interesting. I may be able to oppose the light of his sentinels, using an opposite, ahh ... *vibration*, to nullify its reach."

"You're going to cancel out—" my breath hitched as my body tried to sob and I tried to restrain it, "the wavelength, like sound." Hey, I'd learned plenty in my relatively short lifetime, and my upgraded brain was good enough to put together at least that much. "But is that even possible? You can't think faster than light."

"His light is very steady. You are correct, I may not think faster, but if I can anticipate ahead of time and set up a pattern, perchance it will not matter."

After I relayed this to the rest of them, Adam opened up a hole in the edge of the ink lid, positioned so that the light from outside wouldn't hit any of us directly. It was enough for Torliam to test his theory.

The blue light rippled out of Torliam again, and he reached a hand wreathed in it upward, through the hole up above and over the edge of the crater.

Nothing happened, other than the muscles in his face and neck straining taut. But then the area around his hand started to change. I felt like my eyes were deceiving me in the fading light, but when I reached out with my Perception, I saw the same thing. Between the light of Torliam's power and that of the sentinel was an area of darkness. Not a shadow. A place where the light just … stopped. It ceased to exist. I'd seen quite a bit in the time since I'd become a Player, but this was something else.

Something no human had ever seen before, probably. I stared for a moment, the little involuntary shudders my body was making easing as I became fully distracted from my own mind. It was beautiful, in a frightening sort of way.

Torliam pulled his hand back, and his light faded. His breath came fast, and when he moved back to me and laid his mouth against my temple, I could feel the sweat, cold and clammy on his skin.

Whatever he'd done, it wasn't easy.

"He is strong, so close to the seat of his power. And … loathe as I am to admit it, even in the height of my own power, I would have had difficulty shielding all of us." He paused, and then said, "I am far from the height of my power," with a heavy significance, shoulders drooping.

When she read my Window of explanation, Jacky squeezed my hand, hard enough that my joints protested. The sharp pain of it distracted my mind from both the images and the aching of the rest of my body.

Torliam couldn't get us out. Adam wasn't going to last much longer. Sam and Jacky didn't have any Skills relevant to the situation. And the dirt was as good a shield from the light as any. It didn't take long for me to realize what I needed to do. I kept thinking anyway, because I was hoping to come up with something else. When I didn't, I let out a drooping sigh of my own. "If we were farther away, where the sentinels were smaller and more dispersed, could you shield us all?"

"For short distances, maybe. But we would need places to hide again when my stamina ran its course."

I nodded, then closed my eyes. I didn't really need them closed to send out my Perception anymore, but psychologically, it helped. I concentrated as best I could, trying to calculate the "dimmest" areas nearby, in any direction that could lead us away from the god behind us, who I could practically feel the *crazy* radiating off of.

I found the most advantageous spot, and then with a deep breath, I gestured for everyone to move aside.

Once they'd huddled to one side of the small cavity, I pushed Chaos out with a surge, forming it into a clumsy drill of destruction, though it resisted my attempts to constrain it to any form. Still, it did what it was supposed to, and the dirt in front of me collapsed in a slide of gritty sand. Weariness washed through me. I'd put too much power into it. We didn't need sand. Pebbles would have done.

Torliam understood the plan quickly, but when I moved to start scooping away the sand with my hands, he motioned for us to move back and cover our eyes.

I did so, after making sure Birch was safely behind me just in case, and watched with my Perception as Torliam created a short, hard burst of wind that cleared the tunnel I'd made. I shook my head, letting the blown sand fall off me, and opened my eyes.

The ink lid disintegrated again, and this time, Adam couldn't reform another immediately. I slammed my eyes shut, and hunched flat to the ground, only sitting up again when complete darkness was restored.

—I THOUGHT USING CHAOS HURT YOU.—
-JACKY-

—EVE, THIS WILL ACCELERATE THE TIMELINE FOR CHAOS OVERTAKING YOUR HEALING ABILITIES.—

-Sam-

I closed my eyes, unseen by anyone except maybe Torliam in the semi-darkness. At this point, did it really matter? I'd hoped that the God of Knowledge would be the answer to my problems. Whether he agreed to help me or not, I'd hoped that I'd be able to get what I needed from him, even if I ended up having to take a piece of his Seed core, to mitigate the effects of Behelaino's. But he was crazy. Crazy like the spidermonkey. There was no way he was going to help, and anything from him would be tainted, anyway.

—It'll be okay. I have plenty of Seeds left.—
-Eve-

Torliam and I shared a nod, and I crouched down, shuffling the couple feet into the tunnel and repeating the drill of Chaos with a bit less force, then retreating so he could clear it again.

My knee hurt a bit every time I moved, and Torliam was so big he had to army crawl through the small tunnel, but I couldn't spare the power to make it bigger, if this was going to work. It was a lot of back and forth shuffling, to clear the volume of dirt we needed. Dirt and sand got into my clothes, my eyes, and my mouth.

I grew tired, and Torliam took over digging out the tunnel, though his power wasn't suited to it.

When he grew tired, Jacky crawled down and began to hack at the dirt and rock with her bare hands, digging like a dog. It was surprisingly effective, with her Strength and Stamina. It also peeled back her fingernails, which she ignored until I noticed and forced her to stop, so Sam could at least help her nail beds scar over.

Eventually, we got enough of the tunnel dug so that all of us could fit in it at once—though not comfortably—without being exposed to outside light from above. That allowed Adam to take much needed breaks from shielding us against the sentinels.

Halfway to our destination we stopped and ate some of the rations we'd brought, while I took a couple more Seeds.

It took half the night to reach our destination, which was only a few hundred meters from where we'd stared. "Your turn from here," I murmured to Torliam and Adam, repeating myself with Windows to translate as I spoke. "I don't know if you can tell, but the easiest path—with the least light—takes us in a loop around the line of rocks out there, and then a sharp turn to the right." I gestured without looking over the edge of the tunnel.

We all held hands, and Adam picked Birch up, doing his best not to press on the creature's injuries.

The blue light wafted off Torliam again and spread to cover all of us, and after a few moments, he nodded and took a step forward.

I moved in sync with him, ignoring my kneecap as it grated.

When we hit the golden light, a barrier of darkness immediately spread out where it intersected with Torliam's own. He grunted, but kept moving forward, breathing harder with each step, each exhalation visible in the freezing air. He was trembling as if he'd just completed a race when we reached the spot I'd indicated, and I wasted no time unleashing my own power into the earth, creating a hiding place for us, so he could release his power.

Then, we tunneled only a bit further and took a break, because Torliam would have a much harder time negating the god's light in the full light of the fluctuating sun. And because I needed the rest.

Even so, the spontaneous bleeding started again, right before we reached the end of the second tunnel, and with it came a wave of *agonizing* pain. I flopped onto the hard-packed ground below, twitching and moaning as it washed over me.

Someone put their hand on my shoulder, saying something I couldn't hear.

When the pain passed, I lifted my head from the ground, spitting out the dirt I'd bitten mindlessly into, and wiping away the stringy saliva my mouth had created from the nauseating agony.

"At least I didn't bite my tongue," I muttered, forcing a small smile.

Adam said nothing back, but his hands were exceedingly gentle as he helped me back to my hands and knees, as if I were made of eggshells, or flower petals, or something.

When darkness came, we tunneled again, till morning hit.

I took another handful of Seeds, carefully not looking at Torliam as I did. My supply wouldn't last long, at this rate.

We were going to run out of water soon, and food not long after that. I hoped that we could escape far enough from the god's reach before it became an issue.

I slept deeply, aided by a touch of Sam's hand to my forehead, and whatever he'd secreted through his skin into mine.

When I woke, a Window was hanging in front of my face, from the Oracle.

Chapter 22

I have won every battle but scarred my soul.
— Laodisia

KILL THE GOD OF KNOWLEDGE
DESTROY THIS MANIFESTATION OF THE GOD OF
KNOWLEDGE BEFORE THE SMALL MOON HAS
DARKENED THRICE, DEALING THE FINAL BLOW BY
YOUR OWN HAND.
COMPLETION REWARD: KNOWLEDGE ABOUT THE
SEED OF CHAOS
NON-COMPLETION PENALTY: DEATH

WELL, shit.

I wanted to assume the Oracle was guiding me for the better. I was trying to be smart about it, and not make the same mistakes I had with NIX. It seemed like she'd been aiding me so far, cryptically showing me the path that was best for me.

But I couldn't defeat the God of Knowledge. Even with my whole team, and Torliam, we wouldn't even come close to being better than him. The Oracle had just given me a suicide mission, with the penalty for failure being death.

Perversely, the seemingly insurmountable obstacle actually helped to calm me. It gave me a problem to work on, something to solve and overcome. It was something I could actually *do* something about, and it helped give me the focus to push the memories the god had forced on me from the front of my mind.

Working under the assumption that the Oracle wouldn't give me a quest that was literally impossible to complete, there was *something* I could do. I just needed to figure out what. As far as willingness went, I had no qualms getting revenge on the god.

Especially if by doing so I might be able to save myself from death.

So, I bent my mind to the usual questions. My problem—I wanted to defeat the God of Knowledge. What did I have? What did I need to get where I wanted?

I had myself, probably my team, and maybe Torliam, if he could be convinced. I needed more information about the god, but a preliminary estimation put him at about ten times stronger than *all* of us.

I was forced to admit that I couldn't make the team ten times stronger before time ran out for me. Could I instead make our enemy that much weaker? It sounded nice, but I had no idea how to go about doing such a thing, or if it was even possible. Maybe I could somehow get the Oracle to work against him. She was the one who wanted him dead, after all.

I groaned and rolled over, setting aside my thoughts for the moment. My body protested against the abuse of the cold, damp ground beneath me. An aching stiffness had seeped into my bones as I slept, and I felt like an old, old woman, whose body had been forced to stay on the earth too long.

Birch lay on his stomach in the corner of our little dugout, breathing shallowly.

"Did you sleep at all?" I whispered, leaning over the cub and placing a hand gently on his forehead.

He let out a faint squeak, and I sighed. I turned to Sam, who was already awake, his back pressed against the wall of our little hole. "Is there anything you can do for him?" I said aloud, testing the sound of my own voice in my healing ears.

"I'm pretty much out of juice. And my Skill has never really worked that well on animals, anyway. I'm sorry."

I nodded. "Well, help me out, then. We're going to have to do this the old-fashioned way." I took a few deep breaths and expanded my awareness through my hand, into Birch's body. "This might hurt a bit," I whispered to him. "But try not to move."

Sam lay his hands gently on Birch's body, ready to restrain the small creature if the pain was too much.

I nodded my thanks and gave him a small smile, though my focus remained on the injuries beneath my hand. The bones in Birch's wing needed to be set. I understood vaguely what needed to be done, thanks to the mandatory training I'd received in NIX's classes, but we'd never practiced setting a *wing*.

I unwrapped the gauze, then gripped the feathered appendage in my hand and pulled, using my Perception to make sure the bones within were shifting and meeting back together as they should.

Birch stiffened and I heard the faint sound of his scream.

Sam made sure Birch couldn't move enough to hurt himself in his pain, and I splinted and re-wrapped the wing carefully, so the bones wouldn't shift around.

Birch settled down with a shuddering sigh when I was finished, but after that he breathed easier, and seemed to fall asleep.

We still had a couple hours till sundown, so we sated our hunger with a worryingly large portion of the remaining rations, and then I meditated. I should have done it the night before, but I'd been so exhausted, and distracted, that I'd forgotten. It helped, both with my physical body and with the pseudo-flashbacks.

When the sun set, we continued on, again alternating between tunneling, Torliam's strange light wave negation, and Adam's ink barriers. As we got farther away from the God of Knowledge and his sentinels grew sparser and weaker, we were able to do much more above-ground traveling. We were all hurt, tired, and scared, and my ears were still healing, so I found myself relying even more on my Perception to scan the surroundings.

It took us two days to get close enough for my Windows to reach Blaine again. We'd run out of food by then, and Torliam said it was okay for us to drink the water around us, but only if it was running water, and only if I used Chaos to force it to a boil first.

"I told Blaine not to come meet us," I said, my voice cracking from disuse. "Not till we're away from the sentinels." I didn't know what might happen if the god discovered them coming to meet us, but it couldn't be anything good.

"Good. There is no need to place others in danger. The Sickness has reached so far …" I thought he was finished talking, but he suddenly spoke up again. "I believe we have completed your vision quest from the Oracle, now. It is obvious, I think, that you will not be getting any aid from the God of Knowledge. I do not know the purpose of her revelation, but perhaps when I am home again, this news will bring good somehow. Or maybe, it is just a warning that the end is near."

"We have to come back!" I blurted out.

"We had a deal, human." His voice deepened ominously. "I will not put myself in danger just because you cannot accept that the Oracle did not lead you to salvation."

My stomach soured with apprehension. I needed him, or the whole quest would fall apart. I couldn't let him decide he'd fulfilled the deal and just *leave*. "You'll have to return. The Oracle sent me another quest."

Adam's head snapped around. "What? Why didn't you say something?"

"I was … in shock." I let vulnerability slip into my voice, and bit down on my bottom lip. "Because it's to kill the God of Knowledge. And I have no idea how to do that."

"That was not part of our bargain, and you know it well." Torliam loomed over me, and I'm not ashamed to say the hairs on the back of my neck rose at the sudden sense of danger.

Adam's hands twitched toward the cells of electricity at his waist, and Jacky turned her body sideways to Torliam, for better leverage to block or attack.

"The quest reward is connected to curing the Sickness!" I said.

Torliam blinked. His eyes widened and his lips parted in surprise and maybe even a bit of hope, but then they flattened down again. "You lie."

"I'm not lying. I don't know *how* it's connected, but it says one of the rewards is information on the Sickness. These type of chain quests update when you complete each stage, and the rewards keep growing. Information now, maybe a cure, later."

He just stared at me.

"I mean, why else do you think the Oracle is doing all this? I'm certainly not important enough for her attention all on my own. Maybe she's trying to fight back, through me, through *us*. I mean, she can see the future, right?" I put a few drops of innocent consternation into my voice, and I saw the disbelief break apart in his eyes. For a moment, I felt a pang of shame for my actions, but I ruthlessly squashed it, reminding myself how much I had to have his assistance, no matter how I was forced to obtain it.

However, the way he replied shocked me.

"I did ... suspect, that this might be the case."

Chapter 23

Nothing gold can stay.
— Robert Frost

TORLIAM WINCED at the barrage of questions from us. "I was not certain, of course," he said, raising his hands in a calming motion. "I told you, Eve, that you were likely descended from one of the lines of my people. Matrix is the name of that line, though it seems you call yourself by the name Redding. For many generations, the line of Aethezriel had been bound to serve and protect the members of the line of Matrix, and can never be bound to another in service. Many of the line of Matrix ruled, in times past." He paused for a moment, as if thinking, and then continued, "I knew what you were when I first felt the bond with you, though the last of the line was thought to have died hundreds of years ago. You have their blood. I did not know you were a human." He clenched his fists and looked away, but couldn't quite hide his expression.

Instead of the anger he usually displayed, he was despairing. I almost felt bad, which was ridiculous because I couldn't do anything about being human, or the fact that NIX had forced me to be a Player. I would not have chosen this any more than he. But he must have thought I was one of his comrades, either come to save him, or also captured by NIX.

"Some thought ... that one day they might bring back the one god who could fight back the Sickness. The line of Matrix is descended from a mortal who had relations with the God of ... Life. The Champion." He frowned then, and told me the word he really meant, in Estreyan. "It does not translate, similar to the word for the Sickness. He is the god of order, and form. Shaping. Molding? I do not know, but perhaps you can understand my meaning."

I shrugged, then nodded. "Okay. What are you getting at?"

"There are stories, maybe prophetic, about our salvation. I believe you may be the one who can find that extremely distant ancestor, and bring him back. Many believe he is the only one who can save this world. The Oracle is clearly setting you on a path."

I felt the muscles in my jaw tightening as I held back my anger. "You didn't think that maybe I might be interested in hearing about this?"

Torliam looked away like a scolded puppy, blonde hair falling in front of his face. "I did not believe in the possibility, at first. You may have some distant blood of the line, but you are ..."

"Human? A two-leg-maggot?" One of my eyebrows rose high in challenge.

He didn't rise to the bait. "But with the quest you tell me of, to find knowledge of the Sickness, I am beginning to ... find hope?" He forced himself to meet and hold my gaze with obvious difficulty. "I can help you. If you are indeed the one, you are on the very early stages of the path. You will need to gain acknowledgement from the goddess of Testimony and Lore. Many of my people will follow you, if we can show them the signs. Enough people, perhaps, to kill a god."

Sam spoke up. "Do you think they would agree to help us, though, if they knew that the god was infected? The villagers were so afraid of the Sickness they didn't even want to let us stay inside the walls."

Torliam looked at him, and frowned. "You are right. Perhaps they would not. But we do not have time to train you humans into proper warriors. Chaos is undoing you," he said to me, his voice softening.

I grimaced. It was true.

"We *must* convince my people," he said. "It could mean the salvation of our world. My *mother-lord* may grant us the numbers we need, or at the least allow a force of volunteers to accompany us. And if necessary, we may even deceive those who would not follow us otherwise. The task is too important to fail." His words were coming faster, and he alternated between gazing far away in thought and focusing on me with excitement. "Let us tell people that we are questing for a Bestowal from the God of Knowledge, and he has said we mortals must prove ourselves in battle against him."

"I don't think it's right, lying to people like that," Sam said. "They're going to be putting their lives on the line. They should at least know the truth, so they can make a real decision."

Torliam grimaced. "You are not wrong. But this is too important. In any case ... fighting to kill a god and fighting not to be killed by one while petitioning for a Bestowal are not so different. Both end in death, almost universally. At least the one will give them hope while they fight."

Sam didn't pretend to be happy about it, but he kept any more arguments to himself, having spoken up and thus cleared his conscience of the weight of the decision, I guessed.

Jacky was very quiet, and Adam was already thinking through the possible outcomes in his head, muttering about planning for the worst-case scenarios.

"So, I just have to gain a Bestowal from a couple different gods? Testimony, and Lore?" I asked.

"She is one god, with two aspects. But yes, in essence. Though we will have to find her, first. She, too, has been gone from mortal eyes for generations. I have some ideas, but once we are back in the village, we will be able to use their stores of knowledge to determine exactly where we might search. I have no doubt that we will find her."

Could I do this? Could I go along with this pretense that I was some kind of destined savior, meant to find and bring back the god that could forestall the death of their world? People would die for me. Others would have their soul crushed, when they inevitably learned the truth. I couldn't answer my own question.

I kept asking it of myself, even after we were safely back in the village, we were all healed up at the hand of the Estreyan healer, and the news had started to spread.

Jacky trained like mad, driving herself into the ground every day, only stopping her training to check in with the rest of us and see what progress we'd made in pinpointing the location of the Goddess of Testimony and Lore.

Chanelle's condition improved, and I hoped desperately that enough Seeds would bring back that vivacious girl I'd first met, who looked just like China and who made something inside me cringe every time I saw her looking so incredibly lifeless.

But time was passing, and I didn't have enough to spend waiting and vacillating. It wasn't like me to be so indecisive, but whatever the God of Knowledge had done to me, forcing me to relive all my bad decisions, had made me unsure. I woke up during the night, days after receiving the quest, and the answer was clear in my mind, finally. I would live. I was too afraid to do anything else. I would *live*, and others would pay for my life in blood.

I WOKE with someone's hands pressing down on my mouth, suffocating me. Pressing down, keeping the maggots *inside* me. I clawed across the arm, and they drew back with a hiss.

"Damn it, Eve!" Sam said, the curse sounding strange coming out of his mouth.

I reached those same claws up to my face, barely even feeling the pain as I sliced at my eye sockets, trying to get the squirming parasites out from behind my eyeballs.

My room's light bloomed into brightness, and I sat up. Wraith observed Adam's look of horror, since there was too much blood for my eyes to see directly.

The others piled into the room from down the hall. Blaine held the kids back from entering once he caught a glimpse of my face.

I realized then that I was screaming, and that I'd probably been doing so for a while, if the raw feeling of my throat was any indication. "They're inside me," I said desperately. "Sam, help me, help me! The maggots are inside me, burning cold in my head, behind my eyes, *burrowing* through my *brain!*" The last was a screech, as I tried to impart the desperation of my situation.

My back arched, and I slammed my head against the wall, the starburst of dizziness alleviating the sensation of infestation for a moment.

"Hold her down!" Adam snapped, reaching for my clawed hands.

Torliam was there, a hole in the wall where he'd made himself a door since my own was filled with teammates, and the blue was pressing against me, almost crushing but it hurt the maggots too and they stilled and then Sam was in front of me again, laying his hands on me *oh god thank you thank you help me.*

Then things went dark, even for Wraith, and I fell back into unconsciousness.

Chapter 24

My candle burns at both ends, it will not last the night, but ah my foes and oh my friends, it gives a lovely light.
— Edna St. Vincent Millay

" ... really think that's a good idea? She was trying to scratch out her own eyeballs before Sam put her to sleep," Adam's voice said, almost spitting with vehemence.

"We cannot leave her sleeping and defenseless," Torliam said.

"It's done," Sam said.

I groaned, fighting against the nausea. I didn't know where I was for a moment, but when I saw the diagram painted over the floor in front of me, I recognized the old man healer's house. Torliam, Jacky, Adam, and Sam were with me.

Someone screamed, outside.

I sat up and groaned, "What's going on?"

Adam was already at the window, looking out into the darkness of the night. "I don't ... oh *shit*."

"What is it?" Sam asked.

"One of them just broke down the main gate. They're fighting back, but there are too many monsters for the villagers to kill them all. They're flooding in."

"What?" Alarm crept into my voice. I wondered if I was hallucinating, or maybe in the beginning of yet another nightmare.

"We were attacked by the God of Knowledge," Torliam said. "Mentally. I was strong enough to fight it off. You were not. Your healer forced you to sleep, and we brought you here, to fix the wounds you inflicted on yourself."

I reached up and touched my face self-consciously. The skin on my face, especially around my eyes, was a little tender, but not raw. "Is that related to whatever's going on outside?"

"Perhaps. I wonder that the god is not aware of our intentions, and has sent the attack to ensure we are not able to complete our task."

"How many are there? Monsters, I mean."

"Too many. This village will not last the night, I fear."

"We have to help them," Sam said, moving with adrenaline-rush jitteriness. "There are kids out there. And not all of the villagers are even fighters. I mean, I saw one of them with a Skill in *music*! Everyone's going to die if we don't do something."

"And what will we do, that can make a difference against *that*?" Adam said, flinging an arm out to encompass the village outside.

"We can help them escape, at least!"

The healer bustled into the room, carrying a satchel in both arms. "Supplies for the trip," he said in Estreyan. "Hurry, we must get to the stables."

I climbed to my feet, allowing Jacky to brace me when the room swayed around me. "Where are the others?"

"Back in our rooms," Adam said.

"You must escape, Eve-Redding," the healer said. "No time to pick up those who fall behind."

"No way we're leaving the kids in this shit," Jacky said, her shoulders tightening, as if she expected a fight. "We're going to get them, right, Eve?"

"Of course. No time to waste, let's go," I said, bracing myself on Jacky's arm.

She slammed open the door, and the chill in the air hit me with a sudden shock. I could see fires starting in two different places in the village, and the light of the two moons showed the dark mass of monsters boiling into the streets near the gate, flashes of light and sound flaring from the attacks of the defending villagers.

We ran as a group, the old healer keeping up easily despite the packs he carried on each arm. We passed an Estreyan mother, running terrified in our direction, her young child wailing in her arms. "Go to my home," the healer said to her. "Hide, under the floor. Tell the others."

We had passed each other before she had time to respond, but I could only hope that she obeyed and survived.

We got to the elder's house, and Adam, Sam, and Jacky burst in to grab the others and our supplies, while Torliam, the elder, and I stayed outside to keep watch for attacks on the building. In the distance, a monster with huge bat-like wings flew away, the silhouette of the man in its claws writhing against the moon behind them.

Torliam was trembling faintly, not from fear, but from clenching his muscles too tightly in rage. "The Sickness is an *abomination*. There is no place for it, in a world on which I live. One of us must be destroyed," he said in the poetic lilting of his native language.

The healer turned slightly toward him, eyes still searching outward. "Many have vowed the same. I take heart that this is the first time I have ever held hope that a mortal will be the one to survive a covenant of enmity against the Sickness."

A figure raced up the street, entering the somewhat constrained range of my awareness. The patrol leader. I still didn't know his name.

"Eve-Redding," he said, gasping, once he was close enough. He

269

was holding one arm close to his body, obviously hurt. "Thank the gods you are safe. We must get you away safely."

"Laine?" the healer asked.

The patrol leader shook his head and closed his eyes as if in pain. "No. It was already too late when I arrived at her house."

The healer clapped him on the shoulder, head bowing. "We will repay them in death many times over."

"Their blood will pave her way to the next life." He nodded and swallowed. He turned to me. "You must stop this," he said. "The Sickness has spread through the creatures of the land. The very earth turns against us. You must find the way to cleanse this world. I beg of you. I place my faith in you."

My stomach clenched. I wasn't capable of fixing their world. "I will follow the path," I said. Not quite a promise, and not quite a lie. I couldn't force any more past the lump in my throat.

He nodded tightly, and closed his eyes once again as he swallowed hard. When he looked at me again, the faith in his eyes, the almost fanatical, desperate hope hit me like a blow.

I hated myself in that moment, and not for the first time.

Jacky slammed back through the door, tossing my pack at me. "We're ready."

Kris and Gregor wore their own packs. Though they were pale and obviously frightened, they held Chanelle's hands in comfort as she whimpered with childish fear. Kris climbed atop the patrol leader's back without hesitation when he leaned down to carry her, and Gregor glanced at me, but went with Blaine instead, while Torliam carried Chanelle.

Zed was checking his guns, and with a fluid motion, pulled one out of its holster and shot past my face. The gun sounded with the strange *glup* that indicated an air-burst round. I turned, and saw another of the bat-winged creatures tumble into the top of a house, just entering the edge of my range.

"Nice shot," I said. I pushed the Wraith Skill a little more, since whatever Sam had done to me was wearing off enough that it didn't make me throw up to do so.

270

"I'm awesome, I know. Now let's go," Zed said, his eyes asking me silently if I was okay.

I nodded, but didn't force a fake smile.

We ran, then.

The bird steeds in the stables were panicking, and one had busted through its stall and was barreling around the building, injuring itself as it ran into things in its panic. The patrol leader did something with a Skill to calm some of the birds, and we climbed atop them without even sparing the time for saddles.

We barreled back out through the doors. Jacky glanced over her shoulder, slowing her mount with a pull on the feathers of its neck so she could bring up the rear of our group. "I hate this," she said through gritted teeth, under her breath. It didn't seem like she expected anyone to hear her. "Been working so hard, but I still can't do nothing when it actually matters."

I didn't know what to say to that, or if she would have even wanted me to hear and respond, so I stayed silent. We raced through the streets toward the back of the village, and out through the back gate that led to the training fields.

There were monsters there, too, though not as many, and they hadn't been making a ruckus. When we passed through, they attacked.

Torliam brought his power together into a huge sword-like blade of blue, and slashed with his arm. They fell in a far greater circumference around him than it seemed should have been possible, sliced cleanly through from side to side.

The patrol leader did something, and another huge swath of them fell to the ground, twitching like they'd been nerve-gassed. We ran the birds straight through.

A couple monsters avoided their comrades' fate, but with the Estreyans and my own group, they weren't enough to do more than slow us down a little, and after a while, their numbers petered out. That was when Egon slowed the birds with another simple motion of his hand. "Go on from here," he said. "Do not stop until dawn breaks over the horizon."

"What about you, Egon?" Kris asked, voice pitched high. She didn't speak Estreyan very well, but had obviously picked up on his intention.

"I will go back, and fight to protect my village."

The healer dipped into a short bow from atop his own bird. "Well met, Eve-Redding of the line of Matrix, and Torliam of the line of Aethezriel," he said. "Fight with the strength of our wills behind you."

"Well met, Borogo of the line of Ambercrest," Torliam said, returning his bow.

I copied him awkwardly, and then the two Estreyans turned around, racing back toward the battle.

"No!" Kris yelled. "You're going to—" her voice broke on a sob, "—die. We have to go back!" she screamed. "We have to help them."

"They have saved us," Blaine said. "If we do not do our best to get out of here safely, we will be acting as if everything they have done for us does not matter."

Gregor's hands were fisted in the neck feathers of his own mount. "We won't forget their names, Kris. Like in the story Mom used to read us. We'll remember them."

Kris just sobbed, but she followed along without further protest as we urged the ostrich-like birds into an uncomfortable, loping run. "This world is horrible," she said, breath hitching. "Everyone dies."

Interlude 3

They had all been preparing, ever since the elder felt the rip opening up in the world, and told them that an array had been used. The training grew more desperate, the arguments among them more quick to devolve into violence.

He and some of the others had talked to the elders about making sure their guests were treated with proper courtesy, and now they were often seen moving about the place, though they still weren't permitted to leave the outer boundaries.

The woman had grown bolder, demanding answers from Eliahan and anyone else who wasn't smart or fast enough to avoid her. "What is it that has everyone so panicked? Are you going to attack NIX?"

He laughed. "You know nothing of what is coming. Perhaps that is a blessing, for you."

Chapter 25

It is not the darkness outside that invites the demons, but the darkness inside.

— Darune Imdel

AS EGON HAD INSTRUCTED, we traveled till morning without stopping. By that time, even the ostrich-like birds, which were known for their stamina, were exhausted. Riding them was ... uncomfortable at best. With only two legs, they bounced with every step, and despite my lack of male genitalia, the insides of my thighs and everything between my legs was bruised and aching.

I had wanted a few more days to prepare and gather information about how best to win the Goddess of Testimony and Lore's favor, but we were pretty sure we knew her location, and there was no more village library to search through, anyway. We headed for her, a strange mood combined of sorrow, fear, and helpless determination suffusing the group at first. Over time, though, the mood lightened, growing better conversely with how exhausted we became from traveling.

It took us a couple weeks to make it almost all the way to the edge of the continent we were on, and though the bird steeds could eat almost anything they came across, including smaller animals, we didn't have extra food for them, and they grew noticeably wirier over the course of the trip.

We'd encountered a few monsters along the way, but nothing life-threatening, and since we ate some of them after killing them, we humans were fine for food, even if none of us were gourmet campfire roasters. The type of hunger that makes your hands shake is a wonderful seasoning.

The biting chill of the air froze the insides of my nostrils when I breathed it in straight, so I kept my face hidden behind the fur lip of the coat the villagers had given me. The cold made it difficult to sleep, which I appreciated, as that saved me from the nightmares. But I was so tired I found myself nodding off in the saddle, woken by flashes of screaming terror.

I checked my Attribute Window despairingly. If only I didn't have to put all my Seeds into the healing Attributes, maybe I might have *some* chance against a god.

PLAYER NAME: EVE REDDING
TITLE: SQUAD LEADER(9)
CHARACTERISTIC SKILL: SPIRIT OF THE HUNTRESS,
TUMBLING FEATHER
LEVEL: 38
SKILLS: COMMAND, WRAITH, CHAOS
STRENGTH: 15
LIFE: 67
AGILITY: 22
GRACE: 18
INTELLIGENCE: 28
FOCUS: 23
BEAUTY: 10
CHARISMA: 15
MANUAL DEXTERITY: 9
MENTAL ACUITY: 24

RESILIENCE: 65
STAMINA: 21
PERCEPTION: 25

The clouds above grew thicker and more ridiculously fluffy as we approached our destination. Even the mist showing in the air from our exhalation didn't dissipate like normal, hanging in the air like a puffy trail behind us.

"WE SHOULD LEAVE OUR MOUNTS HERE," Torliam said. "They will not survive in the sky levels."

We left the birds, loosely tied up to a small tree. If we weren't able to return, they would be able to break free.

Then we walked into the wall of fog. Ahead, it thickened, till every gasp made my lungs rattle just a little, and the loose strands of my hair started to float around my head, as if I were underwater. Between one step and the next, my foot rose and didn't touch the ground again. I flailed awkwardly as the foggy substance around me lifted me off my feet, and sent me floating gently upward.

"It is alright. The current will carry us," Torliam said, his voice slightly muffled.

I coughed, and tried to breathe calmly so my lungs weren't overwhelmed.

"Whoa!" Zed said. Instead of the half swim, half run the rest of us were doing, he stretched out in a Superman pose, then started doing flips and stretches.

Kris laughed and joined in, and though Gregor rolled his eyes at first, when Zed pulled him atop his back and pretended to swim like a dolphin, Gregor grinned and tugged on Zed's hair to make them spin different directions.

Jacky started using her Skill to pull herself around, literally zooming through the air like a superhero.

"I want to ride you, Jacky!" Kris yelled.

"That's not fair," Gregor said. "Zed's useless. We're just floating around aimlessly here. I want to ride Jacky, too. Let's take turns."

Zed stuck his tongue out at Jacky, then turned to Adam. "Think you could help me out, here? Flippers, or something?"

Adam smirked and pulled out some ink from a cartridge he'd refilled while we were in the village, and created a mermaid tail that latched around Zed's legs and hips.

My brother reared back, looking down at himself in consternation for a moment. Instead of the protest Adam had probably expected, he flicked his fin and swam through the air over to Adam with Gregor still clinging tightly to his back. "I'm going to need a trident to go with this," he said. "Could you make it spit lightning? To be authentic, you know."

Chanelle laughed, though it might have been at the sensation of floating and the light atmosphere of the group rather than comprehension of the joke. Still, it made us all smile to hear it.

Adam rolled his eyes, and made a normal ink trident that did *not* spit lightning into an unknown gaseous substance. "It'd be just like you to get us all blown up," he muttered.

I hesitated for a moment. It looked like so much *fun*, and there wasn't any danger within the reach of my awareness. Even if there were, a tail would probably help me to navigate what would basically be an underwater fight even *better*. That convinced me. "Could I get a tail, too?"

Adam ended up augmenting all of us, though Jacky got octopus legs that waved through the air randomly, and Blaine got some sort of jellyfish thing that fit around his suit and propelled him in spurts. We played around for the next half hour or so, Adam renewing his Animations whenever they ran out, till the current deposited us on a layer of quartz-like crystal.

Torliam pointed the way, after consulting the map.

I frowned as we began to walk. "Isn't this the way we came? Unless I've made a mistake … but, my sense of direction is amazing. The sky was clear, this way. Wouldn't we have seen clouds? Is whatever this is going to dissipate out from under us?"

Torliam smirked. "My world is not so simple as yours. This is a new layer."

"You know, acting obtuse and mysterious doesn't make you seem cooler," Adam said.

"Trying to explain the science to you would not make a difference," Torliam said. "I doubt you could understand even the necessary vocabulary, much less the concepts."

"Try me," Blaine said. "I am a scientist, and I have been studying the knowledge of your world. Also, I am a genius."

Sam covered his mouth with his hand to hide the smile, sharing a look with Jacky, who snorted in amusement.

"He is also humble and pious," Adam drawled.

Torliam conceded, perhaps more to spite Adam than because he actually believed Blaine, but they quickly fell into a scientific discussion that I, at least, couldn't follow.

As we waded slowly through the thick air, the ground beneath our feet turned more and more crystalline, and increasingly beautiful, glittering all different colors. After a while we noticed that the crystals were letting off light. Despite how beautiful they were, the whole thing gave me a bad feeling. Estreyer was a planet of universal viciousness, in my experience. Anything unusual was probably also dangerous.

I voiced my concerns to Adam, and he agreed that he would give us all ink mermaid tails at the first sign of danger

Despite my uneasiness, I didn't think much of the crystal beneath my bare feet growing sharper and making shallow cuts into my extremely calloused feet. It barely hurt, and I was so used to injury by that point that a few little nicks didn't register. What did manage to alarm me was the quickly growing glow of power in the fog all around us. "Stop!" I called, looking around with my useless eyes while Wraith searched for the source of the power, and found none. Yet it coalesced around us with almost crushing force. "Adam, tails!" I said. "Something's closing in on us."

By then it was already too late.

Chapter 26

Still she haunts me, phantomwise,
Alice moving under skies
Never seen by waking eyes.
— Lewis Carroll

I LET out a squawk as the crystal shifted, slicing into the pads of my feet, and spilling my blood on the ground. It sucked up my blood and shot it forward, blowing mist out of the way to reveal a lump of abstruse crystal. When my blood reached it, it shifted and unfolded, uncurling upward into the form of a woman.

Jacky, Torliam, and Sam closed in on Zed and me in a protective formation, while Adam attached ink tails to Blaine, the kids, and Chanelle, giving first priority to those who had the least chance of protecting themselves.

The crystal creature was naked, but I don't think anybody was really noticing that except a little voice in the back of my inane brain. Her legs were shapely, made of jagged crystal that sharpened down to two points, with spurs, which she balanced effortlessly on. She stretched like an unfurling flower, and turned to look at me.

When our eyes met, a very clear 'Oh, shit,' resounded through my brain. "Get back," I shouted to the team. "Blaine, get the kids out of here."

To his credit, he was already moving, using the tail Adam had given him first to grab a child under each arm. But he didn't get far. The mist thickened a few meters out, and after only a few seconds of trying to swim through it, he began to cough, and then his breaths began to rattle, like he was inhaling half water. He struggled, and the current brought him back, pushing him out of the thick wall of mist.

The three of them flopped gently to the crystal ground, coughing up liquid.

The creature spoke, her voice formed by shattering the crystal gills on the sides of her neck. "Welcome, mortals. Please calm yourselves, and do not try to escape. Only death lies on that path." She spoke in Estreyan.

Torliam answered her back, speaking quickly enough that I missed some of the words. "We are honored, wise—Torliam, son of Mardinest, of the line of Aethezriel—blood-covenant is Eve Redding, of the line of Matrix—by the Oracle."

Zed didn't seem to think whatever he'd said was cause for extra alarm, though to be fair, he already had a gun drawn and primed in each hand.

For the first time, I realized that obviously, alien gods and humans should have a language barrier. I wondered why I'd been able to talk with Behelaino. I wasn't sure if she'd actually been speaking English, doing some weird Seed-thing where she inserted understanding into my brain, or something equally freaky.

"She welcomes us," Torliam relayed. At my questioning look, he nodded. "This is the Goddess of Testimony and Lore, who has long been hidden."

The creature tilted her head to the side. "They are from another world?"

How did she know that?

"Yes," he said.

Crystal tentacles exploded out of the ground and pierced into each of our temples, faster than even Adam could blink.

The surprise and pain caused more than a few screams.

"Be still," Torliam said, and we obeyed. He was the one who was from this world and supposedly had experience with this sort of thing, so I hoped for the sake of my brain staying intact inside my skull that he knew what he was talking about.

The tentacles piercing Chanelle's head broke off instantly, and the crystal ground rippled violently and swept them away from the little clearing. The rest of the tentacles withdrew from our heads after only a few seconds, and pulsed light back to the goddess, as if she was drinking up something through her ..."skin."

She opened her mouth, and her gills shattered and reformed repeatedly, almost faster than my eyes could track, forming sound somehow. "I ... have been waiting here for *so long* without visitors," she said in perfectly clear English. "I did hide myself away, but I didn't expect it to be so ... boring! No supplicants have come to quest for my Bestowals for so long, I decided to sleep so I would no longer have to count the seconds of my loneliness." Her shoulders drooped, needle-sharp fingertips trailing sadly across her thigh. "I was not made for isolation," she said. "And I am glad to finally greet you." She smiled to me. "I have received your offering of blood, and I grant your request for a Trial. You and your followers will be allowed to petition for my Bestowal."

Torliam's eyes widened, and he turned to me, eyes following my own gaze down to my feet.

"Ahh," I said stupidly. "I'm ignorant, and I did not know the ways of this land. I didn't mean to request a Trial." Oh, freaking shit on a stick.

The creature frowned at that. "Do you mean to escape me after petitioning, to abandon the covenant uncompleted after suddenly realizing your fear?" Her voice grew imperious. "You have already entered into agreement, whether by accident, as you say, or not. I will not allow you to leave me again so easily." The wall of choking fog closed in around us, and the rainbow-colored shards of crystal began to pulse with light.

I struggled to breathe, and not just from the quality of the not-quite-air, but from the power pressing down on me. The creature before me could kill us all easily, with the same nonchalance that I would kill a spider or mosquito. There was a sense of age to her, like the feel of mountains that have stood for millennia, or oceans that have lapped endlessly at the ever-changing shores. She would remain, long after we were gone, as she had done for countless others before us.

Torliam was bowing, saying something to the goddess that I couldn't hear, though I wasn't sure if it was because of the terror, or because of the air.

Chanelle had fallen to the ground and was curled up in a little ball, crying.

Gregor was also on the ground. He'd puked at some point, but he was looking at me, and I recognized the emotion in his eyes. Desperate hope. Faith.

I hated it. I couldn't bear the pressure of it. But I straightened anyway. "I will accept the Trial," I said. "But some of my team aren't warriors. They are too weak to participate in a quest for the favor of one so great as yourself." I bowed to her, moving slowly, so that my trembling muscles didn't make me jerk awkwardly.

"All must participate, except the broken one," the goddess gestured to Chanelle, "and the mortal that carries none of our legacy," she said, pointing to Blaine.

"The children will die," Torliam warned in a low voice.

Immediately, everyone shifted forward to guard the children more completely, putting our bodies between them and the body of the goddess. As if that would actually protect them. It was like putting rice paper up to dam the ocean.

"I cannot accept that," I said, my voice growing colder and deeper. "Requesting a Trial was my mistake. But these are my people, and it is my duty to protect them." I settled my heart and released my claws. Maybe if I could distract her long enough, Adam could find a way to get the others out. An ink respirator to filter breathable air, maybe. He was clever like that.

The tension gathered. She stared at me till my heartbeat pounded in my ears from the force of it. Then she smiled. "I am beginning to like you. You play the role of heroine so easily. All must have a part in the story, but if you wish, you may take the burden of protector."

"What does that mean?" I narrowed my eyes suspiciously.

"You and your warrior will take the greater burden of their roles in the story, as well as your own."

Torliam stiffened beside me, but said nothing.

"My warrior?" I echoed her.

"Him, the one with which you have a …?" she turned to Torliam.

"Blood-covenant," he supplied for her.

I didn't mention that many of the others had taken the Seeds as well, fearing it would only make things worse for them.

Torliam nodded to me, and I avoided his eyes. If he, too, was filled with sacrificial hope, I didn't want to see. "I accept," I said aloud. I would die here, or I would die at the hands of Chaos. When I thought of it like that, it was calming. As always, the only way out was *through*.

THE GODDESS RAISED HER HAND. "Let us perform the story of exodus, tribulation, and the … spark-of-hope." She ran the last words together, and I realized it was once again a missing word in English.

I asked Torliam what she meant.

"It is a children's story about our history," he said, "one every Estreyan child knows in some form or another."

I didn't have a chance to ask him for a deeper explanation, because the goddess directed all those participating to stand in various places around her. Torliam and I were placed closest to her, and the non-Players and Chanelle were farthest away.

"I know you do not know the way of this dance," she said in her fractured voice, "so I will lead your movements as we perform the story together." She lifted her hands, and the crystal ground separated and broke outward en-masse, the forms of thousands upon thousands of tiny little fish swimming through the air. Though our footing was gone, we floated.

My eyes widened as I watched the coral-shaded, translucent fish swarm around me in an almost solid wave.

"Begin," she sang, her voice echoing out, seeming to bounce off and through the crystal so that it originated from everywhere, like the best surround-sound system ever invented.

The fish closed in on me, and I jerked when their fins brushed against me and sliced shallowly into my skin. They darted in and scraped up the blood that welled up from the cuts.

I quickly learned to avoid their fins, and in doing so, realized they were guiding my movements. I sent a Window to the others before my full concentration was taken up, explaining the concept in case they hadn't realized it for themselves.

"*Before there was Estreyer,*" her voice resounded, "*our people lived in another place. All lived happily, and in harmony.*"

The crystal fish guided me in smooth, graceful movements. I felt kind of like a ballerina, or an interpretive dancer. I couldn't see the others, and the goddess' power shone so bright and pervasively in my awareness that it blotted out my teammates like the light of the sun might blot out a lightning bug.

"*Then, the unmaking came. It is known by many names. The greater-death, the end, the abhorrent. It began to destroy us all. We could not hold it off, though our warriors fought with all their strength, and many died before it, some falling to madness. So, the people petitioned the gods and the forces-of-existence, and left to create a new world.*"

I was forced to change my movements, jerking faster, in jagged motions that felt awkward and uncomfortable. The fish got some more blood out of me, and as I watched, they began to shine with it in blurry patterns.

"We traveled far and long, hoping to escape the abhorrent by moving beyond its reach and knowledge. Our people voyaged through the breaks, and eventually came to this place."

I split some of my attention away from the strange dance being forced on me and saw images take shape in the light of the swarming crystal. My focus was drawn irresistibly to them, and I watched as people and creatures I'd never imagined left a planet, moving in ships the likes and size of which were almost incomprehensible. I couldn't quite comprehend what I was seeing, as I had no reference for the all-encompassing appearance of space from a wider perspective, and the anomalies which they traveled through. I was sure "break," was another concept that humans had no word for.

"The great champion, enemy of the abhorrent, formed Estreyer of the gods, and we exist in and of the world. But then came knowledge. We would be followed by the darkness, for it was part of us, and we had brought it with us."

I was gazing into the crystal-bright images when a drop of blood fell into my eye. It startled me enough that I withdrew some of my attention from the story and narrative. I realized I was bleeding pretty badly. The dance had progressed, and I wasn't keeping up properly. The fish around me gulped up the thin lines of my blood with their little puckered mouths. I tried to concentrate on their movements, following them so I wouldn't be sliced, but it was hard to concentrate. Something about the images and the sound of the goddess' voice resounding in my head *demanded* my attention.

I concentrated on the fish anyway, forcing myself to split my attention and follow along as their guiding movements became increasingly difficult to follow. I felt like a puppet on strings, or maybe it was the fish that were puppets, and I was the one developing the story.

"We began to search for a way to defeat it, and we built, because

we knew we could not run forever. We traveled far and wide, searching for others like us and sifting through the paths of possibility. For a long time, we found nothing significant, and no force stronger than our own which would aid us. Then, there was a glimmer of hope in the paths."

I couldn't keep up, especially not without my full focus. I couldn't even *see* all the fish! The more blood the fish took into their bodies, the more all-encompassing and imperative my need to concentrate only on the narrative and mesmerizing images became. When I realized the solution, I felt like smacking myself. I pushed my awareness out again despite the almost blinding nature of the goddess' power, letting the Skill observe my body from every direction.

"The glimmer was small, twinkling and weak, and so far away it would be almost too late before we could meet it. Eight would accompany it, completing the Seal of Nine, one for each of the greater Trials."

My part in the dance slowed for a while, thankfully, allowing me to grow accustomed to this new method of following along, and to catch my breath. It also allowed me to faintly catch some sounds of the others, doing dances of their own.

"The Summoner, the Gale, the Gifter. The Tracker, the Struggle, the Shadow. The Black Sun, and the Veil-Piercer."

I could hear the others, faintly. Jacky cursed under her breath in between gasps for air. Someone cried out in pain and surprise. I found it hard to worry despite that, because the crystal fish were showing me things I couldn't even describe. It was like a dream, or a vision. Somehow the words and the images made sense in the moment, but I knew that when I awoke, they would slip from my grasp.

"But as such things happen, misfortune must accompany hope, and the greatest opponent of the abhorrent, our champion, disappeared."

My own movements were forced to quicken again, even faster now, after the brief respite. Even with my awareness extended, I couldn't keep up with the fish. Before, they had been opening a path for my limbs and body to move, but now they sliced into me, though I seemingly had nowhere to move. Greedy bastards. The only areas that were safe were those protected by my armored vest. As I instinctively jerked my cheek away from an almost seamless wall of extended razor-edged fins, the other side of my face pressed against the mass of fish, but pushed them out of the way without being cut. And I understood the way the game had evolved.

I needed to force my way through the correct path, as it would no longer be opened helpfully for me. I panted as the fish drove me to bend and reach and spin in ways that the human body normally never moved. I was more grateful than I thought I'd ever be for China's yoga stuff, and Torliam's training. At least I had some experience with something similar, or I'd have probably fallen and sliced my throat open by that point.

"We searched for our champion and molder of the resistance, but the champion was not to be found. And so, time passed, and the abhorrent caught us, trickling into our midst once more. It poisoned us till flesh turned against flesh, till it seemed that the end was near. The path of deliverance was shrouded, until it seemed to have been snuffed out. Many believed that it had been."

My body shrank inward in sadness, curling and twirling over like a streamer in the wind, in moves I'm pretty sure no human was ever meant to perform. My legs shuddered with the fatigue of forcing my way through the syrupy mass, and my arms went numb. Still, I couldn't quite keep up, and the fish took more of my blood, and the story took more of my mind.

"Then, the inkling of hope drew near, born in ignorance and awakened in pain. Its spark was small, and weak, and many times seemed like it would be snuffed out. And yet, it grew, and grows."

I jumped, stretching like a light that had been revealed in the darkness, if that even made sense. It didn't, really, but it was the image forced into my brain from the crystal fish. My body was nearing true exhaustion, that point from which willpower no longer has any effect on performance. If I didn't fear death, I would have collapsed on the floor in a quivering, bloody heap long ago.

"Our future lies in the spark, in the hope that it will grow into a raging inferno and eat up the abhorrent. And so we nurture the glimmer, which struggles in darkness, known to us by the signs and the blood. Such is our work, and our path, to fight against the abhorrent. Only by this may we one day prevail."

And with that, the swarm scattered, and I was left reaching toward the sky, body stretched out and upward to my absolute limits. The others, except for Blaine and Chanelle, were gathered around me in a circle, each in their own pose. I held the pose for half a second, just long enough to be sure that the goddess was finished with me, then crumpled to the floor like a used tissue, gasping for air.

SAM REACHED ME FIRST, whatever wounds he'd gotten in the course of the Trial already healed. He placed his own slightly bloody hand on my slippery cheek. "Crap," he said. "I can't do much about the cuts. I've got some healing saved up, but I think this is one of those things the village healer was talking about. It's resistant. But it's okay, I'll help your blood clot." He was already doing it, making my skin itch in waves. "It won't be pleasant. Once you've scabbed over, your body can do the rest over time. Thank god none of these are that deep."

Blaine rushed over to Kris and Gregor, flailing his way through the air, all four limbs working to help him move faster. "Are you alright? All I could do was watch as you were stuck in those … *torture devices*," he spat. He picked them up gently, and moved them further to the back of the group, away from the goddess' physical manifestation.

They were alright, though a little cut up.

The horrible *itching* that spread over my skin everywhere that Sam touched distracted me. Whatever he was doing, it had to have been from the destruction half of his Skill, the itching so intense that it felt like burning, and I bucked to get away without even thinking about it.

Torliam and Zed held me down. The former looked like he'd been in a blood-filled squirt gun fight against three or four other people, but Zed was okay, mostly. No serious wounds, just like the others.

"You are the first creatures in a thousand years to petition me and receive the chance to experience the Lore," the goddess said. "It is unfortunate you are so weak. I honestly wondered if you might all die. What has happened, since I have been removed from the mortals? Is this really the best spark the worlds could field?"

I wasn't sure if I should be offended. We were alive, and that was deliberate on her part. Hopefully, if we could avoid offending *her*, we could remain alive.

Of course, Jacky decided differently, on her own. She'd fared better than Torliam or I, but had taken a fair bit of damage. Her clothes hung off her in tatters, almost completely covered in blood. Without Sam, she might end up passing out from blood loss soon. "Well, you can do something about that, right? Make us stronger, if you're so upset about how weak we are," she said loudly, fists clenched.

I'm pretty sure the entire rest of the team froze in horror.

The goddess' mouth fell open for a second, and then her brows drew down in a frown. The crystalfish that had receded swirled up again in agitation. Several shot forward from the storm with such speed I couldn't even *see* them move. Obviously, she'd been holding back on us before. One impaled the base of my throat, but almost all the others were shot through the hand. At my feet, one shot Birch in the forehead and knocked him off his feet with a silent puff of air.

I struggled to move, to attack, or defend, or *something*, but the rest of the swarm was on us already, holding us in place. I pushed against them, heedless of the sharp fins, but didn't get anywhere. It took me more than a few seconds to realize I wasn't in pain, and in fact wasn't being harmed at all. It was more like being constrained in a crystalfish straight jacket than an attack.

I stopped struggling, and the fish released me. "Be still, guys," I called out, my eyes still trained unblinkingly on the goddess.

"You are all quite excitable," she said with a raised eyebrow. "No harm was done to you, except perhaps a little pain. That one," she pointed at Jacky, "asked for your Bestowals. I gladly gave them."

Torliam shot a glare to Jacky, who flexed her hand and point-edly ignored him.

"A seal of nine," the goddess said, waving her hand to the teammates who'd participated in the Trial.

I reached up, touching the base of my throat where I'd been hit. My armored vest rippled away from the spot as if repelled by it magnetically. I couldn't see with my eyes, so I looked at myself with my Wraith Skill, and "saw" the dark scales of armor glinting in the light of the fish that was writhing around under the skin. That was extremely creepy, but it only got worse as the places it touched morphed into faceted sparkles that matched the substance the goddess' own body was formed from. It burned like a brand, forming one line at a time. My body buzzed like I'd mainlined caffeine into my veins.

The fish burst back out, and my armored vest formed back around the crystal so that the symbol it had created was visible.

"With a mark of Testimony," she said, placing extra power into the last word, so it seemed to thrum in the air. "The mark will draw both favor and ill-will toward you. You will be recognized by beings of power, your presence imposed on the book of existence. So I proclaim, as the physical manifestation of Testimony and Lore."

Torliam made a small sound, looking with wide eyes between the crystal in his own hand, the goddess, and me. He had a clear, faceted symbol etched all the way through his palm to the other side.

I opened my mouth, though I wasn't quite yet sure the words I wanted to speak. A question, surely.

"I am eager to end my stay in this place," Testimony and Lore said, before I could say anything. She waved a hand. "I am not meant to exist in solitude." And with that, she left, taking all the crystal with her in a surge that swept past us like the wave of a tsunami, leaving us in foggy half-darkness.

Kris whimpered in pain, and I turned to see the mark etched into her hand, and Gregor's.

YOU HAVE GAINED A NEW SKILL: VOICE

I wasn't the only one to be temporarily distracted by invisible Windows in front of their face.

"She's not even a Player," I said, the words both strangely muffled and echoing. "And I'm pretty sure that just gave her a Skill." I didn't need to state the obvious. If the kids didn't have the gene, something bad was about to happen. Even if they *did*, they'd never gone through the assimilation sickness for that first Seed.

"I'm going to need to find something to hurt, and quickly," Sam said.

ADAM GAVE us fins on our arms and mermaid tails, and Blaine forced the hoverboard thrusters he'd built into his suit to work even in the damaging environment. This time, there was no playing as we raced back the way we'd come, fighting against exhaustion and worry.

It was easier to go down through the currents than it had been to rise, and we arrived back at our bird-steeds quickly. By that time, the kids' temperatures had risen to fever levels.

"I don't want to die," Gregor had said, his hands clenching Blaine's. "I don't want to die. I want to live."

Blaine turned to Sam, and by the flickering movement of their eyes, I knew they were communicating by Window.

Sam paled, then shook his head. "It won't come to that. I'll be able to offset enough through the animals. And if I need more, I'm sure the others will be able to capture some monsters and bring them for me." He untied one of the birds and led it off away from the others, so they couldn't watch what he was doing to their companion.

He placed his hands on its head, and it slumped to the ground, senseless. Then he crystallized its windpipe, so that it couldn't scream out, if it awoke. It didn't even twitch. From there, he moved to the feet, shuddering as pieces bubbled or melted or hardened like stone under his hands. The wings were next, and when the bird twitched, he put it more deeply to sleep. He stopped to throw up before he continued torturing it to death.

I pulled my focus away from him, and turned it to gathering more information. Once again, things had changed.

PLAYER NAME: EVE REDDING
TITLE: BEARER OF TESTIMONY
CHARACTERISTIC SKILL: SPIRIT OF THE HUNTRESS,
TUMBLING FEATHER
SKILLS: COMMAND, WRAITH, CHAOS, VOICE

Then I pulled up my Command Window, checking the new Skills of the others.

PLAYER NAME: ADAM COYLE
TITLE: ONE OF NINE
CHARACTERISTIC SKILL: ELECTRIC SOVEREIGN
SKILLS: HYPER FOCUS, ANIMUS, BESTOW

PLAYER NAME: JACQUELINE SANTIAGO
TITLE: ONE OF NINE
CHARACTERISTIC SKILL: GRAVITATIONAL AUTONOMY

SKILLS: STRUGGLE

PLAYER NAME: SAMUEL HAWES
TITLE: ONE OF NINE
CHARACTERISTIC SKILL: HARBINGER OF DEATH
SKILLS: BLACK SUN

PLAYER NAME: ZED REDDING
TITLE: ONE OF NINE
SKILLS: VEIL-PIERCER

PLAYER NAME: KRIS MENDELL
TITLE: ONE OF NINE
SKILLS: SUMMON

PLAYER NAME: GREGOR MENDELL
TITLE: ONE OF NINE
SKILLS: SHADOW

A LITTLE BASIC deduction told me that Adam was "the Gifter" Testimony and Lore had mentioned. What others remained? The Gale and the Tracker.

One must be Birch, and the other Torliam.

"Hurry!" Blaine yelled, placing one hand each on Gregor and Kris' forehead to gauge their fevers.

"It's almost over," Sam called back, the words seeming to be half for his own reassurance.

"Don't worry," Zed said. "They have the gene, right? I *didn't*, and Sam still kept me alive. It's going to be okay."

"You injected yourself with a Seed from a 'mortal,' not from an *ancient alien goddess*," Blaine said sharply. "Eve was stupid enough to do that willingly, and look where she is. There's nothing Sam can do for her!" His voice rose, until he was practically shouting.

Kris groaned, and tossed her head in obvious discomfort, distracting Blaine from his anger.

"I took the Seed directly," I said. "It's pretty different than getting a Bestowal, which is actually meant for a mortal."

I'd meant the words to be comforting, but Blaine stood and took a single step toward me. "You are the cause of this," he whispered scathingly. "We are here because of you. They did not want any of this. They did not do anything to deserve this fate. Why did you not send them away? Why did neither of us keep them *safe?*" His face crumpled then, and he took off his glasses, pressing thumb and forefinger hard against his eyes. "We failed," he whispered.

Jacky, who had been watching silently, stomped off and started pounding her fists against a nearby tree trunk, hard enough to splinter the bark and shake the trunk. Hard enough to break the skin of her own knuckles.

"Yes," I admitted. "But they're not going to die. I promise." I spun around, quickly spotting Torliam squatting under one of the small nearby trees. "What do the marks mean?" I snapped, moving to stand over him.

"They are symbols representing our roles in the Lore," he said.

"The Lore? You mean this whole supposed prophecy thing where I find the god who's going to save your world? The prophecy that you didn't mention pertained to anyone else but me? The prophecy that just hooked in a couple *kids?*" I found myself leaning over him, claws extended, fingers outstretched.

He hesitated for a couple seconds. "The children's story is known to us all. Most consider it a ... fabrication? A story only loosely based in truth, and made to teach children, while couching the lesson in fiction. But it usually ends at a different place, before the reappearance of the light. I did not *know.*" Despite the inherent contrition of his words, the barely-contained energy I could hear behind them wasn't sad, or sorry. He was excited.

My hand moved almost without my volition, slicing through

the air and cracking against his cheek hard enough to rock his head to the side.

He brought up a hand to feel the furrows my claws had dug into his skin. They healed under his fingertips, as easily as that. "They will not die," he said. "They are needed for you to complete your path."

I leaned down. "You don't know that. *We could fail*," I croaked.

He stared at me for a moment, and then his eyelids flickered, and the excitement drained away. "If necessary, Samuel can use my body to shift some of the destructive side of his Bestowal. I will be able to withstand the injuries, as the rest of you will not."

I nodded without gratitude. "Good."

Chapter 27

It is easy to go down into Hell;
   Night and day, the gates of dark death stand wide.
—Virgil

SAM HAD to kill all but two of the bird-steeds, but he got Kris and Gregor through the assimilation process.

We worried the whole time, Blaine the most out of all of us.

During that time, Jacky asked Torliam to keep training her, and the two of them spent hours sparring, her pushing herself desperately to keep up with him, to get better, to fight back. On the third day, she was throwing up on the ground from a punch in the gut that had literally knocked her off her feet and thrown her a few meters away.

"Rest," Torliam said. "Your human frame is weak. You cannot push yourself like a real warrior."

Not the best thing to say to someone so stubborn. Maybe he knew that, and was trying to push her to break her limits.

She spat, and rushed at him in a zig-zagging manner. Rapid changes of direction at high speed, aided by her ability to adjust the way gravity pulled on her body, both in direction, and in strength. As Jacky often did, she looked like a superhero out of a film, moving in ways so blatantly inhuman.

Torliam kept up with her easily, almost blurring as he met and then parried blow after blow, despite how lazy his movements seemed. He had definitely been holding back against me. And Jacky had improved enough that I wondered just how much she'd been training and practicing when I was too occupied with other things to notice. Even seventy-two Seeds wouldn't cause changes like she displayed.

Still, a lazy kick brought Torliam's shin to her chest, and she went flying back again, skidding when she hit the ground on her knees and forearms. Her back convulsed upward as she struggled to breathe, and Sam stood up, taking a few uncertain steps toward her.

But Jacky didn't stay down. She arched again, and got a leg under her. She *surged* upward, rising taller than she was. Bigger than she was, as if she'd suddenly become part Estreyan.

Torliam's eyes widened, but he didn't have a chance to do more than that, as she threw herself at him again, this time moving even faster. Her steps shook the ground, and when she slammed into his guard, he slid back a few feet. He let out a short laugh of surprise, and showed us all a glimpse of how seriously we'd been underestimating him, despite knowing that every accumulated Seed of ours was only a small portion of his own strength.

He punched and slashed and kicked, all Grace and Strength and Agility. His movement whistled in the air from speed, and when he hit Jacky, it sounded like those fake blows from the old western films. Like someone pounding a slab of raw beef.

She went flying for a third time, and when she stood up, she was bigger than him.

He tried to dodge instead of block when she shot back at him, probably wisely, but she turned on a dime, in a move that should not have been possible, not just for a human, but for any object subject to the laws of physics.

They traded blows that sounded more like the cracks of close lightning, as the rest of us watched in awe. Twenty seconds, then thirty, passed.

Then Torliam blurred, disappearing for a moment.

There was a muffled bang, and then Torliam stood where she'd been, and she was flying forward, bent backward from where he'd slammed into her from behind.

The rush of displaced wind blew past me, making the loose strands of my hair flutter.

Jacky didn't get up a fourth time, and when she shrank back down to her normal size and stayed there, Sam rushed over to make sure she was okay.

"You did well," Torliam said, when she waved Sam off and stood, limping back toward the group.

She laughed aloud, gleeful and snorting. "It's my new Skill! Struggle. I've been trying to figure out how to make it work, 'cause my VR chip wouldn't give me any info."

Sam pressed a hand on her shoulder, encouraging her to sit down on one of the big logs we'd placed around the campsite. Her clothes hung half off her, torn at the seams. He very carefully looked away, and handed her a blanket to wrap around herself.

"This is going to make a difference," she said, practically glowing with joy. "I've been working so hard, and it was just like … every time something happened, I was useless." She turned to me. "I can help, Eve."

I grinned back at her, doing my best not to let any of my dismay show. I'd picked Jacky to be on my team because of her fighting prowess, it was true. And a lot of the things we'd been going up against lately had been ridiculously stronger than us, or something you couldn't fight directly. Looking at her in this moment, it was easy to see how strained Jacky had been acting lately. For a while, actually. She'd been quiet, no longer the first to crack a joke or roughhouse playfully. And I hadn't noticed.

When the kids finally broke through the assimilation sickness,

298

they were almost as happy as Jacky to learn that they had Skills now, too, and just had to learn how to use them.

Blaine tried to convince them to let things lie, and not try and use a power that could potentially harm them, but he had no chance of convincing them.

We traveled toward the capitol, then, taking turns between riding the birds and running along beside them while someone else rode. And I thought. I thought about how smoothly things seemed to be working out. How my lies were becoming truth. And I was deeply suspicious. But by that point, it was too late. I couldn't turn away from the path I'd set myself on. I felt a cold maggot wiggling in the back of my mind, and clamped down on it, doing my best to crush it with meditation, like I did when Chaos tried to overwhelm me.

OUR JOURNEY WAS ... eventful. In addition to the three different types of deadly terrain we had to traverse, we were attacked by monsters over and over again. I had a feeling it was because of my Skill, which was the only one of the nine the group had gotten that started out with a description even before it was actively used.

I suspected this was because the Skill was *always* active. However, the description was nothing more than what the goddess had said when she gave it to me.

VOICE: INCREASES CHARISMA. ACTS AS A BEACON FOR BEINGS OF POWR. ALLOWS PRESENCE AND WILL TO BE IMPOSED ON SURROUNDINGS. SKILL EFFECS WIL EXPAND AND STRENGTHEN WITH PLAYER IMPROVEMENT.

The monsters seemed drawn to us. We had no chance of sneaking past without notice, as if I were constantly emitting some sort of dog whistle that only they could hear. I hadn't had any luck turning it off, but I also couldn't figure out how to actively make it do anything.

On the brighter side, Chanelle had started to talk, and was increasingly hungry all the time, which Blaine thought might be a sign that the Seeds were healing her and intensifying her need for fuel, like me.

I took the last of the Seeds I'd been trying to save for her, when Chaos gave me another bloody nose. I didn't tell anyone. We were already traveling as fast as we could, cognizant of the literal time limit on killing the God of Knowledge, imposed by the Oracle. I could only hope we wouldn't be too late.

I wasn't the only one who was having trouble with my new Skill.

Zed couldn't figure out how his was supposed to work, at all. He was frustrated by this, because whatever the Veil-Piercer Skill was, he was absolutely certain based on the name that it would be "so cool."

Gregor felt pretty much the same way, though Blaine did his best to discourage both of the kids from even attempting to use their Skills.

Adam was banging his head against the metaphorical brick wall, trying every experiment he could think of that involved 'giving' stuff to the rest of us.

Sam hadn't had any strange phenomena occur, but I don't think he was trying very hard, due to apprehension. 'Black Sun' was a worrying Skill name, for someone like him.

Torliam, out of all of us, worked out his Skill, Tracker, with frustrating ease. "I can find anything," he said simply. "If I have a solid idea of exactly what I am looking for, over time I will be compelled toward it." He smirked at the looks he was receiving. "I am familiar with the power of this world. It was not so difficult a task to discern the function, *especially* when provided with a name."

Adam huffed and rolled his eyes.

One night, while we were camping in the midst of a particularly disturbing spot, where the plants whispered and gibbered unintelligibly to each other in a sinister mockery of intelligence, Kris came into her own Skill, Summon. She'd been clutching her moose tightly, eyes squeezed tight and staying as close to the fire as possible, both for the warmth it provided against the frigid night, and for the comforting light.

I'd been on watch, along with Jacky, while the rest of the camp wound down. I was monitoring the surrounding area with my Skill, and we were all very much prepared to be attacked in the middle of the night by that point, since it had happened multiple times.

A particularly loud jabbering of word-like sounds from the surrounding bushes spewed out, in a voice suspiciously similar to some of our teammates.

Kris whimpered, and her moose wiggled. She jumped, letting out a small scream and thrusting the stuffed animal away from her.

It climbed to its feet and walked over to her, circling her and facing outward in a mockery of protective aggression as she stared at it.

A couple of the others had been woken by her exclamation, and we all pretty much just goggled at the plush toy.

Gregor scowled. "What did you do?"

Kris shook her head. "I … I'm not totally sure. I was scared, and I felt something that felt … warm, like … safe, you know? So, I connected it and Moose in my mind. And then Moose started walking around."

"You made your imaginary friend come to life," he said flatly.

"No! Well, not really." She fidgeted, and Moose turned to Gregor and gave a warning toss of its plush antlers. "I think I put a ghost inside Moose."

"A *spirit*, which does not necessarily correspond to the shade of one who was once living," Torliam corrected. "That is your Skill, is it not, Summoner?" He smiled at her encouragingly.

She smiled tentatively back.

Jacky whooped, and went over to give Kris a congratulatory ride around the camp on her shoulders, while Moose ran along at her feet.

Blaine woke up then. After the shock and initial rapid-fire questioning was over, he gave Jacky a good chewing out for encouraging Kris to experiment with "spirit" summoning, when none of us had any idea what dangers could be associated with it.

The rest of us very carefully didn't mention that we might have done a teeny bit of encouraging, too, before he woke up.

AS WE DREW CLOSER to the capitol, Torliam began to teach me how his people interacted in a formal setting, and coach me on how to navigate their politics. "The line of Aethezriel rules, now, but the decision has never been based solely on bloodlines, though often the daughter follows the mother. Who rules is a combination of favors traded and merit."

I frowned. "Wait. Daughter follows the mother? Do only women rule?"

"Not only. A few generations ago, we had a male ruler. This was before my time. But it is customary that the females lead, in the household as well as in the nation." His jaw tightened. "Over time, and as our population has dwindled, it is becoming more widely accepted that a man may be … whatever he wants. In the village, for example, a man could take any position that a female could. Of course, there is still a small percentage who feel that it is shameful for a man such as I to be an explorer and historian."

"I'm pretty sure this is the first time you've ever admitted that Estreyer might have something wrong with it, besides the Sickness," I said. "You know, Earth had the civil rights movements long ago."

"Your people die so quickly, it is no wonder change can be enacted in shorter spans of time," he said, seeming affronted. He proceeded to drill me on the different types of bows I might need to use, nitpicking every little mistake.

Zed thought this was funny, and came over to learn how to bow with me.

Unfortunately, when I collapsed to the ground, cradling my head in my hands, it meant he and Torliam both saw.

I pressed down on temples, trying to stop myself from releasing my claws, resisting the urge to smash my head against the ground. "It's the maggots." I gasped as, stars floated around my eyes from the combination of pressure on my skull and the fact that I'd been holding my breath.

"Sam!" Zed screamed.

"No, no," I said, groaning. "I don't need him. There's nothing he can do."

Torliam knelt beside me, grabbing my hands, and pulling them away from my head. "It is the God of Knowledge."

The others were running toward us. I realized suddenly that the high-pitched keening sound was coming from my own throat, and stopped. This was not the way. I needed to keep it together. At first, I'd thought the flashbacks were just some PTSD. If anyone had earned some, I had. But as it continued, I became increasingly certain that something was very wrong.

"Were you singing?" Zed asked. "You have a horrible voice, Eve. Please refrain from making our ears bleed." He laughed at his own joke, absolutely no real humor in his voice.

I giggled. Once I started, it seemed I couldn't stop, till my laughs sounded more like sobs. My cheeks felt frozen and stiff, and when I reached up to touch them, I realized that behind the concealing rim of the coat around my eyes, I was crying.

I choked down the laughter, and stiffly scrubbed at my cheeks, letting the ice flake away inconspicuously.

Torliam spoke. "I, too, have been experiencing some ... mental 'flashbacks.' His influence lingers. It is apparent that you have even less defense against him than I."

"How do I stop it?" I gritted out. "What do I do?"

"You will have to attack his connection directly. There is a ... Trial, of sorts, in the capitol. It is unpleasant. My people only use it in the most extreme of circumstances. But it will allow you to leave your body and enter your mind, to find the pieces of his power that he has left behind."

"Why didn't you mention this earlier?" I glared at him as the feeling receded and I regained some of my faculties.

"It is *very* unpleasant. Enough to drive someone mad. Only a few have completed it successfully, and there are no Bestowals. Surviving it intact is considered a gift enough on its own."

I looked at him and saw what he wasn't saying. He did not want to attempt this pseudo-Trial. "Is there no other way?"

"None that I know of. Not to remove a mental infestation directly from a god."

"Well then we'd better hurry up," I said. "Knowledge could be watching everything that we do with his little maggots."

Torliam paled.

Chapter 28

Do I fear the sleepless nights?
You have no idea how long the dark lasts when you cannot close your eyes to it.

—Tyler Knott Gregson

THE DREAMS KEPT COMING, and as I grew more tired, it grew harder for me to tell the difference between them and the surreal, cold wilderness we traveled through. I meditated, instead of sleep, but it wasn't the same.

I was trying to meditate as the sun set one evening, curled up in my Estreyan sleeping tube.

Kris tripped over my feet in the twilight, breaking me out of a mutated flashback of the Intelligence Trial, where I'd killed a girl to save myself, and then convinced Sam to do the same.

I shot upward, and she startled back from me and gasped, surprised. "Sorry!" she said. "It's kinda hard to see—"

But I wasn't listening to her words, only noticing the fear on her face, and the way it made me feel. As if I'd done something wrong. I hadn't done anything wrong.

"Do you think I'm going to hurt you?" I snapped.

"Uh …" Her eyes widened. "No, I mean—"

"Why would I do that? I said I'd protect you, didn't I?" My words weren't vicious, yet, but my tone was. "I could have hurt you *long* before now if I wanted to! I'd just slice your throat open and let you bleed out in a few seconds."

Blaine stepped between us then, scowling at me in a way I hadn't seen him do before, even when talking about NIX. "What ridiculous insanity has come over you?" he said in a low voice. "She tripped. It is dark. It was an *accident.*"

Gregor stepped forward from where he'd been watching, little fists balled up tight, thick eyebrows scrunched over his nose. "You're being mean," he said, throat thick with the hint of suppressed tears. "Don't be mean to my sister."

The rage left me suddenly, like a ghost passing through and sucking the air from my body, leaving me gasping. "I—I'm sorry," I said, panting for words, or air, something to fill the hollow in the center of my chest. "I was dreaming," I lied desperately. "A nightmare. I woke up and I didn't quite realize what was habbening—" I broke off, hand shooting to my face, covering my nose.

I turned away, hiding the blood that had made me blubber, and the discordance of emotion. What was *wrong* with me? This was not normal. I could tell that. "I'm sorry," I said again. "I didn't mean what I said. Could you go get Sam for me?"

Kris nodded, wide-eyed, and ran off.

Once the bleeding had stopped, I had Sam force me into a dreamless sleep. When I woke naturally, no nightmares forcing me awake in the middle of the night, I felt better than I had in a long while. "We need to hurry," I said.

"We can be there before daybreak tomorrow, if we do not stop tonight," Torliam said.

We pushed ourselves at an exhausting pace. However, as we got closer to the capitol, excitement overrode some of our weariness. Torliam, especially, seemed to brighten. "I have not seen my family or friends in so long," he said.

We arrived in the dead of night.

I had been half-dozing in my saddle, meditating to calm the effects of both Chaos and the God of Knowledge's attack.

The capitol was beautiful in a way I'd never seen on Earth. Similar to some of the urban ruins we'd been sent to for Trials, the architecture was fantastical, and things seemed to have been designed strictly for beauty. A white wall of marble surrounded the city, but it didn't look particularly useful for stopping attacks—probably because little could be, against an Estreyan or the type of monsters that might attack a city filled with them.

I wondered if they had other defenses. Perhaps advanced technology of some sort was in place, leaving the wall as a symbolic decoration.

Guards called out to us when we were still far enough away that even I with my enhanced sight couldn't make out their forms. I found that surprising for a moment, before I realized that of course Estreyan guards would be picked for their Perceptive powers.

Torliam called back to them, identifying himself.

There was a pause, and then they called out to us again, ordering us to stop. They sent out a group of five to meet us on foot.

Torliam stepped forward, pulling his hood back from his face, so that they could see him.

"Identify yourself!" one called, despite the fact he'd already done so.

Torliam said his full name again.

"He's telling the truth," one said.

"Torliam, son of Mardinest, has been dead for years!" another snapped back.

"I have returned," Torliam said. "I was not killed. Only … detained. Send word to my *mother-lord*. The *warrior-queen* will want to know of her son's homecoming."

With a bit more suspicious muttering amongst themselves, the group of five escorted us just inside the gates, where they set an even larger number of guards on us while someone went to wake the queen.

They took Torliam into a building to the side of the gate, where they had some sort of communication device he would use to prove his identity to his mother. He returned only a couple minutes later, a smile and an excited tension both badly suppressed.

The queen arrived about a half hour later. I knew who she was because of the golden circlet around her forehead, the honor guard of armored Estreyans following silently behind her, and the way her face changed when she saw Torliam.

She threw open her arms and strode toward him, not quite rushing.

He stepped forward, and they hugged each other. It lasted less than a minute, as they both seemed to gather themselves and return to that slightly regal bearing.

She kept a hand on his arm, though, as if afraid he might disappear if she removed her grip. "I thought you were dead, my son."

"I am alive," he said simply. "And I have much to tell you. My quest was not in vain."

Her eyes widened. "You must tell me everything. But first, food." She turned and swept an assessing gaze over the rest of us. "Your companions may stay in the south wing, near the kitchens," she said imperiously. "No doubt they are hungry, and would appreciate a warm meal," she added somewhat more kindly.

"You will be safe," Torliam said. "Eat, and rest." He looked at me. "I will come find you when I have spoken with my mother."

The queen didn't seem to be waiting for an answer. She waved to one of her other companions with a nod, and he stepped forward, holding out a metal staff with lines running through it somewhat like the lines that scored the outside of the Seed spheres. Little rings of metal floated around the top of it, where the crystal ball would have gone if it were a storybook magic staff. It reminded me of the Shortcut.

I realized that was probably not a coincidence, when Torliam stepped forward to wrap a hand around it, below his mother's. The queen wrapped both hands around her staff, and twisted. The metal slid and clicked into place, and they were gone, with only a little breeze as air rushed to fill the space they'd been.

The rest of us stuck together as the guards escorted us through the sprawling city, which was filled with lights even at this time of the night, to the palace kitchens. We ate, gorging ourselves on food with actual seasoning, that hadn't been scalded over a campfire.

The palace staff gave us each a room. They were small, but the beds were almost suspiciously comfortable, and we were all right next to each other, close enough for me to keep tabs on everyone with my Wraith Skill.

Still, none of us quite relaxed, and Adam hadn't stopped jerking suspiciously since we'd passed the city gates. But we didn't want to cause offense in any of the myriad ways Torliam had warned of. So we accepted their hospitality, and set up a watch schedule, so that someone would always be awake to receive and read any emergency Windows.

I'd fallen asleep under this measure of security, only to jerk upright when the door opened.

Torliam slipped into my room, his body making the huge doorframe look normal. "I have spoken with the queen," he said in an odd tone.

I swung my legs over the side of the bed, placing my bare feet on the floor, and waited for him to continue.

He moved to the other side of the small room, placing his back against the wall and sliding down till he sat on the ground. "There is no force heading toward Earth," he said, head bowed.

"What?" My voice was scratchy with sleep.

"Those of my unit who escaped returned to Estreyer about one *irimael* ago," he said, using the Estreyan word for their equivalent to a year. "They told my mother of my fate, knowing that I may still be alive. She did not send a force back for me. Neither to enact revenge or to save me. Not even to confirm the news of my death. Political pressures have been building, she says. Other old families are maneuvering for power, and she could not spare even a scout team."

I didn't know what to say.

"I am her son. But I am not a daughter, and I am not even the oldest. She believed when she allowed me to go that I had been crazed by the death of my sister. I knew that. But I believed she would send for me, when she was able. I spent years within NIX. No rescue was ever coming for me."

I cleared my throat. "You didn't need her to save you," I said. "I mean, that *sucks*. But we escaped all by ourselves. We didn't need to depend on someone else to fix everything for us." I wanted to say something comforting, but I didn't know how. Sentiment was not my strong suit.

He shook his head. "No. I could not escape. I tried. If not for *you* ..." He raised his gaze to mine.

I stayed silent, awkwardly.

"My mother will try to use you to her political advantage," he said, seeming to change his train of thought instantly. "She will want you to bolster her image and strengthen the support of the populace. Fear is a powerful motivator, but it has been turning against her. Hope is even more powerful, and it is the currency you will deal in. Do not bargain cheaply."

"Tell me more," I said, leaning forward.

He smiled, but it wasn't a pleasant expression. That was okay with me.

I MET with the queen in the morning, in what she called her "war chambers." Maps and electronic diagrams, which I couldn't understand the meaning of, glowed out from the walls.

The queen stood at the head of a huge marble round table in the center of the room. She turned to me when I entered. "Welcome, Eve of the line of Redding." She gestured for me to sit across from her, and spoke in Estreyan, which I was gladder than ever I had learned.

I made sure to bow just as Torliam had instructed me. My extended awareness showed me her grimace, which had disappeared by the time I straightened and moved toward the other side of the table. My feet barely touched the ground in the chair sized for Estreyans. "I fear you may have been misinformed," I said. "I am Eve of the line of Matrix."

She raised a hand to her mouth, as if embarrassed. "Oh! I apologize. A simple mistake."

Or a power play. I smiled.

"I must thank you for bringing my son back to me," she said. "I had believed he was dead and lost to me forever. It is a horrible thing to lose a child."

"I could do no less," I said. "The blood-covenant between us allied your son to me irrevocably."

"The blood-covenant which he will be severing," she parried. "Since it was not of his will, and furthermore was spread amongst a whole *slew* of people." She waved a hand in disgust.

"Of course," I said. "That is as it should be. It is not the greatest bond between us now, in any case. Your son has been marked by the Goddess of Testimony and Lore, as I am sure he told you."

"Indeed. What a joyous revelation. He says that the Oracle has set you on the path of the spark. The God of Knowledge has told you to come back with strength and petition before him for enlightenment about the Sickness that plagues our world?" Her voice was dry, but her eyes glittered with intensity, and her fingers clenched around her staff.

"Yes." So he had lied to his mother, too.

"The spark was indeed well hidden," she said with a hint of a smile and more than a dash of irony. She stood then, and walked over to me.

I rose to match her, and she reached forward and undid the bindings on my coat.

She pulled the coat away from me, revealing the crystal mark at the base of my neck, and the gifts of the Oracle on my arm and finger. "There should be three, should there not?"

"There are. I have not yet completed the third. I suspect I will not be able to until I have fulfilled the vision of the second."

She stared down at me. "My son says you may bring hope for my realm."

I stared back at her, feeling the ripple of her power, so close.

"He is surprisingly wise, for a young man. And a human holds no danger to my throne." She stared at me as she said it, gauging my reaction.

"I have no intention of undermining your rule, queen," I said. What was the point in subtlety, for a statement like that? "I have a Quest that may lead to some useful knowledge about how to defeat the Sickness, given to me by the Oracle." That was a lie. Or at least I hoped it was. The quest from the Oracle *could* eventually lead to knowledge about defeating the Sickness, but I had no reason to believe it would. What worried me was the acknowledgement of Testimony and Lore, in relation to a story about defeating said Sickness. But I would go along with it, because I refused to die if there was anything at all I could do to save myself. "I also have a crystal mark embedded in my flesh, given by Testimony and Lore. But the thing I really care about is that I have too much of the gods running through my veins for any mortal of my strength to survive, and I think the Oracle may be leading me to a solution. Your goals and my own meet. For now. So we should help each other."

If she was surprised, she didn't show it. Instead, she laughed. "My son told me you were bold. With you as my champion, I could give hope to the people."

She was laying out the terms of our bargain, I understood. "I would show my support publicly, and you would help me to complete my quest. I will need warriors strong enough to help me defeat a god," I said.

"Do such warriors exist?! At most, I could provide warriors that might aid you in impressing the god enough to gain a small Bestowal."

I shook my head. "It is not a small Bestowal that I need. We must prove that we can defeat the undefeatable, force the unconquerable to kneel. Nothing less will do." I hoped she couldn't hear my heartbeat, or notice it throbbing in my neck.

She drew back. "And what if you fail? It is I that will have to deal with the backlash for having sent the strongest of my forces to die at the word of a foreign girl."

I needed this. She *had* to agree. "I am a godling, progeny to Khaos," I said, enunciating clearly. And the crystal at my throat pulsed, adding an almost physical weight to my words. It was like a vibration, like the brush of wind against you from standing too close to an explosion, or like the feel of a giant foot smashing into the ground too near to you. For the first time, my Voice Skill had asserted itself actively.

Her eyes widened, and she stepped back, the movement almost a stumble.

"I will have the strongest warriors available," I said. "It doesn't have to be a command, you sending men to their deaths. Simply give me your support. Encourage volunteers. Once the hope of your people is proven to be grounded in fact, you will still reap the benefits."

Queen Mardinest raised an eyebrow. "You are not the first to claim connection to the Oracle or Testimony and Lore. Others have created false hope, many, many times. They have all failed, in the end, and my people have grown mistrustful."

"They were not me," I said. "It in my nature to succeed where others fail."

"We will see."

THE QUEEN and I talked for a little while longer. She instructed me on the other bloodlines that might either be allies or cause trouble, sounding somewhat like Torliam did when he lectured, except that she insulted me much less than he would have. Even so, her presence radiated more intimidation than his.

I asked about sending relief to the little village on the edge of Knowledge's domain that had been attacked by monsters. Apparently, Torliam had beaten me to it the night before. A unit was already headed toward the village. I just hoped there was something left to save.

After we were done, I headed to the kitchens to sate my growling stomach. A servant caught me on the way, and told me that Torliam had requested my presence after I had finished with the queen. I tried to get the servant to have Torliam just meet me in the kitchens, but she paled at the very idea of such rudeness, so I followed her with a sigh.

His quarters were on the nicer side of the castle, and *way* bigger than my own. I'm pretty sure he even had multiple rooms. He was pacing across the floor when I entered—which caused the servant to pale a second time and scurry away, presumably so she wouldn't be caught up in the backlash if he got angry.

Instead, he was awkward. "Now that we are back in my … home," he said, "I will finally be severing the blood-covenants forced upon me."

I nodded, giving him a small frown. "Okay. What exactly does that mean?"

"I know you do not fully understand the blood-covenant, but on my world, it is a way to bind people to each other. Historically, it would bind a servant to a master, or two life-partners to each other. Often, a wife and her husband will take the blood-covenant."

I raised my eyebrows. "And we have a blood-covenant."

"Yes. Well, partially. A proper bond goes both ways. My blood has been shared, but I have not received a covenant in return. I am bound to you and many, many others." He shuddered. "The covenant allows power to be shared between the two parties, to a certain extent. You and I have been able to sense each other across distances, before, and I always know where any of those with the bond are, if they are on my side of the divide between worlds. When I break the covenant, that, too, will be broken."

"What will happen to the Seeds already within people's bodies?"

"They will remain. You will not lose all your strength. But there will be a period of … acclimatization. Probably some loss of whatever strength you were drawing continuously from the bond. It can be disorienting, even painful. And as you humans," he said it without rancor, "are undoubtedly the weaker ones in the bond, in addition to not having shared your own blood, you will be affected much more than I. Do you wish to attend the ceremony? There will be healers there, bound to silence about what we do."

"Well, that seems like an obvious 'yes.' Should the others come, as well?" I asked.

"They are welcome to attend, if they wish. You should at least alert them that they will likely be feeling sick in some manner, sometime within the next hour." He turned and led the way down into the bowels of the castle in silence.

I sent a Window to the others, explaining what Torliam had told me, and sending a map of my route and location so they could follow. "How exactly does one break a blood-covenant?" I asked.

His jaw clenched. "By changing that which is shared. The method to do it is one of the old ways. It is forbidden, and highly restricted. But some still know the process, and as queen, my mother-lord has the ability to approve it. If done incorrectly, I will die."

"Whoever's doing this better know what they're doing," I muttered. "Does that also stop the other Seeds NIX took from you from being able to create new blood-bonds?" If not, the problem wouldn't be solved, since new Players could be created at will.

"It does. That is why we must do it this way."

We arrived in a big cavern, with a narrow path cutting through the stalagmites rising from the ground. It led to a large ritual circle in the center of the cavern, surrounded by orbs of colored light that lit up the ground and the tips of stalactites hanging down from far above.

People I assumed were healers stood off in a group to the side, and the queen turned at our arrival and nodded regally at us, though the tension in her body belied the serenity of her expression. Her eyes returned to the people in cheesy hooded robes who moved around the inside of the circle, setting things up.

The other Player members of the team, plus Blaine, arrived by the same path Torliam and I had taken, and though I'd heard them talking faintly before they entered the cavern, they quieted at the oppressive atmosphere of the place. They joined me, and Blaine, ever-curious, sent me a Window.

—Is this some sort of cultural ... ritual magic? Not *real* magic, of course. It is just advanced science. But is it something they treat with ceremony as if it is real magic?—
-Blaine-

I shrugged and shook my head. I knew as little as he did.

The hooded people began to chant ... or sing. I didn't recognize the language, and somehow the lilting, rhythmic way they spoke could have been either. The colored orbs resonated with their voices, seeming to reflect and throw them, till they seemed to come from everywhere at once, and the hair on my arms vibrated with every word as it throbbed through the air.

Torliam let out a sharp pulse of his blue misty power, and suddenly he was bleeding from the middle of his left forearm. He walked around the circle, filling the little lines that surrounded and connected the base of all the orbs with his trickling blood, in one continuous path that ended with him standing back in the middle without ever walking over the same blood-filled line twice. He looked a bit pale, and I knew that a comparatively smaller human would probably have passed out from blood-loss already.

The lilting chants grew louder, and louder, the sound of it a physical thing, kind of like the way the Boneshaker moved me from the inside.

The lines of blood flared with white light, and the orbs seemed to explode. With the flash of light and sound, something *shattered*. Like a crystal chandelier breaking forever in slow motion.

When the spots cleared from my eyes I noticed that the blood was gone from the circle. Torliam knelt in the middle, sagging from exhaustion while a couple of the healers worked on him.

I looked over at Jacky, who was hunched over and looking pale and slightly green, like really old fish.

Without warning, I bent over and threw up what little was in my stomach.

Chapter 29

I have been one acquainted with the night.
— Robert Frost

ONE OF THE healers came to make sure my team was all right, and Blaine questioned her. "I have two kids, and they were both given Skills from a goddess. I am very worried that the power is too much for them, and might backlash. Is there something you might be able to do for them? Or at least examine them to see if my worry is founded?"

The healer refused. "That is beyond my realm of ability. Beyond most healers, in fact." She left.

"Ifkana," I said, turning to Zed, who'd barely seemed to be affected by the bond-breaking ritual. "Isn't that the name the healer from the village recommended? He said he'd be one of the few able to extend my life."

Zed didn't even have time to nod before Blaine jumped in. "We need to see this Ifkana, then. As soon as possible."

I nodded. "I agree. We should take Chanelle, too, just in case.

If he's able to do something for me, he might be able to help her, too."

I passed along the plan to the others, and would have asked Torliam to accompany us, but the other healers had taken him off somewhere, presumably to rest after his ordeal and significant blood loss. I tried to ask the queen, but she'd disappeared, too. When we returned to the palace, I asked a servant to tell the queen I'd like to meet with her, but they said that she had left the palace, and they did not know when she'd be back.

We waited around for an hour, then grabbed another servant, and asked if they could take us to Ifkana the healer. They hesitated, but agreed, noting that no one would turn down an audience with Eve of the returned line of Matrix, even if an appointment hadn't been set up ahead of time. I was amazed by the wildfire spread of gossip, but if it would smooth the way for what I needed, I guessed I didn't mind.

We grabbed the kids and Chanelle, and followed the servant through the streets. The percentage of people walking or riding huge animals rather than vehicles surprised us.

The servant explained to Blaine that vehicles not meant for long distance travel, goods transportation, or attack were considered lazy. "It is as if one is making a statement that they are not powerful enough to travel on their own strength," he said. The servant brought us to a mansion almost as opulent as the palace, though significantly smaller.

We were then forced to wait in a room with very uncomfortable chairs that were too big for all of us.

Jacky leaned back in her chair, half-sliding off it. "Is this person busy healing half the population of a small country all at once, or are they just ignoring us?" she whined.

Chanelle spoke. "We are waiting to see a healer?" she asked, looking at me.

We all turned toward her, weariness instantly gone. It was rare that Chanelle could speak coherently, though increasing in frequency.

"Yes." I nodded. "He's supposed to be the best. Maybe even good enough to help you and me." It would be a wonderful thing, if Chanelle's mind could be returned to her.

She smiled, a jerky stretching of the mouth that didn't look very practiced. "That's good. I can't stay …" she paused, searching for the word, "*awake* for very long, still." She sniffed, a little like a dog. "I'm hungry. Is there any food?"

I dug out a fruit from my pack and tossed it to Chanelle.

She caught it, and grinned brightly at her success, the expression looking just a little more natural this time. She stayed lucid and kept eating until the healer finally deigned to see us.

One of his servants escorted us to a larger room filled with a couple jacuzzi-like tubs of water, strange devices, and a fat woman wearing an extremely long sheet that had been wrapped around her several times in artful ways. The translucent fabric glowed, and strands of what looked like gold glittered among the rest. Obviously, she was rich, and she wanted everyone to know it. Ifkana was not a man, I realized belatedly.

She turned to us with a smile, as if she'd been distracted from something, though I saw nothing she could have been working on. "Welcome, Eve of the line of Matrix," she said. "And companions, bearing the marks of Testimony and Lore, I hear?" She tilted her head like a little bird, eyes seeking out the crystal symbols on us.

Birch coughed at her, and she cooed over him, snapping her fingers at one of her servants and instructing them to go grab a snack for the, "darling little creature. And so *rare* a species, too!"

"Thank you for meeting with us on such short notice," I said, giving one of the bows Torliam had taught me for someone who wasn't socially above me, but who I respected. "I have heard you are the best, and we are in need of your services."

She tittered, waving a sausage-fingered hand. "Oh, of course I am the best. Queen Mardinest has been trying to retain my services since she first came into power, you know." She smirked. "I hear our *great* ruler is supporting your claim of heritage and Testimony?" The words were tinged with a hint of derision.

I raised an eyebrow. "It would be hard for her to deny it, with the abundance of proof. You are certainly well-informed, though. We only arrived in the city yesterday."

"Oh, I have my ways, you know. I am a *powerful* healer," she said, a kind of smug significance in her tone. She asked me who needed healing and of what, and then motioned me forward. She waved her hand about, and a bright purple light arced from it, almost like ribbon unfurling. It spun around me, changing colors, and making patterns which she seemed to pay only passing attention to, more interested in making conversation with me. She wanted to know about my connection to Torliam and the queen, my quest from the Oracle, and the gifts Testimony and Lore had given my team.

I felt strangely reluctant to reveal too much information, because her questions had sharp teeth, hidden behind her facade of pleasantry. I wondered if she was one of the people who wanted Queen Mardinest removed from power. They weren't allies, that was definite.

Finally, the purple ribbon returned to Ifkana, disappearing into the hand that had created it. "Your regenerative power is strong," she said. "I will boost it, but there is not much more I can do for you at the moment. When that wears off, you come back to me, and I will keep you healthy a while longer. You know that no mortal can stave off the effects of a greater god's power indefinitely, though?"

I nodded.

Kris and Gregor were next, and she told them to come forward together. Once again, she waved out the purple ribbon, and it began to swirl and dance around them, as she asked them about their Skills from the Oracle.

Gregor pouted while Kris exclaimed excitedly about summoning spirits and putting them into bodies to play with her or complete tasks.

When Ifkana tried to get Gregor to talk about his own Skill, he scowled down at the ground and refused to speak.

Ifkana seemed to find this more irritating than endearing, but was distracted by Jacky, who was more than happy enough to talk about her own new Skill. The purple ribbon, still focused on the kids, let out a pulse of red halfway through one of Jacky's sentences, and Ifkana's attention snapped toward it as if it had slapped her.

"What?" she said aloud, waving her arms and moving her fingers in complicated motions that seemed to control the ribbon. It turned all red. She gasped, and stepped back, hand over her heart.

"What's wrong?" Gregor asked. "Is the Skill killing us after all?"

Adam took a step forward, but froze when Ifkana screamed, "Do not move! Everyone stay still." Once her back was pressed against the wall, she spewed out another purple ribbon, this time sending it weaving among the rest of the group.

It stayed purple, until it reached Chanelle, where it turned an instant bright red.

Chanelle looked down, blinking at the ribbon of light circling her. "That's ... not good, is it?"

"You are infected," Ifkana said, her voice wavering. "It is not the Skills you need to worry about, but the Sickness."

Chapter 30

A star shines brightest at the edge of collapse.
— Omar Thornton

"THAT IS IMPOSSIBLE!" Blaine said. "Kris and Gregor do not have your world's disease. They are not even Estreyan!"

"It is early," Ifkana said, "but I do not err. I am the best healer on this side of the seven seas! The children have the Sickness, and the fair one," she pointed at Chanelle, "will soon succumb to it."

"We have been here a long time, now," Chanelle said, in a soft voice. "And some of us much longer than that. Maybe the weakest of us picked it up along the way." She spoke in English, and Ifkana flinched from her words, like they might somehow hurt her.

There was silence, then. My mind was reeling. Of all the things we could have learned, and all the bad news I had braced to hear from Ifkana, I had not expected this.

"What does this mean?" Gregor asked. "I'm going to die?" His breath came a little too fast.

"No," Blaine and I both said immediately.

"You should go," Ifkana said.

Blaine shook his head desperately. "Is there nothing you can do?"

"No one can heal the Sickness! It has no cure, and—" she calmed herself with a visibly shuddering breath, and looked at me. "You may find the cure for them, if you are what you say, Eve of the line of Matrix. The very marks on their hand set them on the path to save themselves." She straightened. "You should go. It is not safe for you to be here, only in part because the Sickness may spread. The *warrior-queen* may pardon those with the Sickness. Otherwise, the solution is always death. To reduce the chance of it spreading, or the affected going on a rampage and killing indiscriminately, those with the Sickness are to be killed, everything that they are and have owned obliterated from the face of the planet."

Kris whimpered, and Blaine knelt down to hug her and Gregor, glaring at Ifkana over their shoulders. "I swear I will not let that happen," he said.

"Go," she said. "Take them back to the palace."

"Don't say anything about this," I ordered her. "I don't want anyone doing something stupid."

"I will not tell anyone," she agreed, nodding rapidly enough that her second chin jiggled.

We'd waited so long for her to see us that it was night out when we excited the house.

Gregor grabbed onto my hand as we hurried through the streets. "You really can fix this, right?"

"Yes. It's going to take me a bit of work, but don't worry. We won't let anything happen to you."

Sam and Blaine shared a look, and then Sam sent out a group Window, connecting everyone but the kids and Chanelle to it.

—Your quest isn't actually to stop the Sickness, though, is it? Just to get information about it?—
-Sam-

I ground my teeth together. My quest had nothing at all to do with the Sickness, but everyone in the world, and now even my own team, needed my lie to be the truth.

—No. But Testimony and Lore seemed to think I had something to do with this "spark" that they think will find the way to save them. Maybe the third puzzle will have information about that, or I'll get another Quest.—
-Eve-

—Do we actually have time for that? How fast does the Sickness progress?—
-Adam-

—I need access to a lab. There's no way a cure is not possible without some alien god's help. Science does not work like that.—
-Blaine-

We were almost back to the palace when the blast knocked me off my feet. We'd been walking through mostly deserted streets, with what were probably shops and warehouses, since there weren't any people in their beds within.

My body and face smashed into the wall of the alley I'd been blown into, and I bounced off, dizzy and *burning*. I scrabbled blindly at my unprotected arms and neck, ripping off the smoldering remains of my clothes and pack.

"Get into the alley!" Adam screamed, throwing up a broad ink shield in the direction the attack had come from.

I rose to my feet, looking around frantically. Wraith lashed out, but found no others—wait, no—"There!" I screamed, spinning around to face the form rushing from the alley's other opening.

Zed's guns were out and shooting in half a second, but the person *dodged* the bullets as I watched, racing inevitably closer.

Adam threw out another shield, this one covering the other end of the alley.

The attacker stopped before it for a second.

Another explosion from behind made me stumble, and Adam's first shield disintegrated. He frantically created a replacement, layering multiple shields instead of just one.

"What's happening?" Sam screamed, the children and Chanelle pressed up against the wall behind him, protected by a human barrier formed from himself, Blaine, and Jacky. They'd boxed us in, attacks coming from both ends.

"We were betrayed," I said, the words coming to my mouth as soon as they formed in my mind.

The speedster took a few steps back, and jumped at the wall, bouncing off it onto the other wall, and then tossing himself over the top of the ink shield.

"I will not let you hurt them!" Blaine screamed, reaching for his own gun, and pointing it at the attacker falling straight toward us. The bullet shot out, spinning, and fragmenting outward and inward simultaneously in a way that baffled even the Perception of my Wraith Skill, and threatened to give me a headache if I focused on it too hard.

The wall of the building behind Speedster *ruptured* when the bullet hit, but he was no longer in its path. The stone statue that had replaced his form mid-fall exploded outward, chunks raining down on us.

Instead of being pulverized by Blaine's weapon, Speedster stood atop the building above, looking down on us, beside another huge form, which was so wide and muscular it looked like an orc.

"Agh!" Adam screamed, as his multi-leveled ink barrier against the street attacker failed. The heat grew dizzying. He was blown back when his last ink shield disintegrated under the touch of the floating female form made of magma.

My eyeballs burned as the water evaporated from them, and I smelled burning hair.

Blaine shot at the creature, and it threw a hand forward.

A blast of fire pulsed out and engulfed the bullet, the two attacks meeting above Adam. The bullet released its effects, which were enough to blow the fireball apart and tear into the magma creature, blasting her stomach apart and blowing pieces of her everywhere.

Adam *screamed* as the heat of the exploded fireball hit him, turning him pink instantly, and sizzling away the hair on his face. He scrambled backward, pushing himself along the ground with his legs, covering his face with his arms.

Blaine shot again, but the huge form up above gestured, and the slow-moving bullet was replaced by some pebbles which fell impotently onto the ground. In the air far up above, the real bullet exploded, with a similar lack of damage to anything important.

Zed shot at the two on the roof, but most of his bullets were stopped by the orcish Estreyan, and the others were dodged by Speedster, who nudged his comrade out of the way when necessary.

Jacky let out a frustrated scream, crouched down, and launched herself up and at the wall, imitating speedster's zig-zagging jumps to much greater effect.

I slipped back to take her place protecting the kids, broadcasting out a Window to everyone. It displayed everyone's location, and any danger I thought might go unnoticed, updating as fast as I could process the same information. I didn't have any long-distance Skills, except Wraith, and maybe Voice, but neither of those were helpful, and I didn't want to leave the kids or Chanelle unprotected. If only Torliam were with us, this fight would be going very differently.

Jacky distracted Orc long enough for Blaine to get off another couple shots against Magma, but when Sam took the opportunity to try and grab Adam off the ground, it left an unprotected spot in our shield wall around the kids and Chanelle.

Blaine was distracted by the way the pieces of Magma he'd blown off her were inching their way back to the main body, globules burning snail-trails across the ground and walls.

Speedster took that opportunity, shooting himself straight down off the top of the wall toward us.

Zed clipped him in the leg with a bullet, I think, but it didn't change his trajectory.

The kids were huddled down, heads tucked into their knees and arms up for protection, but Kris looked up, and screamed. She thrust both hands out and up, as if she could stop the falling attacker in mid-air.

The crumbled statue from earlier that had taken Speedster's spot slammed itself clumsily back together, rising to fill the spot Sam had left. It thrust a fist forward to meet Speedster, but when they collided, the soft sandstone-like material of the statue crumbled and broke.

Speedster pushed off the statue to launch himself toward Sam instead, who was crouching over Adam. He smashed his feet into the back of Sam's head, knocking the boy out cold.

Adam launched an arc of lightning from underneath Sam, catching Speedster with enough force to throw him back down the alley.

Up above, Jacky had grown to match Orc, and was using her Skill to great effect, flashing all over the place, hitting him again and again with enough force that I could feel the vibrations traveling through the walls and the ground.

Even so, Orc seemed to be withstanding the onslaught, and the occasional blow he returned hit just as hard.

Blaine ran out of the cool ammo, then, and things went to hell.

Magma floated forward, her pieces reconstituting back into the whole, ignoring the normal rounds that impacted into her body with little ripples. She raised her hands slowly, and the temperature rose with them, as if she were calling up Hell from the depths of the earth.

"Cover the Speedster," I snapped, targeting him on both Zed and Blaine's maps. I stepped around toward Magma, trading places with them as she thrust a hand forward, aiming at Adam.

He threw up another shield, but I knew it wouldn't be enough. This had to end *now*.

I lashed out toward her with my own clawed hand, feeling Chaos scraping against my insides as it bubbled up gleefully, rushing out in a wave of dark-tendrilled destruction.

She fell apart where it touched, and launched herself backward to escape my reach, her body slagged half away in the front. That didn't stop her, though. In fact, it seemed like it just made her angry. She flew upward, dripping little pieces of liquid heat.

Up above, Orc reached for Jacky.

I realized what was about to happen, and updated her Window with the coming attack and her possible escape trajectory.

But it was too late. Orc's hands clamped down around her shoulders with unnaturally long arms.

She lifted up her feet, kicking him in the face, but though his head rocked back, he didn't let go.

And then Magma was above them, streaming fire down onto Jacky.

Jacky screamed, first in pain, then in desperate rage. Her hair crinkled and burnt from the ends.

Adam rolled Sam's unconscious form off him and sprayed out the ink from a canister with a swing of his arm.

Jacky's body shuddered, as if trying to grow even more, but the fire streamed down on her, going from dark red to orange, to bright yellow.

I screamed in denial.

Jacky sagged, and her body began to shrink.

A human-sized ink bird slammed into Magma from the side, dissolving even as it forced her over the side of the roof and slammed her into the street below.

Speedster was gone. He'd escaped out into the street while we'd all been distracted. He was out of my range, but I could follow the vague trail of his blood from where Zed and Blaine had gotten a few shots in. Not enough blood.

The sandstone statue under Kris' control, still missing an arm, grabbed Sam, and dragged him back toward us.

"Go save her!" Kris screamed.

Adam, skin blistered and hands shaking, limped over to us. "I've got this!"

I leapt away, my claws sinking into the stone of the wall, puncturing it with a sound almost like gunshots as I crawled up the wall like a spider, muscles straining as I pushed myself faster and faster. I threw myself over the side, leaping for Orc with my claws extended. I scratched across his face futilely, and he released his grip on one of Jacky's arms, punching out at me.

I was already throwing myself back, but his punch caught my leg, and my knee buckled, hyperextending backward. I screamed. I caught myself on one foot, never so grateful for my high Grace level as at that moment. I leapt forward, lashing out once more.

Then I was slamming face down into the ground below, halfway down the alley.

Up above, a sandstone statue of me impacted harmlessly against Orc. The bit of Chaos I'd managed to get out before he teleported me away wasn't so harmless. It ripped into his chest.

He released Jacky in shock, and toppled backward off the roof, falling toward me.

I rolled.

He slammed into the ground next to me.

I shaped my hand like a spear, leaning over Orc, throwing my whole body into a jab toward the hollow of his throat.

Speedster slammed into me, crushing me into the alley wall at high speed. My head slammed into the stone with a crunch that I felt as well as heard.

Someone screamed. I couldn't move.

Orc got up, moving over to the group still huddled against the wall.

Zed shot at him.

"Adam, can you get them out of here?" Blaine screamed. "Just grab one kid in each arm and run for it!"

Speedster didn't give Adam a chance, jerking jaggedly around the shields Adam which threw up with shaking hands, before they could even fully form.

Adam must have been almost out of ink. And almost out of energy.

Blaine stepped forward to meet Speedster, and was thrown out into the street, his fingers and hand breaking around his gun grotesquely.

Adam plunged both his hands into his electricity cartridges, and stepped forward away from the kids, arcs of lighting shooting off him in a pincer movement, grasping for Speedster from every angle.

Speedster went down, but Adam's knees buckled along with him.

One of the residual arcs of electricity lashed him, and Sam woke up with a dramatic gasp.

Gregor slapped him across the face, screaming at him to "get *up!*"

Orc reached Zed, unhurriedly slapping his guns aside. He smashed his forearm into Zed's neck, pinning him against the wall, and then dragging him upward against it, so they were looking eye to eye.

The sky above us filled with firelight, again.

Sam stood up, standing with arms spread in front of the kids and Chanelle.

I coughed, twitching my fingers. I had to move. I *had* to *move*.

Kris pointed, screaming. Had she ever stopped screaming? The sandstone statue obeyed, slamming into Orc, beating on his arms, kicking at his legs, destroying itself in a futile attempt to free Zed.

Zed, who was kicking and scratching, and turning purple.

Another sandstone statue dropped down close to me, its legs crumbling up to the knee when it landed. It was shaped like me, and it carried Jacky in its arms, bringing her to Sam. It dropped her on the ground in front of him, and turned to aid its counterpart in attacking the Orc.

Sam dropped to his knees to heal Jacky.

Kris ran toward me.

Gregor hesitated, then followed.

They each grabbed one of my arms, trying to help me up, or to drag me.

I lifted my head, looking up to the bright body of flaming, molten heat above.

It streaked down like a falling star, landing in front of us.

Kris was blown back, landing on the ground. She scrabbled away.

Gregor caught himself on my body, and was still within reach of Magma.

I twitched my fingers, letting Chaos spear out of me. "No," I whispered. "I won't let you."

She threw herself out of the way, losing only a few pieces of her arm.

Then she reached again for Gregor.

My arm moved, pushing me upward. But not fast enough.

Gregor screamed, but there was nowhere for him to escape.

Her molten hand sizzled through his shirt, and then sank all the way forward.

I screamed.

But Gregor didn't. He didn't make a sound. The pitch-black form of darkness that lay where he had was unharmed. It stood up, moving around Magma's arm like she didn't exist. Or like *it* didn't.

Her head turned to stare in astonishment, and then snapped around, as a rip opened up in the world.

Zed fell backward into the void, and Orc slipped through it with him, my brother's hands still clawing at his wrist.

The rip in the face of the world closed up behind them, as if it had never been. One second passed, and then two.

The world ripped again, and Zed crawled out through the

crack headfirst, flopping onto the ground. His clothes were frosted over. His lips were blue and chattering. He was alive.

Orc didn't come with him.

Magma spared another glance for Gregor's black form, and then turned toward Chanelle.

Jacky was awake, after Sam's ministrations, but she couldn't stand.

Sam had propped her up next to Chanelle, muttering "oh god no" over and over to himself.

Magma shot herself toward them, spewing flames from an outstretched hand.

Sam stepped straight forward into it, screaming like a broken thing. Screaming defiance, and hatred, and death. He was burning, and healing himself, and burning some more. Then he changed, power pulsing from him under the sight of Wraith.

Magma stopped. Her feet touched the ground. She tried to backpedal.

Sam stepped forward, his hand grasping her forehead.

The magma turned to flesh.

He grasped her head between both hands, pressing down.

I could see her fire-bright eyes reflected in his own. But his were just black mirrors. No white, no blue. All pupil. All sucking devouring *apathy*.

She burst and crumbled and melted and was eaten away.

When he rose, he stood over half-melted stone, and a pile of pieces that didn't seem as if they had ever resembled a human form. He looked at his hands, then up to me. "I don't feel ... anything," he said, his voice echoing as if it had come from a deep place.

Behind him, Jacky called softly. "Sam? Are you okay?" Her voice was small with fear.

He turned to her. "Of course. I can heal you better now. But before I do that ..." he turned to Speedster. "I'm going to kill him."

Chapter 31

All is not lost, the unconquerable will,
and study of revenge, immortal hate,
and the courage never to submit or yield.
— John Milton

SAM DID INDEED KILL SPEEDSTER, reducing him to another small pile. Then he healed the rest of us, easier than he'd ever done it, even when I had first met him. "Should we go after the betrayer?" he asked, directing those black holes that his eyes had become toward me.

I resisted the urge to shudder. "Yes."

He nodded. "I think I'll be able to get her to talk. We need to make sure she didn't alert anyone else. And that she won't have a chance to do so again."

Gregor slipped out of his shadow state back into normal flesh and blood, and promptly passed out. Kris did the same, as soon as she gave up control over her two mostly destroyed golems.

Chanelle had a brief moment of lucidity just before we left the alley, and looked around in shocked confusion. "What happened?"

"We got in a fight," I said simply. It probably hadn't been more than ten minutes since the fight started. Fifteen at the max, still ... "We need to hurry," I said. "Estreyan enforcers might be coming. People had to have heard the noise, or seen the lights."

I dug the Oracle's third gift out of the charred remains of my ruined pack, and then we gathered together any obvious evidence of what had happened that we could find.

Zed opened up another rip in the world and tossed everything through.

I stumbled back from the feeling of cold death, and he closed the rip.

I took only Sam and Jacky with me when we returned to Ifkana's house, leaving the others hidden a few streets away. A short exploration with Wraith found Ifkana in an upstairs bedroom, pacing back and forth.

Jacky jumped up with Sam, and then with me, and we entered through the balcony.

Ifkana didn't have time to let out more than a yelp before Jacky clenched her hand around the healer's throat.

Ifkana waved her hands, dark green ribbon coming out, and Jacky spasmed.

Sam pulled Jacky back to safety.

When Ifkana's eyes met his, the woman's knees buckled under her, bringing her height to just below his.

"Those three you sent after us are dead. Did you tell anyone else?" he said, staring down at her.

She shook her head slowly, face going slack. "My personal guard. I thought ... they would kill you," she said.

Sam killed her. She didn't scream.

Jacky flinched, but I couldn't look away.

Zed slipped through a crack in the air above Sam. "I got a Window. You called?" he said.

Sam pointed to the ground. "Cleanup." He turned to me. "Should we kill the servants, too? One of them might have heard something."

I hesitated, then shook my head. "It's not worth it. If even one of them escapes while we're doing it, we'll be caught. The longer we stay here, the greater the chance. And we need to get the others back to the castle where it's safe. As it is now, it would only be our word against a servant's."

He nodded, and we left. It wasn't till we'd gotten back to our rooms at the castle that the black faded from his eyes. He stumbled, and passed out, too.

Jacky tucked him into bed. Unlike the night before, we all packed into three adjacent rooms instead of all along the hallway. We'd been shown how little time there might be to react if an Estreyan attacked us. Not enough time to make it all the way down the hall.

When I opened my door, Torliam was sitting on my bed with Birch, scowling. "Where have you been?"

"We had to kill some people," Jacky said. "Hope we're not gonna get in trouble for that."

He eyed her hair, which had been burnt short, then turned to me and sighed deeply, rubbing his face. "Explain."

Chapter 32

We are born only with the adored knowledge of self-destruction.
— Kaiser Fell

I WAS hesitant to tell Torliam that Chanelle, Kris, and Gregor had the Sickness, but he didn't react like Ifkana.

He paled, but the next words out of his mouth were, "We have to save them before it is too late. The Oracle must have known this would happen. It does not mean hope is lost."

I wondered if that were true.

Torliam told me that after what had happened with his sister, his mother no longer had the authority to pardon someone from death if it was revealed that they had the Sickness. Ifkana had lied to us. It was hard to feel any remorse for her death, so I didn't try.

"Is it going to be a problem? We killed the most powerful healer this side of the seven seas, by her own words. Along with three other Estreyans. There's a good amount of property damage."

He leaned back. "Some will try to use this to their advantage. We will just have to move first, and set the tone of the situation. You were attacked by enemies of my mother when going to see

Ifkana the healer to make sure the children were able to withstand their new powers. These enemies killed Ifkana before coming after you, but you were able to defeat them. Perhaps these people had the Sickness, or had been affected by it in some way."

I frowned. "Will people believe that?"

"No, not all of them. The ones who don't will notice that a powerful rival of my mother's was killed the day after we returned. They will likely see it as a statement. A power play."

"What about the servants? We didn't kill them. What if one of them heard something? Does your city have surveillance cameras? There have got to be investigative forces that will be assigned to something like this."

"Queen Mardinest is powerful. We will give her a modified version of what happened. One of her people will make sure that nothing certain ever makes it out."

I sat back, feeling somewhat mollified, but not completely satisfied. I never liked letting other people handle important things in my stead. But I didn't really have a choice here, since I had no idea how to fix the problem myself.

"Once the people believe in us," he said, "something like this will not sway them. You ... we are going to save this world. Anyone who stands against us stands against our salvation. There is no one who would excuse that, for any reason. Once they believe."

"So how do we get them to believe?" I asked.

"Give them hope. If we can make them truly hope, they will believe as a function of that, rather than the other way around. It will be too painful for them to doubt."

Like Egon the patrol leader, and the old healer who had helped us escape from the village. I nodded, and said, "Before we can proceed, we need to enter that Fear Trial you mentioned before. It may all be for naught, if we can't remove the God of Knowledge's influence from our minds. I, for one, cannot continue to function with his maggots—" The very thought it made them wiggle a bit. I clenched my jaw so hard my molars creaked.

Torliam didn't respond right away, and didn't meet my eyes. "I will take you there. Tomorrow. Tonight, I will speak with the queen."

WHEN TORLIAM LEFT, I took my mattress over to the next room, where Zed, Sam, and Blaine were.

Birch was pretty irritated at me, and took every opportunity to flatten his ears or look pointedly away.

"I'm sorry we left you behind," I said in a low voice, since Sam and Blaine were asleep. "You were with Torliam anyway. Didn't you have fun today?"

Birch snorted and grabbed my pillow, pulling it over to the corner and stamping on it emphatically before plopping down on top of it with his back to me.

Zed chuckled. "You didn't need a pillow anyway, right? It's not like you were planning to sleep with it."

I rolled my eyes. "Of course not. I brought my only pillow for the sole purpose of not using it."

"Well, you can't have mine." He paused. "We could probably get one of the servants to bring us another."

I sighed. "Forget it. I'm tired."

"Me, too." We lay in silence for a while, and then he spoke again. "Veil-Piercer. It's pretty much as cool as I imagined. It's like … I can see these cracks in the world. And if I concentrate hard enough, I can slip my fingers into them and peel them back. It's like our world, but … not. I've been calling it the Other Place in my mind. It's cold there. Like warmth has never existed. And I noticed it started leeching all the feelings out of me. I don't mean because it was cold. It was like it was freezing my *emotions* out." He paused. "I admit it's dangerous. I could get stuck over there."

"I wish I could tell you not to use your Skill," I said. "But I can't. And I'm not going to try. Just be careful, okay?"

"Umm, I feel like I could be saying that to *you*. How many times did you use Chaos today?"

"Three times? I'll meditate before I go to sleep. That healer Ifkana boosted my Resilience earlier. It might have been bad, if she hadn't."

"What's the plan for defeating Knowledge?" Zed asked, following the obvious train of thought.

"Gain lots of strong Estreyan supporters who are willing to risk their life against him," I said. "I'm going to do that Fear Trial Torliam talked about tomorrow. Got to get Knowledge out of my head first."

Zed snorted. "When did any knowledge ever get *in* your head?"

I knew he was worried for me, but there was nothing either of us could do about it. "You're lucky Birch stole my pillow. Otherwise you'd be getting a face full of feathers right about now."

"*You're* lucky Sam and Blaine are sleeping it off, or being pillow-poor wouldn't save you."

With a grin, I turned over and tucked my arm under my head, meditating for a while before I fell asleep.

When I woke in the morning, both Zed and Blaine were gone, and Sam was straightening his bedding. He noticed that I was awake, and said, "I'm okay," over his shoulder.

When I didn't respond, he continued. "I know you were probably wondering. Considering … what I did last night. I mean, it was pretty horrifying."

When he turned around, I examined his face. "Are you really okay?"

"I've decided I'm not going to feel bad about it. If I hadn't done what I did, those people would have killed Kris, and Gregor, and Chanelle. I could never live with myself if I didn't …" He sat across from me.

If only just deciding not to feel bad about something actually worked. My own life would be much easier. "You saved us," I said.

"This time." His voice had grown hoarse, and he laughed self-consciously. "But it wasn't even *me*, you know? The Skill took over. I remember what happened, and that person wasn't *me*. If it had been me, I would have frozen, and they would have died, just like China."

I shook my head. "Sam, that's not—"

"Don't lie to me!" he said angrily. "We both know it. But the kicker is, I don't even know what it is that I did. I don't know how to turn Black Sun on, and I don't know how to turn it off. What if —if I need to be that other person again, and I can't? Or what if I can't turn it off, and I do something that I *should* regret? When that Skill is active, I don't care about anything. It's like I've got this sucking emptiness inside me. I wasn't saving the kids because I wanted to save them, I was just doing it because ... I don't even know why. Because I'd wanted to before the Skill activated? Because it was interesting?"

We sat in silence, while I tried to figure out what to say. If Sam did something horrible under the influence of his Skill... "That would be bad," I said.

He snorted.

"It would be," I said. "But there is nothing outside of our control. I have to believe that. If we push hard enough, search far enough, and fight harder than we think we're capable of, we can change things. If that happened, we would just have to find a way to fix it. Maybe you'd need another Skill to balance Black Sun out. Or maybe we'd need to get the you who's under the influence of Black Sun to *agree* to act in a manner that normal Sam can live with."

He stared at the ground for minutes. When he finally raised his head, his eyes didn't glitter with agitation anymore. "That's how you do it? You just believe hard enough that you control your destiny?"

I shrugged. "Then, you have to actually *act*. Belief doesn't do much, in a vacuum. But the point is, there's no use worrying. If you need to fix something, fix it. That's all there is to do."

Sam laughed. "When you say it like that, it seems so simple."

I laughed. "I wish!"

"Anyway." He cleared his throat. "Blaine said his genius was needed elsewhere, and I think Zed went to go train with the others. Torliam stopped by while you were sleeping. He said to meet him in airship field three."

It was a testament to how exhausted I'd been the night before that I hadn't woken up while any of this was happening, despite how paranoia normally interrupted my sleep on a regular basis. I nodded, and left to go find Torliam.

He had been working while I slept, if the bags under his eyes and the crustacean-shaped ship I found him in were any indication. "We leave when you are ready," he said. "I have alerted the media, and they will meet us on the mount of Phobos and Deimos. The Estreyan people will want to see this."

The idea of people spectating as I subjected myself to a Trial made me uncomfortable, but I climbed in anyway.

I'm not sure what I had expected, but Torliam set the ship on autopilot while he took a nap, and we flew silently to the top of a peaceful mountain range. Soft green grass, totally out of season, grew from the ground at the top of the tallest mountain. Black spheres, as large as a person, floated unmoving above the grass. They made my Wraith Skill hurt to look at them, and reminded me of the way Sam's eyes had looked the previous night.

"You will enter one," Torliam said, slowing the ship so that it hovered above the edge of the mountain. "It will show you the monstrous depths of your mind. If you can make it through, you will gain control, and be able to fight back. Remember, the things it shows you are not real. You have control over everything."

Behind us, the dots of other ships began to fill the sky. The Estreyan equivalent of reporters, coming to document our success or failure.

"I'm guessing it will be harder than you're making it sound?"

"Significantly. Telling yourself there is no reason to be afraid when you are terrified is not always useful."

It would be different, at least, than being forced to acknowledge that I had every right to be terrified, and having to press onward anyway. "You'll enter one of the other spheres?"

He hesitated. "Yes."

I frowned, turning to peer at him. "You don't want to do this." I said it as a statement, though I meant it as a question.

"On the God of Knowledge's mountain, when the light of his sentinels reached my eyes, he showed me ... something that had happened in the past. My sister died of the Sickness, as you know. I was much younger then, and though I had known those who fell to its grasp, none of them had been so close to me. Her death spurred my search for a cure, though everyone thought I was crazed by grief, obsessed with a futile goal. The God of Knowledge showed me her death, over again. But I knew, with every day, how she felt as her mind turned against her, her body blackening and growing putrid. As we all hovered over her, and the connections she felt toward us, her family, and the people she loved ... they were severed, and twisted, till she could not tell love from hate, family from ... food." He shuddered. "I felt it all, knew it all, as if I *were* her."

"You're afraid to go through that again."

"Yes. I know it must be done, but ... I fear I will not leave with my mind intact. I have experienced many things in my life. When I was within NIX, before they forced you into blood-covenant with me, and then again when I thought you were one of them created to torture me, I came closer than I like to think to losing my grip on the strings that connect me to myself. I am not invincible. I have almost lost myself before."

I reached out and grasped him by the elbow. "This is different," I said. "Because you have hope." I raised his hand, looking pointedly at the mark of crystal branded all the way through. "Your suffering was not in vain. You found the descendant of the line of Matrix. And we are going to fix everything." I was lying, in a way. But I wished it were the truth.

He clenched that crystal-marked fist, and stared at it. "Sentimental drivel," he sneered. But a smile followed the words, and he settled the ship down on the grass at the edge of the mountain.

The reporters swooped in, landing all around, the more eager ones hopping out of their ships before they had even settled. They carried small tubes that beamed light out toward us.

"Those devices will record everything we do and say, in three dimensions. Others will watch it, later. Be careful that you do not lie. It will be found out, under scrutiny," Torliam said, walking with me towards the black spheres.

"What?!" The word popped out of my mouth, full of alarm.

He sighed deeply and shook his head, as if continuing to talk to me would drain him of all energy. He stopped near the edge of a sphere to call out to the reporters, "Today, we conquer our minds. Tomorrow, what can hold us back?"

They burst out with questions, all talking over each other, not so different from reporters on Earth, even if their equipment was way more sophisticated.

Torliam ignored them.

With one last look towards each other, we stepped forward, into the black.

Chapter 33

It isn't the light you want to recover, it's the certainty that there is only darkness.
—Paulo Coelho

INSIDE, it was dark. I blinked compulsively, instinctively trying to get my eyes to adjust till they could see, but the light just wasn't there. I jerked when I felt the fog intruding on my mind, sifting through it.

I very likely would have panicked just from that, what with the God of Knowledge doing something so similar and all the pain it had caused me, if not for Torliam's earlier words.

I held back the instinctive shudder when the darkness started to lessen, and I felt little tiny, hairy legs—spider legs—running over my body, around my neck and down my back, in my ears and hair.

I didn't panic when that changed, and I was suddenly sitting on the ground, with my fingers resting on something that felt like finger bones.

It must have been pulling memories from my Characteristic Trial. A good place to start, I agreed, though maybe not the best.

I still didn't panic when the bones clacked to life around me, grabbing on and wrapping themselves around my body, and dragging me backward into dark water. The illumination grew, just enough that I could see things—large things—moving through the water at the edges of my vision. I'd been scared of whales and sharks as a small child, and had had this nightmare before. I held my breath, and willed myself to remember that this was nothing more than a dream.

My heart started to beat faster as I held my breath, the organ attempting to distribute oxygen to my burning muscles, and the beats brought with them a sour feeling, like the beginnings of real fear. Not good. The longer I could stay calm, the better. I knew things could only get worse from here. So I breathed out, and then sucked in, drawing the water into my lungs, and continuing to suck even as they cried out with the unnatural burning sensation. There was no water. I only perceived water.

And sure enough, my heart stopped pounding so hard, and as I breathed in and out, it calmed and returned to normal, the only tension in my body the discomfort of my lungs. The water slipped away, not as if it was draining from some big tub, but as if it was just deciding to be air instead.

I was on the ground, then, the area around me lit by what seemed like a spotlight, though I could see no source for the light.

Jacky walked into the spotlight with me. Without saying a word, she spat in my face and walked away.

Were they trying to make me angry? Just trying to get any emotional response out of me so that another one would be closer to the surface? I wiped off the spit and listened to her footsteps echoing away till it was silent.

There was a scrabbling beyond the sharp edge of darkness. Panting.

I grimaced, sensing a hint of what was to come.

Fingers, bent and twitching, entered the ring of light. A nose, a mouth, and a face with blue eyes and blonde hair. Chanelle, or maybe China.

She slobbered, looking crazed. Her eyes were full of hunger. Chanelle, then.

I reached out and petted her on the head as if she was a dog, and she rolled over onto her back, still panting and slobbering but now with a silly smile on her face as she tried to get me to rub her belly.

Then she straightened and jumped up, reaching out for me, suddenly coherent and worried. "Run!" She screamed, and then her body twisted and broke, falling to the ground in slow motion as her gaze stayed locked on mine.

I took a shuddering breath and looked away. Not real. It wasn't real. We were going to save Chanelle, just like China had wanted. And China wasn't here.

"It's your fault," she whispered from the ground, blood bubbling from her mouth.

I turned back to her, gently straightened her out a bit and crossed her arms over her chest, then pushed her back out of the light. I waited.

Zed stumbled forward, bleeding from the eyes. "Help ... help," he gasped, reaching out for me desperately.

My arms lifted to stabilize him almost involuntarily, and he collapsed forward, no longer able to support his own weight. I wanted to help, but as blood bubbled from underneath his eyelids, silver-grey foam frothed up from his mouth. The nanites that NIX had invented. I'd known they needed maintenance, but we'd stolen some of their nutrient paste! He had been taking it, hadn't he? When was the last time I saw him do it? He hadn't run out, and not told me, right? That sounded like something *I* would do, I thought ironically.

"You've been eating their nutrient paste, right? Right!?" I slapped his cheek gently, trying to get him to focus as his eyes rolled back in his head. I was breathing faster, and my heart was definitely beating faster than normal. "Oh, god," I said aloud. This Trial was better than I had hoped. Or worse.

I laid him gently on the ground. "I would never let this happen to you in real life," I murmured, and walked away into the darkness. I didn't look back.

The ground fell out from under me, and I was plummeting down toward the God of Knowledge, my claws out and Chaos lashing toward him. "Ahh!" I screamed. I could see into his open mouth.

He reached out to me, hand smashing through the air, slamming into my side, fingers folding around me, crushing. He brought me down toward his mouth, which yawned open, unnaturally wide in a way that would have caused human cheeks to rip open at the crease of the lips. I could see bits of human flesh within, stuck between his teeth and rotting away.

I opened my mouth to scream again, and somehow, it, too began to open wider and wider, till it eclipsed my body, and then his. My gigantic mouth crashed downward around his head, the teeth ripping and grinding till I'd severed through his neck. I chewed the crunchy metal of his head and swallowed, and his rusting golden body fell to the ground, lifeless.

My stomach roiled, first in nausea, and then in something else. Light poured out of my eyes and mouth in laser-like beams of brightness. Chaos reacted, roiling like the sea in a storm, darkness fighting light, still my body began to break apart, the power bursting through my skin, throwing dancing light and shadows onto the world around me.

I didn't recognize this fear, but it must have come from within me, because I couldn't help the dread and almost overwhelming desire to reject what was happening. I wanted to scream my denial, to turn away and hide, but I couldn't.

The world around me began to crumble. The earth, the God of Knowledge's senseless body, the very air, disintegrating around me. Where it was destroyed, it revealed a ... *lack*. A nothingness, behind the veil of the universe. I screamed, then, and somehow forced my eyes shut. I knew I would die if I kept looking.

I could sense it, though, even with my eyes closed. I screamed again as I began to lose my sense of self, Chaos and the power of the God of Knowledge bursting outward till my body ceased to exist.

"We have met, and we will meet again," a faint voice whispered to me.

I closed my eyes and just concentrated on my breaths, which came ... increasingly slowly. And finally, I began to ... *vibrate*. It started subtly, and then grew more pronounced, till I was jerking out of my own skin with every shake. I struggled to open my eyes, and when I finally did I stood, and looked back at my peaceful body.

"Interesting." I turned, then, and walked out into the world of my mind, leaving my body behind.

THE ATTACKS KEPT COMING, and I kept moving, for a long time. I didn't sleep, didn't eat, and I didn't rest. Though my mind grew weary, my body did not. I tried not to stop, because I had a feeling that if I lost focus on my goal, I would forget that I had a body outside of this place that I needed to get back to.

Finally, I found what I was looking for. A huge golden gate, beyond which a great golden column reached out from somewhere in the distance, thrusting up toward the sky and piercing a hole in the ... *ceiling*. It was huge, and corrupting, and it shouldn't be there. Not in my mind. It was creepy, and made me feel violated.

I bared my teeth at it, and ran forward. But before I could open the gate, a small golden boy stood up from where he'd been crouching in front of it.

I almost ran into him, and panicked for a second, lashing out with my claws.

He winced at my attacks, but didn't fight back.

I backpedaled and stood staring at this creature, who looked quite like another fear of mine.

The boy uncurled his body from its defensive posture, and opened his golden eyelids. The eyes within glowed with a teeming mass of writhing lights. "I've been waiting, Eve. You certainly took long enough." He spoke in English, and though his voice was a conglomeration of many, it originated solely from his own mouth, unlike the God of Knowledge.

Still, I instinctively wanted to attack.

"I mean you no harm," he said in a rush, raising his hands to ward me off and flinching back a little. "And I have little strength to defend against you. Please, calm yourself."

"Who are you?" I said.

"I am a manifestation of Knowledge."

"*A* manifestation? A separate one?" Was this how the gods had babies? Even the males?

He quirked his mouth up, as if amused at my thoughts. "A *very* small one, but yes. The Knowledge that you have seen and I were once the same. Part of me—*I*—noticed an anomaly within myself. Processes being corrupted, dissociation with things that were once meaningful—I would reach for them, and find the connection within my thoughts, my memories, and my 'emotions' had been severed. Or, more insidiously, redirected. I immediately attempted to isolate the affected areas, in an attempt to amputate them, but they'd grown too much already, while I had been made *ignorant*," he spat it like a curse, "by my own power. This," he gestured to his child's body, " was all that I could do. I have enclosed what little I could safely determine was untainted, and have been trapped within myself as the rest of me fell to the abomination. When you came into my domain, I transferred a small part of myself to you, riding along my greater counterpart's attack."

"So, you're the part of the God of Knowledge that doesn't have the Sickness?"

"Yes, in a way. The being you see before you is but a simulacrum. A tiny, tiny piece of my power. All you could bear without dying, and all I could spare without losing my fight against myself, and being re-assimilated. So much has been lost, you see. I saw you, though my diminished range of power. I have done all I could to thwart my corrupted manifestation. And I have waited for you to return, and cleanse me." He said the last with an expressionless face, but a voice that sounded heavy, tired, and resigned.

"Cleanse you ..." I said, narrowing my eyes. "You mean kill you?"

He raised his eyebrows. "That is what my daughter asked of you, is it not? Death is but a metamorphosis, though admittedly quite unpleasant. You of all creatures should understand that, scion of Khaos." He stared at me with those eyes of bright power. "Oh. You have no idea." He grimaced in distaste. "No wonder your power rebels against you. My old friend did not do a good job of preparing her progeny. I'm not so surprised as I should be, unfortunately. She has no patience for such things."

"Do you know ... how to stop it from killing me?" I asked, trying not to let hope bloom prematurely.

"Of course. Knowledge of a thing is power over it. But that is the reward of the quest, and you have not completed it yet."

"But if I kill the big Knowledge, you'll die too, won't you? How will you tell me, then?"

He pointed beyond the gate. "The knowledge is hidden within his sentinel. Conquer and cleanse, and it will turn to follow you. When you have need of it, it will reveal itself to you."

I looked up at the golden sentinel. "What?"

He just stared blankly back at me, as if he hadn't heard my question.

"What about the Sickness?" I tried. "Do you have any information about how we can cure it? Or where I can find this other god that can fight against it?"

"Much has been lost," he said again. "You must follow the path. It has been traveled, once before. The first time."

"I'm not sure I understand. Could you be less cryptic?"

He sighed. "No, I could not. Just do what you came here to do." Then he stepped back, and sank into the gold of the gate, melding together with it till the form of the boy was gone.

I shook my head, feeling a little disoriented. Almost woozy. It was hard to concentrate. When I tried to take a step, the ground pulled at my feet, releasing me with a suction-cup *pop* only after I threw myself forward. I realized I'd been standing still for too long.

The gate gave under my claws like butter, and where it broke apart, tiny little motes of light flew into me. I ran forward, toward the distant glare of the sentinel.

WHEN I FINALLY EXITED THE black sphere, the reporters bombarded me, shining their little pen-light recorders at me, talking over each other.

My stomach cramped from hunger, and my muscles trembled faintly, as if I was coming down off a horrible caffeine high.

"What did you see within the Trial of Deimos and Phobos?!"

"You are the first to emerge. Are you worried about Torliam of Aethezriel?"

"What is the relationship between you and Torliam of Aethezriel?"

I straightened, hoping that their cameras wouldn't catch my weakness. "Torliam of Aethezriel will be finished when he is finished," I said, not-answering as best I could. "As for what I saw …" I paused, meeting their eyes, as Torliam had instructed me would appear best for their recorders. "I saw my own fears, and my own failings, and traversed the depths of my own mind turned against me." I hesitated, wondering whether to mention that I had met with a small piece of the God of Knowledge. It was true, but if I couldn't lie … they might ask more questions than I was able to answer truthfully.

"There are rumors that the Oracle has given you three gifts, and the Goddess of Testimony and Lore has marked you! Is this true?" another reporter asked, yelling to be heard over his counterparts.

"It is true," I said.

"There are reports that Testimony and Lore has been seen traveling amongst mortals once more. Did you free her?"

I laughed. "She did not need me to free her. She was never trapped."

"What is your quest? What do they bid of you?" another yelled.

I paused for a breath, thinking of the proper answer. "I will follow the path." There, a nice cryptic answer for the media to go crazy over. I walked away, getting into the ship to wait and worry for Torliam while munching on the snacks he'd packed.

Torliam emerged after sundown, falling to his hands and knees and gasping.

I rocketed out of the ship and ran to kneel beside him.

He murmured, "Thank the gods, it is done," in Estreyan, and then collapsed.

I caught him, and maneuvered him back so he didn't fall on his face. I snarled at the reporters pressing in. The press of potentially dangerous strangers, all yelling and jostling close to us while Torliam was too weak to defend himself, made the hair on the back of my neck raise. "Get back!" I growled in threat. Voice pulsed with the command, and they stumbled back, as if it had been a shockwave. I would have to learn how to use it consciously more often.

Torliam was almost delirious, but he wasn't unconscious. After a bit of water, he got to his feet, using me as an armrest to support himself. "Let us go to the edge," he said.

The reporters kept their distance, though their recording penlights stayed trained on us.

"From here," he said, sitting so his feet hung off the side of the mountain ledge, "they will not be able to hear, only to see."

"Same for the cameras?"

He nodded. "If you are willing, Eve Redding of the line of Matrix, we might give them else something to talk about."

"You're not going to try and kiss me, are you?" I narrowed my eyes at him.

He snorted. "Your beauty and power are irresistible," he scoffed. "No, idiot."

I huffed. "Well, they were all asking what our relationship was, if I was worried about you, how I felt about your mom, given our 'delicate' relationship, and stuff like that."

"This will make them chatter more than that." He hesitated, then cleared his throat. "I severed our bond. But you are more of what I originally hoped than I thought, though you are a human. As a descendant of the line of Aethezriel, it is my duty ... and my honor, to offer my bond again." Less formally, he continued. "If we complete it properly, it will return some of the power you lost when the bond was broken before, and it may help to stabilize you against Chaos."

I flexed my fingers, trying not to pounce on the idea of more power, anything that might help me survive. I'd seen what the blood-covenant had meant to Torliam. "Do you really want to do that?"

"Yes."

Well, I wasn't going to *argue* about it. "Okay, then. How do we do it? I don't have any Seeds left."

"We will complete this *properly*," he said, emphasizing the word. "Do as I do." He slashed his forearm with his power, and I followed suit on my own arm with one of my claws.

"The life is in the blood. And thus, I bind mine to yours." He dipped his thumb in the blood, and wiped it on my forehead, and down over my lips, so that I tasted the tiniest hint of iron and salt on the tip of my tongue.

I repeated the process on him, having to stretch up to reach his forehead.

He grasped my forearm, so our wounds touched. "So be it."

I felt the rush, then, extremely different from before when

NIX had done this to me. But I didn't have time to examine the feeling, because the reporters broke out in a roar, their voices mixing together in a jumbled wave that was no longer recognizable as speech.

I turned to look at them over my shoulder. "Should we make a statement, or something?"

"No." He grinned and stood up, not bothering to offer me a hand. "People find the mysterious much more interesting. This is the time to run away!"

I laughed and ran after him.

Chapter 34

There is a dark place underneath the world.
— Sha Du

I'D SENT the others a Window to let them know I was okay while I was waiting for Torliam to emerge, but as we flew back to the palace, I got a few more.

—WHAT THE HELL WAS THAT?—
-ADAM-

—THE NEWS PEOPLE WENT CRAZY WHEN YOU GUYS WIPED BLOOD ON EACH OTHER'S FACES.—
-ZED-

—IT ITCHES, BUT TORLIAM SAYS I CAN'T WASH IT OFF. BECAUSE TRADITION. AND PUBLICITY.—
-EVE-

The queen was waiting with Birch in the airship landing field when we arrived. Her face was pale and foreboding, and her mouth tightened when she saw the dried blood. But what she said was, "I have called a mandatory assembly of the court, for tomorrow evening. We cannot wait. After a spectacle like this, rumor spreads quickly. We want to make the announcement when it will still be a political boon to do so, and before any of my detractors have time to prepare arguments or subtle ways to undermine me. They must all be shocked and caught off guard."

We spent most of the night planning, despite how exhausted Torliam and I were.

Birch bit me on the hand for leaving him behind again, and then struggled to stay awake. He failed, and ended up curling up in Torliam's lap, snoring lightly.

First thing in the morning, Queen Mardinest summoned the rest of my team and drilled them with both questions and guidance about what might happen at the announcement, and the small part they would play in it. She included Birch in this, and didn't seem surprised by how he appeared to acknowledge her instructions.

Then she sent us off to be prepared for the assembly.

I was given a room with a bed that looked fluffy and comfortable. I wanted nothing more than to fall down into it and sleep, but the woman the queen had assigned to preparing me took one look at me and vetoed that.

"I will have to put glamour on your face. Oh, my, those dark circles under your eyes. You look like a *pordok!*" She *tsked* her concern.

A *pordok* must be a panda or raccoon equivalent, because I was pretty sure that's what I looked like.

By that night, the girl in charge of my wardrobe and appearance had driven me crazy with her demands, but I looked amazing. My almost-black hair hung straight down my back. She'd put some paste on my face and magically removed my dark eye circles and the unhealthy hollow underneath my cheekbones, and given my skin a healthy tinge of color.

The armorer had given me a dark grey set that made my pale eyes stand out, but kept my left forearm, fingers, and my neck uncovered to display the sparkly "gifts" I'd been given from the gods.

I was pretty in love with the armor. It fit over my—now clean —vest, was light-weight and non-reflective, and still allowed me full range of motion, so it would actually be useful for battle and not just decoration. I wondered if there might be a way I could sneakily "forget" to give it back.

The servant led me toward the back entrance to the ball room, or the throne room, or whatever it was, muttering about how she'd "tried her best."

The queen was waiting with Torliam, a little removed from the rest of my team. She waved me over and threw a long, almost-black cloak over my shoulders. It went well with my armor, and covered all my sparkly gifts, no doubt so she could dramatically reveal them in front of the assembly later. She wore one of the Estreyan style dresses, but had obvious knifes both at her belt and strapped along her thigh. The outfit looked like something she would have no trouble fighting in.

Torliam had been properly groomed and made fancy, too, almost like a different person than the one I was used to. He didn't make any snarky comments or even grimace at me. He held himself proudly straight, his hair swept back and held in place by a thin circlet much less elaborate than his mother's.

With her nod of acceptance, we entered the throne room through a back door, my team following a few steps behind the three of us.

Jacky shot me a grin, pointing to her pixie haircut. The short style only served to accentuate the lines of her cheekbones and jaw.

Contrary to my expectations, none of the reporters along the walls burst out with questions, and the huge crowd of high-ranked Estreyans did no more than murmur surreptitiously amongst themselves.

Queen Mardinest took the throne above Torliam and I, who

stood to the side of her raised dais. She wasted no time starting her speech, thanking them for coming on such short notice. "I have summoned you here tonight for a joyous announcement," she called out in a voice that had no trouble reaching to the far ends of the room. "My son, Torliam of the line of Aethezriel, still lives."

At her motion, he joined her on the dais, bowing shallowly to the crowd.

"I sent him on a mission some time past, to search for an answer to the seemingly indomitable Sickness that plagues our land and people. Two nights past, he returned from his mission, *successful.*"

There was a long beat of silence, after that. Then they broke out in sound. People exclaimed in shock, chatted to each other disbelievingly, and shouted questions, talking over each other such that my rudimentary grasp of the language failed to distinguish their words.

The queen raised her hand for silence, and didn't speak again till it was quiet. "As it is said in the Lore, my son has discovered a descendant of the line of Matrix."

I joined her then, and the hair on the back of my neck raised as my subconscious reacted negatively to the weight of so many powerful stares.

The noise died down quicker that time, as people were no doubt eager to hear what she had to say.

"This is Eve-Redding, last of the line of Matrix, and my own champion."

She'd added the last part for political gain, I knew. But I was okay with it, because as far as I could tell, what was good for her at the moment was also good for me.

"Our world has been ravaged by the Abhorrent, and we waited for the spark in the darkness. Our hoped waned, and we grew weary and disbelieving, and perhaps some of us even forgot that such a thing might one day come." She paused, for effect, and I did my best to project confidence and power. To look like someone they could believe in.

"Finally, we may wait no longer. Despair no longer. Stand helpless and frightened no longer." Her words thrummed with power, and for a second, it seemed like the crystal in my chest pulsed in response, a physical sensation, like the rumbling of a huge, slow heartbeat.

Eyes were drawn to the crystal, and from it to me. I wasn't quite sure whether or not to be grateful for the strange gift of Testimony and Lore, but at times like this, it was helpful to claim legitimacy.

Torliam stepped forward, then, and from the way the queen stiffened, I was pretty sure they had not agreed on this.

"I am of the line of Aethezriel," he said loudly. His voice didn't carry that same thrum of power that his mother's had, but his words caught the court's attention all the same. "For generations, my line has served the line of Matrix, bound to them in blood-covenant. Until the last died, and they were thought to be no more." His eyes traveled over them, and he waited till the last was silent, waiting for him to continue. "The line of Aethezriel stands before you, once again bound in blood-covenant to the line of Matrix." He bowed to me then, deeply and formally, dipping to a knee and baring his neck.

I did my best to act unsurprised, and reached out a hand to lay gently on his shoulder.

He rose to his feet.

The queen snapped the cloak off me with a flourish, like a stage-magician, drawing attention back away from her son. "She has been given three gifts by the Oracle." She held up my hand, displaying first the ring, and then motioned for me to lift the other arm, showing off the band wrapping around my forearm, and the unsolved gift wrapped around my waist and clasped with a dark grey brooch. "And the mark of Testimony." She touched a finger to the crystal in the hollow at the base of my throat, and it reacted on its own, thrumming a pulse of power outward that washed through those of the crowd closer to the throne. "Her companions have the Seal of Nine." She waved a hand, and my teammates lifted their hands, showing off their own crystal-embedded skin. "She is here, with a quest from the Oracle, to defeat the Sickness,"

It was a strong exaggeration, even based on what the queen believed, but I wasn't surprised.

It took even longer for the noise to die down, that time.

AFTER HER ANNOUNCEMENT, some of the higher ranked court members, judging by how rich they looked and their level of arrogance, moved up before the throne to ask official questions in front of the court.

"How do you know *she* is the one talked of in the Lore? Or even a Matrix? Has she taken the test of genealogy to prove herself?" one man asked. He kept a veneer of politeness, but his eyes were narrowed, and he looked at the queen with a kind of greasy hunger when she wasn't watching.

"There is no doubt she is a Matrix. My son has a blood-covenant with her. But we will gladly allow a test of lineage."

His cheeks twitched in what might have been a smirk if he'd allowed it to form fully. "That will alleviate some of my doubts. However, wasn't your line in *service* to the Matrixes?"

"Indeed," she said severely, as if what he was insinuating didn't bother her. But I felt an almost unnoticeable pulse of power roll off of her, and knew she'd been angered. "My *younger* son has the honor of fulfilling the historical traditions."

After him, others asked similarly leading questions, as if trying to trip the queen up, and there were many among the crowd that frowned and muttered to each other, as if suspicious. However, just as many others were staring at me with interest, or crying even as they smiled, or hugging each other with overwhelming emotion.

Finally, someone asked how we were going to defeat the Sickness.

Queen Mardinest smiled with triumph. "The God of Knowledge has met my champion, and given her a quest to gather strength, so that she may prove the worth of the mortals on this world, and gain knowledge of our path to *victory* against the Sickness!" Her voice had raised in both volume and power, and she raised a fist into the sky to punctuate the end of her sentence.

The mood washed over the assembly, and they responded with a cheer of their own, which she egged on this time rather than trying to quiet. Her Charisma levels must be off the charts. "I ask that those willing to lend their power to this quest come join us. I believe that we may eradicate the Sickness completely during my reign, and I will not rest until it is done!" She once again pumped her fist in the air, and let out a war cry laden with that almost physical intensity particularly powerful Estreyans seemed to be able to imbue into their voices. "Tonight, we celebrate!"

The whole place exploded with festivities after that, and even if anyone had wanted to ask more questions, they wouldn't have been able to over the overwhelming noise. People were crying, laughing, hugging each other and dancing.

My group stayed with the queen, talking to the people who lined up to meet me, or pledge something to the cause. The Estreyans kept thanking me, reaching out to touch me or one of my sparkly gifts.

I'd reacted a bit harshly when one chubby man tried to touch the crystal at the base of my throat.

He'd been surprised and half fearful at first, but quickly laughed off my firm grip on his wrist, and the claws that pressed against his skin in warning. "We have a warrior in this one!" he called out to the people around him, which caused another irritating cheer to rise up.

I had to stay at the dais, but after a while Torliam was allowed to leave and mingle in the crowd, surrounded by a large group of people demanding his attention. He looked truly happy for the first time I'd ever seen. His shoulders were thrown back, not in arrogance, but as if the lack of burden they carried made him stand straighter. It made me uncomfortable, though I wasn't sure why.

Two weeks after that night came the day where we officially accepted applicants for the fight. The line of non-rejected applicants stretched all the way through the castle, from the huge throne room to the streets outside, and plenty of people were trying to sneak their way into the line, though they hadn't been accepted by the queen's vetting process. It was chaos.

The queen had sent out word after the Trial that we would be accepting warrior applicants to go challenge the God of Knowledge's main manifestation. Many, many people applied to follow me, but her analysts had sorted through them, only allowing the best to be accepted. "There will be limited battlegrounds in a physical sense," she said. "Even with those who can fly and do not need room on the ground. It is better to have a smaller group of those who have a real chance of defeating the God of Knowledge than clutter the place with well-meaning weaklings who will be dying like gnats all over the battlefield."

She'd also found me another healer who could boost my healing Attributes. He had seen me a few times, and warned me that I didn't have much time left before Chaos overtook me.

Even if my body could have withstood it, the time limit given by the Oracle was approaching—the smaller of the Estreyan moons had already darkened twice.

The queen stood in front of her throne, with me beside her and the rest of my team kind of milling about the room with varying levels of watchfulness. "If I were wise," the queen said, staring at the Estreyans milling about and standing in the too-long line, "I would kill you now."

My head snapped around toward her as I registered her words, and I stepped back in sudden wariness. When someone so powerful made a comment about killing me, it wasn't something I could take lightly.

She noticed my alarm, and gave a slight smile that was less than reassuring. "With the number of my citizens ready and willing to throw their lives away for you, you could become the leader of a fanatical uprising. Some people place all their faith in the Lore."

She meant that I could become a religious cult leader. "That sounds like way too much work for me," I said. "I just want to finish this and retire somewhere in peace. Or something."

"Or *something*." She raised one eyebrow sardonically.

I wasn't quite sure what the joke was, but she walked away then, and I was happy to let the subject lie dormant, but not forgotten.

I stood at the front of the line of accepted warriors, listened one by one to what their strengths were—basically whatever had gotten them accepted—and formally received their pledges of alliance. It took a few hours to get through the whole line. Some of my new allies were stoic and determined, some prideful, and some looked at me like I was the messiah-figure they believed me to be.

Just when I thought it was over, the queen stood up and dramatically announced for the cameras that she was lending me two squads of her own elite fighters. You know, seeing as I was *her* champion.

Still, who turns down two squads of elite fighters? Not me. I smiled and thanked her prettily.

Chapter 35

Weep not for the shore, but become the wave.
— Sha Du

I LET out a scream of challenge toward the God of Knowledge, not really meant to intimidate him, but to release some of my own tension. He had really messed me up, and I'd only recently felt fully recovered from that, at a time when I already had too many problems to deal with.

In a move we'd practiced many times, my group started to move forward from the edge of the valley toward the God of Knowledge. They stayed in the shadows and kept a protective formation around me, since I had to live to make this work.

Though my eyes were closed, I watched the battlefield with my Wraith Skill.

Ahead of my group, the heavy-hitters attacked with abandon. They paused for a moment, to allow an Estreyan with two huge, beautiful blades as tall as he was to attack without taking friendly fire.

He slung the blade off his back and pointed it toward the god with one smooth motion of his arm. A point of light shot out the end of it, connecting to a spot on the other side of the god.

Half a second after that, the Estreyan had moved there, so fast even Wraith barely registered an after-image. The sound reached me, then, like a bell ringing as something shattered.

The Estreyan's blade broke into pieces and fell to the ground.

The God of Knowledge paused, as if surprised, and started to turn to the Estreyan. There was a line scored across the back of his golden knee. The same one that was already rusting away.

The Estreyan was already pulling the second, backup blade from his back, and repeated the process before the god could even complete his pivot.

The blade broke again, after cutting across the exact same spot on the back of the knee as the first slice.

The Estreyan landed, back where he'd started, and fell down dead from the blow Knowledge had landed on him as he passed.

But my fighters didn't lose focus just because of that, instead redoubling their attacks, focused on the god's pelvis, stomach, and lower back.

At the timed command, they all stopped attacking simultaneously, and I rushed forward, surrounded by my still mostly fresh team.

I neared the target quickly, stepping over ground that was simultaneously melted, frozen, and a half dozen other residual effects. One patch glowed an almost comical, radioactive-green. I avoided that spot carefully.

Torliam was counteracting the light for my group, I could tell, and Adam kept his hands touching the disks his strongest shields had been painted on, in case he needed to activate them instantly.

When we neared, Adam and other forcefield and barrier-makers tossed the results of their Skills up around the god, hoping to trap him for just a moment.

The God of Knowledge tore through all the shields around him as if they were paper, raised his hand, and brought it down flat, smashing me and the rest of my group like bugs.

"Damn it!" I gritted out. A loud horn blared, and I stood up with the others, as the simulation lost some of its terrifying realism.

One of my Estreyan warriors kicked a golden tree, making it flicker and getting his foot stuck halfway inside the hard-light construct.

"Damn it," Gregor also muttered as he drew nearer.

Blaine gave me a pointed look. "Your cursing is rubbing off on an eight-year-old."

"You did well, young one," a female warrior said to Gregor. "Was it three people that you saved from death, this time?" She smiled at him with obvious affection, just one of my many warriors who'd grown fond of the kids.

Gregor scowled. "But we still lost!"

Birch coughed agreement, walking beside the boy with tail and ears drooping.

"I'm going to go review the logs," I said, walking toward the viewing room. "Maybe we can get more efficient with taking out the sentinels in the beginning."

The Estreyans I passed bowed or smiled at me, despite the fatigue and vague sense of shameful failure I knew we all felt.

My team and a few of the more Intelligence-focused Estreyans, or those that had large scale battle experience, followed me.

—I BELIEVE THAT CABIN WHERE WE FIRST ARRIVED WILL BE THE BEST PLACE TO TAKE THE KIDS WHILE YOU FIGHT. WE WILL BE SAFE FROM THE RELATIVELY WEAKER MONSTERS THERE, AND HOPEFULLY WE WILL NOT BE FOLLOWED.—
          -BLAINE-

I nodded.

—THE PALACE HAS QUITE A FEW SHIPS. YOU'LL WANT TO DISABLE THE COMMS AND TRACKING SYSTEM IN ONE AHEAD OF TIME.—

-Eve-

The Estreyans expected the kids to fight along with the rest of us, because they had the Seal of Nine, but neither Blaine or I were okay with putting them in such extreme danger.

The preparations to fight the God of Knowledge took up most of my concentration, anyway. I'd been researching past supplicants and successful Bestowals, even though gaining his approval wasn't exactly the goal, I hoped to gain clues about how to win.

People all over Estreyer were doing their best to contribute even if they weren't warriors. I had become the somewhat bemused owner of several properties, air-ships, living steeds of different breeds, and tons of advanced armor and weaponry. I had someone whose *only* job was to manage the donations!

The city even had a much cooler version of NIX's simulation chamber. My team and myself were the only recorded people to see the God of Knowledge in recent history. We'd helped some of the technicians made a passable model of him for us to mock battle.

The Estreyans and I had been trying to come up with a plan to defeat him. We gathered at the simulation chamber every day and pitted our strength and strategy against the modeled God of Knowledge, over and over again.

Unfortunately, we kept failing. No matter what we came up with, when we tried it out, we always lost.

Our training had made us all stronger, but without a ready supply of Seeds from an outside source, progress was slow.

PLAYER NAME: EVE REDDING
TITLE: SQUAD LEADER(9)
CHARACTERISTIC SKILL: SPIRIT OF THE HUNTRESS,
TUMBLING FEATHER
LEVEL: 38
SKILLS: COMMAND, WRAITH, CHAOS
STRENGTH: 18

LIFE: 71
AGILITY: 25
GRACE: 22
INTELLIGENCE: 29
FOCUS: 23
BEAUTY: 11
CHARISMA: 25
MANUAL DEXTERITY: 9
MENTAL ACUITY: 25
RESILIENCE: 67
STAMINA: 24
PERCEPTION: 27

I paused the three-dimensional simulation of the battle we'd just gone through, just as the God of Knowledge batted one of my most important fighters out of the air in a move that would have killed, or at least incapacitated her in a real fight. I growled under my breath, and let the playback continue, watching the tiny three-dimensional image of her body hit the ground and turn red.

"He's too strong," I said aloud. "He can take whatever we throw at him. His inherent power makes him the worst possible opponent, because not only is he stronger than us, but he knows everything we're doing or just about to do, as long as it's within the range of his divination."

"Why don't we just make him weaker, then?" Jacky said.

I looked up at her in surprise.

She'd gone back to being too quiet, after our fight with the assassins. She trained harder than ever, but that was *all* she did.

I'd been worried about her, but when I asked her if anything was wrong, she'd told me that she was weak, and had to get stronger. "There's nothing you're gonna say or do that's gonna change that," she'd said. "I don't need mushy gushy friendship and feelings right now. I know we're friends. What I *need* is to get stronger before it's too late, so we can all *keep* being friends."

I hadn't been able to retort to that, because I understood how she felt all too well. Still, it was a surprise that she had spoken during the strategy meeting, other than to ask about thing she could be doing better.

"If I knew how to do that ..." I glared at the simulated god reduced to human size in front of me.

"Maybe I'm being stupid," Jacky said, her shoulders hunching in a little.

I caught something in her tone, and narrowed my eyes at her. "Do you have an idea, Jacky? Tell me. I need all the ideas I can get." This hesitance wasn't like her.

"Well ... why don't we poison him?" she asked simply.

Adam, and Blaine, who were working with Chanelle in the corner of the room, looked over, their attention drawn.

"He's made of Seeds, right? Or something like that."

I nodded. His body was probably a manifestation, kind of like Behelaino's, but there was probably a core of Seed material somewhere in or near it that was powering his form. In essence, the God of Knowledge *was* really just Seed material, gathered in one spot.

"That thing NIX did to Chanelle, didn't it get rid of her Seeds?" Jacky asked simply.

My eyes widened, and I'm pretty sure I gasped like a landed fish. "Jacky. You're a genius." I turned to Adam and Blaine, who were sharing similar looks with each other. "Could that work?"

Chanelle frowned, scratching her forearm. "Are you going back to NIX? I want to come."

We conferred for a few minutes, but Blaine was pretty positive it would work, and as he was the one with the most experience, I was inclined to trust his judgement.

The Estreyans were more than a little alarmed at the implications of anti-Seed weaponry, and the fact that the military force of a hostile—though primitive—planet had been developing it. Blaine's explanation of how it was almost certainly meant to allow NIX to attempt to create Players out of those humans without the necessary Estreyan gene to accept the Seeds, and not necessarily to attack Estreyans, didn't mollify anyone.

Still, we took the idea to the queen. She stood up and started tapping on the table, calling for some of her official underlings. "Call *door-makers* to me. I need experts in the old connections, those beyond the void. I have an immediate decree," she announced to the room. "I am re-opening the portal to Earth."

People gasped.

THE ESTREYANS who learned about the queen's plan over the next few days had the same universal reaction. Horror.

"Why is this such a big deal?" I asked. "The arrays are there for a reason, right? I mean, it worked just fine for us, and we didn't even have a *complete* one."

Torliam didn't look at me. "It is forbidden."

"*Why?*"

He hesitated. "The array technology is knowledge we brought with us, before Estreyer. We do not fully understand it any longer. There are two reasons why it is forbidden to use it, and why the doorways were blocked. The first is that we feared to spread the Sickness to others. The second … do you remember that I told you there are powers beyond that of the gods?"

I nodded.

"Some call them the eldritch. We do not understand them. Some even believe that the Abhorrent, which causes the Sickness, is one of them, and that is why we cannot stop it. Long, long ago, we discovered that the arrays work both ways. I do not mean between world to world. The arrays pierce through the divide. The void between worlds. When we open them, things from between may slip back through."

I vaguely remembered the glimpse of that break in existence that I had seen in the Trial for Testimony and Lore. I shuddered, suddenly absolutely sure that *something* coming from there was a really, really bad idea. "How did you know how to make the array work, if they're forbidden?"

"I am a historian, and an explorer. I know many of the old things that others have forgotten."

I started to nod, then frowned. "Wait, weren't you worried that the array on Earth would let something from between through?"

He smirked. "The array opens a door to the void from the world that *initiates* the doorway. Estreyer was never in danger."

"So ... we could go back to Earth only to find it's been invaded by some ... eldritch cthulhu monster?"

He nodded. "Yes."

I stared at him. "You're an asshole, you know? There are plenty of innocent people on Earth. *Children.*"

His jaw tightened. "Well, it is only a possibility. And we had no other choice at the time, so do not condemn me for it now."

I conceded, though irritation simmered in my blood. "Are you coming with us?"

"I ... will cross through, but I will not go back to NIX. I will stay close, and if you have need of me, I will raze the place to the stones of its foundations. But I cannot see it and restrain myself to pleasantries and subtle threats. It will be nothing at all, or death."

Shortly after that, all of us making the trip piled into the two-person Estreyan ships that were small enough to fit through the array on Earth's side. I squeezed into one with Adam. Blaine and the kids were staying behind for this venture.

A group of people activated the stone circle, which glowed bright and kept glowing.

Adam flew us through, the ship flitting down from winter and up into autumn in a disorienting twist.

It didn't take long for the others to join us, and we flew toward NIX over the course of a couple hours, our tiny ships piercing through the night like crustacean-shaped bullets. When we got close enough, we exited the ships and stood around as a group, Estreyans and humans stretching our legs in tense camaraderie. We all wore full armor with no skin exposed, along with masks that covered our mouths and noses to keep from breathing in any anti-Seed warfare, which the Estreyans feared NIX might have aerosolized.

I thought they were being unnecessarily paranoid, but just shrugged and went along with it. It did make us look even more intimidating, so that was a plus.

Our goal was to both retrieve the meningolycanosis, and make sure NIX didn't have access to it any longer. Along with any other interesting or suspicious substances we happened to find. I'd convinced the queen not to order the small force of Estreyans that had agreed to come with me to wipe NIX out completely. Not that I had any sympathy for the organization, but many of the Players were just … people. People forced into this, just like I had been.

Besides, too few Estreyans wanted to risk travel through the highly stigmatized arrays, so I convinced her that if possible, we would do this through diplomacy. What a novel idea.

Atop a mountain about a mile out from NIX, our group looked down on the base.

Torliam's hands clenched so tight that his knuckles creaked, and he glared at the compound without blinking.

I turned to one of the Estreyans and nodded, huddling together with Adam, Jacky, Chanelle, and Sam.

With a loud *pop,* the five of us stood in the center of NIX's courtyard.

There was an instant of surprised silence, but only an instant. Alarms blared. People rushed into action. A group of Players sprinted inside before the doors slammed shut behind them, guards scrambled, and most surprisingly, the Shortcut fell straight down, concrete sliding over the part of the courtyard where it had stood. The gun turrets on the walls—new ones, since we'd destroyed many of the old—turned all the way around to point down at us.

Less than thirty seconds after we'd arrived, a group of people in the darker bodysuits of the special ops Player units dashed out of one of the doors, which opened only long enough for them to slip through.

I raised my hands above my head. "I'm not here to fight, guys," I called. "I just want to speak to Commander Petralka. If you find you can't resist attacking us … you *will* regret it."

They hesitated, and didn't attack, though one of them spoke in a low voice, probably talking to someone on the other end of a microphone.

I realized as I looked around that NIX seemed so much smaller, so much *less* than it once did. Always before I had been afraid, within this place.

Chanelle sidled up beside me, gripping the side of my utility belt for reassurance. "It feels weird, to be back on Earth. My family is here. They probably think I'm dead, though."

I bit the inside of my lip. "After this is over, we'll come back again. We'll find them, and make sure our families are okay."

It didn't take long before another of the doors slid open, and a man in crisp military uniform exited, striding over to us. He stopped a few feet in front of me, definitely not a safe distance from someone with my abilities. He was a tall man, almost as tall as me. "Commander Petralka has been … removed," he said. "She proved herself incapable of fulfilling her duties, multiple times. You may have some idea of the instances I am referring to," he said with just a hint of a smirk, his piercing glare and the way he held himself more than a little aggressive. "I am Commander Britt. You can just call me Britt. Why are you here?"

I smiled. "I'm here to make a bargain. A trade, if you will. You have something I want … and I have something *you* really *don't* want." I looked around, noticing the faces peeking out of windows, some of them being herded away, presumably to safer places. "Why don't we go somewhere where we can talk? Your office, maybe? Don't worry, we're house-trained."

He stared at me for a little, then his eyes flicked over my small group of teammates. "You first. I think you know the way."

I led the way to Petralka's old office, escorted by a pretty large contingent of guards and special ops Players.

Britt opened the door with a complicated series of scans and identity checks, and stepped into the room, moving to sit behind a large marble desk.

A pale man with too much pudge to be considered skinny, but too bony to be considered fat, sat in the corner, his twitching hands sunk into bulky gloves. He muttered when we entered, but didn't look up at us, staring at the smartglass tablet on the walled table in front of him.

I was curious, but my Wraith Skill was really bad at deciphering how electronic displays would appear to the human eye, even at close distances like this. "Your security is much better," I said. "And you've obviously been running response drills."

Jacky, Chanelle, and I sat in the chairs in front of Britt's desk, while Adam stood with his back to the wall, eyes darting around, though for once his hands were still. Sam stood behind me.

"Thanks for noticing," Britt said again with the decidedly mean smirk. "What do you want?"

"I want your anti-Seed experiments. Doctor Blaine Mendell coined the term 'meningolycanosis.' I believe you're familiar."

Chanelle coughed pointedly, her big blue eyes narrowed into a glare.

The man in the corner's fingers twitched, and Britt's eyes flickered. Window communication. Interesting.

"I am. What do you want with them?"

"I believe that should be obvious," I said flatly.

He leaned back. "You're actively an enemy to NIX. My superiors have authorized me to kill you on sight, if I feel the need. If I successfully capture you, I'd get kudos for that, too. Though ... I would worry that you're just allowing me to apprehend you as part of some ridiculous plan to steal even the damn Shortcut out from under our noses."

Jacky snorted.

His eyes narrowed. "Though, it would seem you don't need it.

How did you get here? We found no trace of you on Earth. And we looked."

I shrugged. "Maybe you don't know all the hiding spaces."

Britt read another Window.

I had an idea, and sent Wraith out toward the man in the corner. Instead of concentrating on the screen, I read the reflection of the smartglass tablet in the shine of his eyes. The numbers flashed across so fast I could barely read them, then settled.

"12% chance they hid on Earth."

Very interesting. I sent a Window to Adam, telling him what I'd just learned.

"You didn't hide on Earth," Britt said. "Maybe, if you'd like to share, I could get authorization to release the 'meningolycanosis.'"

"This isn't that kind of trade. Petralka got "removed" because she couldn't handle me or my team, and she didn't realize it early and kill us while she could. Well, her Thinker didn't realize it either, as far as I could tell. But you've got a new one now." I looked at the man in the corner, who twitched. "Maybe you won't make the same mistakes. Because it's too late to just kill us."

"This is obviously a threat."

Sam stiffened behind me, and then relaxed, his posture changing to something more resembling warm toffee.

I turned to look at him, and had to suppress the instinctive flinch when I saw his black eyes.

His new Skill liked to kick in without his permission, especially when he felt stressed. Once it did, it didn't let him go until it had to. "This is why I should have gone to see if I could heal that group of people that had been infected by that mind-control hive bacteria. You wouldn't have to go to all the trouble of bargaining," he said.

"You're the one who vetoed that idea," I said. "When you had your morals."

"I was being stupid." He turned to Britt, staring at him with a complete lack of expression. "And yes, this is a threat."

Britt flinched back from the windows into emptiness that had taken the place of Sam's eyes.

I nodded. "I want the meningolycanosis, or I'm going to attack this base, along with help from some of my alien friends."

The Thinker's fingers twitched.

"98% chance of alien collusion."

"10% chance of attack."

I changed my mind.
The Thinker's eyes widened.

"27% chance of attack."

I changed it again.

"63% chance of attack."

Britt's eyes flickered, and he frowned.

"You see, Britt, the aliens didn't care about us Earthlings. They didn't come here to attack, at first. But we made them angry with the whole, 'imprisonment and torture of one of their own,' thing. They'll kill you and everyone here if I don't stop them."

"84% chance of truthfulness."

"If you just give me what I want … we'll go away."

"95% chance of truthfulness."

"In event of attack, 7% chance of base survival."

Britt's teeth ground together audibly.

"No one could fault your decision to comply with me, with percentages like that," I said.

He jerked.

A few minutes later, I was walking unimpeded through the lowers corridors of NIX. Estreyan guards had joined my team to make sure Britt didn't decide to betray us halfway through completing our "trade."

Chapter 36

...that which we are, we are;
   One equal temper of heroic hearts,
   Made weak by time and fate, but strong in will
   To strive, to seek, to find, and not to yield.
— Lord Alfred Tennyson

ADAM LED us down into the bowels of the compound, moving quickly.

We turned the corner on a surprised guard at one point, and my Estreyan escorts slipped in front of me faster than he could draw his gun up.

The guard stared at my group, and then slowly lowered his gun, stepping back toward the wall for us to pass.

Sam, still under the influence of his Black Sun Skill, brushed a hand against him on the way by, and he crumpled to the ground.

I was beginning to see what the queen had meant about becoming a cult leader. It was strange, but I can't deny I liked the sense of security that came with not having to worry about dying all the time, when people were willing to literally put themselves between me and danger.

On the way to the meningolycanosis stores, we passed the Player containment area where they'd kept Chanelle. Cell doors ran along the hallway, and almost all of them had viewing windows through which we could see the condition of the Players within.

I'd known vaguely where they were, but this was my first time actually exploring the area.

Some of the Players looked sick, or depressed, or just generally unhealthy. But some were worse. Their bodies were bloated, veins turning black as the skin turned gangrenous in places. They tore at their own skin with nails and teeth, or wore restraints to keep them from doing so, straight-jackets and human muzzles. They babbled soundlessly behind the walls, and twitched in seeming paranoia at things that weren't there.

Watching them made me ... extremely uncomfortable. I had a feeling my mind was trying to remind me of something, a sense of vague deja-vu.

The Estreyans were even more shocked than I, and the group slowed from a jog to a walk as we all became distracted by what we were seeing.

One of them turned to me. "Your world is touched by the Sickness, too?"

I wanted to deny it on instinct, but realized that was what I'd been comparing the prisoners to. They reminded me of the infected spider-monkey I'd seen on Estreyer. "We didn't, before," I said instead, lamely, trying to ignore the horrible suspicion forming in my mind.

Sam had no compunction in blurting it out when the same thought came to him. "NIX has been experimenting with it, I bet."

There were gasps all around. Jacky shuddered, and Adam and I shared a worried look with her. Was this what had been done to Chanelle?

"What is *wrong* with your people?" one of the Estreyans asked, still staring through the windows.

"They know not with what they play," I said, slipping into the Estreyan speech pattern in my own distraction. These people were injected with meningolycanosis, if the medical charts on their doors weren't lying. The same as Chanelle. But she was different from them. Not normal, but she didn't act *insane*.

Chanelle whimpered, grabbing my hand as she looked through the observation windows. "They cultivate the abhorrent, like flowers growing in the soil. Growing in the flesh of our own kind," she whispered, eyes half-vacant, though I wasn't sure if she was losing lucidity, or if she was just in shock.

We continued on to the storage room for the meningolycanosis. We took it, and everything else in the room that wasn't bolted down, including the documentation. The Estreyans stored everything breakable extremely carefully, doubly wary of human creations now.

"I know Queen Mardinest did not order it," one of my guards said, "but it would be a kindness to these poor creatures if we razed this place to its standing stones, and killed them all. They are suffering, and the Sickness will spread."

"Nothing stops the Sickness from spreading," I said. "And maybe … maybe we will return with a cure, and these people will not need to die."

He shrugged. "If it is not soon, they will die anyway."

Chanelle squeezed my hand harder. This fate would be hers, if I couldn't find a way to stop it.

I resisted the urge to slide down the wall and hide my head in my hands. When did saving the world become something I was seriously considering?

As we left, I carefully did not listen to the sound of the subjects' screams of pain.

AS WE WALKED out into the courtyard, which still bristled with security, I saw two faces that I never expected to see again.

I stopped in my tracks, and the others followed my gaze, up to one of the hallway windows that looked down on the circular courtyard.

Jacky *hissed*. "We don't need NIX anymore. Can we kill him now? We've gotten a lot stronger. I bet we could do it."

Kilburn looked down on us, his too thin form standing nonchalantly with his hands in his pockets.

Sam smiled, especially surprising because of his usual stoic nihilism under the influence of Black Sun. "I would like to melt his eyeballs out," he said.

Adam looked around. "It'll have to be quick. Could you guys cover for us?" he asked the Estreyans.

"No," Chanelle said.

We turned to her. She stared up at Kilburn with the kind of piercing focus so rare for her even now. "I want to kill him," she said. She turned to me. "I want to do it. But I'm not strong enough yet. Will you bring me back … later? After?" The unspoken question, whether I would bring her back after she wasn't sick any more, hung in the air.

I grimaced, forcing my claws back into their sheaths, and nodded. "You have more right to his death than any of us," I said reluctantly.

I looked up again, but Kilburn had gone.

Near where he had been, another person who should have been dead looked out on us, pressing his hand against the glass. Vaughn glared down at me, mouthing one word very slowly. "Traitor."

I turned away, and with a signal of my hand in the air, we were gone from the courtyard, back to the mountainside with Torliam and the Estreyan teleporter.

The flight back to the array barely registered. As we passed through, I sent out a prayer that neither world had been or would be noticed by the things in between. Though I didn't know what gods might be listening.

Chapter 37

There is no chance, no destiny, no fate,
  Can circumvent or hinder or control
  The firm resolve of a determined soul.
  — Ella Wheeler Wilcox

THE NEXT COUPLE weeks were a blur of exhausted, desperate training, and sleepless nights of strategy and worry.

Blaine and the Estreyan scientists—that he grudgingly admitted were somewhat intelligent—had taken the samples we'd appropriated from NIX, and went to work testing and weaponizing them for use against the God of Knowledge. They'd also been developing visors that they thought might cancel out his light-based psychological attack. Blaine had gone without sleep for days and commandeered every useful Estreyan he could find to help him build them.

Birch discovered how to use his Skill, which with the name Gale, was unsurprisingly an aerokinesis Skill. Its first use allowed him to fly, after he displayed incredible foolishness in jumping off one of the palace balconies, only to discover that his wings were not, in fact, ready to carry him just yet.

I scolded him for his stupidity and recklessness till he crouched to the ground, whimpering with his ears flat to his head.

He poked me with his nose, sending a flashing image of a pitiful, mewling kitten into my mind. Then, walking meekly behind a figure with two long legs and a smell of strength, then a flash of my own blue eyes and the taste of dark blood.

The two-legs was me, and it seemed to be his way of saying he was sorry and he would be good in the future.

I sighed and gave him a flank of raw meat, with a short congratulation on discovering how to use his Skill.

After that, he "flew" everywhere he could, creating a constant updraft below himself to keep afloat.

Gregor spent a lot of time training with a pair of blood-activated Estreyan daggers, which were more like swords compared to the boy's size. They'd been donated by one of my many supporters, and when Gregor spilled a few drops of blood onto their hilt, they would phase in and out of corporeality with him. They were incredibly deadly. While in shadow form, they could pass through anything, and when they returned to reality, they retained their momentum for a short while. Gregor tested this by cutting through trees and blocks of marble, phasing back into his physical form with the blades halfway through an object.

An Estreyan puppet maker who learned of Kris' Skill came to the palace and volunteered to design and build bodies to house her summons, and they worked together creating bodies out of steel and platinum. Bodies that wouldn't crumble from the power of their own attacks, and that could kill a hundred different ways.

Blaine got into quite a few arguments with Kris and Gregor, but he couldn't stop them from training. Not without alerting the Estreyans who gleefully supported said training, and fully expected the kids to have to fight against the God of Knowledge.

At that point, only Adam had yet to figure out how to use his new Skill, Bestow. He was frustrated enough about this that he considered allowing a specialist to be brought in for a consultation, but a simple request from Kris led to the answer.

Adam could gift his ink constructs. Not just creating them to attach to someone else, only to expire within the next couple minutes. With a bit of focus, his Skill allowed him to transfer ownership of his paintings to the person whose skin they were drawn on, to be Animated at will by them.

Too quickly, the last days of the countdown passed, and despite everything, I did not feel prepared. How could we be, when our goal was to defeat a god?

Still, the Estreyans looked at me with hope.

We gathered before the airships on the night before the final day, all of us nervous, checking our gear and running though the previous mock battles in our heads, over and over. Some people grew quiet, some people chattered or joked uncomfortably, and a couple people walked away to puke inconspicuously behind a tree or around a corner. Every warrior was kitted out in the most powerful weapons and armor that we could provide.

I stood a little apart from the crowd, and pushed my Voice Skill to add weight to my words. "This is not a night for fear," I yelled. "This is not a night for doubt. Those nights have passed. That time when you did not know if you could ever be saved is passed. This is a night for hope, and triumph, and joy." Voice pulsed from my throat in time with my words, and I could feel the weight of the crowd's unwavering gaze on me. "Because now we know what we have to do, and it is very simple. The first step in the path has been swept clear before us. If you have fear, or doubt, throw it away. Tonight, we defeat a god. Tomorrow, the Sickness."

I wasn't any good with speeches, but Voice helped with that, and the Estreyans still cheered me, stomping their feet and clanging their weapons against their armor.

I didn't see Blaine or the kids among the crowd, and I wished them a safe escape as we filed into the ships, and our fleet lifted off, heading towards what would be the death of most of us.

When Blaine's Window appeared in front of me, dread filled

my heart.

—I cannot find the children. They were in the ship I had decommissioned. I left for a moment, and when I came back they were gone. I fear they may have been attacked, but perhaps they went with you? They are not answering my Windows.—
-Blaine-

—I didn't see them before we left. I will check for them.—
-Eve-

My Wraith Skill had trouble exiting the air-tight ships, and then reaching another at such high speeds, as if the passing wind were trying to blow it away. I sent a Window to Kris and Gregor instead, including Blaine in it.

—Where are you? Are you okay?—
-Eve-

—We're fine.—
-Kris-

Blaine interjected, then.

—Where are you!? I thought you may have been attacked again, or kidnapped!—
-Blaine-

—We are going to fight with the others. Don't try to stop us, it's just a waste of time. We already made up our minds.—
-Gregor-

—It's not safe. You should stay away. This isn't a game. It isn't even like when we were attacked by those assassins. A lot of people are going to die.—
-Eve-

—If we can't win, we're going to die, too, anyway.—
-Kris-

—We have the Sickness. And we have the Seal of Nine. We're part of this, and you can't do anything about that. We have more right than you do to be involved in this.—
-Gregor-

—You are children. As an adult, I cannot allow you to put your lives in danger.—
-Blaine-

—We're flying our own ship, so there's no one to make us turn around. And I was telling the truth when I said you can't stop us. Physically, you can't stop us. We have Skills. And all we have to do is tell all the other Estreyans that you're trying to stop us from fighting the God of Knowledge, and how it might make us lose the war against the Sickness.—
-Gregor-

—We're not doing this to spite you. But we have to fight.—
-Kris-

—I'm not going to sit back and let myself die.—
-Gregor-

—We're not going to attack Knowledge directly.

WE'LL STAY ON THE EDGES OF THE FIGHT, SAFELY OUT OF THE
WAY, AND JUST ATTACK THE SENTINELS AND RESCUE HURT
PEOPLE. WE HAVE THE ANTI-LIGHT VISORS, AND ARMOR AND A
MED-KIT, AND WEAPONS AND MY MARIONETTES.—
-KRIS-

—EVE, DO SOMETHING ABOUT THIS! THEY WILL LISTEN TO
YOU. IF THEY WON'T, *MAKE* THEM LISTEN. STOP THEM.—
-BLAINE-

I HESITATED.

—I CAN'T STOP ANYONE FROM FIGHTING FOR THEIR OWN
LIFE, BLAINE. EVEN IF THEY ARE KIDS. HOWEVER, IF YOU
GUYS ARE GOING TO JOIN THIS BATTLE, YOU WILL OBEY ME AS
IF YOU ARE SOLDIERS. MY ORDERS ARE LAW. YOU OBEY. YOU
DO NOT ARGUE, YOU DO NOT QUESTION. YOU WON'T BE
RECKLESSLY ENDANGERING YOURSELVES FOR NO REASON.—
-EVE-

If I could guarantee that we could win this and keep them safe,
it would have been different. But I couldn't. No child should be
subjected to the horrors of battle. But no child should be subjected
to a dissociative wasting disease, either.

MY ATTACK FORCE converged in on the God of Knowledge
from all around, the larger ships carrying ten or twenty people,
while the smallest bore only individuals. We did our best to avoid
the light of the Sentinels, but of course it was impossible to do so
completely. There would be no element of surprise—one of the
downfalls of increased military force. The God of Knowledge had

to know we were coming, but he hadn't tried to attack or given any indication that he was aware of our approach. Perhaps he was confident in his own dominance, and *wanted* us to attack. So he could kill and eat us.

I ran through a last series of tests on the tracking and communication system we'd implemented, making sure everything was working properly. The anti-light visors Blaine had created allowed the Estreyan Thinkers and battlefield generals to assign tasks to individuals. It aided in extracting wounded soldiers, assigning higher priority ratings to certain objectives, and notifying people of incoming danger or attacks.

Sunrise was about an hour away, and the darkness made it easier to see the god's power. The valley of pure gold where he resided shone like a beacon in the night, the light of the sentinels cutting through the darkness with an almost palpable harshness. What I saw surprised me. Many of the sentinels had fallen to that strange bubbling. The god stood in the middle of the valley, his condition worsened in the time since I'd last seen him. The back of his knee was half eaten away, his skin flaked away all over, and his "hair" was lopsided, as if he was going bald starting from the side.

—HANG BACK UNTIL STAGE ONE IS OVER. THEN, STATION
HERE.—
-EVE-

I sent Kris and Gregor a mapped location through a Window. It was as safe a position as I could choose without removing them from the fight altogether. From the spot half-covered by a ridge of rock on the side of the mountain, they would be able to see the battle, but still escape quickly if necessary, and there was a natural barrier against the light of some of the sentinels. Kris would be able to see to direct her summons, and Gregor wouldn't have too far to travel to reach the heavier clusters of sentinels, which he would be removing.

Stage One started. Fast-moving ships flew over the valley in a wave, dropping dark grey spheres as they went, concentrating them around the god, the bigger sentinels, and the sentinels in higher or more strategically defensible areas. When the spheres hit, they exploded spectacularly.

This had been a human idea. Estreyans preferred to do things under their own power.

Then, another wave of ships, dropping pouches that exploded into fine dust that would float endlessly in the air, and make the path of the light even easier to see, like sun beams through dust motes.

Stage Two. My fighters with enough immediately destructive power attacked the remaining larger sentinels, while small, darting ships and long-range attackers harried the god. Few were strong enough to do serious damage, but some were, and others worked together to chip away at the bases of the sentinels. It worked for less than a minute.

Knowledge picked up one of the broken, dimmed chunks of sentinel, and hurled it toward one of the attacking ships as it passed by overhead.

The pilot dodged, but not nearly quickly enough. The ship careened out of the sky in what was probably the worst possible way, smashing into both another ship and a free-flying warrior on the way down.

All three crashed, but the god grabbed the flyer as he plummeted toward the ground. He shoved the mortal's body headfirst into his mouth, biting down on their stomach and ripping away, so their intestines broke and spilled out.

He chewed slowly, a look of pleasure on his eyeless face. Then he twitched strangely, like a robot with a glitch, or an old tape recording with a scratch on it. "So ... hungry," he murmured, swallowing, and then popping the bottom half of the body into his mouth and repeating the process. "I will not pass from existence!" he suddenly screamed shrilly. "I am—erumpant—to—widdershins —" He twitched like he had a nerve disease.

That had distracted people. There was a moment of silence, stillness, as the God of Knowledge spasmed, little flecks of his body floating away like really bad dandruff.

Then the comms blew up with commentary, as people realized. One of their gods had the Sickness.

I overrode their voices on the system, and spoke calmly into everyone's ear as I watched them both in my mind's eye, and out of the windshield of my ship far above. "This is the path laid out by the Oracle," I said, hoping that would give them some comfort. "We must win this battle, for the future of the world. This is our only chance. It can be done, so we must do it."

I didn't know if my words would be enough, especially as the god reached one of the downed ships and began to tear into it to get at the person within.

One team leader on the other side of the valley let out a battle cry, the sound echoing off the mountainsides, and resumed attacking his assigned sentinel frantically. His team followed suit, and then the rest of the advance attackers followed, cheered on by those watching and waiting their turns.

Once the God of Knowledge was done eating the three people he'd downed, he lifted a hand, palm facing upward, and grew a golden column out of it. He hurled it, and killed the team leader who'd encouraged the others, the chunk of sentinel piercing through him and still clipping the arm right off one of his team members.

Knowledge tried the same on another group, but one of them stepped forward, throwing up a shield that ate the sentinel as soon as it touched the shimmering patch of air.

The god laughed, his strange, conglomerate voice echoing smoothly off the mountainsides all around. "You stupid, stupid mortals. You—cabal—your strength to be added to my own."

None of the Stage Two teams hesitated in their attacks.

He seemed to take that as a challenge, growing and launching the sentinels with blurring speed, despite his size, and the obvious limp from his bad knee. He spun and lunged, and we died. Sometimes, the Thinkers gave warning in time for the fighters to throw themselves out of the way, or one of the team members was able to dodge or block the attack. More often, we died.

Still, where we succeeded in cutting down some of the sentinels, their light cut out like that of a crushed lightning bug.

The god lunged toward one of the closer groups.

They retreated immediately, sprinting away at full speed.

He almost snapped up the slowest of them, but one of the extraction team waiting on the mountainside saved the trailing warrior, reaching out with a lash of power that grabbed and snapped the Estreyan forward like the tongue of a frog snatching a bug out of the air.

The God of Knowledge turned to his prey's rescuer, and with an almost nonchalant toss of gold, their brain was smeared across the rock behind them.

We changed tactics, then. Some teams rushed in to act as decoys and distract the god, while others continued to take out the sentinels, but this time moving in arcs that took them back to safety quickly after they entered the battlefield, and made it harder for the god to focus on any one team.

The power the Estreyans held was truly astounding. Some flew through the sky under their own energy, attacking from above or rescuing others below when escape wasn't possible on foot. Some lashed out with Skills that flashed through the air like light-shows, or created golems that pried themselves out of the ground and rushed forward into battle, or flashed walls and barriers into existence for a moment to protect their comrades.

It was sound, and light, and beautiful chaos, as we removed the god's source of control over the battlefield.

It lasted only for a couple minutes.

Knowledge pretended to be distracted by a flashy attack from above, only to suddenly turn and take out an entire team halfway across the valley. The limited attacks on the sentinels became counterproductive then, as he killed relentlessly, only pausing to eat a couple people here and there.

Time for Stage Three.

Chapter 38

In the end,
   I will win.
   — Eve Redding

I SENT OUT THE SIGNAL, and my ship flew to the edge of the valley, flitting low to the ground. The floor dropped out from under me, sending me plummeting toward the golden ground below.

Two other medium-sized ships did the same, my attack group falling with me. We tumbled when we hit the ground, and the ships flew away.

All around the valley, other teams did the same.

I worked best with my own team, so despite the protests of some of the Estreyans who felt they would be better able to protect me, Adam, Jacky, Sam, and Torliam crouched in the relative darkness with me, along with a few Estreyans hand-picked for their Skills.

An Attribute-boosting healer, still just a boy, laid his hands on my back, maximizing everything he could, and then pushing even harder.

When he finished with me, he moved on to the others, till his Skill was exhausted, and he collapsed to his knees. A flicker caught him, and he was gone, extracted on the orders of one of the Thinkers.

I resisted the urge to straighten and hold my head high in challenge. The rush of multiplied power made me feel as if I'd just had a shot of caffeine straight to the veins, while listening to my own personal film track of epic music. However, I was aware the feeling was an illusion, as people much stronger than me were being killed like mosquitos in front of me.

I had thought the display of powers was awe-inspiring before, but now it was truly astonishing. This was the wave of heavy hitters. The attackers who could damage a god directly, and who aimed to kill or at least incapacitate him. Plus, there was me.

I stood, finally, and let out a scream of challenge toward the God of Knowledge, a familiar action from our mock battles. The Voice Skill thudded, sending out my scream in a rolling wave that shivered through the ground. Other voices joined me, first my own team, and then the others, and the valley echoed with our screams of defiance.

Patches of light and darkness flared, strange effects from esoteric Skills. They gave me a headache when Wraith tried to make sense of what was happening to the laws of space or time within them.

We moved forward as a group, traveling through sentinel-free patches whenever possible, and shielded by either Adam or Torliam when it wasn't.

In a particularly flashy move, a gigantic flower of frost-threads and blue light bloomed from the god's head, moving through the full lifecycle from bud to decay in the course of a couple seconds. The wave of cold hit me hard enough to induce a shiver, even halfway across the valley.

That was followed up by a phoenix of fire, the sudden temperature change causing hairline fractures in the god's face, the cracks sounding like cannon-fire as they formed.

It didn't even faze him, except to make him angrier.

We passed an Estreyan dragging himself across the ground, missing his legs, and Sam stopped to seal off the wounds and signal for extraction.

One of Kris' summons bounded past us, picking up the Estreyan without even slowing down. It would carry him to safety.

I noted the group forming into a wide circle around the god, each standing at equidistant points, and seemingly unnoticed by him, what with all the other attacks. Good.

Several of the fighters in this stage, including most of my own team, carried meningolycanosis samples, in the hopes that someone would get the chance to administer it to him. I fingered the cartridges of meningolycanosis around the belt at my waist, each of them with a different delivery system, at least one of which we hoped would work.

I watched as a couple warriors tried to dagger the god with it, but the injectors, though they were of various designs and materials meant specifically to pierce him, just broke against his golden skin. They died for their failed attempts. But at least we knew that there was no way we would infect him that way.

One Estreyan with some sort of flight ability had an idea, and after a particularly vicious attack by the others, launched himself right at the god's face. Once in the air, though, he couldn't move or maneuver quickly enough.

He was moving through the light, and the God of Knowledge noticed him far too soon. The flier had no chance of getting the meningolycanosis into his nose or mouth, but he threw the breakable vial anyway.

The god caught him inside one perfectly sculpted golden hand. The fingers clenched, and the Estreyan man was squeezed out between the fingers like red putty.

I shuddered. At least his death was probably instant. It wasn't a bad idea, on the Estreyan's part, but it probably wouldn't have worked. The golden body may be a manifestation of the God of Knowledge, but it was *not* the God of Knowledge. Like Jacky had said, the God of Knowledge was the gathering of Seeds that held his power and consciousness. And that's what I needed to get to.

Once my group was close enough, but still behind both the main attackers and the group who were working in a wider circle around them, we paused for a second in an area of relative shadow, crouched down almost flat to the ground.

I pushed my awareness out, trying to see past the glowing ground and sentinels, the flaring bonfires of power darting all around and expending their power, and the overwhelming brightness that was the God of Knowledge's body. I needed to see the point from which his light emanated.

I closed my eyes behind my visor, but even so it felt like my retinas burned in the light. My eyes prickled with involuntary tears.

I vaguely saw the sun, though, hidden deep-seated within the God of Knowledge's belly, near his pelvis. I bit my bottom lip. How would we get to that? We could barely damage his skin. Despite my misgivings, I announced my findings through the communication system.

The news lent renewed energy to their attacks. A miniature sun burnt itself out against his torso from one person while tendrils of octopus-like darkness grew out of the ground around him and stabbed at his stomach from another.

Wraith saw attacks that weren't visible to the visor or my human eyes. Rents in space that ripped small pieces out of him. One person got close enough to touch his stomach with their bare hand. They were dead an instant later, squished and then eaten, but the patch they'd touched stayed frozen in midair when Knowledge stepped away, ripping off him.

Torliam fogged up with blue, building and building his power, then attacking with a lance that scored a small divot into the golden skin.

We died almost as fast as we attacked.

Finally, though, the surrounding barrier group's technique was ready. Bands of shadowy red appeared in the air, huge concentric rings that floated over the heads of the barrier makers, matching the size of their circle.

With their shout, the bands snapped inward, constricting around the god.

He jumped in surprise, but wasn't quick enough, and they tightened like a wriggling snake, then hardened, trapping one of his arms halfway bent at what looked like a painful angle. He struggled a bit against his bindings, but didn't seem to be making any headway.

A surge of elation went through me, and I'm sure the rest of us mortals. But my fighters didn't lose focus just because of that, instead redoubling their efforts.

We had a minute at most to work, and the technique the barrier makers had used was not repeatable. The red bands were created somehow from the blood and will of a group of highly trained specialists, who worked in tandem to pull off a technique that was pretty much a lost art. It hadn't been performed in over a thousand years, and for good reason. Even if the barrier makers had enough blood to try again, they wouldn't have the minds to do so. Somehow, they traded their Intelligence and Mental Acuity over the course of a long period of time for the binding. They would be almost retarded, and need daily care, for the next few *years*, until the faculties which they'd traded for an instant of power finally returned to them.

The extraction team immediately removed them from the battlefield, so they wouldn't be sitting ducks.

The Skills converging on the God of Knowledge overlapped and even merged with one another. Everyone still standing was giving their all, down to the last drop of power, and the god was writhing in pain, which hopefully meant they were successfully eating away at his metallic body, opening a path for me to his Seed core.

The seconds counted down. Since we didn't know exactly long

we had, we'd tried to plan within the margin for error. Like we had practiced, the attacks stopped, and the shielders used their Skills, a backup protection in case the red bands failed sooner than expected.

I saw a couple Estreyans drop to the ground in exhaustion, and just hoped the extraction team could get to them in time.

I sprinted forward, flanked by my unit. At a motion from me, one of the more powerful teleporters transported us to within a few meters of the god. The Skill residue cleared up, and I could sense that his pelvis was not fully open, or eaten through, whatever you wanted to call it.

A wave of simultaneous terror and rage at the terror ran through me, and with a snarl, I brought forth a surge of Chaos which smashed like a hungry animal into the wounds the others had created, setting gleefully to the task I'd set it. Destruction.

It seemed to be doing a surprisingly quick, effective job of it. Sometimes I felt a camaraderie with Sam, having a power so destructive I couldn't quite trust it, or trust myself with it. This was not one of those times.

The God of Knowledge twitched, tensing up as if to try and somehow move away from Chaos. But then he relaxed, somehow shrinking in on himself, and sliding his awkwardly bent arm forward, which created a bit of space within his hardened bindings.

Then, with the tiny bit of momentum that extra space earned him, his arm burst outward, striking one of the barrier rings.

It shattered, and its companions burst apart with it, even though they hadn't been touched.

The backup force fields and shields crumbled when he smashed his hands into them, even the one that had previously eaten his sentinel.

I backpedaled, my claws digging into the ruined ground as I slid, attempting to stop as if in slow motion.

The god turned to face me directly with its perfect, eyeless face, seeming to see into my own eyes despite the visor. It *grinned*.

Adam had reacted as quickly as me, as had the Estreyans. He threw up a shield, and another, and another, layering them in the air only centimeters apart, two walls at an angle pointing toward the god like a giant arrow, close enough together that he couldn't step through them, and facing so the broad side would stop his huge arms if he tied to swing at us.

Torliam threw up misty blue shields of his own, reaching for me.

Time seemed to slow. My toes were still digging into the golden ground, struggling for purchase.

Torliam's hand slapped over my face, a precaution, as he pushed his Skill into creating a canceling shell of darkness around us, shielding against the light.

Others in my protective group were throwing out Skills of their own, some meant to protect, and others to attack or force the god back.

I saw one of the Estreyans in my group, whose job was extraction and rescue, reaching out for me. His Skill gathered its brightness in my mind's eye, preparing to lash out.

I had a moment of rejection, where I wanted to stop him, when I realized he could only save *me*. But it didn't even matter, because the ground *erupted*. Even with the artificial expansion of time caused by my panic, it happened so fast I could barely follow it.

Golden sentinels shot out from every direction.

One speared right through the Estreyan that had been going to save me. I was disappointed, because that meant I was going to die after all.

Things snapped back into normal speed.

The sentinels sprouted like Sam's crystal attack, bursting in every direction like a mass of coral. They killed some instantly, and trapped others within.

Adam had been close beside me, but his body was gone, as were his shields.

Torliam's hand was still wrapped over my eyes, but it made no difference. I could see everything without my eyes. He was contorted painfully, but not seriously injured. Already, his power was slicing and pushing at the sentinels, to limited effect.

A small chunk of my thigh seemed to have been ripped off, but it wasn't much deeper than the skin, and wouldn't impede me in the short term.

One of the Estreyans had been speared through the stomach. He was held suspended in the air by his wound.

Sam was trapped behind me.

Jacky was meters away, but not badly hurt, and her body was growing already.

There was no time for caution. I let out a sharp burst of Chaos, as small and precisely formed as I was able, to disintegrate the sentinels holding nearby allies in place. As before, it was effective, more so than many of the other Skills I'd seen.

But it drew the god's attention. He reached forward, the sentinels moving aside for him and releasing me and those nearest me, though they still formed a mass of impenetrable brambles everywhere else. "You want freedom?" he asked, his smooth voice making cold sweat burst out over my skin. The god leaned downward, his massive body blocking out the sky. "Knowledge is power," he said, in what would have been a soft voice if not for the sheer *volume* of it, echoing from everywhere. It was coming from the sentinels, the golden ground, and even the golden plants.

The whole valley was part of his body, I realized. How foolish we'd been, to think we could attack him like this and win. He'd been humoring us.

"When you know—fogey—thing, completely, you have complete power over it." He didn't even seem to notice the way he'd glitched out. It didn't matter. If anything, it made it even more terrifying. "And I know you, Eve Redding," he said. The grin hadn't left his face.

I was about to die. I understood that. But I couldn't quite accept it, my heart still pounding frantically, my power screaming out to be used, as if I might fight my way free, or somehow find a way out of this.

Jacky screamed, and slammed into me from the side, her massive body sending me flying.

The god brought a hand down, and she activated the shields Adam had painted onto her, all at once.

His hand smashed through them, and with another scream, she lifted both arms to block, catching his blow, though the force of it made her knees buckle.

I landed, dizzy and disoriented, the golden ground beneath me seeming to turn white.

He lifted his arm back for another attack, and I screamed at her. "*Move!*"

A tear opened in the world, a couple meters above the ground, and Zed's hand came out, reaching for her.

Threads burst upward from the ground in sheets, surrounding me in the space between a blink. They formed a familiar shape around me, like a smooshed ball, with helixes, bridges, and wandering arches filling the inside haphazardly.

I howled in rage.

Chapter 39

But one by one we must all file on
   Through the narrow aisles of pain.
   — Ella Wheeler Wilcox

THE ORACLE CRAWLED out of the floor, detaching herself from the string and turning to look down at me, the sound of wind over glass bottles floating out as she moved.

"What the fuck are you doing?" I snarled. "They're getting killed out there!" I couldn't actually tell, since Wraith had been confined, just as surely as I had, but even an idiot could make basic deductions based on facts.

"Yet you are in here."

"That's my *team*!" My shriek pulsed with Voice, echoing off the walls, tearing at the threads. "Save them! Shield them inside one of your spiderweb egg sacs!"

"That would defeat my purpose." Her stone eyes were somehow still sad, though they did not weep like they had when I first met her.

"I can't do this without them." My voice broke, the enraged demands turning to a plea.

"If my goal was for you and your team to defeat the God of Knowledge, that would be true. But my father is much too strong for you."

"He said I was supposed to kill him, too."

She smiled at me, just a little, tilting her head to the side like I was a cute puppy, or a stupid child.

"Why are you doing this?" I whispered. "What do you want?"

The Oracle ignored my question. "I am a meshing of many of the different aspects of those who begat me. The lesser aspects of Knowledge and Time allow me to see a web of existence. Possibilities. Percentages, you might call them. But the strands of the web are always shifting. My goal is to save my world," she said simply. She bowed her head in a semblance of sadness, and the sound of the movement through the lines of her body was somber, but her stone face showed no expression. "There are paths to deliverance, among the mortals. You are not the only one, Eve-Redding. I see you succeeding more often than the others. But the paths are difficult, and many things must happen for yours to pierce through. You must make the right choices, and through them, *change.*"

"Get to the point."

She frowned at me. "You are naive. You have not yet learned how to *lose*. In this way, you will learn, but with my intervention, may continue living."

"What about the others?" My eyes were trained on her in an unblinking stare that was already halfway to a glare.

"That is the loss." She shrugged, the motion letting out a few notes into the air that quickly died away. "It is more likely that you find your way if they die here. But do not worry. I will still give you the promised reward. You will not die from the power of Khaos." She touched her chest, in that same spot that had once folded away to reveal the puzzle rings.

My heart pounded, and I clenched my fists, careful not to let my claws slip back out and puncture my own skin. "You want me to accept defeat, and give up. If I do, I'm more likely to save this world, and you'll consider my quest completed successfully, even though the terms have suddenly changed completely? But everyone out there is going to die, including all the others with the seal?" I touched my throat. "My brother? The kids?"

Her features twisted once again, into a mask of compassion. "This will be hard for you. But it will make you great. Besides, they will all die eventually, if you do not stop the Sickness. On this path, their loss just comes a little sooner, and the number of those you may save is so much greater."

Rage ate at my insides, eroding my control. "People will die if I don't? Lots of people? I don't care! I'm not some savior, some martyr who's come to fix all the problems of this world just because you want me to. All people were not created equal in my eyes. I could trade a million empty numbers for one member of my team, one life I care about. Did you really think this would work? If you wanted me to work for you, you should have offered me a better deal," I snarled, panting for breath. Chaos begged to be released, to *destroy* her.

She stared at me, as if bemused at the actions of a strange animal. "There is no point to your anger. You must accept defeat. It is inevitable either way. You cannot win against the God of Knowledge, and if you refuse my offer, you will only die alongside those you place such unbalanced value on." She smiled, gently amused, and too assured of herself. "I have seen your future in the web, Eve-Redding. I know you."

"You don't know me," I said hoarsely. The crystal at my throat began to thrum again. "If you did, you would know that I don't give up. I *win*. I don't care what you see in your little future webs." The crystal was thrumming along with the beat of my voice, and almost physical pulse that pushed at her angrily. "I will bend the world to my will. I swear it." I took a deep breath, and straightened to my full height, which wasn't much compared to her twelve feet. "Now, you are going to send me back down there to kill your father. And when I win, you're damn well going to give me the reward we agreed on."

The Oracle's frown formed crags along her stone brow. "I cannot choose the path for you, you *foolish* mortal." She let out a sharp grunt that still sounded lovely, and with a musical shake of her head, the egg-shaped web folded and sank away as quickly as it had come, leaving me standing in the middle of a ravaged battlefield, right back in front of an enraged god.

Chapter 40

I am the master of my fate,
I am the captain of my soul.
— William Ernest Henley

MY CONVERSATION with the Oracle hadn't taken that long, but I hadn't really believed there would be anyone left for me to rescue. I was wrong.

I lunged to the side, claws scrabbling futilely at the golden ground for extra purchase.

The sentinels rose to block me.

I gestured forward with a clawed hand, as if drawing something from my chest, and a mass of Chaos parted the impenetrable forest like a beam, cutting a tunnel straight forward.

My awareness swirled out, and I took stock of Adam lying trapped within the sentinels, too far away to reach with Chaos. He was badly injured, one of them having punctured right though his back, from side to side. Basically, a chunk the size of his arm was just ... *gone* from his lower back. His spine was definitely severed.

If not for the sentinel still pressing into him, he probably would have bled to death already.

Gregor was cutting his own path through the sentinels toward Adam, in direct violation of my prior orders. Three of his sister's summons escorted him.

Sam was ... *melting* a path of his own with his bare hands, moving toward me.

I could feel the effects of Black Sun on him through my Wraith Skill.

Jacky was almost as noticeable as the god, her Struggle Skill still in effect, though one arm hung limply, blood dripped from her head, and she looked like she could barely keep her balance in the fighting stance she'd taken. Her visor was gone, so she was fighting with her eyes closed, and that was even more impressive. She was half as big as Knowledge, far bigger than any Estreyan I'd ever seen.

Torliam's blue mist lashed out from beside her, giving her a moment to recover while he harried the god with enough force to make Knowledge take a step back.

A ship zoomed past overhead, shooting two missiles at the god as it passed. They folded inward and outward simultaneously in a familiar manner, and when they hit, Knowledge was blown completely off his feet, tumbling through the air and smashing through his sentinels, snapping them to bits in a huge swath.

I should have known Blaine would be coming, with the kids here and in danger.

The ship came around for another pass while the god was down, this time smashing straight into him in an even more spectacular explosion, while two small forms were expelled out the back.

A flying Estreyan streaked by, catching the bigger form, and carrying Blaine away from the battlefield.

The smaller form, Birch, flew down to one of the people trapped within the sentinels. His fur and feathers bristled up, and he let out a wave of wind that carried a black-tendrilled power I certainly recognized. It cut right through the sentinels, and the Estreyan fell free. How much of my blood had Birch consumed, even back before he'd even hatched? I hadn't even considered what it might be doing to him.

I formed a plan in my head, and I hoped that I had the power to pull it off.

The long-range and flying Estreyans still able to fight took the opportunity to lay down a barrage on the god, keeping him down.

I sprinted forward, creating a tunnel through the sentinels at the same rate I moved. I passed a couple Estreyans along the way who weren't dead, and I let out pulses of Chaos to help free them.

One of them still had the visor on, and seemed to realize when she was released from the sentinels, though she moved slowly, as if fighting against her own body.

The other stared into nothing, still trapped within their own mind.

I reached Sam, and he turned without hesitation, running with me. I overtook Gregor along the way, wishing I could spare a moment to glare at the boy.

At some point, Adam's blood had bubbled up around the sentinel. He took advantage of it, using his own blood as ink, which formed into bandages to staunch his wounds. He let out a shuddering gasp, the air rattling in his lungs. Punctured by his broken ribs, probably.

Sam didn't hesitate.

I left Adam suspended, because he might bleed out too quickly even for Sam if I didn't.

Adam lifted a hand, reaching for me.

I stepped forward. "I don't have much time—"

His hand touched my forehead, the blood on his fingers spreading onto my skin. "Kill him," he whispered.

I grinned. "Okay." I ran away, requesting a pickup for Gregor on the comms system.

Jacky had shrunk, the break in the pressure of the fight while the god dealt with Blaine's attack removing the necessary conditions for Struggle to stay activated.

I ran toward her and Torliam.

She was still conscious, and had turned to make her way toward the god, good fist still clenched as if she were ready to fight.

Torliam turned to me as I neared, and when Jacky saw me, she let out a shuddering sob.

I slipped under her good arm, helping to support her. "I still need your help," I said. "So I hope you're not too tired."

"We don't get tired," she lied with an ironic grin. "What's the plan?"

"Get me into position, save a bunch of people, then get the hell out of here. Far enough that Knowledge can't reach you. I am going to kill a god. Chaos seems surprisingly effective against it. I'll just need to use more of it. A lot more. My power isn't controllable in large amounts. I don't want you anywhere near when I unleash it. Grab a long-range extractor, if you can. Maybe ..." Maybe there would be something of me left to save, afterward.

Knowledge rose to his feet, roaring. His main body was very much worse for wear, but most of it was scratches, sometimes gouges, and other than his knee, which he braced with a quick growth of sentinels in the eroded area, none of the injuries were even enough to slow him down.

I explained the plan to Jacky and Torliam as quickly and simply as possible, and then the three of us ran forward.

———

THE GOD of Knowledge knew we were coming, obviously, and it was turned to face us by the time we arrived. "Your power is impressive, Eve," he said, his voice conversational, as if we were having tea instead of a fight to the death. "Quite different— amygladin—those of the others. It reminds me of ..." He looked down and away for a second, as if he'd been reaching for a word, or a memory, and had just forgotten what it was. He looked back to me. "I will add that power to my own strength."

I gave him a feral grin. Perfect. "My power will never be yours," I yelled, loud enough that he, along with anyone who might be trapped but still conscious within the growth of sentinels, could hear me.

I rushed forward, a boost of Torliam's Skill behind me pushing me faster. I moved close to the god, but shot past him, with a lash of Chaos to the back of his bad knee along the way.

He swiped for me, but was just slightly too far away to reach me.

There was a puddle of blood on the other side of the clearing his tumble had created, and a couple of my fighters were trapped beyond, alive.

I pulsed a wave of Chaos their way, weakening the sentinels around them.

I turned abruptly, body tilting low to the ground as my toes dug in for purchase, and sprinted back toward the god. This time, I aimed Chaos at his pelvis on the way by.

He was prepared for it. He took one smooth, sliding step in my direction to cover the distance between us, and reached for me.

A blue, misty light slammed into me from between the god and I, and tossed me aside, to safety.

It was a bit painful, but I twisted easily in mid-air, landing half-sideways on the wall of sentinels. I let out a bit of Chaos around my lower body to stave off their attempt to grow around me, and jumped off at an angle, making it into safe range once again.

Jacky pulsed, growing larger, and then larger again. She jumped high and dropped down with a punch so forceful she cracked a sentinel with her bare hands. She spun, throwing the chunk at the god like he had been doing to others earlier.

I shot past the god again, attacking like a dog nipping at his heels, with Torliam acting as my safety net, protecting me when Knowledge got too close to catching or hitting me. When it was feasible, I aimed my trajectory so that I ended near someone who was trapped within the sentinels. Slowly, I freed people, and if they were uninjured and still aware, they struggled their way out.

The remaining fighters converged on the god, doing their best to cover me, to distract him, to stay alive for just a little longer.

"I see through your plan, tiny one," he said, his voice seeming to come mainly from behind me, though I was facing him. "Did you—trickle—you could hide, within my light?"

The hair on the back of my neck prickled, and more cold sweat dripped down my back, under my armor. Shit.

"You cannot save them. When you are dead, I will capture them again, and they will become part of my strength as well."

I exhaled, and turned to Jacky. We sprinted toward each other. When we got close enough, I jumped, she grabbed both of my hands in her one good one, and used her Skill to root herself to the surface of the planet. She turned our combined momentum into a spin, so fast that I felt like my shoulders might pop apart as I flew through the air.

She released me, mid swing, throwing my body like a discus at the god.

In this way, my direction changed in an instant. It was almost enough to catch Knowledge off guard. But he slid his foot forward like a dancer, and lifted it, slamming the top of it into me relatively gently, like I was a ball.

The abrupt change in momentum *hurt*. My internal organs protested, and my bones creaked.

Torliam threw up a shield for me.

I jumped sideways off of it.

The god's hands were too quick, and I was caught inside gigantic bands of gold as he wrapped his fingers around me, once again almost gently.

This was the moment of reckoning. If he squeezed me, it was all over.

But I was guessing he would want me to fear, and scream. I struggled, clawing and letting out ineffectual, random bursts of

Chaos that intentionally didn't do much damage, staring in my best imitation of terror at his mouth.

Sure enough, he brought me close to his mouth, almost in slow motion, opening wide so I could see the tombstone like teeth that would be grinding into me in a moment.

I waited till the very last second, then released the huge breath I'd been holding along with a whispered, "Animus," and relaxed my slightly angled arms and legs, using the same trick he'd demonstrated earlier to create space.

Blood wings snapped to life, a single great flap and every bit of strength I had in my legs shooting me straight forward into his mouth, with a little swirl of Chaos around my body to grease the way.

His teeth snapped together halfway down my armored feet, biting through the metal.

I scrambled forward, losing some skin and ripping the claws off my toes. But I was already inside, and I wasted no time being surprised, or disoriented, or focusing on the pain. I scuttled away from his teeth, down his throat, stopping myself with claws and spread-eagled limbs pressing against the walls of his golden esophagus, just before the opening to the stomach. The stench hit me first.

The god's internal design had abandoned all resemblance to mortal biology. A ball of light sat on a small pedestal at the bottom of the stomach chamber, with little glowing sparkles flowing in and out of it like a swarm of ever-glowing fireflies around a nest. His Seed core. It was significantly bigger than Behelaino's. My muscles clenched in a subconscious desire to retreat, as I realized once again how strong he was. I also felt a hint of greed. Power like that could do so much for me. But I wanted no part in it. Both because my body would probably just burst apart if I put any more of the gods into it, and because it was Sickness-tainted.

The assaulting stink came from the pieces of bodies scattered about. Some were well-chewed and soupy, while I recognized whole limbs in other places. The light particles swarmed over them, growing brighter before returning to the main ball. Like bees collecting honey.

I growled angrily at them, and dropped down to the bottom of the chamber, wading toward the Seed core through the putrefied human flesh sliding off the bones. I resisted the urge to throw up, once again. Breathing through my mouth didn't help. The taste of death and disease coated my tongue and throat, and I gagged, so hard I couldn't breathe past it. I reached the sphere, and took the two cartridges of meningolycanosis from their spot at my waist. I injected both of them into the sphere, hoping that it worked as we'd anticipated.

The light of the sphere pulsed strangely, as if it the Seed substance was spinning in every direction at once, and had become unstable. The little particles of light swarmed out of it, dipping in and out like bees disturbed from their hive.

An overwhelming feeling bubbled up from my stomach, and I let out a gleeful laugh that echoed off the walls of the stomach chamber, making me sound crazy. I ignored the little voice in my head that was telling me it wasn't the echo that made me sound crazy.

I opened the door to room of serenity, then lifted the lid of the box of silence, and unlocked the chest of stillness. Chaos shattered outward, tearing at me from the inside. I turned it on the core, and the god *screamed*.

That was the key, it seemed.

Chapter 41

He who fights with monsters might take care lest he thereby become a monster. And if you gaze for long into an abyss, the abyss gazes also into you.

— Friedrich Nietzsche

KNOWLEDGE WAS A TERRIBLE, beautiful thing. I could feel it flooding me, changing my brain with a physical sensation. Synapses fired, pathways of thought and knowledge forming. I found myself knowing things in a way that seemed like I'd known forever, memories and understanding from before I was born. Some of it, relevant in the moment, came to the forefront.

"Knowledge of a thing truly is power over it," I whispered in a voice so low even I could barely hear it.

Little eddies of Chaos swirled over me, around me, for the first time like a caress instead of a burning lash. I clenched my hands, then flicked those clawed fingers forward.

Dark flames, almost identical to those I'd seen from Behelaino, flashed to life in my palms. It burned.

I ignored the pain. My mortal body would not channel the

power needed without being consumed. It was going to hurt a lot more. But that was okay. This was a pain I could find some peace in. Fear of death had kept me alive. But to live a worthwhile life, there have to be some things worth dying for.

I threw the almost solid flames at the core. They ate at it, disintegrating pieces of it in flashes of blinding light.

The chamber bucked around me as the god did, throwing me and the other contents around within his stomach cavity.

I shuddered as a half-digested eyeball slid out of my hair. I was alright, but I knew I couldn't take my time with this. I didn't have the power to draw it out, and the god would find a way to stop me if I tried.

I unleashed more of the flames, letting them spill forward from me, building upon themselves, multiplying under my direction. They were a wild, feeding mass that I would never be able to create piece by piece, or without the aid of the uncorrupted piece of Knowledge.

The god screamed, loud and animalistic, and began to rip his own stomach open to get at me.

Too late, I hoped. I lifted my arms and let the black fire wash over my skin. I threw all my power into it, watching idly as the first layer of my skin peeled away and disintegrated immediately within the grip of my power. I closed my eyes, then. Because the visual was disturbing enough to be distracting from my task. It kept hurting, as I raised the firestorm higher, feeding it with my power and unintentional pieces of my own flesh. At some point, it hurt too badly, and I was too weak to continue, but by then it didn't matter.

Chaos knew what to do.

My eyes burned away, shortly after the lids protecting them disintegrated. But I didn't need them. I watched with the last bit of my Wraith Skill as the storm consumed the God of Knowledge's corrupted manifestation.

The towering cone of black fire grew from within, as if from nothing, and then expanded, exploding outward into the valley, burning and eating away.

"Don't hurt ..." *the living,* I finished silently. My lips had gone, and it hurt too much to talk with a ruined neck.

The fire ate through the gold, and the dirt and rock, deep into the mountainsides all around. An unparalleled force of destruction.

Then, Chaos turned, and moved beyond destruction. Oh, how little I had understood it, before. The fire died out, smokeless, and left behind something new wherever its devouring tongue was felt.

It pulled inward, back towards the center. Towards my meaty stump of a body, which was barely hanging on to life. I was stubborn.

Then, it was gone. And with it, the pain.

QUEST COMPLETED!

Chapter 42

I rise.

— Maya Angelou

I ROLLED ONTO MY STOMACH, gagging and coughing up blood. Despite that, my brain was bursting with chemical euphoria. I had almost died. I had *felt* myself dying, my consciousness partially slipping away, and partially fading out of existence, while my body ignored its wounds, slipping into bliss.

I touched my face, my eyelids, my lips, whole once more. I stood up, looking around in disorientation. Something was wrong with me. Things moved too fast, and too slow. I stumbled forward, catching myself on one of the new trees.

My left arm caught my attention. "Well, that's weird." I flexed my six fingers, and then looked up slowly, interest drawn away from the strange way my body felt and moved, to the land around. I stood in a weir wood.

It reminded me of the exact opposite of that horrible forest from my very first Trial. The angled sunlight of dawn shone sideways through the widely spaced trees. I walked up to another one, almost stumbling at first, seeing the wood, grown into the shape of a warrior. He had the semblance of a sword in his hand, which grew bright leaves at the end of the flat branch of wood. I looked up to his face, and vaguely recognized the features replicated in bark. Golden threads ran through the wood, veins that sparkled slightly when the sun hit them through the leaves. It was beautiful.

But I didn't want everyone to be trees.

I sobbed, once, and turned. An Estreyan was standing in the midst of the newly created wood, watching me. She looked shaken, to say the least. Pale and wide eyed, and a bit bloody.

I laughed with relief. "You're alive!" Voice pulsed out of me, sharing my joy. Hopefully the others would be alive, too.

When our eyes met, she dropped to the ground, pressing her face against it.

She must be exhausted, I knew. I walked on, my thoughts skipping dizzily. I passed more Estreyans as I went. Most of the non-trees were relatively unharmed, but I found a couple who were severely injured. "I'll send a healer for you, I promise," I said. My visor was long gone, and even my VR chip seemed to be malfunctioning. Or else I'd forgotten how to use it.

It didn't take me too long to find a clearing, where people were gathering. This had been where I fought the god, before being "eaten."

Adam and Sam were there, both lying on the ground and looking horrible. But they were alive, and an Estreyan healer hovered over them.

Jacky stood to the side, tears running down her beautiful, grimy face. She made almost no sound in her sadness, aside from the occasional hitching breath.

Torliam lay against a mossy rock over to one side, surrounded by some concerned Estreyans, a couple of whom I recognized as healers. He was letting out seemingly uncontrolled, and accidental, bursts of Skill-blue mist.

"Healers?" I asked. "Injured," I said, pointing back the way I'd come. My voice sounded really strange. And it felt strange. I reached up absently to touch the base of my throat, which was vibrating a little too much to be normal. Was that Voice again?

Heads turned to stare at me, eyes widened, emotions that I couldn't quite decipher crossing their faces. Were they afraid to go? Maybe they didn't understand me.

"It is okay," I added, making sure I was speaking Estreyan, and not English. "It is over. Go save them."

One of the healers bowed deeply to me, and rushed off in the direction I'd come from.

Well, at least *someone* was listening.

I swirled my awareness outward, and fell over when the world tilted, the Skill overwhelming me with the sudden rush of information. I reined it back in, but didn't bother to get off the ground. "Everyone important is okay," I said to Adam. "And a lot of the Estreyans. Make people go get them and bring them here." I waved my hand limply. "I'm too tired to do the ordering."

"Are you in shock?" Adam muttered.

I ignored him. No need to bicker, after everything.

"The god is dead?" Torliam asked.

I nodded, rolling onto my back to look up at the sky, the stars fading away into pink and blue light. "Death is but a metamorphosis," I said, sounding quite wise, in my own opinion. "But yeah. That one is gone. Maybe another one will gather here in a while, but he won't be sick."

People shifted, and I heard someone whisper, "It *is* her."

I turned to Jacky, who had fallen onto her butt, and was staring at me. "That reminds me, I have six fingers," I said, lifting my left hand to show her what I'd discovered. I frowned at it. The skin was darker and harder, segmented in geometric patterns that looked like a cross between honeycombs and scales. The fingers were clawed, and abnormally long and angular, almost like they'd tried to grow one more joint. "Weird."

"You're bigger, too," she said.

"Really? Maybe that's why it's hard to walk—Torliam, why are you flashing?" I was distracted by how irritatingly bright he was being. "Stop that."

"I cannot."

"You should probably work on your control. You desperately need it," I said.

"I think some leniency could be afforded me, as I am bound to a godling twice over, and the backlash makes control difficult." He raised an eyebrow deliberately at me as people reacted to his words.

I rolled my eyes at him, and turned to Jacky. "Excuses."

As if she'd been waiting for the eye contact, she launched herself forward and slammed into me. "Idiot!" she half yelled at me. "I really thought you were dead this time."

I hugged her back, and resisted the little burning tingle in my eyes. It felt good to get a hug. I was tired, really tired.

Birch arrived with Kris and Gregor, all three of them looking a bit worse for wear, but uninjured.

The injured and the Estreyans that had been separated from the main group started to join us, Blaine among them. He didn't yell at the kids, just gathered them into a crushing hug.

The clearing filled up with people, but there were so many less than there had been when we left. Still, we'd killed a god. And the people-trees made of the dead were pretty, at least.

Interlude 4

When the *scryer* finally worked out the requirements and finished preparation to open up a brief viewing window onto Estreyer, Eliahan brought the woman to watch..

The *scryer* located their target, and in the serene pool of water carved out of the stone floor, a moving image appeared.

She took a single, startled step backward, but stopped when she felt his hand on her arm.

He dropped his hand.

"What is this?"

"It is our child, grown strong. Sadly, it is also the beginning of the end."

"What are you saying?" An uncharacteristic waver entered her voice, perhaps brought on by the almost physical atmosphere of foreboding from his people.

"Words were spoken, a long time ago. A prophecy, *some* think."

"A prophecy? Like telling the future?" Her mouth twisted up on one side, but fell again when no one responded with similar amusement. "One of your...*quirks*," she said, with a resigned air of understanding. "What did this prophecy say?"

"Despair follows hope," he said simply.

"You don't believe in this prophecy?"

"They are a slippery thing. One cannot truly know the future, I believe, unless they are the God of Time, and perhaps not even then. We are no match in strength for what is coming. But the will of a mortal can be a powerful thing."

Chapter 43

I am become Death, the destroyer of worlds.

— J. Robert Oppenheimer

WE HAD MORE than enough empty ships to take the survivors back to the capitol, and I slept the whole way there. I slept for the next three days, in fact.

I awoke to an opulent room with paintings on the ceiling of people using their Skills.

An Estreyan woman had been sitting beside my bed, and she squeaked when I awoke, then scrambled out of the room backward, bowing repeatedly as she went.

I got up and went straight to the bathroom, peeing for what was probably a straight minute. When I finished, I looked at myself in the mirrors on the main room's walls.

I'd grown a little bigger. Enough that I wasn't just an abnormally tall woman, but big enough to stand out as strange. My eyes had changed—upgraded to match my beyond-human levels of Perception. My facial features, too, though it was hard to say exactly how they were different. A little more angular. A little more striking. And blemish-free.

I still wore the armor from the battle, though Chaos had changed it, too, and apparently made it impossible to remove from the outside, though it had been cleaned.

The skin of my entire left arm, the one that had been turned into hamburger and was never quite the same afterward, was dark, with those honeycomb-scales, though the rest of me was still mostly normal. The arm didn't hurt anymore, at least. The Oracle's gifts were still there, sitting as comfortably as ever, despite my larger size.

My body was beautiful, in an alien, *interesting* kind of way. But not attractive in the way I often used to wish I could be. I could feel Chaos unbound within me, swirling around calmly. It didn't hurt, though it rippled at my attention, as if readying itself to be used.

I shrugged experimentally at my new reflection, and pulled up my Attribute Window.

PLAYER NAME: EVE REDDING
TITLE: SQUAD LEADER(9)
CHARACTERISTIC SKILL: SPIRIT OF THE HUNTRESS,
TUMBLING FEATHER
LEVEL: 38
SKILLS: COMMAND, WRAITH, CHAOS
STRENGTH: 23
LIFE: 74
AGILITY: 32
GRACE: 28
INTELLIGENCE: 31
FOCUS: 24
BEAUTY: 16
CHARISMA: 32
MANUAL DEXTERITY: 10
MENTAL ACUITY: 29

RESILIENCE: 70
STAMINA: 26
PERCEPTION: 33

The new body was a bit of an upgrade, if my levels were to be believed.

The door opened, and Queen Mardinest slipped into the room.

"They are calling you the godkiller," she said without preamble. There were bags under her eyes, and her skin looked thin and pale.

"It is what we set out to do," I said.

"It is not what *I* set out to do. Nor the warriors who followed and died for you."

"I know. But who would have agreed to help me kill a god?" Especially, when the reward was only to be my own salvation. It was ironic coincidence that my own power, used properly, also happened to be the thing that could cleanse the Sickness, literally burning it out.

"The world has already forgotten your treachery," she said. "They rejoice, and say the loss of life was well-spent. The celebrations spill into the streets, and your name is on every tongue. The warriors who lived exult in their good fortune, not to have lived, but to have battled with you." She stepped forward, holding up a vial. "But I will not forget," she promised.

I stepped back quickly, but she didn't move to attack, and after a couple moments of confusion, I realized what was in the vial. Meningolycanosis.

"Yes," she nodded. "I know what your people have done. I know how they prepare to kill us, steal our power, and violated my son. I know that he is likely not the only one. But most importantly, I know that they cultivate the Sickness, for use in war." She spat on the floor, turned to the door, and left.

I stood still for a moment. My stomach burned, though I wasn't sure whether it was with hunger or apprehension.

The next day, the queen called a press conference of sorts. The media had been clamoring to get at me and the team, and what had happened at the battle with the God of Knowledge was being publicized everywhere. The warriors who'd been there had been taking interviews.

News about NIX was also circulating. Estreyan scientists had talked to the media about the meningolycanosis samples they'd worked on. Uproar over that was almost as great as the hubbub over the defeat of a god.

I stayed holed up in the castle with the rest of the team. The servants bowed to us all as we passed, and the more courageous of them asked questions.

While I ate in the kitchen with some of the others, the young man who served us asked nervously, "Will you have to kill all the infected, to cleanse the world of the Sickness?"

"There may be other ways," I responded vaguely.

Chanelle smiled at me sadly, and I almost choked.

It wasn't like I'd really killed a god. I'd just dispersed it, or removed its physical manifestation, or something. The gods of Estreyer were forces of nature. Of existence. They weren't something that could be literally killed. Enough of Knowledge would form together again at some point, and he'd reform a physical manifestation. There could already be another one, somewhere else, that had been there all along and just hidden from the mortals.

The only way I knew how to stop the Sickness was to burn it away. And Chanelle wasn't like a god. She wouldn't reform over time. Neither would Kris and Gregor.

Sam watched my face, and then bowed his head, hands fisting into his hair.

"We'll find another way," I said.

Blaine's fingers clenched around his plate. "I will need to study your power, how it works. Perhaps the effective part can be duplicated, without the need for destruction," he said to me.

Adam stared at my scaled arm. "And while you're at it, maybe you could burn me some new legs?" His upper lip curled back, a mix between a sneer and a snarl.

Sam flinched. He hadn't been able to heal Adam's wound, because it was created directly with the power of a god, and had invaded Adam's body. Unlike when we'd gone through the Trial with Testimony and Lore, the wound was deep. Just clotting the blood and waiting for Adam to heal up on his own wasn't going to work. Which meant that Adam was still missing a piece of his spine, and though Sam had kept him alive, he might never walk again.

Adam shoved back from the table, an ink dog with a broad back springing into existence under him, carrying my teammate out of the room before anyone could stop him. "It's time to go to the throne room," he snapped over his shoulder.

Jacky shook her head at him. "Whadda we do about him?"

Blaine stood, pushing away from the table and following after him. "We hope that association with Eve does not cause the same level of harm to the rest of us."

I sat up straighter, face slipping into a stony expressionlessness.

Blaine was angry at me. Kris and Gregor hadn't been hurt during the fight, but they could have been. He thought I was a destructive and dangerous influence, and he wanted to keep them safe from me. If they didn't have the Sickness, and he could just run away and live somewhere peaceful and normal with them, he would have already done so.

I understood that.

But he needed me. We were in this together, now.

I shook my head at Jacky and Sam's looks of concern, and stood. "Let's go. Torliam's on his way to come grab us." I could feel his location like a tickle on the back of my neck, always.

Torliam stepped through the doorway, sagging when he saw the three of us. "Where are the others? It is time to speak to the media." Fatigue dripped from his voice. He had had almost no rest since we returned from the fight. In absence of his siblings, and with his new role as media darling, it fell to him to help his mother navigate the roiling politics of the court.

"They're already on their way," I said, confirming my words with a pulse of awareness.

The information about NIX had been a blow to the queen's approval rating, despite her association with me. Her detractors were using it against her, cultivating fear. They publicized the queen's lack of involvement in the progress we'd made, how she had left her son for dead, and wasn't even aware of the forces of Earth torturing him and plotting against us.

As we paused at the back door behind the throne, Torliam visibly steeled himself, covering up the fatigue. "Are we all ready?" he asked the team.

"Let's just get this over with," Gregor said with a groan. "We love the queen, yadda, yadda, hurry up so we can get back to doing something useful. Like fixing the Sickness."

Kris nodded, but her lips were white. "Are *we* going to have to answer questions?"

Blaine put a hand on her shoulder. "That is unlikely. If they make you uncomfortable, I will step in."

She nodded, and with a last moment to brace ourselves, we entered the throne room.

I noticed the crowd first, then the big screen hung over the wall on one side, though it displayed nothing. I looked around for the queen, but her throne was empty, and I didn't see her.

The reporters didn't seem to mind, peppering us all with questions.

"How did you kill the God of Knowledge, Eve-Redding?"

"Eve-Redding! What can you tell us about what the Earthlings have been doing to the Estreyan descendants upon their planet?"

"Torliam! How do you feel that the queen left you for dead among the Earthlings?"

"How do you plan to stop the Sickness?"

"Has the Oracle given you any more tasks, Eve Redding?"

"Eve-Redding, now that you can eliminate the Sickness, do you still plan to find the Champion?"

They didn't have time for any more questions, because the queen threw open the main doors. The sound echoed, and silence rippled through the crowd as everyone turned to look at her. She strode through the crowd up to her throne. "I have come before you today because I, too, am shocked and outraged at the actions of the Earthlings," she cried out.

Alarm bloomed in my stomach hard enough to make me nauseas. That wasn't what she had told us this was about.

—I HAVE A FEELING SHE'S ABOUT TO SCREW SHIT UP.—
-ADAM-

She continued talking. "We have not harmed them, and yet, they covet our power. They prepare for war, and the Abhorrent allies with them. They are creating weapons that will destroy the power and blood of our people, allowing the Sickness to eat it away, just as it eats away at our hearts and minds. This cannot be allowed." She gestured to the screen on the wall, which came to life, displaying a huge Stonehenge look-alike. Its stones were different colors, obviously newly repaired.

I moved to step forward, but Torliam grabbed me by the elbow, his eyes trained on his mother. "It is too late," he said, lips barely moving. "If you speak against her now, it will only harm you."

"Did you know about this?" I whispered severely.

"I swear I did not."

The queen raised her voice over the clamor. "Before they can destroy us, we must destroy them. We must stop them, before they strengthen and spread the Sickness even further! For the hope of our future, I hereby declare war on the Earthlings." Her hand slashed down.

On the screen, I watched as large Estreyan ships flew through the activated array, disappearing in a blink.

The crowd gasped.

I counted two ships, then five, then seven. I stopped counting. My hands started to shake.

If you enjoyed this book, please take the time to leave a review on Amazon or Goodreads. It doesn't have to be more than a sentence or two, and it really does make a difference.

Want to get an email when my next book is released, or when I'm running book giveaways and contests? Sign up here: http://bit.ly/SeedsofChaosNewsletter

Also by Azalea Ellis

Seeds of Chaos Series

Gods of Blood and Bone

Gods of Rust and Ruin

Gods of Myth and Midnight — Coming Soon

Sign of for my newsletter to get news about new releases.

http://bit.ly/SeedsofChaosNewsletter

About the Author

I am an author of science fiction and fantasy. I love to hear from my readers, so feel free to reach out to me.

For more information:

www.azaleaellis.com

author@azaleaelis.com